TRUE SIGHT

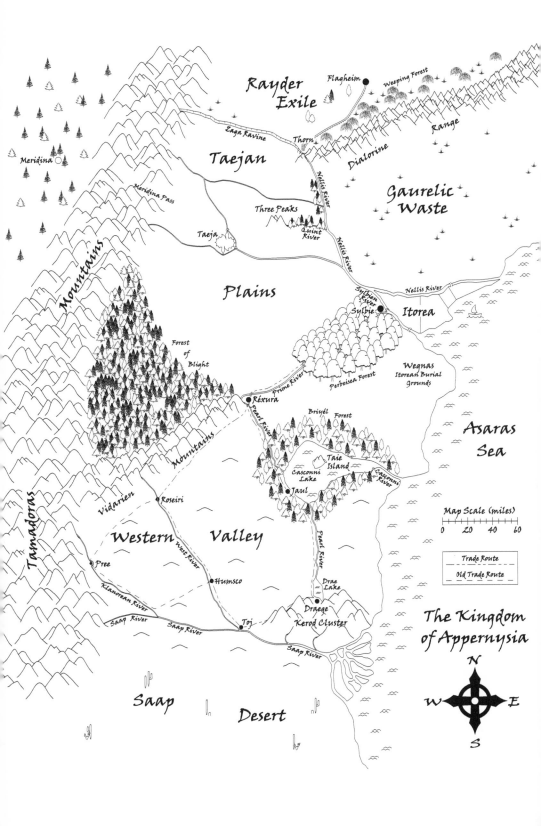

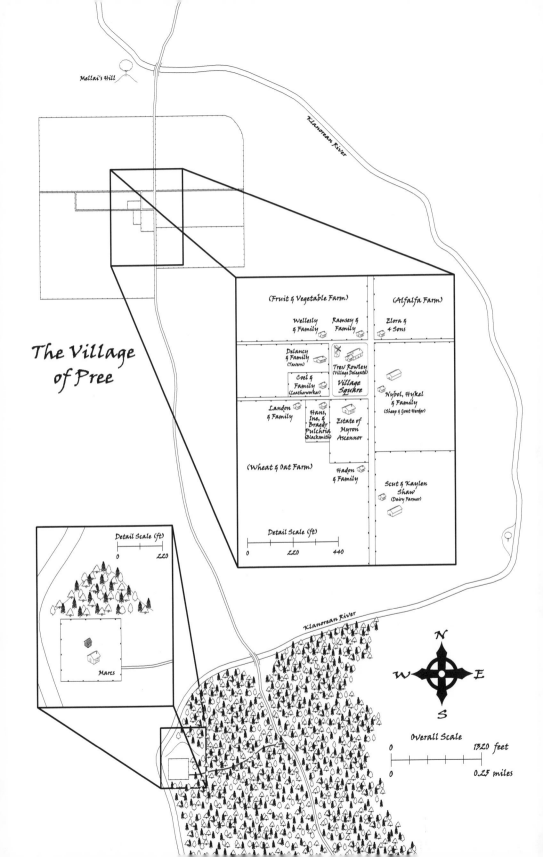

Mellai's Hill

Klanorean River

The Village
of Pree

(Fruit & Vegetable Farm)   (Alfalfa Farm)

Wellesly   Ramsey &   Elora &
& Family   Family   4 Sons

Delancy   Trev Rowley
& Family   (Village Delegate)
(Tavern)
                        Village
Coel &   Square   Nybol, Hykel
Family   & Family
(Leatherworker)   (Sheep & Goat Herder)

Landon   Hans,   Estate of
& Family   Ine, &   Myron
                Braedr   Ascennor
                Pulchria
                (Blacksmith)

(Wheat & Oat Farm)   Hadon
                                & Family
                                              Scut & Kaylen
                                              Shaw
                                              (Dairy Farmer)

Detail Scale (ft)

0   220   440

Detail Scale (ft)

0   220

Marcs

Klanorean River

N
W   E
S

Overall Scale

0   1320 feet

0   0.25 miles

Gaurelic Waste

Nellis River

Nellis River

Sylbien River

Sylbie

Prime River

Prime River

Cavalier Crook

Agricultural Lands

Keep

Asaras Sea

Itorea
City of the King

Wegnas
Itorean Burial Grounds

Perbeisea Forest

Hook
Tip
Blade
Halberd

Trade Route
Main Road
Canal
Aquaducts

N
W   E
S

Map Scale (miles)
0   5   10

Taeja
2nd Age
of Appernysia

Three Peaks

N
W — E
S

Map Scale (miles)
0 1 2 3 4 5

Old River Path

The Swallows

North Gate

Keep

Arena

Armory & Barracks

South Gate

BEHOLDERS: True Sight

First edition published in February 2015 by Jolly Fish Press, LLC
Provo, UT

This edition published in February 2018 by Nypa Distributing, LLC
Tooele, UT

Printed in the United States of America

ISBN: 978-0-9997400-4-0

0 9 8 7 6 5 4 3 2

*To my dad, Allen. Without you, I would
have given up years ago.*

Acknowledgments

My queen, Crystal Lyn, the inspiration of benevolent Queen Cyra and the Lynth Pendant of immeasurable sacrifice.

Llen, Dawes, Duncan, Dax, and Duke. From witty remarks to unimagined attack techniques, you've never ceased to influence my writing. I'm the luckiest father in the world!

Marcs and Casconni, my most efficient critics. Thank you for your meticulous genius.

Humsco, still supporting my creative passions with your mastery of graphic design.

Sévart, who I can always turn to if I need a ray of sunshine. No, that's an understatement. You're the whole sun.

My fans, who have patiently (and not so patiently) waited on pins and needles. Thank you for sharing your enthusiasm!

My junior high students. Every last one of you knows how much you mean to me. It has been a pleasure thrashing you with my red pen.

Prologue

Spectators filled the cobblestone square outside Itorea's keep. Civilians and soldiers alike stood shoulder to shoulder, craning their necks to view the solitary platform at the base of the castle. The platform had been used to make public declarations for centuries, but never had so many people gathered inside the keep.

A solitary man stood at the center of the platform, clad in shining plate armor with the Lynth Flower etched onto its breast. A dark green cloak hung from his shoulders, nearly touching his ankles. His light brown hair hung loosely to the middle of his neck. His blue eyes, calm and confident, scanned the crowd.

Kaylen Shaw stood amid the throng with her friend, Aely. She anxiously watched the nearby platform as another man stepped forward with a sheet of parchment in his hands.

"Kamron Astadem," the man boomed with a low voice, "protector of the Lynth and general of our king's army. You are hereby found guilty of desertion and ultimate treason."

A low rumble surged through the people as many voiced their opposition to the accusation.

"He didn't leave without cause!"

"He saved tens of thousands of lives!"

"This proclamation is treason!"

The herald paused only a moment before continuing. "General Astadem, your sentence for your cowardice is public execution by beheading."

The rumble of dissent suddenly gave way to shouts of outrage. Kaylen gasped as twenty soldiers rushed the line of armored halberdiers guarding the platform. Though they had no weapons, they ran at the sentries without reservation. Seven were speared on the lowered halberds, but the other thirteen slipped past the deadly weapons and hurled themselves against the halberdiers, battling ferociously to free their general. One soldier stepped onto the angled shield of a sentry and leaped toward the platform's edge, but his flight was cut short as four crossbow bolts pierced his chest. In little more than a minute, all twenty soldiers lay dead on the cobblestone.

The sentries gripped their shields and halberds as they tightened their line and glanced around with grim faces. The herald stepped down from the platform, seemingly unshaken by the attempted rescue and subsequent violence. An armor-clad man took his place, a large broadsword in his grip.

"This is wrong," Kaylen said, looking to her friend for a response.

Aely's eyes softened. "I don't know what to tell you. I've heard that he deserted his troops when they needed him most."

Murmurs of disapproval continued through the crowd, but the rebellion had been quelled. General Astadem knelt, but held his chin high. "I have a message for King Drogan, who ironically was too much of a coward to witness my sentence himself. I pity him, along with anyone else who goes to battle with the Rayders. Had he courage enough to fight with us at Taeja, he would know this for himself."

As the executioner gripped his sword with both hands and prepared to strike, Kaylen grabbed Aely's arm and fled the courtyard. She couldn't watch.

General Astadem's voice filled her ears as she ran. "Know this. As long as a Beholder leads the Rayders into battle, they cannot be defeated."

Chapter 1

Transition

"W hy are we sneaking?" Mellai whispered to Kutad as she hid behind a tree, peering through the darkness.

"We need to get you into your grandparents' house undetected. Your grandfather and Theiss were supposed to be hunting together." He pointed through the darkness at the two distant men just before they disappeared behind a house. "They can't be seen coming back with you. Can you imagine the questions that would raise?"

Mellai smiled at the tradesmen and slumped against his shoulder, weary from travel. For the second time, Kutad had selflessly journeyed into the Vidarien Mountains to rescue a helpless young woman. Only this time, it had been her instead of Kaylen, and he had the help of her grandfather and Theiss.

"We can't reveal the truth to the villagers either," Kutad continued. "If they couple your disappearance with Kaylen's kidnapping last winter, they would demand you leave and take your troubles with you. I'd have to adopt you back into my caravan, *Linney*." His expression sobered. "Why would you go back there, Mellai? Of all places in Appernysia, why there?"

"The clearing?" Mellai asked. "I don't know. It's just where I ended up."

She turned away from Kutad, hiding the tears in her eyes. She wanted to forget everything—the letter from Kaylen, Lon's betrayal, the Jaed—everything that made her heart ache and her stomach churn.

A shadowed figure waved them forward, and Kutad led Mellai through the tall reeds. Soon the four travelers were huddled together in front of her grandparents' house. Despite their care, the front door creaked open as soon as they arrived.

"Dhargon, is that you?" an aged woman whispered as she poked her head out of the house.

Mellai's grandfather nodded, then the woman stepped outside and flung her arms around Mellai. "You don't know how happy I am to see you alive. Now come inside before somebody sees you!"

"One moment, Grandmother," Mellai said with a smile, then turned to Theiss. "Are you staying here tonight?"

"I should go home," Theiss replied as his face flushed red. He kissed Mellai on the forehead. "I'm glad you're safe." He nodded at her grandmother, then turned down the dirt road.

Mellai's grandfather snickered as he watched Theiss's outline disappear into the darkness. "How about you, Kutad? It's not safe to travel this late, especially by yourself. Can I convince you to stay until morning?"

Kutad shook his head. "I need to hurry back to Réxura. My caravan will be anxious to leave. I'm already worried we won't make the full trade loop around the Western Valley before winter. I have no intention of repeating last year's misery."

"Which means you won't stop by Pree again?" Mellai asked, forlorn. "I was hoping to give my parents a message, but I can't send Theiss again. He's travelled there two times already this year. Hunting excuses can't hold out forever."

"I'll see what I can do," Kutad said. "What would you like me to tell them?"

Mellai frowned. "I don't know. I would rather keep everything about Lon a secret, but my parents are going to find out when the villagers get back from their annual journey to Itorea."

"Your parents should know the truth," Kutad said. "I can't promise I'll make it to Pree, but if I do, I'll fill in the blanks of what they already know. Roseiri is always the last stop on our way home to Réxura, so I'll bring you word then. How does that sound?"

Mellai hugged Kutad, then stood on her tiptoes and kissed his cheek. "Thank you, Kutad. You're a true friend, and you've done so much for my family."

The corners of Kutad's mouth dropped slightly as he nodded.

Before Mellai could ask him what was wrong, Dhargon stepped around her and clasped Kutad's hand. "I owe you everything for helping bring my granddaughter back safely."

"Think nothing of it," Kutad answered, but his smile seemed forced.

Mellai's grandmother also gave Kutad a warm hug, then moved back to hold her granddaughter. "Your wagon and team are out back, Kutad. I fed them and loaded a fresh supply of hay in the wagon, along with a basket of food. Sorry I couldn't do more."

Kutad put his fist over his heart and bowed low. "You have done too much already, Allegna. I'll see you in a few months."

Once Kutad disappeared around the corner of the house, Mellai's grandmother led her into the house and closed the door.

"Let me look at you," Allegna ordered as she held Mellai by her shoulders. A warm glow from the fireplace filled the room. "My goodness! You're as frail as a newborn foal."

"She could use a hot meal," Dhargon added. "Poor girl has eaten nothing but dried biscuits for almost five days."

Allegna shook her head. "Honestly, Mellai, how am I supposed to take care of you when you disappear like that?"

"I'm sorry, Grandmother. I just needed to get away." Her face fell as she recalled the closing message in Kaylen's letter. *I'm sorry, Mellai, but your brother has betrayed us all.*

Indeed he had, and after the Jaed's visit . . . she feared what role she would play in her brother's future.

Allegna's eyes softened. "Sit down and rest while I bring you something to eat."

As her grandmother busied herself with a late dinner, Mellai listened to Kutad's wagon moving slowly down the dirt road. "Kutad doesn't seem like he's in a big hurry to get back to his trading caravan, despite what he said."

"Can you blame him?" Allegna called from the kitchen. "The loss of family and friends would be hard enough, but now the tradesmen have savages—no disrespect to Lon—living nearby. Life was easier when Taeja was abandoned. Even in Roseiri, I don't feel like we're far enough away from the danger. I've even wondered if we should pack up and join your parents in Pree, Mellai."

"Are you serious?" Mellai asked excitedly. "That would be wonderful."

"Our roots go too deep here," Dhargon interrupted. "I've spent my whole life taking care of this land, and so have my fathers five generations back."

Allegna stopped and turned toward Dhargon. "And who's going to take care of it after you're gone?"

"Maybe a future great-grandson," Dhargon answered with a smirk as he glanced at Mellai.

"Stop it, Grandfather," Mellai said, shaking her head. It wasn't the first time he had fabricated a marriage proposal from Theiss. The initial teasing had made Mellai giddier than a pig buried in slop, but the anticipation had dissolved to irritation. While marrying Theiss was an exciting prospect, Mellai knew better than to give such remarks credence when they came from her grandfather.

"A man learns to appreciate what he has when he almost loses it. Theiss and I just spent two days together searching for you. That leaves a lot of time for a heart-to-heart."

A large smile grew on Allegna's face as she returned to her cooking with an extra bounce in her step. Mellai only rolled her eyes. "You're just trying to change the subject. Why won't you move to Pree, Grandfather? It just seems right. Even Grandmother wants to go."

"It's not up for discussion," Dhargon grumbled. "If you and Theiss want to run off together, that's your own choice, but Allegna and I are staying here." He lit a small lantern and stormed out of the house, slamming the door.

Mellai turned to her grandmother. "What was that all about? Is it because I ran away?"

Allegna stared out of the back window and sighed. "That didn't help, but no. This isn't the first time the subject of leaving Roseiri has come up. He's irritated because I brought it up in front of you. He doesn't like being pressured into things."

"That makes two of us," Mellai said. She soon heard her grandfather behind the house, chopping wood.

"The truth is," Allegna continued, "your grandfather is afraid of leaving Roseiri. He has a good reputation here, but he knows he's getting old. He can't do what he used to. From what you've told me about Pree, it would take a lot of effort to earn their trust. I don't know if either of us has that kind of energy left."

"You wouldn't have to do anything," Mellai countered. "Our house has more than enough room for you. You wouldn't need to worry about your reputation either. If my parents say you're trustworthy, the villagers would gladly welcome you."

Allegna nodded. "I know. I've thought this through already, but your grandfather wouldn't accept charity. He'd work himself to death, literally."

Mellai frowned as she listened to the repeated sound of metal splitting wood. She knew her grandmother was right, but Mellai wasn't going to give up. Staying in Roseiri presented too many problems. If Theiss really was about to propose marriage, she wanted her parents to be part of the ceremony. That couldn't happen if she and Theiss stayed in Roseiri. And she'd have to continue hiding her identity. Yet, returning to Pree would pose problems as well. Theiss would have to leave his family behind. His father would never forgive him, and his younger brother . . . well, Theiss's leaving would break his heart.

Bringing her grandparents to Pree might even be dangerous. Someone might connect their family to Roseiri, where the Beholder rumors had started in the first place. The Rayders didn't care about the rumors anymore, but the Appernysians definitely would. If King Drogan discovered Lon's identity, he would hunt their entire family down.

Mellai sighed and laid her head on the table, closing her eyes. Her life was becoming an ever more complicated knot of deception.

A dazzling light suddenly filled the room, piercing her eyelids. Mellai jerked back, her mind flashing back to that night in the mountains. She shaded her eyes with her hand and peered out through squinted eyes. A glowing figure hovered in the air in front of her, like a shadow floating in the middle of the room, but emanating light instead of darkness. A familiar pair of brilliant, shining eyes pierced her with searing light.

Terrified, Mellai turned to her grandmother, but saw a similar glow filling Allegna's body as she bustled about the kitchen. Allegna seemed oblivious to the figure hovering next to Mellai, and she did not appear concerned about the dense fog filling the room.

Mellai turned back toward the glowing shadow and opened her mouth, but a voice cut her off before she could speak.

"Do not speak, Mellai. Your grandmother cannot see or hear me, nor could she understand what you are witnessing."

Then how am I supposed to talk to you? Mellai thought. *I have so many questions.*

"I know your thoughts," the figure said. "All will be well."

Mellai nodded slowly, recognizing the voice. *Llen?*

"Yes."

I thought only Beholders are supposed to be able to see Jaeds. Why do you keep appearing to me?

"Have you no assumptions?"

The implication was clear. Mellai squirmed and stared at the floor, pushing her thoughts to the back of her mind.

"I will not dictate your life's journey," the Jaed continued, "but one unavoidable path lies at your feet. You have been chosen."

What does that mean? Mellai silently screamed, her head jerking up to glare at the Jaed. *Am I doomed to a life of misery like my brother? Do I have to join the Rayders, too? Am I going to help Lon destroy Appernysia?*

"I will not speak of Lon at this time, nor his chosen path," Llen answered calmly. "Only you can decide whether or not to stand next to him. Your future is your own."

Mellai clenched her jaw. *Why are you here, then? Did you want to rub this curse in my face? Did you do the same thing to Lon?*

Piercing light poured from the Jaed's eyes, causing Mellai to wince in pain as she covered her face with her hands.

"A visit from a Jaed should not be taken lightly," Llen said.

Tears flowed down Mellai's face. *You said yourself that you know my mind. You know where my anger comes from. Why have you allowed my family to endure so much pain? Why didn't you help Lon? Why did you let him join the enemy?*

"I have not come to answer your questions tonight, but to bestow my gift. Unlike Lon, your transition will complete within a month."

My transition?

"Your suffering will be far greater than your brother's, and you must endure it alone." Despite Llen's resonating voice, Mellai heard a touch of sympathy as he continued. "No one can know the cause of your pain. If anyone discovers the truth, the consequences will be far beyond your comprehension."

I don't understand, Mellai thought as she peeked out from behind her hands. *What consequences? What transition?* Her mind reeled with panic. *What suffering?*

Llen glided forward. The oval outline of his eyes slanted down with compassion as he reached out and touched her forehead with the palm of his hand.

"I will visit you again."

As he finished speaking, a jolt coursed through Mellai. The energy stabbed through her eyes and down her body, burning her fingertips and the ends of her toes before reversing up her body once again. Her blood felt as if it had turned to boiling tar, her heart forcing the searing pitch through every inch of her body.

Mellai toppled from her chair and thrashed on the wooden floor. Her screams sliced through Roseiri.

Chapter 2

Despair

Sweat poured from Mellai's pale skin, soaking through her clothes and dripping onto the floor. Perspiration fell through Dhargon's fingers as he held her, forming a small pool on the timber under Mellai's head. Allegna mopped the sweat from Mellai's face.

Already, a crowd of villagers was massing at the front door, Theiss and his father foremost among them.

"Linney's burning up," Allegna told Theiss as he burst through the front door.

"Help me," Theiss said as he took hold of Mellai under her arms. Dhargon held onto her legs and together they carried her to the bedroom.

Allegna entered the bedroom moments later with Theiss's father. She handed him a cup of hot water and crushed herbs, then he hurried to the bed. "Tilt Linney's head back and hold it still," he said. "We need to get as much of this . . ."

His voice faded when he saw Mellai's unveiled face. He looked up at Dhargon, having obviously recognized her.

"Not now," Dhargon whispered intently. "Please, Gorlon. Help me save my granddaughter's life."

"Please," Theiss added.

"You knew?" Gorlon asked his son.

"Please, Father."

Gorlon glanced back at Allegna, who was wringing her hands nervously. He sighed. "I'll help, but you owe me an explanation."

"I'll owe you more than that," Dhargon added as Gorlon stood next to Mellai's head and placed the cup against her lips. He drizzled the elixir into her mouth and, although unconscious, Mellai immediately gagged and coughed up the mixture.

"Suggestions?" Gorlon asked.

"Pour it in and force her mouth and nose shut," Allegna snapped back. "She has to drink it!"

Gorlon handed the cup to Theiss, then pinched Mellai's nose with his left hand. "Go ahead."

Theiss poured some of the elixir into her mouth, then Gorlon clamped her jaw and lips shut with his right hand. Mellai's eyes shot open and her body contorted, but the three men held firm. Mellai's eyes bulged in panic, until she finally swallowed. Gorlon removed his right hand, Mellai gasped for air, then her eyes fluttered shut again.

"How much did she take?" Gorlon asked.

"Only half," Theiss replied, shaking his head. "I can't do this."

"It's saving her life," Dhargon said.

Theiss's jaw line tightened, but he complied. He poured the remaining elixir into Mellai's mouth and Gorlon forced her to swallow it. She reacted just as violently, but once again returned to her comatose state.

"What now?" Gorlon asked.

"We wait," Allegna answered, her expression drawn. "The rest is up to her."

* * * * *

Gorlon sat next to Allegna. "What did I make her drink?"

"It's a strong sedative that should also help reduce the fever." Allegna's brow furrowed. "I don't understand where this came from.

We were having a normal conversation, then she started to spasm and the fever overwhelmed her—all within minutes."

Gorlon nodded, understanding the severity of the situation. Allegna was a wise and experienced healer. If she couldn't help her granddaughter, no one could. Gorlon turned his attention to Mellai's motionless figure on the bed, wondering what brought her back to Roseiri. Where was the rest of her family? Why was she hiding?

As Gorlon watched his son and Dhargon at Mellai's side, he cursed himself silently. When had Theiss discovered who Mellai was? Why had he kept her presence a secret? What was *he* hiding?

* * * * *

"Make room so I can check if her fever is gone," Allegna said after a while. She turned to Theiss's younger brother, who had taken up position in the doorway. "Bring a lantern, Reese. I'll need the light."

Dhargon and Theiss moved away from the bed, while Reese hovered at Allegna's shoulder with the lantern. The orange light flickered across Mellai's pale face. Her lips were slightly parted, and her closed eyes looked dark and sunken.

"Is she dead?" Reese asked.

"Shut your mouth," Theiss growled. He pushed past his brother, lifting Mellai's torso to cradle her in his arms. He turned to Allegna.

Allegna lifted her hand toward Mellai, but Theiss flinched back. "She's still alive," he growled through clenched teeth.

Allegna forced a reassuring smile and placed her hands on Mellai's forehead and chest, then closed her eyes and held her own breath. Mellai's head was cold and clammy. There was no movement in her chest. No breathing. No heartbeat. Allegna remained motionless, praying for the life of her granddaughter. Minutes passed in silence, but Mellai's condition did not change.

Allegna reopened her eyes and looked up at Theiss. He searched her face, but she could not hide the truth.

"I'm sorry," she whispered in a trembling voice.

"No!" Theiss shouted, pulling Mellai closer and laying his cheek on her head. "She was fine when I left! She didn't . . . she couldn't . . ." His voice broke and he wept fiercely, rocking Mellai in his arms.

Allegna slumped, but Dhargon caught her and helped her to a chair, then knelt in front of her.

"Allegna?"

She stared at the ground in shock, unable to return his gaze.

"She's dead?" Reese asked again. His bottom lip quivered.

Allegna finally looked up and nodded, too overwhelmed to speak.

Reese dropped the lantern and fled from the room. Theiss touched his forehead to Mellai's, quietly whispering under his breath as his tears wet her face. Allegna wrapped her arms around her husband and stroked the back of his balding head.

"Mellai," she cried. "My sweet, precious Mellai."

Chapter 3

Preserved

Lon Marcs gazed at the ominous forest far to the south as he traveled along the edge of a dry riverbed. His squad followed his eyes.

"Are we in danger, Beholder?" Wade Arneson asked.

Lon sighed. It had been two weeks since the Battle for Taeja. The surviving Rayder soldiers, along with four thousand Appernysian peasants, had bowed themselves before Lon, hailing him as the first Beholder to appear in more than twelve hundred years. He still struggled to accept his new status. The way everyone looked at him expectantly, like he would solve all their problems, was a difficult burden to bear. And the dissention. It wasn't out in the open, but Lon could tell by the way people acted around him, speaking in hushed whispers, that many of the Rayders didn't like him—his quick rise to power, an ex-Appernysian endowed with True Sight, the power Rayders believed was theirs by right of inheritance. And they probably thought Lon got his way with everything because of his close friendships with Acting Commander Omar and General Tarek. They couldn't be more wrong.

"This is the closest I've ever been to the Blight, Lieutenant," Lon answered. "Actually, I hadn't seen this forest before yesterday."

"Nor had I," Wade said with a nod as he stared at a line of towering trees forty miles to the south. "I had always wondered why Appernysians were so frightened of a measly forest, but now that

I see it with my own eyes, there is little anyone could do to make me enter it."

Lon looked back at Wade with raised eyebrows. "Really? Not even with a Beholder leading the way?"

Wade frowned as he watched Lon until a smile formed at the corner of Lon's mouth. Lon could see that Wade wasn't sure if he was jesting, but soon Wade's face brightened and he chuckled. Soon, Lon and his squad joined in the laughter.

"Don't worry," Lon said as he patted Wade on the shoulder. "I wouldn't lead you into the Blight, even if we were trapped against it with no retreat. At least in battle, you know what's coming for you."

"And your enemy will not start eating you before you die," Thad added from behind, his hand on his sword and his sharp eyes glued to the south. A somber mood fell on the squad again.

"Very true," Lon agreed as he shifted his gaze to the nearby peaks looming overhead to the west. "Though we won't be much safer in the mountains. Hopefully we'll be able to find the diversion without having to travel very far into them."

As Lon led the Rayders west, he reflected on his responsibilities, grateful for the chance to get away from annoying politics. He enjoyed following orders much more than giving them. After the Battle for Taeja, the Rayders had created a strict outline of duties to follow if they hoped to survive the coming winter. Their most pressing need was water. Taeja had once been fed by rivers from the Tamadoras Mountains, but when the Rayders were banished at the end of the First Age, the Appernysian king had ordered the destruction of their city and the rerouting of the rivers running into it. Over the centuries, the Taejan Plains had faded from rich green to dry, dusty yellow. For the returning Rayders, the closest source of fresh water to Taeja was a lake at the base of Three Peaks, but that was forty miles northeast of the city.

After helping care for the wounded and cremating the dead, Lon and his squad had received the assignment of finding where the water's flow had been diverted, and returning the flow into the riverbed. Lon's ability to mold the earth made it an easy task to complete by himself, but Omar considered it too dangerous to venture into the Tamadoras Mountains alone—even for a Beholder. And so, Lon and his men had followed the winding riverbed for two days, traveling over sixty miles from Taeja.

Lon glanced over his shoulder and followed the winding path of the riverbed. Along the way from Taeja, he and his squad had discovered a distributary of the main river about twenty-five miles east of the Tamadoras Mountains. The alternate path ran south, angling directly toward Réxura. If the Appernysians decided to attack from Réxura, they would have to cross more than a hundred miles of barren plains. Lon didn't want to supply them with water along that route, so he had closed the southern fork of the dry riverbed before continuing west.

"What is the plan, Beholder?" Wade asked, breaking Lon out of his reverie.

"We'll make camp here for the night," Lon answered as he slid out of his saddle. He gauged their distance from the dense forest at the base of the mountains. *About two miles away.* "We'll find the source of the dam tomorrow while the sun is up. Gather firewood. I'm not going to camp this close to those mountains in the dark."

The squad uttered their agreement. They galloped to the nearest oak tree, cut it down, and dragged it back to the camp. A large pile of cut wood was soon collected, and the men retrieved their bows and bedrolls from their saddles. Wade piled a few logs together, then sat on his own bedroll and turned to Lon.

Lon was still standing by his horse, feeding him dry reeds out of his hand. He ignored Wade's stares as he spoke loudly enough for the lieutenant to hear. "See, Dawes. This is exactly what I told Omar before we left Flagheim. Rather than building a fire properly—with a tinderbox—they pile a few logs together and expect me to ignite them. They're getting lazy already."

Dawes nickered and snorted, drawing a smile from Lon. "I knew you'd understand."

Wade immediately walked to his own horse to retrieve his tinderbox, then gathered some yellow grass and knelt by the log pile.

"Why does he refuse to light it?" Preton complained to Wade, but not quietly enough. Lon heard every word. Intervention crossed his mind, but he pushed the thought aside. Wade would take care of it before Lon had the chance to turn around. Such loyalty filled Lon with reassurance. "After what he did to the Appernysians," Preton continued, "lighting a small fire should be—"

Before Preton could finish, Wade drew his sword and placed its tip against Preton's neck. "Do not question your First Lieutenant," he ordered, "*especially* when he is a Beholder."

Preton brought his chin up, and Lon could see his blood pulsing in his neck. Preton glared at Wade.

Lon grimaced as Wade's eyes narrowed. He had seen this encounter many times before with various Rayders throughout Taeja. Wade's tactics were effective, but his people couldn't be ruled by fear eternally. Something had to change, and that bothered Lon the most. He had no idea what.

"You might have been loyal before we left the Exile," Wade said, "but your change is obvious. I have seen the way you watch him— that mix of jealousy and hatred. Now finish lighting this fire." He stood and stepped to the side.

"Yes, Lieutenant," Preton answered as he held out his hand.

Wade sheathed his sword. "With your *own* tinderbox."

Preton nodded, retrieved his tinderbox from his horse, then knelt over the dry wood and started a small fire.

"You have also earned the privilege of first watch, Preton," Wade added as he sat on his bedroll, "but I will be watching you. Remember that."

Preton licked his dry lips. "Yes, Lieutenant," he replied, then sat twelve paces to the west, facing the nearby mountains.

An awkward silence settled over the camp. Wade was staring at Preton, his lips pulled tight as he breathed heavily through his nose. Lon only shook his head, still wondering what he could do to change the Rayders' hearts.

* * * * *

Well into the night, Lon awoke to a gentle nudge on his shoulder. He turned his head and saw Wade prodding him with a long branch. This had been their detailed arrangement for two reasons: one, to keep Lon from a panicked awakening, and two, to ensure the safety of whoever woke him.

Lon stretched his arms over his head and sat up. All but the two watchmen had fallen asleep, their prostrate forms orange in the flickering firelight. Preton was arranging his own bedroll on the opposite side of the fire. His shift must have just ended.

"I am sorry, Beholder," Wade said, "but I am too tired to maintain watch, and I trust no one else to keep you safe tonight."

"I understand," Lon said as he stood. "How long did I sleep?"

"Three or four hours."

Lon nodded. "Lie down, Lieutenant. I'm rested enough."

Wade saluted and curled up on his nearby bedroll. His exhaustion soon overcame him and his eyes drifted shut.

Lon was truly glad to take over watch. Because True Sight enabled him to see far past the light of the fire, he was the best person for the job. As usual, he summoned his power and began to survey their surroundings.

A solid line of glowing figures, too far away to distinguish clearly, had completely encircled the camp. Only a hundred-yard buffer separated them, putting the beasts dangerously close, but at a protective distance outside of the firelight.

"Defensive positions!" Lon shouted immediately, his voice loud and commanding. "Circle the fire!"

While Lon pivoted around and around, searching for the nearest threat, his squad scrambled. They were half awake, often stumbling into each other in their hurried efforts. Wade was the first to Lon's side. He dropped a pile of gear at Lon's feet, then sprinted back to his horse. Lon quickly dug into the pile. He slung his bow over his shoulder and lashed a full quiver at his waist, opposite his sheathed falchion. He then stood facing away from the fire, his diamond-shaped shield held in his right hand and a glaive in his left. Another thirty seconds passed before the rest of his squad was similarly assembled, a solid defensive line encircling the fire.

"What is it, Beholder?" Wade said. He stood to Lon's right, peering over the top of his diamond-shaped shield for something to kill.

"We're trapped," Lon replied, his voice loud enough for his whole squad to hear, "completely surrounded. I can't tell if they are man or beast, but it's obvious they aren't here to swap stories. Ready yourself for an attack. A hundred yards off." He glanced at the nine Rayders, calculating a quick and desperate defense. "Stagger archers, every other man. Prepare to duck behind your shields."

Lon gripped his glaive tighter, debating whether to cast his shield aside. Although a master swordsman, Lon liked two handed pole weapons more. He felt at one with the glaive as he twirled it around his body. It felt . . . natural.

"I can't see anything," Wade said. "How can we know what to defend against?"

The same thought had crossed Lon's mind, and their only source of light was the fire. With only a few logs at their disposal, they needed more fuel. Knowing the best solution would be to use True Sight to bring the wood to them, he concentrated on the closest pine tree. Using the surrounding air, he ripped it out of the ground and brought it back toward their camp. The glowing line of enemy watchers reacted.

A volley of stones arched into the air from the beasts, soaring toward them. Seconds turned into hours, as they had when Lon first used his power to protect his twin sister in Pree. The approaching threat distracted Lon, enough that the hovering tree escaped his grasp. Its momentum caused it to twist sideways, hurtling toward them and threatening to crush them all in one sweep.

Lon tried to recapture the pine tree, but he was too panicked to concentrate. All he could manage was a quick shout of warning.

"On the ground!"

The Rayders obeyed instantly, dropping flat to their chests. The tumbling pine twisted over them, branches and needles whipping at their backs before crashing somewhere in the distance.

"Shields up!" Lon shouted again, rising to one knee and holding his shield angled over his head.

The barrage of stones dropped moments later, pummeling their shields with loud clangs. Lon's arm stung when one smashed directly into his shield, then a stone the size of a man's head sunk into the soft soil next to him. One landed in front of them and rebounded to his left. Dovan barely dropped his shield in time to stop the mortal blow. Shouts poured from the squad. Pain. Warnings. Their situation was desperate.

"Should we charge?" Wade shouted over the noise. He was crouched low, supporting himself with his fist on the ground.

Once again, Wade was right. No one would survive if the barrage continued. It had to stop, and a counterattack was the only solution.

Lon took a deep breath to calm himself, then dropped his shield and raised a high wall of thick dirt directly in front of himself, his default response to most needs. After stepping against it for protection, he turned and located the nearby pine tree. With a desperate surge of power, Lon raised the tree over the fire, shattered it into manageable pieces and dropped them into the flames. With the aid of True Sight, he made sure the lumber quickly ignited, their light widening the field of vision for his squad.

"Look out!" Wade shouted, shoving Lon aside just before a boulder struck his head. It bounced off the dirt wall and landed in the center of the fire.

Lon regained his feet, berating himself for being so careless. He had to think fast. He had never attempted to use True Sight on something hundreds of yards away, but he had to distract their attackers somehow. He picked a spot in front of the enemy's glowing line as he pulled energy into his body through his feet, then forced it out his hands. With a ground-shaking crash, he thrust up an earthen wall fifteen feet high.

The attackers disappeared behind the dirt, but quickly reappeared over the top and around the sides of the barrier. Their movement on top of the barrier was just clear enough that Lon could see they were throwing the boulders at him, head-sized rocks from further than three hundred feet away. These attackers were no mere humans, but something worse. Something far more powerful.

Lon picked another spot ahead of the line. Using the air again, he lifted a large section of rock out of the ground and dropped the rubble on top of their attackers.

A terrible roar erupted, and the stone barrage finally stopped. Where Lon dropped the rubble, the attackers were clustering together. The Rayder squad similarly repositioned themselves near Lon, taking cover behind his earthen barrier.

"Jaeds protect us!" Wade shouted over the creatures' din.

Lon gave no reply as he turned and lowered the dirt wall. It provided protection, but hiding behind it would allow the beasts to sneak up on them unimpeded. "Bows at the ready, Rayders. Circle the fire and shoot at anything you see."

The fire, Lon thought. "Change of position. Everyone stay behind me. If I turn, you turn, and keep loosing those arrows." Lon faced the fire, standing so close he could smell the stubble on his unshaven face melting in the heat, despite the sweat coating his skin.

Moments later, an ear-piercing cry sounded from the enemy line, causing Lon to wince. Through the fire, he watched the glowing line attack, barreling toward them like stampeding horses.

"Attack," Lon ordered. "Aim at ninety yards."

While his squad emptied their quivers, Lon drew spheres of flame from the fire and hurled them at the advancing line. Bursts of flame ignited the grass when the spheres hit the ground, but the oncoming force easily dodged them. Lon pivoted to face another front and sent a jet of fire out into the field. It ignited a long line of grass with high flames, but the glowing attackers pushed straight through it.

"Seventy yards," Lon shouted, then reached for his glaive. The weapon slipped from his sweaty palms, shaken loose by his trembling hands. Lon cursed, partly in frustration, but mostly in desperation. Only a miracle would save them, and only he could provide it. No other solutions. He clenched his jaw, grabbed the glaive off the ground, and turned away from the fire, abandoning the flames. "Sixty yards," he shouted as he lowered the glaive and pulled energy into himself.

The roars continued to intensify as the glowing line of beasts tightened their perimeter. Lon carefully gauged their speed, waiting for them to cross an imaginary mark forty yards away. When they touched the mark, Lon forced another wide row of rock upward, underneath the line in front of him, sending the creatures hurtling through the air toward his position.

"Can't maneuver without the ground," Lon shouted defiantly as he swung the glaive around his body. "Stand ready, Rayders. I'll only get one chance at this."

Ear-shattering snarls and growls pounded in Lon's ears from all sides, even directly above. It was unlike anything he had ever heard before, mingled with the terrified whinnies of their tethered horses, but Lon focused on the approaching danger in front of him. He continued to swing his glaive in front of himself in a figure eight, building speed and drawing energy into himself. He peered at the helpless attackers, but their glowing energy was still too condensed to distinguish. Just before they hit the ground—not twenty strides in front of Lon—he swung the glaive over his head like an ax and struck the steel blade on the grass. The ground shook at the impact, and a wave of energy surged outward in a blinding flash of light only Lon could see. It filled his vision, obscuring everything else.

Moments later, as the light subsided, Lon jerked his head down as two massive creatures came into view. They came from above, skimming just above the squads' heads. Lon felt a burst of air upon his face as the beasts flapped their massive wings.

Lon's jaw dropped as he watched the beasts attack the fleeing enemy in all directions. Terrified snarls erupted each time the beasts dove into their midst, followed by deafening cries. Over and over, the two beasts attacked, pushing the line of danger farther away, until they reformed into a cluster and disappeared into the forest.

Lon blew out his breath and dropped to his knees, his body sapped of energy and his senses failing. *What just happened?* he thought as he glanced around and found himself surrounded by his men. They stood with their glaives outward in all directions, ready to defend their Beholder with their lives. But the squad remained motionless, obviously unsure of what to do with themselves.

"Are they dead?" Wade asked.

"Not all of them," Lon answered, "but the survivors fled."

Wade eyed him, but seemed satisfied. "What you did was amazing, Beholder."

"Perhaps," Lon replied, "but I had a little help from two flying beasts." A strange feeling overcame him, tugging at his memory. Despite the peril, he felt strangely soothed. Suddenly, he remembered. He had experienced such a feeling once before, on his journey from Pree.

"Blue eyes . . ." Lon muttered to himself. He shook his head and glanced around. The burning timber, once a large pile of raging heat, was now scattered around them in all directions. He had been so caught up in the moment that he hadn't noticed. "What happened?"

"When you hit the ground," Wade continued, "the logs bounced up and flew around like dead leaves in a windstorm. All of us but Dovan fell to the ground from the shaking. What did you do?"

"I don't know."

Indeed, Lon had no idea what he had done. He had run into desperate situations before and worked his way out of them through some inexplicable show of force. When he hit the ground with his glaive, he had trusted the same to happen again.

But I desperately wish I knew, Lon thought. *The blast . . . it wasn't air or fire, so what did I do? It looked like raw energy.*

When he pulled out of his daze, Lon noticed their horses were missing, having ripped their tether stakes from the ground. He searched the surrounding darkness and saw Elja's glowing form. The Rayder was on one of the horses, with a couple in tow and many left to catch.

"What was that roaring?" Thad asked, squatting next to his First Lieutenant and peering into the darkness. Aside from Lon, Thad's vision was the best of their squad.

"I think the roaring came from our rescuers," Lon said. "They must have been circling high above us before they rushed in and chased the danger away. They may have been the reason we weren't attacked sooner. I think they were ghraefs, but I wish I knew for sure."

"I wish I knew what *attacked* us," Thad continued. "I only saw a faint shadow of the beasts before you struck the earth and forced them away. Could you see them, Beholder?"

"No," Lon answered, releasing True Sight. The answer wasn't completely untrue. He couldn't distinguish any specific physical details about them, except that they could sprint faster than horses. "We'll inspect their dead in the morning."

"I doubt you will recognize them," Channer added. "That forest and those mountains are full of creatures most people have never seen before."

Lon breathed deeply, trying to force his anxiety out with his lungs. Although he didn't know what had attacked them, the danger was undeniable. Had the ghraefs not come to their rescue, even he and his squad's unrivaled skill would not have saved them. Whatever those attacking beasts were, they needed to be fought at a distance. That was where Nik and Riyen would most benefit them. Their skill with a bow was unmatched by any Rayder.

It was then that Lon notice his two sharpshooters were not among them, but barely visible in the ring of firelight. Nik was kneeling on the ground, his left arm limp at his side. Riyen was lying on the ground next to him. Nik held Riyen's head on his lap.

Lon summoned True Sight, dreading what he would undoubtedly see. Riyen's motionless body was dim in contrast to the glow that filled his friend. His essence had left him. Riyen was dead.

When Lon tried to walk toward the fallen Rayder, he staggered. At first Lon thought he had gone numb with sorrow, but quickly realized that his own body was injured. The left leg of his pants was torn open, his exposed thigh bruised. A boulder must have hit him, but not badly enough to hinder him in the whirlwind of the attack. Now with the excitement gone, his thigh throbbed.

He turned back to the rest of his squad. "Sound off injuries."

"I think my shield arm is broken," Keene said, holding his left bicep with his good hand, "and Channer hurt his ankle trying to dodge the boulder when it bounced off my shield."

Channer punched his cousin in the face. "Keene has a broken nose."

"Enough," Lon ordered before Keene could retaliate, not in the mood for their games. He doubted any of them knew that Riyen was dead. "Others?"

"Mostly scratches and bruises," Wade replied. "Dovan has a deep gash on his cheek."

"From the tree," Dovan said, "but it is not serious."

"Good." Lon hung his head, weary with pain and sorrow, then turned back in Nik's direction. "Follow me."

He limped forward and sat at Nik's side. With the limited light of scattered fires, he could see that Riyen had received a blow to his head. Even if Lon had found him sooner, there still would have been nothing he could do.

"It should have been me," Nik muttered as he cradled Riyen's head with his good arm. "I had my bow drawn, unaware. He shouldered me out of the way. The rock still hit me, but Riyen . . ."

Wade knelt and placed a hand on Riyen's chest. "His sacrifice will not be forgotten."

Nik slid Riyen's head to the ground and stood. He began picking up fragments of wood and placing them over Riyen's body. The squad soon joined him, Lon and Channer limping about.

Lon knew better than to use True Sight in such a circumstance. It would diminish the honor of Riyen's death to effortlessly cover his body in timber, but Nik still requested Lon's assistance to set the corpse ablaze. Lon reluctantly complied, allowing his tears to flow freely. Three of his squad had died in his service, and in such a short period of time. How long until the rest of them followed?

When the embers of Riyen's pyre ceased to glow, Lon took Nik aside. "Can you continue?"

"Yes, Beholder."

"Are you sure? There is no disgrace in returning to Taeja, especially with your injured shoulder."

Nik tried to raise his left arm, but could barely move it. "I think it is only dislocated."

"Allow me," Wade said, still shadowing Lon's every movement. "I have dealt with such injuries many times."

"As you wish," Lon said, then turned to address his squad. They were in no condition to travel, especially in the dark. They had to trust that the danger had been chased away for the night. "We need rest, now more than ever. Thad and Dovan, take watch. Make sure Elja gets back safely, then keep a wide perimeter. I don't want anyone or anything getting that close again, understand?"

"Yes, Beholder," the two answered with a salute.

Although he knew he should remain on guard, Lon was too weary to stay awake. Even as he retrieved his water skin, he fought to keep his eyes open. After a quick splash of cool water to his face, Lon caught sight of Preton. He was studying Lon intently with his arms folded across his chest. Lon shook his head and rearranged his pad on the ground.

Wade obviously didn't trust Preton, but Lon wasn't sure what to think. Even as a Beholder, Lon had plenty of weaknesses, as the attack just proved. Preton had many opportunities to kill Lon, but hadn't taken them. Confused, perhaps, but rebelling? Seeking solitude didn't make Preton an enemy. Lon had been doing the same thing for months. Sometimes silence and meditation were the only cures to confusion and strife. Preton would work it out. He just needed space.

Chapter 4

Onward

The next morning, the Rayders struggled into their saddles and followed Lon as he led them out to investigate the previous night's attackers. Two walls of stone and earth still stood where Lon had raised them. Patches of charred grass showed where fireballs had landed. Even with their own injuries and the sorrow of Riyen's death, Lon's squad asked many questions about the previous night. They had only witnessed Lon using True Sight a handful of times. It obviously still astounded them.

Aside from what Lon had done, there were obvious disturbances in the soil where pairs of sprinting claws had dug up the dirt. There were pools and trails of blood everywhere, yet no bodies were left behind. When the Rayders came to the spot where Lon had dropped boulders on the creatures, they found tunnels dug under the rocks, but no corpses.

It was the tunneling that especially caught Lon's attention. His stomach churned as he thought back to a lesson from Omar, specifically the illustration of Appernysia's most feared enemy: Seven-foot beasts with bulging muscles covered in fall-colored fur; fierce claws for digging complex underground fortresses; razor sharp teeth; two-foot bone spikes jutting from knees and elbows. Lon shuddered. The calahein had been wiped out over twelve hundred years earlier, yet he couldn't ignore the obvious signs of their return.

"What is your order, Beholder?" Wade asked as they sat upon their horses, looking into the deep holes in the ground. After resetting Nik's shoulder, Wade had returned to his Beholder's side. Lon doubted the Lieutenant got much sleep.

"We have a job to do," Lon answered, trying to remain calm as he searched for the nearby riverbed. He turned Dawes to follow its dusty path into the mountain forest, shifting as much weight as possible to his right stirrup to ease the pain in his opposite leg. His torn pants showed that the purple bruising in his thigh had deepened in color. It would take at least two weeks before he completely healed. "Taeja needs water, and it's our duty to provide it for our people. We can only hope that what attacked us last night has been scared away for good."

"Not to mention every other danger living in those mountains," Keene added with a smirk at his cousin. Keene's broken nose was still swollen, but had been reset sometime during the night. His broken arm, however, would not heal so easily. It was bound against his body with a cloth torn from his bedroll, as was Nik's.

Lon repositioned himself next to Channer and looked at Keene. "Lead the way, Keene."

The Rayder's grin dissolved as he saluted, then he took point and led the squad toward the mountains. Lon stayed at the rear of the column with Channer.

"How is your ankle?" Lon asked as he signaled with a slight gesture to allow some distance between them and the rest of the squad.

"Manageable. Your leg?"

"Not as bad as it looks," Lon said, then lowered his voice to a whisper. "What have you decided?"

"About what, Beholder?"

"About last night. You've seen the evidence. What do you think attacked us?"

Channer frowned. "I only have assumptions, Beholder, but they are far-fetched."

Lon nodded. "As are mine. Speak openly."

"From what I have read," Channer said, shifting in his leather saddle, "my best guess is that kelsh attacked us."

"I was afraid you'd say that." Lon thought back to the sketch Omar had shown him of the kelsh—the nightmarish soldiery of the calahein. "Could it really be true? Could the calahein be alive?"

"It should be impossible," Channer countered. "They were exterminated at the end of the First Age."

"So the books say."

Channer cast a sideways look at Lon. "If they really were kelsh, then we are in serious danger. What if there are seith nearby? We don't have enough arrows to protect ourselves from the flying calahein, and there is only so much you can do, Beholder."

"What can we do? We'll just have to trust that our flying protectors are still nearby."

Lon glanced up at the sky as the squad moved into the forest. He thought back to the previous night. *No*, he resolved. *I wouldn't have felt so calm if they had been seith, and they wouldn't have attacked their own kind.*

His last thought stuck in his mind. *Ghraefs. Could it be?* Despite its impracticality, the thought made sense. He hadn't checked the sky, but he would never make that mistake again. If kelsh were alive and attacking, seith wouldn't be far behind. He would have to change his tactics, too. With their vast, membranous wings, seith didn't need to touch the ground to maneuver.

Lon remained tense as his squad followed the dry riverbed through the dense foliage, weaving between large pine and oak trees, and dense clusters of thorny shrubs. They traveled slowly, but gratefully found the river blockage within just a few hundred yards of the forest's edge. A mound of rocks and dirt had been piled across the original river and a new channel had been dug leading south through the forest.

Lon looked at Dovan with a teasing smirk. "Want to climb up one of these trees and see where that channel leads?"

Dovan saluted, then leaped from his saddle and grabbed hold of the branch of a nearby oak tree. He swung himself up into the tree and started his ascent.

"Amazing how he does that, isn't it?" Lon commented, mostly to himself, but still earned a response from Channer.

"Ironic that a tree was the only thing that injured him last night."

A minute later, Dovan's voice echoed from the top of the oak. "It is hard to see through the trees, but it looks like the channel continues south for miles toward the Forest of Blight."

"Well done, Dovan," Lon called, then turned toward the dam, anxious to complete their task and leave the forest. "The Blight doesn't need this extra water."

"How may we help?" Wade asked.

Lon smiled. "You can find higher ground, just in case."

While the squad moved away, Lon summoned True Sight and thought through his strategy. It would have been easiest to move the dam straight from the dry riverbed to the water channel. However, Lon wanted a burst of water to help force the river down its old path. The only way he could successfully transfer the power of the moving water without slowing its flow would be to perform both actions at the same time. Lon knew how to coordinate two separate flows of energy while creating fire, but then he combined both flows together to accomplish one task. This situation was different, and much more difficult. He had to perform two separate tasks at the exact same time, completely independent of each other.

As he led Dawes to the rest of the Rayders, Lon thought about a mind game he used to play as a child. He would rotate his right foot in a clockwise motion, then tried to rotate his right hand around counterclockwise in the opposite direction. Inevitably, Lon had always started turning his foot in the same direction as his hand. If he used his left foot and his right hand, or his left hand and his right foot, he could do it, but never on the same side. He had passed the challenge on to other children, but no one had ever succeeded at maintaining the opposite motions on the same side of their body—except Mellai.

Lon cringed at the thought of his sister. He hadn't heard from either her or Kaylen for nine months. What were they doing? Were they happy? Safe? He closed his eyes and reached for his connection with Mellai, hoping to learn something—anything—about her or Kaylen's lives. *Nothing.* Lon breathed deeply, clearing his mind, pushing aside his devotion to the Rayders and his drive to unite them with Appernysia. *Mellai,* he thought, *where are you?* Despite his efforts, no response came from his sister. Anxiety filled his mind. Had he lost his ability to feel her emotions? Or even worse, had something happened to her? If she was hurt or in danger, what about the rest of his family? What about Kaylen?

Wade's voice interrupted his thoughts. "Beholder?"

Lon opened his eyes and shook his head. He had to push the thought aside, just for a moment. He had to remain focused. Lon slid out of the saddle and stood a few feet from the dam. He held out his hands at their separate targets, then began cycling energy from the earth through both halves of his body—in through his feet and out his hands into the soil. No manipulation, just cycling, and in the same direction. Once he was comfortable with the flow, he tried alternating the direction on his right side—in through his right hand and out his right foot. He failed miserably.

Lon ground his teeth in irritation and tried again. Another failure. Time and time again, he was unable to maintain the two opposite cycles. In his frustration, he uprooted a nearby tree and hurled it over the canopy of the forest.

Wade clicked his tongue at his horse and moved next to Lon. "What is wrong, Beholder?"

Lon rolled his eyes and sat on the ground as he rattled off the dilemma. Failing was frustrating enough, but reliving it through a tedious explanation to a Rayder who thought his abilities to be limitless was even worse. Wade was an invaluable member of Lon's guard, but he offered little privacy. Sometimes Lon wished for Tarek's companionship, a man who was more interested in punching someone than the inner workings of True Sight.

"I do not understand," Wade said. "Why do you have to rotate . . . whatever it is in opposite directions?"

Lon blew out his breath. "Because I need to force down the blockage at the same time I raise up a dam in the channel. Opposite actions in opposite directions."

Wade nodded. "I see." He paused, glancing back and forth between the channel and the dry riverbed. "Begging your pardon, Beholder, but perhaps we should do this the Rayder way."

Lon studied the Lieutenant's face. It was full of zealous excitement, as it had been weeks ago while working on the siege bridge, Justice, that the Rayders had used to escape the Exile. Lon couldn't help but smile at his enthusiasm. "What do you have in mind?"

*   *   *   *   *

A short time later, Wade's idea was put into practice. While a portion of his squad kept watch for danger, Lon had used True Sight to create a bridge over the water with thick logs. A large mound of rocks and dirt had been piled on top of the collapsible platform. Elja and Preton were on their horses, each with a rope wrapped securely around the horn of his saddle, the other end lashed to a wooden dowel on the side of the platform. When they pulled out the dowel, the platform would buckle in the middle and drop the dirt and rocks into the water. It was a simple and effective design. Had they created the platform and piled the rubble by regular means, it would have taken days. But with the skills of a Beholder, it had been completed within an hour, even with three of them too injured to assist.

"Your thoughts, Beholder?" Wade asked, smiling proudly at his own ingenuity.

"A blind man would be happy to see that," Lon jested, then took his place on the opposite side of the blocked riverbed, facing the new platform. "As soon as I see the dowel pop out, I'll remove this barrier. If we time it right, the water will transfer smoothly to the old riverbed."

Lon summoned True Sight, curved both hands in front of himself, then nodded at Elja and Preton. They urged their horses slowly backward to increase the tension on the ropes, which crackled in protest. Just when it looked like the rope would break, the dowel popped out of the platform and the dirt and rocks dropped into the channel. With a great surge of True Sight, Lon tore the barrier out of the riverbed and the flowing river transferred routes without interruption. After a moment's satisfaction, Lon dropped the barrier on top of the dirt and stone in the southern channel, reinforcing the dam.

The Rayders cheered as they watched the water claw through its old home. Trees and shrubbery that had filled the old path offered little resistance as the water forced its way through. Within a few days, the stirred mud and debris would clear, and Taeja would have a constant source of fresh water once again.

While the Rayders watched the river wind its way toward the Taejan Plains, Lon turned his attention to the new barricade blocking the water. He pulled energy from the earth and forced it into the dam, strengthening and solidifying it. He also raised its top level with the sides of the channel to ensure there would be no overflow.

"Shall we keep going?" Keene suggested after a few minutes. He was carefully prodding his bicep, wincing when he pushed on tender spots. "These mountains are a little too wild for my taste."

Channer locked eyes with Lon as everyone else agreed with Keene. Lon knew what Channer was thinking, and he was right. They had to make a quick stop on their way to the next river diversion.

Lon dismantled the platform they had used to fill the channel, then placed a few logs together as a bridge over the water. He crossed the river, threw the temporary bridge aside, then climbed into Dawes's saddle. After scanning the area one more time for threats, he released his power.

"We need to check the Meridina Pass," he said, turning his horse down the mountain.

Wade tapped his heels against his horse and moved next to Lon. "What lies in the pass, Beholder?"

"I hope I'm wrong, Lieutenant," Lon replied without looking at Wade, "but I have a terrible suspicion that the calahein have returned from Meridina."

"But the burrows were destroyed, along with every beast."

Lon shrugged skeptically. "And none escaped?"

Wade's eyebrows lifted as he pieced together Lon's anxiety. "If that is true, we must hurry back to Taeja."

"Not yet," Lon said. "We'll confirm our suspicions first."

Wade nodded and Lon urged Dawes to a quicker pace. His assumptions quickly spread through his squad, and he could tell from their posture and hushed tones that they shared his anxiety. When they escaped the tangled web of the mountains, the Rayders forced their horses into a gallop. The Meridina Pass was twenty-five miles north, but they didn't ride directly there. Lon led his squad northeast, away from the mountains. He didn't trust the luck that had saved them the previous night, and wanted to put extra distance between them and the mountains. They rode all day and into the night before they finally stopped to camp ten miles east of the pass. At daybreak, he would send a scout party of uninjured men into the pass—Thad, Dovan, and Elja. If they didn't return before nightfall, he would have his answer.

Chapter 5

Pendant

The keep of Itorea was the stronghold of the Fortress Island. Its surrounding walls stood three hundred fifty feet tall, fifty feet higher than the perimeter wall protecting the rest of the city. Reinforced drum towers, like the tower Kaylen and Kutad had climbed her first day in Itorea, littered the keep's wall. Flanking towers protected the east and west gates of the keep, and five-hundred-foot watchtowers stood inside the wall at each of the keep's four corners. At over a hundred square miles, the keep could hold a significant portion of Itorea's population. Should the blade or hook of Itorea fall to an enemy, the keep provided a heavily defensible fallback where the Appernysians could make their final stand—one worthy of song.

In the center of Itorea's keep was a fortified donjon. It was in this castle that Drogan Jagonest, King of Appernysia, dwelt with his court. Kaylen Shaw and her friend, Aely Leeran, were among the many servants of the court. They functioned as handmaidens to the nobles, performing a wide variety of tasks. Most of their duties were simple and monotonous, but not always. A few times every year, the lords and ladies of Itorea's Cavalier Crook—the southwest region of Itorea—would stay in the fortress. This was one of the many traditions of the king's council.

"I don't know why they're making us do this," Kaylen complained as she knelt over a large basin of soapy water with a washboard. "These were already cleaner than anything I've worn my whole life."

Aely pinned a finely knit gown to a drying line, then grabbed another gown and knelt beside the basin. "Tomorrow is Council," she said as she plunged the dress into the soapy water. "Our ladies will be wandering around the castle flirting, gathering information, and trying to sway the lords of the council. They need to look *extra* beautiful."

Kaylen only grumbled as she scrubbed the gown.

"It really is ridiculous, though," Aely finally agreed. "A bunch of single women wandering around and batting their eyelashes at perverted lords. I can think of a lot better things they should do with their time. But unfortunately, girls like us will never be pulled into Itorean politics." The corners of her mouth drooped with disappointment.

"Why would you *want* any part of that? My head spins every time you try to explain the council." Kaylen stood to pin a dress on the drying line. It was smaller and wider than the others and ornamented with an overabundance of lace and silk. She fingered the edge of the lace running across the chest, where she had spent a half hour tediously cleaning some sort of red sauce that had been spilled on it. The owner of the dress was the most ornery and demeaning person she had ever had the displeasure of meeting. "Why did Lady Netsey bring us this dress herself instead of sending a servant?"

"If there's one characteristic that defines Lady Netsey, it's telling people what to do," Aely growled with contempt. "Wait until you meet her father. Lord Tyram is ten times worse. The two of them have only been in the keep for a day, but everyone already knows they're here. It will be nice when they return to the Crook."

Kaylen returned to the washbasin, her thoughts shifting to Kutad. She had heard of Lord Tyram before, but had never met him. She couldn't help but wonder if he was one of the men who trampled

Kutad's daughter, Linney. "So all forty-seven lords of the Cavalier Crook are part of the council?"

"Yes," Aely replied, "but a few choose not to participate."

"Why?"

Aely shrugged. "Perhaps to guard their land from bandits."

Kaylen paused to look at her friend. "Why don't King Drogan or Queen Cyra go to Council?"

Aely stood to hang another gown on the drying line. "It's too dangerous for them, especially since they have no children."

Kaylen lifted an eyebrow. "I've heard they had a son that died very young. What a heartbreaking thought. Do you know what happened?"

Aely didn't answer until she was kneeling again. "Officially, he got very sick when he was two." She leaned closer and spoke in a whisper. "But I suspect foul play."

"My goodness," Kaylen said, her wet hands covering her mouth. "From whom?"

"Lord Tyram, for one," Aely said, shaking her head. "But that's just speculation. What's more important is that without any other children, King Drogan has no rightful heir to the throne. A perfect recipe for disaster, if you ask me. Not all the lords of the Crook are honorable, and they've been rallying other nobles to their own ideologies. I suspect many of them are aiming to be the next monarch. Council isn't as safe anymore. King Drogan is a skilled fighter, but neither he nor Queen Cyra can risk exposing themselves to an assassination attempt. They spend most of their time locked in the royal chamber with their own special group of servants. They even have their own personal barber."

"That makes sense," Kaylen said with a nod. "I've run into Lia many times over the past few months."

"Lia's nice," Aely said, "especially for a royal chambermaid. I don't envy her position, but I'd still rather empty the royal chamber pot than deal with the likes of Lady Netsey."

"That's not all she does," Kaylen said, stifling a laugh. "She actually does a lot of the same things we do, just for the royal chamber."

Aely gave Kaylen a sideways glance. "Do you even know what the royal chamber is?"

"Upstairs."

"Not *where*. I asked if you knew *what* it is."

"Oh," Kaylen replied, her cheeks hot. "Well, it obviously includes the chambers of the king and queen, but I don't know what else. I've never been up there before."

"Neither have I, but I've heard there's an enormous library up there. I'd do almost anything to get my hands on those books. I'm dying for something new."

"You might have a chance someday," Kaylen said.

"I seriously doubt it. The royal chamber members are descendants of generations of loyal servants. Our great-grandchildren might have a chance of getting in there, but only if all their predecessors are perfectly obedient."

Kaylen shrugged, thinking of how drastically her life had changed over the previous nine months. "You never know."

As she finished speaking, Kaylen reached deep into the basin for a bar of soap. Her fingers touched something unusual—a chain perhaps—but it disappeared into the sodden mass of clothes before she could grab it.

Aely noticed Kaylen jerk forward. "What's wrong?"

"I felt a metal chain, but I can't find it anymore."

"What was it?" Aely asked, peering into cloudy water.

"I don't know . . . jewelry maybe."

"If it's jewelry, we need to get it out of the water before it's damaged—if it's not ruined already." Aely set her gown aside and fished around through the deep water with her hands. "I can't find anything. Maybe it sunk to the bottom of the basin."

Kaylen plunged her long arm deep into the water. Her fingertips barely touched the bottom as she moved her hand back and forth.

When she felt a chain against the side of the basin, she hooked a finger under it and carefully lifted it out of the water. Her jaw dropped when she saw what emerged. Kaylen was holding a polished silver chain. Dangling at the bottom was a glowing, thumb-sized diamond. The brilliance of the pendant was unlike anything she had seen, sparkling with every swaying movement.

"That's Queen Cyra's necklace," Aely nearly shouted.

"Where did it come from?" Kaylen whispered, her eyes demanding that Aely do the same. She had never seen the queen, but stories of her necklace and its dazzling inner light were well known throughout the court. It was a coveted one-of-a-kind diamond, and she was holding it in her hand.

"It shouldn't be here," Aely continued in a lowered voice while glancing over her shoulder. "The only way it got here is if someone stole it."

Kaylen gripped her fist around the necklace and hid it underneath her apron.

"What are you doing?" Aely hissed.

Kaylen returned her friend's terrified stare. "Did you steal it?"

"Of course not."

"Then someone else did, and they'll be looking for it."

Just then, the wooden door to the washroom flew open, its metal hinges creaking as it slammed into the stone wall. Both girls jumped to their feet at the startling crash.

"Where's my gown?" a short pudgy woman demanded, her gaze whipping about the room and her face covered in a thin layer of sweat.

Fortunately, Kaylen had kept her hands behind her apron, one fist clutching the queen's necklace. While she gawked at the intruder, Aely dipped her head and pointed to the gown hanging on the drying line. "It's cleaned and drying, Lady Netsey. It will be ready and in your chambers by tomorrow morning."

The woman bustled to the drying line, slipping across the wet stone floor, then frantically dug into the many folds of her dress. As the seconds passed, her eyes grew wide with hysteria. She tore at the fabric, splitting seams and ripping lace, until she finally yanked the dress from the drying line and threw it to the ground.

Kaylen tried to swallow, her throat dry with suspicion as Lady Netsey moved to the large washbasin and squatted at its side. Her pudgy face turned beet red as she tried to hoist one side. After a couple failed grunts, she glanced at Kaylen and Aely as if she had just realized the two servant women were still in the room with her.

With a labored breath, Lady Netsey stood, raised her chin, and jabbed her fat finger at the washbasin. "Dump it."

Kaylen didn't dare question her. Lady Netsey's intent was obvious. She had been in possession of the necklace and must have just realized she misplaced it. The big question on Kaylen's mind was how Lady Netsey came into possession of the necklace in the first place.

Aely wore a worried expression as she knelt with Kaylen and gripped a ridge wrapping the wood basin.

Kaylen finally gained enough control to carefully stow the necklace into a pocket of her dress, then grabbed the other side of the basin. It was heavy, but with the two women working together, they raised one side just enough that the soapy water began to spill across the floor.

"Out of my way," Lady Netsey ordered once the basin was empty. She bumped Kaylen aside with her wide hips and kicked the washbasin over, then drew a hidden dagger from her dress and sliced through the folds of wet material.

Kaylen jumped to her feet and backed against the wall, terrified of what Lady Netsey would do when she couldn't find the necklace. Aely soon joined her and gripped Kaylen's hand, whether to give or receive comfort, Kaylen couldn't be sure.

Many minutes passed before Lady Netsey finally seemed to give up, but not before scraps of material had been scattered across the room. Every article of clothing, both clean and soiled, had been shredded. She stood and glared at the two servant women, holding

CHAPTER 5: PENDANT ✦ 55

their gazes for the most uncomfortable ten seconds Kaylen had ever experienced, then sniffed with derision and waddled back to the drying line.

She paused to examine her ruined dress on the floor with squinted eyes, then wiped her finger along the dirty stone wall and rubbed it across the wet folds. "Look at that smudge. Whoever cleaned this dress did a pathetic job. I ought to have her banished from the keep."

Netsey stood and scurried out of the room without even glancing at Aely or Kaylen. "And close that door," she ordered from down the hall. "I don't need to listen to you slop that filthy wash water around."

Aely closed the door softly, then slumped to the floor. "I thought we were dead."

"So did I," Kaylen barely managed to whisper. She sat silently next to her friend, both of them heaving enormous breaths while she pondered the situation. Her hands drifted back to the royal necklace hidden in her pocket, the source of Lady Netsey's madness. Netsey hadn't found what she was looking for, but how long would that last? When would she return, and who would be with her? Kaylen bit her bottom lip with concern. "What are we going to do?"

"There's only one thing to do," Aely spat, her usual spirit returning. "Lady Netsey is a thief, and we're going to make sure Queen Cyra knows it."

"How? We can't send a messenger. Anyone could be on Lady Netsey's side."

Aely stood and placed her hand on the doorknob. "Then we tell the queen ourselves."

*   *   *   *   *

Kaylen and Aely struggled through the lower halls of the keep, each burdened with a heavy bundle of the wet and damaged clothing.

"Are you sure you know where you're going?" Kaylen asked. She glanced over her shoulder, grateful that the torch-lined hallway was empty. "It's easy to get lost in this place."

Aely only nodded as they rounded another corner. They had reached the bottom of a spiral staircase, the entrance into the royal chamber. Four sentries stood shoulder to shoulder in front of the stair. They were clad in full plate armor with green cloaks hanging from their shoulders. Each man had one hand resting on the pommel of his sheathed sword, while the other hand held a halberd vertically at his side.

The sentries didn't move as Kaylen and Aely approached, nor did they respond when the two women curtsied.

"Umm . . ." Kaylen muttered uneasily as she set her bundle on the floor. "We would like to speak with Queen Cyra, good sirs."

The sentries stood motionless without answering.

Kaylen glanced at Aely and raised her eyebrows in question. "Should we just leave?"

"We can't," Aely answered as she dropped her own bundle on the polished stone floor and turned to the sentries. "Didn't you hear us? We need to speak with the queen." She spoke respectfully enough, but her voice was rising in volume. Kaylen could tell her patience was wearing thin.

A young man appeared around the corner of the stairs. He wore lavender linen pants tucked into polished black boots, and a dark green tunic with a white halberd stitched into the front. His hair was slicked over, perfectly flat against the top of his head. "What's this about?"

Kaylen curtsied. "Forgive us. We were just telling these guards that we have a message for Queen Cyra, but they didn't respond. We didn't know what to do."

"Don't mind them, my ladies. These men are under strict orders. Things are more . . . intense around here than normal. Now give me your message and I'll make sure it reaches our queen."

"We can't," Aely replied, her fists on her hips. "This message is for Queen Cyra's ears only."

The young page stared at them, his head tilted contemplatively. "Do you know how many people come to me with similar requests every day? What makes yours different?"

"Someone has defaced these ladies' dresses," Kaylen interceded as she opened her bundle, quickly formulating an excuse in her mind. "Queen Cyra needs to see the damage, and only she will know how to deliver the bad news to the ladies."

The page moved past the sentries and examined the contents in Kaylen's bundle. He was visibly struck by the extensive damage to the fine material. "How did this happen?"

"We're not sure," Aely continued, obviously catching on to Kaylen's story. "We came back from eating and found our washroom destroyed. The washbasin had been tipped over and the clothing cut to shreds."

The page shook his head. "You've come at the wrong time. Most of the ladies are with Queen Cyra right now. They will certainly recognize their ruined dresses."

Aely placed her hand gently on the young man's arm. She spoke softly, her eyes pleading. "There's more to this than just torn clothes. *Please* try to understand. We need to see Queen Cyra."

The young man eyed Aely. "You have a suspect?"

"We do," Kaylen replied, "and an explanation too large to pass between messengers."

"Convincing," the page replied, "but not reason enough to bypass the royal guard. Let's hear that explanation."

From the set expression on the page's face—tight lips and furrowed brow—Kaylen knew their only option was to reveal the queen's necklace. She slowly reached under her apron so as not to alarm the page, took hold of the silver chain, and pulled it out just enough that only Aely and the page could see the diamond's ceaseless glow. "This was among the rags," she said, then quickly stowed it again.

An uncomfortable silence followed, long and poignant. Kaylen's anxieties grew as the page's expression transformed from determined to guarded. Aely didn't look pleased at Kaylen's action, either, but she also kept a careful eye on the page. The air became so oppressive that Kaylen began to consider options for retreat. She would grab Aely's hand and drag her away if she had to. She refused to be held responsible for something they didn't do.

"Very well," the page finally said, formal and suspicious, "but leave your bundles behind. I will attest to the damage." He turned to the four sentries. "Ric and Duncan, follow us. These women have a token for the queen." One of the men pivoted on his right foot, moving the left side of his body to create a small opening. Kaylen couldn't help but tremble as she and Aely passed the sentries, dropped their bundles at the base of the stairs, then followed after the page. If the ladies were in the Royal Chamber, that would include Lady Netsey. This could be a complicated encounter. And what if this page was on Lady Netsey's side? Kaylen glanced back at the two sentries, wondering again if she should abandon her quest and return to the washroom.

The young man looked over his shoulder and smiled. "Try to relax. Ric and Duncan are only tagging along to keep everyone safe. That's all."

Kaylen nodded, unconvinced, but determined to conceal her anxieties. "It's not that. We were just saying yesterday how lucky we'd be to ever see the royal chamber. I know I haven't actually seen it yet, but we're a lot closer to it than most of the other servants in this castle will ever be."

The page laughed a little too loud for the situation, and a drop of sweat trickled down in front of his ear. "I don't blame you. I remember my first time up these stairs. It was years ago, when I was just a small child, but I can still remember the churning in my stomach. There's nothing quite like it, is there?" He looked at Aely as he finished his sentence.

One side of her mouth curled up in what Kaylen easily recognized as a forced smile. "Yes, my lord."

The young man threw up his hands defensively. "I'm not a lord. Just a page. Call me Snoom."

Aely lifted an eyebrow.

"It's a long story," Snoom replied. "It's not my real name, but has stuck with me since I was little. I like it."

"Aely," she replied with a gruff curtsey. "Kaylen and I aren't ladies, either."

"Aely and Kaylen . . ." Snoom said to himself as he turned and continued up the stairs.

Kaylen's hands became sweaty as they climbed for another five minutes, pausing momentarily at three more intimidating sentry posts along the way, until they reached a flat area in front of a closed door. Kaylen knew they had lost any chance of retreat. Their fate was now completely in Snoom's hands. She had to do something to increase his trust in them, to show their loyalty to the queen. She searched the area and noticed the unique door, its surface a polished stone-like material few would probably recognize.

"Furwen," Kaylen observed.

"Impressive," Snoom said as he turned to look at her. "Most people think it's just made of stone."

Kaylen smiled as sincerely as she could muster. "I had a knowledgeable guide when I first came to Itorea. He pointed out the Furwen gates at the west entrance into the city."

"Massive things, aren't they? Too bad we can't get them to budge." Snoom ran his hand along the chamber door. "This door, however, opens just fine, but only when we want it to. No one gets in the royal chamber unless they're invited."

Snoom took a feather quill from a suspended shelf, pulled a long, skinny piece of parchment from his pocket, and scribbled on it with the quill. He folded the parchment in half and slipped it under the door, then yanked hard on a heavy rope at the side of the door. The faint sound of an iron bell sounded on the other side.

Kaylen speculated about what was written on the note. Something like a password, or was it a warning? Her tension was thick and daunting, pressing on her like a falling tree.

The door finally opened, revealing a large broad-shouldered man blocking the entrance.

Snoom placed his right fist over his heart and bowed. Aely dipped her head and curtsied. Kaylen stood speechless, her jaw hanging open. Standing in front of her was General Kamron Astadem. She had heard rumors that he had escaped his execution, but from unreliable sources. What's more, no one had seen the general since that day. She had no reason to believe he was still alive.

Even with the necklace hidden in her pocket and the potential threat of their own safety, Kaylen's mind flooded with questions she wanted to ask the Appernysian general. At the forefront were questions about the Beholder. She wanted to know what the Beholder looked like—if it truly was Lon—and what he had done to frighten the Appernysians away. Last Kaylen had seen him, Lon was on the edge of death with no control over True Sight. What had he learned to do? What damage had he caused? How many deaths were on his hands?

"Please close your mouth," General Astadem said with a hint of amusement, then turned to Snoom. "These are the two servants?"

"Yes, General."

"Follow me." General Astadem motioned to Aely and Kaylen. "Don't attempt anything foolish." He paused and looked past the two women. "You, too, Ric and Duncan."

As soon as the general led them into the room, Kaylen's anxieties temporarily faded from her mind. The large chamber was adorned with extravagant decorations and the opposite wall was spotted with many oak doors. King Drogan sat at a desk on one side of the room, his silver crown and matching silver hair barely visible above tall stacks of parchment. Two young men stood on each side of the desk, dressed in uniforms similar to Snoom's.

Queen Cyra was seated in the middle of the room at a beautiful oak table. Her crown matched Drogan's in design, except it was smaller and imbedded with three dazzling, square-cut diamonds. Her satin gown was equally stunning, and streaks of gray ran through her brown hair, treasures of her years of experience.

The queen was surrounded by scores of ladies dressed in fancy clothes, all of them chattering as they worked their sewing needles through piles of loose material on their laps. Much to Kaylen's chagrin, Lady Netsey was sitting in the midst of them, her stubby legs too short to touch the floor. Two other women dressed in servant clothes were moving around the room, cleaning here and polishing there. Kaylen recognized one of them as Lia.

On the wall opposite King Drogan's desk was a two-story bookcase filled with hundreds of books and rolls of parchment. Kaylen turned to point it out to Aely, but her friend was already staring at the bookshelf with wide eyes. She was so entranced by the vision before her that she didn't realize her escort had stopped.

She bumped hard into General Astadem's back. He whipped around, his sword half drawn, obviously startled by the contact. Aely cowered to the floor, while King Drogan jumped to his feet. In his haste, the king knocked his pewter goblet over the side of his desk and spilled red wine onto the white stone floor.

"I'm so sorry," Aely said with tear-filled eyes as she untied her apron and offered to clean up the spilled wine.

While General Astadem sheathed his sword with a few muttered curses, Lia hurried across the room. "Don't you worry about it," she said as she placed her own apron over the spilled wine.

Aely smiled weakly at Lia. The chambermaid was older, probably just in her forties, but she was beautiful nonetheless. Her kind hazel eyes sparkled through the shallow wrinkles on her face.

"Where do you find your servants?" one of the ladies called from across the room. "I'd gladly give you a handful of mine, Queen Cyra. You deserve better treatment than this."

"That girl *almost* ruined my gown today," Netsey added, her eyes smoldering with warning hatred. "I'm lucky I caught her in time or it would have been damaged beyond repair."

At this comment, Snoom turned to face Kaylen. She returned his gaze, silently begging him to understand the lies wrapped in her response. *It's her! Lady Netsey stole the necklace. She ruined the clothes. Please understand!*

Snoom's unreadable countenance faltered, just brief enough for Kaylen to notice. His eyes were the most telling. Compassion. Understanding. Kaylen released a final tremble as she realized she was no longer a suspect.

Queen Cyra placed her sewing on the table, then stood and crossed the room to stand in front of Aely and Kaylen. The ladies paused in their gossip, obviously watching for the punishment that was sure to fall.

Aely quickly stood and curtseyed. "I'm sorr—"

"Let me help you," Queen Cyra interrupted as she took Aely's apron, then stepped behind her to retie it.

By then, King Drogan had also approached from his desk. "Don't worry about the spill," he said to Kaylen with a nod. "Now, to what do we owe the pleasure of your visit?"

Chapter 6

Uprising

Kaylen glanced over the king and queen's shoulders at Netsey, who glared back with a mixture of tension and spite. With her and all the other ladies watching, Kaylen's mouth became dry and sticky. She uselessly sought for words that never reached her tongue. A quick glance at her friend gave her no reassurance. Aely looked just as stupefied.

"These women have made an important discovery," Snoom finally said as he stood between them. He placed his calm hands on their backs and gave them a nudge forward. While the action was ineffective on Kaylen's part, the gentle push broke through Aely's befuddlement.

"Alright, alright," Aely said, stepping sideways out of Snoom's reach. "I'm sorry to disturb you, my queen, but we found something in our washbasin this morning that belongs to you. Show her, Kaylen."

Kaylen forced her gaze from Lady Netsey to her queen. She knew Queen Cyra must be agonizing over her lost royal pendant. Even with the ladies present, the necklace needed to be returned. She jabbed her hand beneath her apron, wanting to reveal the truth before she lost her courage.

She must have moved too quickly, enough to warrant suspicion by Queen Cyra's protectors. Even Snoom, who knew what Kaylen had in her possession, moved to protect their queen. He grabbed Kaylen's dress and yanked her backward, while at the same time stepping between her and Queen Cyra. Kaylen's left hand had barely hooked the necklace chain hidden in her pocket before she stumbled and fell onto her rump. She flailed her hands to her sides for balance, and with the motion, whisked the queen's glowing pendant across the polished stone floor.

Many of the ladies gasped at the crude unveiling, including Lady Netsey, but Queen Cyra's mouth only slightly parted in a stunned gape as her hands drifted to her bare neck. "Where did you find that?" she finally whispered.

"I knew it," Lady Netsey interceded, bumbling off her chair and hurrying across the floor. She carefully lifted the necklace from the polished stone and held it up with a straight arm. "My servant was ill this morning, so being the caring lady that my father, Lord Tyram, worked so hard to raise, I made her rest while I took my laundry to the washroom." She spoke slowly and deliberately, but Kaylen could see the anxiety hidden in her gaze, the same panic from the washroom.

A single clang interrupted Lady Netsey's monologue. It came from the bell beside the Furwen door. Someone in the stairwell must have pulled the rope.

"Send them away," King Drogan said.

General Astadem nodded and turned, eyeing the floor. He must have been waiting for a note similar to Snoom's to slide under the door. There was no such note, and after a brief pause, General Astadem raised a questioning eyebrow back at the king.

"I found these two servants there, nervously splashing clothes into the washbasin," Lady Netsey said with renewed confidence, recapturing everyone's attention. She kept her arm up, displaying the glowing crystal as she crossed the room toward Queen Cyra. "I thought their behavior suspicious, but I did nothing at the time. I'm sorry, my queen. I should have followed my instincts and questioned them immediately. They were obviously hiding the royal pendant in their filthy wash water."

As she finished speaking, Lady Netsey lowered her raised hand to the queen. Her tactics were well performed, so much that no one seemed to notice as her other hand slipped into a fold in her dress. No one except Kaylen and Aely, who had already pinned her as the thief. All eyes were locked on the glowing crystal and Queen Cyra's hand as she reached out to take it.

"A knife!" Kaylen screamed, pointing at the glinting silver of a blade emerging from Lady Netsey's dress. At Kaylen's warning, Snoom threw himself between Netsey and the queen. The thrusting dagger buried itself in his side instead of Queen Cyra's.

Chaos ensued. The rows of watching ladies jumped from their seats. Many rushed into the fray, surrounding Lady Netsey protectively and moving her away while others hurried to their queen's aid. Some ran around screaming, seeking safety from the bloodshed. Snoom dropped to one knee, wincing as he gripped the dagger and yanked it free. King Drogan drew his long sword and stood defensively in front of his wife. Seconds later, General Astadem, Ric, and Duncan, joined him with their own swords drawn, along with one of the two pages that had been standing at King Drogan's desk. They watched carefully as Lady Netsey's circle of women shuffled farther away.

"I do not wish for more blood," King Drogan finally said, "but by my honor, I will kill every last one of you if Netsey doesn't step forward immediately. Women or not, you are aiding a traitor."

Cries for mercy and forced tears echoed through the stone chamber so loudly that Kaylen was tempted to cover her ears. She still sat on the floor, watching helplessly at the encounter. She worried most about Snoom. He gripped his stab wound with his free hand, but blood still leaked through his fingers and dripped to the floor. Kaylen was no healer, but she could at least help. She rolled to her side to stand up.

"Stay where you are," General Astadem ordered. He pointed his sword directly at her.

"We're not the enemy," Aely replied, standing next to Kaylen.

"No? Just bad timing?"

Kaylen shook her head. Arguing would get them nowhere. He was right. Their timing was terrible. The only option left for her and Aely was to flee. She looked over her shoulder at the Furwen door, her only exit from the royal chamber, just in time to see four ladies lift the crossbeam and begin opening the door.

Several men forced their way in, shoving the door aside. They were garbed in fine clothing only lords would wear and their faces were covered to hide their identities. Sounds of fighting echoed from the stairwell, metal clanging and men screaming.

One of the ladies was crushed between the heavy swinging door and the stone wall, and two others were immediately dispatched by the men. The only surviving lady, a woman Kaylen didn't recognize, ran past the men and fled down the stairs.

Aely grabbed Kaylen and dragged her sideways, out of the path between the attackers and the king. King Drogan, General Astadem, and the two sentries worked their swords with unmatched skill, quickly killing five attackers and pushing the others back into a corner of the room. Snoom and the other page remained to protect their queen. Snoom swung his dagger threateningly at the women still in the royal chamber and ordered them to flee, while the other page edged the queen toward King Drogan's desk. Kaylen didn't blame Snoom for such rash actions. They couldn't trust anyone, most especially those protecting Lady Netsey.

It was then that Kaylen noticed the women protecting Lady Netsey were also rushing toward the staircase. Their protective cluster had dissolved into a line, with fat Lady Netsey fumbling at the back. The stolen necklace was still swinging from her fist. Kaylen wanted to go after her, to retrieve the necklace and return it to Queen Cyra, but the task was dangerous. Too dangerous. Lady Netsey could have more daggers hidden in her dress.

Aely must have come to a different conclusion, because she grabbed an oak chair from the table and ran toward Lady Netsey, screaming with the chair raised over her shoulder. Lady Netsey's pride broke. She dropped the necklace to the floor and scurried toward the staircase, her pudgy hands lifting the front of her dress to avoid tripping. Aely was still undeterred. She chased after Netsey and at the last second, hurled the chair after her. The chair struck Lady Netsey on her back and knocked her to her face in the pooled blood at the top of the staircase. She slid through the doorway and tumbled headfirst down the stairs, screaming as she vanished from sight.

Leaving Aely to her mission, Kaylen went after the abandoned necklace. But she had barely picked it up before Snoom approached her, dagger raised.

"Give it to me," Snoom ordered, his face pale from lost blood.

"Of course," Kaylen replied and held her hand up, the glowing crystal resting in her palm and the silver chain dangling off the side. "Please, take it." She searched for Queen Cyra, but she had disappeared, along with the second page. The only sign of their escape route came from the fluttering tapestry behind King Drogan's desk. It must have been hiding a secret door. The third page was still standing at the desk. He hadn't moved a single step since the fray had started.

Snoom moved his hand from his abdomen and reached forward cautiously. His bloodied hand trembled and his forehead beaded with sweat, until finally his eyes glazed and he collapsed forward. Kaylen hooked her arms under him, barely catching him before his weight forced them both to the floor.

"Help," Kaylen shouted as she rolled Snoom to his side. His green tunic was soaked red around the slit in his side. After placing the queen's pendant back in her pocket, Kaylen took the two-inch blade from Snoom's hand and tossed it away, removed her apron, and pushed it against his wound. She turned her head and shouted again. "Please help!"

The fighting in the room had ceased. The clustered assassins had all been killed and Ric and Duncan were dropping the Furwen beam back into place. General Astadem was standing to one side, a bloody sword in one hand and his other arm holding Aely back. She was fighting to get past him, shouting venomous curses at Lady Netsey.

King Drogan was the first to Kaylen's side. He lifted Snoom in his arms and nodded toward his desk. "Pull the drapery aside."

Kaylen did as she was instructed, and discovered a solid oak door hidden behind the drapery.

King Drogan kicked the door twice and shouted, "Open, by order of the king." A loud clank sounded inside, then the door opened to reveal a searching eye, which stopped on the injured young man dangling in King Drogan's arms.

"Bring him in," Lia shouted as she flung the door open. King Drogan followed her through the doorway.

Kaylen remained outside, staring after King Drogan for a moment, then clasped her hands anxiously, hoping Snoom would survive. She ignored the blood covering her hands from Snoom's wound.

"Thank you." The voice was General Astadem's.

Kaylen turned to the general. He smiled weakly at her. He had an arm around Aely, who stood next to him with tears pouring from her eyes. He squeezed her reassuringly.

"I didn't do much," Kaylen said.

"You've done more than you realize," General Astadem replied. "The royal necklace, Lady Netsey, Snoom . . . I must apologize. We should have trusted you from the beginning."

"How is he?" Aely asked, her voice weak. "Is Snoom dead?"

"I hope not," Kaylen said, suddenly realizing the gravity of the situation. She was lucky to be alive. Snoom had been stabbed protecting Queen Cyra. So many traitorous ladies. And who were those men with the masks? Why did they attack? Only one answer seemed logical. This had been a well-organized assassination attempt. She and Aely had only stumbled into it when they found the stolen necklace. Or had they? Had Lady Netsey planted it in her dress? Intended on them bringing it back to Queen Cyra? It offered the perfect distraction, and fit the timing of the men that attacked the stairwell. They could have followed her and Aely to the royal chamber.

No, Kaylen thought, dismissing her conclusion. *Lady Netsey was genuinely upset in the washroom. Frantic. She didn't mean for us to find the crystal. Fate just tossed us into the middle of this.*

The page that had helped Queen Cyra hide suddenly appeared from the hidden room and saluted General Astadem with a fist over his heart. "How can I help, General?"

"Ever the faithful page, Ernon. Carry a message to Lord Haedon and Lord Anton. They should still be at Council, but be discreet about it. We don't need everyone knowing there has been an attempt on the king and queen's lives, and there's a good chance many lords at Council helped plan this attack, even if they weren't physically part of it. Tell Haedon and Anton to return to the royal chamber. The king will need his advisor and the queen her chancellor. And be careful."

After another quick salute, Ernon sprinted through the chamber. Ric and Duncan temporarily opened the Furwen door for him and he disappeared down the stairs.

General Astadem ordered the third page—still standing at the king's desk—to hold his position, then turned to Kaylen and Aely. "Let's check on Snoom."

"All of us, General Astadem?" Kaylen asked apprehensively.

"Please, call me Kamron." He helped Aely through the hidden door, his arm still around her, and Kaylen followed awkwardly after him.

They had entered the royal bedchamber. A large bed was positioned against the far wall, dressed in layers of fine linens. Queen Cyra was seated in a chair next to three other women. All four held spanned crossbows on their laps. King Drogan paced the floor in front of them, his sheathed word clanging at his side with every step.

A hunched, old man stood nearby with the aid of a steel cane. Spectacles clung to the end of his sharp nose and his white beard nearly touched his belt. He was dressed in the same royal garb as Snoom, his clothing sagging from his scrawny figure.

Snoom was lying on the floor on a white blanket, his tunic cut away to reveal a narrow gash on the side of his abdomen. Lia sat next to him, having just finished cleaning the blood from his wound with a wet cloth. The old man stood over Snoom, carefully examining the injury.

"Deep, but not fatal," the old man said.

Another woman appeared from a side room and set a large leather bag next to the old man.

Lia nodded at the woman. "Thank you, Jude."

"We will need more clean rags," the old man continued as he crouched onto his hands and knees at Snoom's side, "and strong liquor."

Jude disappeared into the side room again while King Drogan walked to his bed, lifted the mattress, and produced a small steel flask. Queen Cyra scowled at her husband as he crossed the room and handed the flask to the old man. "Here you are, Henry."

"Thank you, my king," Henry squawked as he rolled onto his rump and took the flask. After removing the cork and pouring a healthy amount onto Snoom's abdomen, Henry took a swig for himself and set the flask aside.

Kaylen watched in awe. Henry was easily the oldest man she had ever met—well beyond seventy—yet his hands were perfectly steady as he stitched Snoom closed with a long hooked needle and strips of dried pig tendons from his satchel. Kaylen had heard of the king's personal healer and the miracles he performed, but she had never known he was so old. Yet as Kaylen watched Henry, his old age only made her respect him more.

Jude soon returned with clean rags and helped mop up the blood while Henry finished stitching the wound closed.

"Now he needs to rest," Henry said as he poured more liquor over Snoom's wound and covered it with a dressing.

"Move him onto our bed," Queen Cyra ordered while the king retrieved his flask. She scowled at her husband again.

King Drogan shook his head, took a swig from his flask, and resumed pacing across the floor. "Any further news, General?"

Kamron placed his right fist over his heart. "None, my king. Ric and Duncan are stationed at the Furwen door and I've sent Ernon to collect Lords Anton and Haedon from Council."

"Excellent. What about Verle?"

"He still stands at your desk, my king."

King Drogan shook his head as he watched the women hoist Snoom onto the bed. "I should have given my pages weapons, Kamron. This could have been avoided."

"Perhaps," Kamron replied, "but there is little you can do about it now. Don't worry about Ernon, either. He's light on his feet. I'm sure he'll return safely."

Queen Cyra set her crossbow on the floor, walked to the bed, and placed her hand on Snoom's pale face. "I hope you're right, General. He's only a boy."

"A knight in training," Kamron said as he moved to the door. He closed the bedchamber door softly. "He knows how to protect himself."

"Perhaps you're right." Queen Cyra leaned against the tall bedpost and sighed. "They're getting rash."

"I know, my dear," King Drogan said, "but do not fret. We will equalize their boldness with our own attentiveness."

"Why did they try to kill you?" Aely asked. Kaylen's jaw dropped at her friend's audacity, but Aely was undeterred.

Queen Cyra returned to her seat between the three other women. "Drogan and I have our theories. Please sit down, both of you."

"You can sit here by me," Henry wheezed from the floor. "I'm not getting up anytime soon."

"Let us help you up, my lord," Kaylen said as she crossed the room with Aely close behind.

Henry laughed. "Standing up means I have to find somewhere else to sit down again. Don't worry about me. I'm fine right here."

Kaylen rolled up the bloody blanket and placed it near the door, then she and Aely sat next to Henry.

Henry smiled. "Cozy down here, isn't it?" he whistled through missing teeth.

They were sitting on a hard stone floor, but Aely and Kaylen smiled at Henry's sweetness.

"Let's clear the air first," King Drogan said from across the room. "We don't suspect you two were involved with any of this, so there's no need to worry. Your actions have proved your loyalty."

Suddenly Kaylen remembered the queen's pendant hidden in her pocket. She took a deep breath, then brought her fist forward. The glowing diamond dangled from her hand by the silver chain. "This belongs to you, your Majesty."

Queen Cyra gasped and rushed across the room to take the necklace. "How did you get this from Lady Netsey?"

"Aely fought her for it, my queen," Kaylen replied. She nodded toward her friend then bowed her head, lowering the crystal into her queen's outstretched hand.

Queen Cyra unclasped the chain and lifted it around her neck. A lady-in-waiting stood and glided across the floor to secure the chain behind the queen's neck.

"Thank you for returning this to me," the queen whispered, her chest heaving with deep breaths. Tears were flowing from her eyes. "And thank you, Aely, for fighting to keep it. This necklace has been handed down from queen to princess since the First Age. It's invaluable to me."

Aely glanced at Kaylen, who nodded in return. She knew what Aely was thinking, and completely agreed. Their queen desperately needed help, though Kaylen still wondered what use the two of them could actually be.

Aely turned to the queen. "We'll gladly assist you in any way we can, your Majesty."

Queen Cyra's chin trembled, then she wrapped her arms around Kaylen and Aely in a warm embrace. "You don't know how much this means to me."

They awkwardly returned the hug, unsure of how to respond. The queen held them for nearly a minute before she finally leaned back with her hands on their shoulders.

"How can we help you, though?" Aely asked, fighting to control her own emotions. "We're just laundry girls."

"Your comment answers your own question," Queen Cyra said. "Neither of you know what's really going on in the keep, which makes you perfect candidates."

Kaylen tilted her head in question. "Candidates?"

Queen Cyra smiled, though a hint of sadness slipped through. "You have been faithful servants without asking for anything in return. The situation is even better because you are servants at the lowest level. No one will suspect you."

"Suspect us of what?" Aely asked, her frustration starting to show.

One of the three women next to the queen blew out her breath. "Queen Cyra, are you sure this is the best idea? They're so naive."

Queen Cyra smirked. "Their ignorance is what makes them perfect. Trust my judgment, Ryndee. This is not a task for a lady-in-waiting."

"Yes, my queen."

King Drogan walked across the room and stood in front of Kaylen and Aely. "The important question is, how dedicated are you to your king and queen? Are you both willing to die for Appernysia?"

The king's pointed question surprised Kaylen. Had she been asked a day earlier, she would have easily said yes, but after the attack she had just witnessed, with Snoom lying unconscious nearby . . . the possibility of sealing her loyalty to King Drogan with her own blood was all too likely. Did she want to die? Of course not, but she didn't want her king and queen to die, either. So back to the king's inquiry: would she die for Appernysia? Most likely, if such a sacrifice was crucial and unavoidable.

Aely was the first to reply. "Forgive me, your Majesty," she said, glancing over her shoulder at the nearby general, "but I can't make that decision while I have a concern of my own."

"What concern is that?" King Drogan asked with obvious apprehension.

"Why is General Astadem still alive? The law says—"

"I know my law," King Drogan interrupted, "and a lot more about the circumstance than either of you. Not all is as it appears to be. My kingdom is divided, and General Astadem is one of the few people I can trust."

Aely dipped her head respectfully, but did not speak. Kaylen knew her friend was holding back her true opinion for another time, without the general or king there to critique her.

King Drogan paused, rubbing his chin. "Before we continue, I would like to wait for Ernon's return. Haedon and Anton will offer valuable input on this circumstance."

Chapter 7
Enlisted

Through the open door to the royal bedchamber, Kaylen heard a single clang from the signal bell at the Furwen door. The sound was alarming, breaking the suffocating silence that had plagued the bedchamber for half an hour. Moments later, the scraping of a crossbeam and the opening of the door reached her ears, then light and uneven footsteps approached the royal bedchamber. She knew that whoever approached would have to pass the sentries, Ric and Duncan, but Kaylen still felt uneasy at the unknown visitor's approach.

"Permission to enter the royal bedchamber," a voice called.

"Granted, Ernon," King Drogan replied.

Ernon entered the room, limping heavily on his right leg. "I apologize, my liege, but I have failed. Sergeant Ched wouldn't let me pass the door into the great hall. I tried to force my way in, but he slammed the door on my foot."

"A rash reaction," Queen Cyra said, "with only two possible explanations."

"My thoughts exactly," Ernon replied, "but I'm afraid the worse is the only possible reason. My foot might be broken, but not pointlessly. I caught a glimpse of Lords Haedon and Anton through the door. They were lashed to chairs at the grand table, and I saw Lord Tyram strike your chancellor with his fist. I'm sorry, my queen, but I panicked and hurried back here as quickly as possible."

"You made the best choice," Queen Cyra replied. "There was nothing you could do there, and now we have confirmation of the treason we've long suspected."

"Indeed," King Drogan agreed, "and if Lord Tyram is doing the beating, it is only under the direction of Chamberlain Ramik. The situation has matured, as we feared it would. Kamron, bring Verle in here."

The general called out the door and Verle quickly entered. "How may I serve you, my king?"

"I have need of your haste," King Drogan said. "Do you remember the identity of . . ." He glanced briefly at Kaylen and Aely, then returned his attention to Verle. "Of our informant?"

Verle nodded. "Of course, your Majesty."

"I need men here I can trust, but he is abroad. Ride to . . . *his contact* positioned at the perimeter wall, and send him with all haste to summon our informant. And speak to no one of your quest."

"By my honor," Verle said, pounding his chest once with his fist. "I will leave at once."

Kaylen watched the young page depart, wondering at the king's hesitation. Who was their informant, and who was his contact? She didn't blame King Drogan for his secrecy, but the way he hesitated, eyeing her and Aely, made her wonder. Would she know their informant?

Snoom's weak voice interrupted Kaylen's thoughts. "What's happening?"

"The chamberlain is trying to take control of Itorea," Lia said, who was still sitting at the bed. "Glad to see you awake." She gently stroked Snoom's forehead—not romantically, but maternally, in the same way Kaylen's father used to comfort her when she was ill. The thought tugged at Kaylen's heart. How was her father doing? Why hadn't he replied to her letter? Was he angry that Kaylen served the king?

"You think Lord Ramik ordered the attack?" Aely said, bringing Kaylen's mind back for the second time.

"We *know* he did," Queen Cyra replied. "The attack wasn't only from outside the chamber, my dear. We were betrayed on the inside, too."

King Drogan pulled his longsword a foot out of its scabbard and slammed it back inside, but he said nothing as he paced the floor.

General Astadem left his post at the bedchamber door and stepped to the side of Kaylen and Aely. "Our king's frustration stems from the attack. He blames himself for not preventing it."

Kaylen cleared her throat and wrung her hands nervously. "We still don't know what happened, your Majesties."

"Since you now have the confidence of our queen," Kamron replied, "I believe an explanation is in order." He paused. "My liege?"

"Go ahead," King Drogan replied.

"Yes, my king." Kamron returned his attention to Kaylen and Aely. "Lord Ramik has been manipulating our laws and commands for quite awhile. It was only a matter of time before he resorted to something like this, which has forced us to seek refuge in this royal chamber. He wants our king and queen dead so he can assume the throne. Now we know he controls many of the ladies of the Crook, too. The assassination attempt was coordinated almost perfectly."

Queen Cyra shifted in her chair. "I wish I knew why Lady Netsey's dagger found Snoom instead of me. Perhaps our deaths have been reserved for Lord Tyram or the chamberlain." She shuddered. "What a frightful ordeal."

Kaylen leaned against Aely. "My apologies, your Majesties, but I feel faint. So many people have died."

The queen's countenance dropped. "I know, and I'm sorry to pull you into this."

"But this all seems far beyond us, my queen," Aely said. "What can we possibly do?"

King Drogan crossed the room and stood directly in front of Kaylen and Aely. "Two things. First, you need to trust us—no matter what happens and what you hear. Can you?"

Both women nodded, though Kaylen could still read apprehension in Aely's expression.

"I would like to hear you say it," King Drogan continued.

"I promise to trust you, my king," Kaylen said with a reverent curtsey.

Aely hesitated, but finally voiced her loyalty, too. "As do I, my king."

"Then the second thing you need to do is be patient. You will find out soon enough. In the meantime, keep about your regular tasks and stay out of trouble."

"Stay out of trouble?" Aely replied cynically. "How exactly are we supposed to do that?"

"A valid question. We cannot protect you, but we won't leave you defenseless." Kamron pulled two four-inch daggers from his belt. There was nothing ornamental about their design and each was sheathed in a slim leather sleeve. "Take these blades. Keep them hidden, but easily accessible. They might save your life."

Aely grabbed hers and hid it behind her apron. Kaylen was more hesitant. She looked at the remaining dagger warily.

"No one expects you to use it," Kamron reassured her. "It is for the sole purpose of defense. Please, take it."

Kaylen reached out a trembling hand and accepted the dagger with her index finger and thumb. "I don't even know how to use one of these."

Kamron smiled warmly, then placed his hand on Aely's shoulder. "You both must leave now. You've spent too much time here already. Come. I will walk you down the stairs."

Kaylen watched as Aely and Snoom exchanged a prolonged glance. Snoom was obviously the oldest of King Drogan's three pages, perhaps a year older than Kaylen. He gave Aely an encouraging smile and motioned with his head that she should go. Aely returned his smile, then she and Kaylen curtsied to the king and queen before following after Kamron.

Their journey from the Royal Chamber was harder than Kaylen suspected. The sentries at the three positions along the staircase were all dead, surrounded by twice as many corpses of attackers. Sticky streams of red blood flowed from their bodies, staining the polished stonework. Kaylen wept as she moved past the bodies, trying vainly not to look at them. The expressions of terror frozen on pale faces haunted her, memories she'd never be able to purge from her mind.

They turned the final corner and stopped short. Kaylen gasped, focusing everything she could on not passing out from the gruesome scene. Two sentries were on the ground, their breastplates punctured by multiple crossbow bolts. They were surrounded by seven other motionless bodies. Blood pooled on the stone floor.

"Such unnecessary death," Kamron said to himself, obviously struggling to contain his grief. Kaylen and Aely pulled up their dresses and tiptoed through the gore until they had entered the corridor. As they disappeared down the hall, they heard Kamron's muffled sobs echo off the stone walls.

Kaylen did not speak on their way back to the washroom. Her thoughts were plagued by fear and doubt over her unknown responsibility to King Drogan. She feared what the future would bring. Uncertainty breeds the very worst possible imaginings, and Kaylen was brimming with questions.

Chapter 8

Awakening

Gorlon stood behind his son with a hand on Theiss's shoulder. Theiss sat motionless on a wooden chair, his eyes swollen with sorrow. He stared unblinking at Mellai's motionless body on the sofa. Dhargon slumped in a chair while Allegna wandered aimlessly around the dark house, looking for something to do. Many villagers had tried to visit, but Theiss's younger brother, Reese, stood outside the front door, redirecting everyone back to their homes.

Gorlon finally broke the silence. "It's been two hours, Dhargon. Time to make some decisions."

Dhargon nodded absently.

"Where do you want to bury her?"

Dhargon didn't answer.

"Do you want to send for her family?"

Again, no answer.

"Look at me, Dhargon," Gorlon ordered softly.

Dhargon lifted his pained eyes.

"Where's her family?"

"I can't tell you, Gorlon. You know that."

Gorlon blew out his breath. "They deserve to know about Mellai. You're in no condition to ride, but I could send Reese. Tell us where they are, and he'll be on the road in ten minutes."

Dhargon's gaze shifted back to his granddaughter. "She was perfectly fine. We found her and brought her safely home. This came out of nowhere."

"I know. You've told me ten times already. You need to accept what's happened and move on. Don't burden her journey to paradise with your sorrow."

Allegna crossed the room and stood next to her husband. "She never should have come here. She would have been safe with her parents."

Gorlon stood and paced the floor. "I've been more than understanding," he said, his voice rising. "But I've had enough. You owe me an explanation."

Theiss turned. "Father—"

"Silence," Gorlon demanded. "You'll get your turn when we are home."

"Calm down," Allegna interrupted. "Mellai came here because she missed us. That's all."

Gorlon glared at her. "Then why did she pretend to be a tradeswoman?"

"She wanted a normal life. Is that too much for a girl her age to ask?"

"Yes, when it involves my son. I should have been informed."

"Look at the way you're reacting," Theiss growled. "She just died and you're complaining about secrets. Can you blame us for not telling you?"

Gorlon stammered and ground his teeth, filled with a mixture of rage and sorrow. His pride finally took control and he stormed out of the house, slamming the front door.

* * * * *

Gorlon's voice roared through the shut door, ordering Reese to follow him home. Reese's head appeared in the window.

"Go," Theiss called. "I'll be right behind you."

Reese nodded, his tired eyes full of empathy, and disappeared. Theiss listened as both men hurried away.

Sorrow overtook Theiss once again. Tears poured from his eyes as he stared out the dark window, wondering if he had just lost his birthright. His sense of loss was overwhelming.

Allegna sat on the edge of the sofa near Mellai's head and brushed aside her granddaughter's curly hair.

"I still hear her screaming," Theiss whispered through his teeth.

Allegna nodded. "I know. Many things about her death are almost too much to bear, but I'm glad she's not in pain anymore. She looks peaceful, doesn't she?"

Theiss lifted his chin and looked at Mellai. "I suppose, but—" He stopped short and jerked forward in his seat. "Did you see that?"

Dhargon sat up in his chair. "See what?"

"Did you see it, Allegna?"

Allegna's mouth hung open as she watched her granddaughter. It happened again.

Theiss jumped to his feet. "She opened her eyes."

Dhargon hurried across the room. "What's he talking about, Allegna?"

"I . . . I . . ." Allegna stammered.

Mellai opened her eyes a third time.

"I'll be a goat buried in garbage," Dhargon shouted.

Theiss reached for Mellai, but Allegna stopped him. "Leave her be, Theiss, and stop your jabbering, Dhargon."

Allegna placed her hands on Mellai's head and chest as she watched for movement. Stillness consumed the room. Minutes passed, during which Mellai opened her eyes two more times.

"I don't understand," Allegna said, removing her hands from her granddaughter. "I can't find anything that makes me believe she's alive. She doesn't even appear to be breathing."

Theiss stared at Mellai. He did not speak, but his eyes must have said everything—pleading for the impossible to be true.

Allegna shook her head. "I don't know, Theiss. I just don't know."

As if to answer the question her grandmother couldn't, Mellai grunted—like someone had slugged her in the stomach—then she gasped for air.

"Out of my way," Dhargon ordered as he leaped out of his chair and fell to his knees in front of his granddaughter. He took her hand and squeezed it, while Theiss held the other. "Mellai . . ."

Although Mellai's eyes remained closed, Theiss felt a very subtle squeeze from her hand. Suddenly he was crying again, tears streaking over his dirty cheeks before dropping from his chin. He nodded at Dhargon, then turned his head toward Allegna. "She's alive."

Theiss was stunned. He wanted to pick her up in his arms and swing her around in circles, even though he knew it would be foolish. Mellai's breathing was constant, but labored and shallow. Every breath wheezed in the back of her throat, then rattled as her lungs forced it out again. All Theiss could do was hold her hand as she hovered between life and death.

Minutes passed slowly as the three of them watched Mellai. Color returned to her cheeks, but with it also returned the hot sweats. Her skin became clammy.

Allegna stood to make another elixir, but Dhargon stopped her. "I don't think this is something herbs are going to fix, Allegna. We need to let her body work it out."

"I agree," Theiss said. The circumstance was beyond their control.

Allegna stood behind Dhargon and placed her hands on his shoulders. "Go to bed, you two. You both need sleep. I'll stay with Mellai."

Dhargon withdrew his hand from Mellai's and placed it over Allegna's. "Keep both eyes on her. If she progresses at all, let me know."

After his wife agreed, Dhargon exited to his bedroom. Allegna returned to her place on the sofa in front of Theiss.

Theiss shook his head. "There's no way I'll be able to fall asleep."

Allegna took Theiss's hands and led him to Dhargon's padded chair, then draped a thick quilt over him. "Sit here with your eyes closed. If you can't fall asleep by the time the fire burns down, I'll let you take my place."

Theiss nodded and closed his eyes. By the time he heard Allegna return to the sofa, he could already feel his mind wandering. Just before he fell asleep, he heard the soft whisper of Mellai's grandmother.

"Come back to us, my little girl."

∗   ∗   ∗   ∗   ∗

It wasn't until an hour after sunrise that Dhargon shuffled out of the bedroom. He paused to look at his wife and Theiss. Although the eastern sun poured through the front window of the house, both were sleeping soundly in their chairs, their faces droopy and careworn. Dhargon crossed the room to check on Mellai. Her fever was gone, and her breathing had calmed. Dhargon was overjoyed with her progress, especially considering what she had been through the previous twelve hours.

Dhargon allowed everyone to sleep while he brewed their morning tea. Allegna stirred first. She rubbed her weary eyes with the back of her hands, then smiled at him. "I think this is the fourth time you've ever beaten me to breakfast."

Dhargon chuckled. "I'm a lucky man." He handed a filled cup to Allegna. "How'd it go last night?"

Allegna sipped her tea. "She hasn't regained consciousness, but she's doing much better."

"Should I move her to her bed?"

"No. Whatever is going on inside her, it's fixing the problem. I think it's best to leave her undisturbed until she wakes."

Dhargon nodded, then retrieved his own cup of tea and brought another chair from the table to sit by his wife. They basked in the rays of the rising sun, sipped tea, and watched their granddaughter sleep. Dhargon leaned back, allowing the tea to sooth his aching body.

"What a journey we've been on the past few days," Allegna commented. "Lon is fighting for the Rayders, and Mellai almost dies in the mountains, recovers, really dies, then comes back to life."

"It worries me to think what tomorrow will bring," Dhargon said with a sigh, nodding toward Theiss. "I don't think he can take much more of this."

Allegna held the cup in her lap. "Neither can Mellai."

Chapter 9
Flooded

Acting Commander Omar Brickeden stood knee-deep in mud, a scowl fixed on his aged face. The top of his bald head was scorched bright red from endless hours under the ruthless sun.

The piercing whistle from one of his Rayder soldiers caught Omar's attention. He looked up and saw a man with bulging eyes, his muddy hand pointing north at what should have been an inspiring sight. In addition to the southern river that had reached their city a week earlier, another source of water was making its way toward Taeja from the north, creeping south through the dusty riverbed. Riding alongside the approaching river was Lon and his squad.

"I will kill him myself," Omar growled as he trudged to his horse. He was barely able to pull himself into the saddle, but lost his left boot in the process.

Another nearby Rayder fished the boot out of the mud and squished it back onto Omar's foot, then stepped back and saluted. "What should we do, my Commander?"

"Keep looking for the source," Omar answered, then turned his horse north. "I need to stop this from getting any worse."

Omar forced his horse through the quagmire, wishing all the while for Dawes and his experience in the Gaurelic Waste. His own horse, Dax, nearly fell into the mud on several occasions, catching himself at the very last moment before Omar toppled over his head.

The process was tedious. When Omar reached the north end of the city, he kicked Dax into a gallop out of the mud and toward Lon. Mud flipped from Dax's legs as he ran. The squad was only two miles north of the city—at the head of the approaching river.

✳   ✳   ✳   ✳   ✳

"Stop the water!" Omar shouted.

Lon glanced at Wade. "Did he just tell me to *stop* the water?"

"I believe so, Beholder."

Lon urged Dawes into a gallop until he reached Omar. "Why?"

"The south river flooded the city," Omar replied, pointing back at Taeja. "If you had come back before moving on to the next dam, I would have warned you."

"How was I supposed to know this would happen?" Lon said defensively. "Did it overflow the banks?"

"Yes and no. There are water channels throughout the city that are fed from the river. Some of them are on the surface, but many are underground. The underground channels must have deteriorated. Water is seeping up through the ground all over the city."

"Then I'll just close the inlets from the riverbed before the water reaches them," Lon replied.

Omar shook his head. "We have already looked into that option, but the inlets are not visible from the surface. You have to reroute the water out of the riverbed."

Lon raised his eyebrows. "This water will reach Taeja in an hour. You're asking me to reroute an entire river around a whole city. It needs somewhere else to flow. I can't just remove one of the banks and let it flood out the side."

Omar picked a clod of mud from Dax's mane and flung it to the ground. "Trust me, Lon. It will create an even bigger mess when it reaches Taeja. This riverbed flows straight through the center of the city. Taeja is already flooded with mud and silt. If you do not stop this river, we might as well move into the Gaurelic Waste because Taeja will become just as uninhabitable."

Lon glanced back at the river, creeping closer at a slow, but unrelenting pace. The mountains would feed the river with a constant supply of water. If something was to be done about the pending disaster, it had to be done fast. "Show me where to start rerouting the river, Omar. We don't have much time."

"Bring your squad, too," Omar replied, looking over the Beholder's men. "Who are you missing? I count only eight."

"We were ambushed by something," Lon said. "We lost Riyen, and many of us were injured, but my explanation can wait. Let's reroute this river first."

Omar grimaced, visibly struck by the loss of such a valuable soldier, then kicked Dax around and galloped south. By Lon's command, he and the eight members of his squad followed the acting commander.

They had all been recovering in their own respect. Dovan's gashed cheek had morphed into an inflamed scab; he would carry a significant scar for the rest of his life. Lon's left thigh was bruised and ugly, still visible through his torn pants, and troubled him with a slight limp when he walked. Channer's right ankle was swollen nearly too big to fit in his boot. He claimed he was fine, but he was incapable of putting any weight on his foot. Nik and Keene's injuries were the most debilitating of the survivors, though Nik's dislocated shoulder would recover quicker than Keene's broken leg.

There had been no sign of the calahein at the Meridina Pass, which Lon both regretted and appreciated. No one else had been injured and they had not been attacked again, but the empty pass left a hole in Lon's deduction. Without complete proof, he'd never know for certain that calahein had attacked them.

Omar led them to a spot a half-mile north of Taeja.

"Close the riverbed here," Omar said, then pointed southeast. "Create the new path at least a half-mile away from Taeja. There is no sense in risking more leakage into the city. I will position your squad ahead of you to mark the path."

Lon heaved a sigh at the thought of so much walking and looked at Wade, who had stayed behind. When Lon gave him a questioning glance, Wade placed his hand on his sword. "I swore to keep you safe, Beholder."

"Don't worry about me, Lieutenant," Lon replied. "I'll be fiddling with True Sight. It would be foolish for anyone to venture too close, especially right now. I have a lot more on my mind than just keeping Taeja from flooding."

Lon shifted in his saddle and surveyed Taeja. Most of the Rayders were busy in the south half of the city. The only people close to their location were the Appernysian peasants Lon had rescued during the battle three weeks earlier. They were clustered together at the north edge of Taeja, a few hundred yards from Lon and Wade.

Wade must have also been watching. "General Tarek will never forgive me for leaving you alone so close to them—even if they are indebted to you. Do not forget what happened to Commander Rayben." Wade kicked his horse and chased after the others. "Keep an eye behind you, Beholder."

Lon understood the underlying meaning to Wade's last comment. As a Beholder, Lon was only capable of wielding the energy he could see. Although he trusted the peasants, Lon decided to take Wade's advice—just in case someone was foolish enough to attack. He positioned himself so Taeja would still be in his line of sight as he carved out the new riverbed.

Lon checked the position of the approaching river. "An hour away," he complained to Dawes as he slid carefully out of the saddle, grunting at the pain in his thigh, "and many more hours of work ahead of us. Well, there's no sense in delaying the inevitable. What do you say we give it a try?"

Dawes nickered and tossed his black mane, then moved to stand behind his master while Lon summoned True Sight. Lon first closed the path of the existing riverbed by pulling up and solidifying a thick wall of earth and stone. He curved the wall away from Taeja, angling it gradually to prevent a sharp turn in the river's new path.

After plotting his course by the positions of his squad, Lon started the same rotating pattern of energy he had used in the mountains—in through the feet and out the hands. He forced down the existing bank of the dry riverbed and hardened the bottom and sides of the new path by compacting the dirt. He made the new riverbed thirty feet wide—the same width as the old path.

"Here we go . . ." Lon muttered, then took a step forward with his right foot. When it touched the ground, he pushed down the next section of dirt and hardened it. He continued this pattern with his left foot, making sure at least one foot was on the ground to keep the cycle of energy flowing. The process was slow and tedious at first, especially with the pain in his thigh, but Lon's confidence and skill increased as he continued forward.

The eight members of Lon's squad were positioned about every two miles along the full length. It took Lon less than an hour to reach the first post, manned by Wade. At every successive post, Lon would take a small break to rest his mind and body—making sure to leave plenty of room between himself and the oncoming river.

By the time Lon had created nine of the seventeen miles required, four hours had passed. It was far past sunset and darkness filled the Taejan plains. Those with Lon volunteered to retrieve torches and light the path for their Beholder. Although Lon didn't need the extra light, he allowed the squad to fetch the torches. Wade, however, refused to leave the Beholder's side.

Although Lon felt taxed to the edge of his strength, he successfully created the new riverbed within seven hours. It took another three hours before water filled the channel and joined with the southern river. Lon had accomplished an amazing feat, yet neither he nor his squad had the energy to celebrate. They unraveled their bedrolls at the fork of the joined rivers, and collapsed into slumber.

Chapter 10

Water

Light was just beginning to appear in the east. Lon pushed his arms high above his head, surprised that his muscles weren't sore after the previous days' labors. He was even more grateful when he heard Wade deep in slumber. To ensure Lon's safety, Wade had lost a lot of sleep during their journey.

"Your lieutenant rivals Tarek with his rumbling snore," said a familiar voice.

Lon sat up to see Omar sitting on a partially buried boulder. His eyes were droopy and bloodshot.

"Didn't you sleep?" Lon asked.

"No," Omar drawled. "Sleep is not something I will be able to enjoy until a commander is selected."

Lon slipped past the sleeping Rayders and sat next to Omar. "Has someone tried to kill you?"

"Not yet, but I can see it in their eyes. Desire for power can twist the mind of even the most stalwart man. Their lust will settle once a commander is selected, but now we have a rather significant delay before a tournament can be held." He released a long sigh. "How did Riyen die?"

Lon's face fell. "We were attacked by beasts from the Forest of Blight. I was almost certain they were kelsh, but we traveled deep into the Meridina pass on our way to the north river and didn't find any sign of calahein tracks. All I know is that a large cluster of extremely aggressive creatures attacked us. I never had a close look at them."

Omar's expression remained unreadable. "Did you examine their dead?"

"No, and that's partly why I suspected kelsh. They tunneled under a heavy stone to extract their dead. All I could see were prints in the soil."

"Two claws?"

Lon nodded.

"This is grave news," Omar said. "Their behavior sounds far too calculated for a typical beast. You may be correct, yet you survived the attack. How?"

"I injured and killed many of them while they were approaching, but nothing I did seemed to daunt them in the least. They launched a barrage of melon-sized stones at us from over a hundred yards away. I did little to save us. We only survived because two massive beasts flew down from the sky to intervene. I'm almost certain they were ghraefs."

"That would be marvelous news," Omar replied, "but it also worries me. Both ghraefs and calahein should be extinct. Our history shows that they were mortal enemies, so it would be beyond coincidence that both return at the same time."

"True," Lon said, "but I can't say it was either of them for sure."

Omar nodded. "I understand, but the important thing right now is that, calahein or not, something dangerous is living in the Blight. I will send squads to patrol the plains west of Taeja. We cannot afford to be caught unaware. Our situation is dangerous enough as it is."

"I also suggest we send a runner to Tarek. His soldiers should be on guard, ready to protect our people while they travel here."

"Excellent recommendation, Lon. I would prefer Wade go, but I expect he would refuse unless you went with him. As soon as Dovan wakes, I will send him instead. Is he well enough to travel?"

"Just cut on his cheek. He'll be fine."

"Good." Omar sighed as he looked west. "I am sorry to put more pressure on you, Beholder, but we are even more pressed for time than I had originally suspected. Now we are in danger from the east *and* the west. We need to rebuild this city's defenses as soon as possible."

Lon nodded. "You mentioned a significant delay. What is it?"

Omar stood. "Follow me." He led Lon a short distance to the remains of the earthen staircase Lon had created during the Battle for Taeja. It had eroded away into a misshapen pillar, destroyed by successive rainstorms.

"Would you mind creating another one of these, but a little higher?" Omar asked.

Lon summoned True Sight and complied, then released his power and followed Omar up to the platform fifty feet in the air. Omar turned and gestured to the west with an open hand. "What I am referring to is this."

Lon looked passed him and into the heart of Taeja. Stone ruins were scattered for miles across the muddy terrain. Piles of the stonework had already been hauled to the center of the city for the construction of storage chambers.

Lon squinted as he searched the city. Aside from the nearby squad, not a single person was visible. "Where is everybody?"

Omar frowned. "All of our tents, wagons, and supplies are positioned on the west side of Taeja, along with our soldiers. The flooding has made it impossible to survive inside the city boundaries. There is no fresh water or vegetation for the livestock. Your efforts last night were successful, but as you can see, our situation is still hopeless. Taeja is lost to us until we can drain the excess water."

"I'll reroute the south river," Lon suggested. "Once the source of water is removed, it shouldn't take long for the soil inside Taeja to dry."

"You are talking about over a hundred square miles of land," Omar replied, shaking his head, "and Tarek will arrive with the rest of our people by the end of September. That is only two months away, Lon, and winter will not be far behind them. We still have to build fortifications, storehouses, and shelters for our entire nation. I have six thousand soldiers, four thousand Appernysians peasants, and two months to do it. We don't have time to wait for the ground to dry. We have been delayed a week already."

Lon's heart ached for Omar. He was in a terrible predicament. Moving the city outside the original boundaries of Taeja was not an option. Rebuilding the city was a point of tremendous pride to the Rayders. Even if their new city was constructed right next to Taeja, it might as well be thousands of miles away. The location itself was everything to them. As illogical as it sounded, Lon knew the Rayders would rather die than give up what they had taken.

"Let's back up a step, Omar, and think through our tasks. We have unblocked the rivers, so fresh water is no longer a problem. Tarek took four thousand of our soldiers with him to the Exile to escort the rest of our people to Taeja. Did you send someone to Three Peaks yet?"

Omar nodded. "Do you remember Thennek Racketh?"

Lon rubbed the stubble on his face. "Isn't he part of Lieutenant Warley's siege group?"

"Correct. I made him lieutenant and sent him to Three Peaks with forty men. After they restock the signal fires with oiled wood, Lieutenant Thennek will oversee the strengthening of its defenses. Five Rayders will man each peak and twenty-five will occupy the guardhouse at the mountain's base."

"Excellent idea," Lon replied.

"Perhaps, but only a small one," Omar countered. "Their signal fires will do little good if no one is alive to defend Taeja."

"What are you doing with the peasants?" Lon continued.

"The Appernysians? Keeping them as far away from the Rayders as possible—for their own safety. Many of the Rayders hate having them here, but that is beside the point. The Appernysians do not know how to conduct themselves in our society. They will get themselves killed. I assigned them the task of disposing of the dead Appernysian soldiers. Even with the damage it has caused to Taeja,

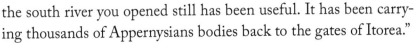

the south river you opened still has been useful. It has been carrying thousands of Appernysians bodies back to the gates of Itorea."

Lon frowned as he considered the horrifying image from Itorea as they saw clusters of their fallen comrades floating toward the city. "How about Braedr?" Lon asked to change the subject. "Has he been causing any problems?"

Omar smirked. "I have kept him busy. There is no time for trouble-making when you are busy with waste management."

"Waste management?" Lon asked with a furrowed brow. "What kind of waste?" A laugh erupted from Lon's throat as he realized what Omar meant. "He's in charge of digging holes for people to squat over?"

"Basically, yes," Omar chuckled "Until we drain the water from Taeja and can figure out a more permanent solution." Omar's face fell as he finished speaking.

Lon searched the western horizon for the Rayders, then shifted his gaze to the flooded city. He had turned Taeja into a quagmire, and he was the only person who could reverse it. The thought concerned him because it would require wielding water. Although he had often thought of the conveniences of such a feat, Lon had pushed his curiosity aside because of Omar's warnings. But this situation required action. He could delay no longer.

"It's time for me to learn how to manipulate water."

Omar remained silent, obviously considering Lon's declaration.

"I admit that the thought has crossed my mind," Omar finally said as he eyed the Beholder, "but do you realize what you are suggesting—and risking? Lon, you are the only reason we beat Appernysia's army. If you pull the blood out of your body while doing this, then our situation becomes even more desperate."

"I need to reroute the south river first," Lon said as he hopped to his feet, "so we have all day to think about it."

Without waiting for a response, Lon returned to his bedroll and packed his gear. Dawes was awake, watching Lon with anticipation.

After Lon secured his gear to Dawes's saddle, he pulled himself onto the horse.

Omar's voice reached Lon as he galloped away. "Perhaps you should stay in your saddle today, Beholder. You have an enormous task ahead of you. You will need all the strength you can muster."

As Lon followed the south river to the east edge of Taeja, Omar's parting words echoed in his mind. Above his need for strength, Lon was desperate for more time. Riding Dawes while using True Sight was the obvious solution, but to manipulate energy through another living creature? He didn't know what to expect.

When Lon reached the east point where he wanted the new river to return into the original riverbed, he dismounted and searched the plains for animal life. Finding none, he summoned True Sight and resumed his search, hunting for a bright cluster of energy hidden among the dry grass. He found a ground squirrel twenty feet to the left, its head barely poking out of a hole in the ground. Lon focused on the earth surrounding the squirrel, then quickly compressed it to hold the squirrel captive from its neck down. The squirrel squeaked and chattered in protest, but it was unable to free itself. The action was cruel, but Lon believed it a necessary sacrifice to speed things along.

Lon ran to the rodent and placed two fingers on the squirrel's head. The squirrel snapped at Lon, but its body was completely immobilized. Lon closed his eyes and drew a deep breath, then opened them again and focused on the energy of the tiny critter. The energy was bright and complex, similar to Lon's own essence. Slowly, Lon pulled energy from the earth and through his helpless victim. The squirrel froze. Its eyes bulged and darted around while Lon pulled a constant stream of energy through it.

After a few seconds, Lon stopped the stream of energy and released his extra supply through his palm, then stepped back and freed the squirrel. It slumped to the earth, and its tiny body twitched with quick breaths. Just when Lon feared he had killed the helpless creature, it jumped to its feet, ran around the hole in a wide circle, then dipped back underground.

Lon laughed at the critter's erratic behavior, then stood and turned to Dawes. He climbed onto the horse and together they crossed through the river to its southern bank. "We'll start here," Lon said when they were about ten feet away from the river's edge. He calmed his mind and body, then using Dawes as an extension of himself, pulled energy from the ground.

Dawes's neck tensed and his shoulders shuddered. Lon created the circular cycle of energy toward the ground. He pushed the soil down in front of them and hardened the dirt to create a new riverbed.

"Imagine that," he said exuberantly, then tightened his lips. "Here we go again . . ." He clicked his heels on Dawes's sides, then together they moved forward, creating the south river's new path.

An hour into the task, Lon was joined by Wade. "I am sorry for sleeping late, Beholder," Wade lamented. "I have failed to keep my oath to protect you."

Lon only shook his head. His concentration was focused on creating the new riverbed, but he thought it pointless to stop and reassure Wade. Besides, the time away from his personal protector had been therapeutic, giving Lon a kind of peace and clarity that he hadn't experienced since he first arrived at the Exile. Although Wade's presence was usually necessary, it was also a constant reminder of the discontent amongst the Rayders. For just a moment, Lon had forgotten the constant threats against his safety.

Although it had taken Lon seven hours to create a new seventeen-mile riverbed the previous night, it took him less than half that amount of time to cross the southern twenty miles while riding Dawes. By the time the sun moved three hours above the eastern horizon, Lon had opened the west entrance of the new southern riverbed and closed the existing river's path. He and Wade galloped ahead of the water to connect the east end of the riverbed, then the two of them waited.

Wade shook his head as they watched the existing river fill the new path. "It is remarkable what you can do with your power, Beholder."

"I'm only using the basics of it," Lon replied. "There's so much more I should be able to do."

Wade watched him with a sidelong glance. Lon recognized his desire for information. "What is it, Lieutenant?"

"I have been wondering," Wade said, shifting in his saddle. "Is this power something that can be learned?"

Lon folded his arms across his chest. "Are you referring to me or you?"

Wade looked down and fidgeted with the horn of his saddle. "Both, I suppose."

Lon nodded and sighed. "I don't know the answer to either question. If we want to stay in Taeja, I need to learn how to manipulate water. I just don't know how to do it. It's really dangerous." Lon paused and watched Wade. "I have no idea if anyone else can just *learn* how to use True Sight. That's not how it happened with me. It came on me without my asking for it. I considered it a curse for many months."

"How could it be a curse?" Wade countered. "Look at what you have done to help us."

"I couldn't control it at first. Before I met Omar, it almost killed me. It was dangerous to everyone around me, too."

Wade's eyes softened, and he looked up at Lon. "Is that what happened to Kaylen?"

Lon flinched at Wade's question. "I'm surprised you remember her. I haven't talked about her since we were on our way to Three Peaks."

"You talk in your sleep," Wade said, sounding a little embarrassed.

Lon suddenly became very anxious, fearing what Wade and the rest of his squad knew about his past. "What have you heard?"

"Most of what you say is incoherent. I hear Kaylen's name most often. Sometimes you mention the village Pree. Lately, you have talked a lot about a girl named Mellai, but nothing specific. Mostly just yelling her name, as though she is in danger."

At the mention of sister, Lon slumped. In his haste to investigate the Meridina Pass and unblock the north river, Lon had forgotten his previous experience while reaching out to her. How could he have forgotten? He wondered if his dreams were a result of that connection forcing its way through. Was Mellai in trouble?

Lon closed his eyes and felt for his sister. It was difficult at first, but after a few slow breaths, he was able to empty his mind. Sudden agony shot through him like a thunderbolt, and he nearly fell off Dawes's back. Although Lon couldn't actually feel what was happening to Mellai, he could sense her excruciating pain. Tears flowed from his eyes as her pain and fear washed through him.

Wade's voice severed Lon's connection. "I am sorry again, Beholder. I have pushed too far."

"Mellai is my sister," Lon responded. His body still trembled.

"Your sister?" Wade asked. "I thought your family was dead."

"I lied," Lon whispered. "I had no choice."

Wade watched him for a moment, looking stung at Lon's deceit. But Lon didn't care. As with countless previous times since joining the Rayders, he couldn't afford to feel. His Rayder brothers were relying on him. He looked over the flooded ruins of Taeja. His anxieties redoubled at the task before him.

"How am I going to drain the water?" he muttered.

As if in answer to Lon's question, Omar appeared from the north, galloping quickly from a cluster of Appernysian peasants.

"This conversation stays between you and me," Lon ordered before Omar was close enough to hear. Wade firmly assented.

When Omar reached them, he smiled. "Sorry I was delayed. I was placing the rest of your squad with the Appernysians. Those peasants need escorts they can trust."

Wade tensed. "Did you leave Preton with them, my Commander?"

"I understand your concern," Omar replied, "but your comrades are with him. He will not cause any problems." Omar paused to examine what Lon had accomplished. "Swift work, Beholder."

"This was the easy part," Lon complained. "Taeja still needs to be drained."

Omar's eyes smiled. It was obvious he had found a solution, but he didn't speak.

"It's fine," Lon said to the acting commander. "Wade knows I don't know how to manipulate water. Continue."

"With your permission," Omar acknowledged. "Try this exercise." He dismounted and indicated for Lon to do the same. When they were standing on the ground five yards apart, Omar grabbed a nearby rock and tossed it up into the air. "Catch."

Lon watched the rock fall to the earth at Omar's feet. "You have to throw it closer to me than that."

Omar retrieved the same rock and shook his head. "Catch it the *other* way." He threw the rock into the air again. Lon summoned True Sight, caught hold of the rock's solid matter, and suspended it motionless in the air.

Omar nodded. "Now retrieve it."

Lon pulled the rock to his hand and wrapped his fingers around it.

"How did you do that?" Omar asked.

"I connected myself to the rock to control it."

"Did you cycle its energy through yourself?"

"No . . ." Realization dawned on Lon.

Omar smiled. "Do the same thing with the water. Do not cycle it, but extend your essence to *it* instead. Wade and I are watching you carefully."

Wade sat bug-eyed upon his horse. "I may be watching, but I cannot believe what I am seeing."

"It's not the first time you've seen me work," Lon countered.

Wade nodded. "But I could not see what you did near the mountains. You are the only one with the ability to see clearly at night, Beholder."

Omar retrieved a cup from his saddlebag and filled it with water from the river. He placed the cup on the ground in front of Lon. "Now try the same with this water. Extend your essence to it."

Lon cocked his head to the side and took a deep breath, then focused on the slow moving energy in the cup. He extended his essence into it and tried to grab the water. A hollow sphere formed in the center, displacing the water around it. The fluid itself avoided Lon's efforts and splashed over the sides of the cup. He had failed.

"Do not be discouraged," Omar said as he refilled the cup with water. "Try again, but with less aggression. Up until now, True Sight has supplied you with power and force, so you will have to change your approach. Treat the water gently, like the delicate bristles on the end of a wheat stalk."

Despite his frustration, Lon relaxed his mind and body and focused on the water. Using his essence, he probed at its edges and tested its reaction. The water responded with indifference at Lon's presence, so he pushed in farther, scooping the water with an invisible hand and pulling it from the cup. It rested in his essence, swirling around passively as Lon moved the water through the air toward Dawes. The horse reared his head back as the water approached, then finally lurched forward and bit through it in protest.

"Very well done," Omar exclaimed as the water splashed out the sides of Dawes's mouth. "Now try to form a constant stream."

Lon did as Omar suggested, forming a tunnel with part of his essence, while scooping the water and dropping it into the invisible trough. The task was tedious and ineffective. He thought through every circumstance where he had used True Sight, and remembered when he and Tarek had discovered Braedr hiding up a tree in the Dialorine Range. He had pulled wood from the tree that morning, but differently than other situations. He had not grabbed hold of any particular object and retrieved it, but had pulled its energy through his own.

Lon tried this new tactic, siphoning the water's energy toward himself, but stopping before the water reached his body. With a little encouragement, the water started gliding through the tunnel and emptying into the dirt. In just a few seconds, the cup was empty.

"Excellent," Omar congratulated. "Before the final step, however, I must know how you have been moving the water."

"I siphoned it with my essence, but with little effort. Once I got the water moving, it just pulled itself out of the cup."

Omar's eyes lit up. "An effective technique. Now let me ask you, is your essence the only element that can hold water?"

Lon pondered the question before answering. "I suppose not. I would have to get it started myself, but things like wood and metal can hold water, too. I don't think that's the solution, though. It would take a long time for our men to build channels in the city."

"Maybe for us," Wade commented, obviously caught up in finding a solution, "but you just created a twenty-mile riverbed in just a few hours, Beholder."

"Even so," Lon said, shaking his head, "it's not practical to layer Taeja with a web of water channels. Travel would become almost impossible—not to mention the drainage problem. The whole city is flooded, which means there must be buried channels everywhere. Whatever I create will just drain back into the underground system again."

"I agree on all fronts," Omar said. "What about creating new channels, above ground, and removing them when you are done?"

Lon furrowed his brow with speculation.

"Have you considered that you might be able to channel water with air?" Omar continued. "If you can use air to stop a man from breathing or form a pocket to block out mosquitoes, you should be able to hold water with it."

"So I could use air to form the siphoning tunnels, get the water moving with my essence, then the water will drain itself into the new river channels." Lon bubbled with excitement, his anxieties about his sister again forgotten. He climbed into Dawes's saddle and turned to ride into Taeja. "Wish me luck."

Omar put up his hands. "Slow down, Beholder. This old riverbed needs to be closed off on this end first."

Chapter 11

Council

Kaylen knelt over the laundry basin, sweat pouring from her face as she scrubbed clothes. Aely stood guard behind the open door into the washroom. She gripped a dagger in her right hand, but kept it hidden behind her apron. Two days had passed since the attempt on the king and queen's lives, yet the two handmaidens had heard nothing. King Drogan had asked them to be patient, but Kaylen's patience was wearing thin.

"Time to switch," Kaylen said as she pulled a chemise from the basin and hung it on a drying line.

Aely heaved a sigh, then took her place at the washboard. "This is torture."

"I know," Kaylen said as she wiped the sweat from her face with her apron, "but it's the only protection we have. One of us needs to keep watch so Lady Netsey doesn't sneak in and cut our throats."

"She fled," Aely growled, "and with one of us standing guard, we're getting half as much work done."

"There's nothing we can do about it. We're not supposed to know our king and queen. We have to act completely oblivious."

"Easy enough for you," Aely grumbled, "but I guess you're right. I don't want to end up like all those dead people at the royal chamber."

"Don't talk about that," Kaylen said as she thought back to the carnage. "I never want to see something like that again. I'd rather be here, washing clothes, where I have some sort of control. No matter how dirty these clothes get, I can always wash them clean again."

Aely held up the gown she was scrubbing, revealing a dark stain in the bottom hem. "Well I've had enough of this," she said, followed by a string of curses.

Kaylen nodded absently, her thoughts still on the royal chamber. "What are we going to do, Aely? I'm so confused."

"I don't know. There's a lot they aren't telling us."

"But can you blame them? They have to make absolutely certain we're on their side. Think about it. The violence we saw can't be an everyday occurrence. Something really bad is happening."

"I agree, but what are we supposed to do about it? The only person in the keep that I talk to anymore is you, Kaylen. We don't know anybody. Where can we find answers?"

"That's what Queen Cyra seemed to like about us, though. I say we help." Kaylen took her place behind the door and wrapped her hand around the dagger hidden under her apron. "I don't think Lady Netsey is gone, not if Lord Tyram is still locked in the great hall with the council. She wouldn't leave her father behind."

Aely stood and hurled the garment she was washing into the soapy water. "We have no idea what she's capable of doing. She's pure evil."

Kaylen was about to answer when a woman slipped into the room. Before Kaylen could react, one knife was at her throat and another jabbing into her ribs. The woman must have known Kaylen was hidden behind the door.

"Do you know how easily sound travels through stone corridors?" the woman said, facing Kaylen. "You might want to be more careful about what you say."

Aely ripped her dagger from under her apron.

"Tsk tsk," the woman said with a glance over her shoulder, pushing the knife harder against Kaylen's neck. "That was a horrible mistake, Aely."

"Please. Let her go." Tears filled Aely's eyes. "She's my best friend."

The woman stashed one knife, reached under Kaylen's apron and pried the dagger from Kaylen's hand, then stepped back. "Better. Drop your dagger and kick it over here."

"Who are you?" Aely asked, doing as she was told.

The woman smiled. "My name is Kat Jashfelt. I believe you've been waiting for me—patiently, I hope. I am King Drogan's spymaster."

Kaylen put her hand to her throat, afraid the blade had pierced her skin. "Can I have my dagger back, please?"

"Not until we're friends," Kat said with a laugh, "even if their Majesties trust you."

As with Kaylen and Aely, Kat wore a servant's dress with a white apron tied in front. She looked to be in her mid-twenties, and her short black hair was only a few inches long. It stuck out from her head in spikey clusters.

"You're a spymaster?" Aely said. "I've never heard of such a thing."

"As it should be," Kat answered with another laugh. "I wouldn't be doing my job very well if everyone knew me, would I?"

Aely's brow furrowed. "How do we know we can trust you? You could be feeding us lies."

"Very true," Kat answered, "which is why I came with a token." She held up the same glowing diamond Kaylen had returned to Queen Cyra.

Kaylen gasped. "How did you get that?"

As quickly as it had appeared, the diamond disappeared behind Kat's apron. "Don't pretend to be such a fool," Kat said as she returned the dagger to Kaylen. "It doesn't suit you."

Kaylen held up the dagger and aimed it at the mysterious woman. Kat only laughed. "You can fetch your dagger, too, Aely, if it makes you feel safer."

Aely hurried across the floor and retrieved her weapon. She sheathed it, but kept her hand wrapped around the grip.

Kat's eyes suddenly became very serious. "I'm glad to see you're at least *thinking* about being cautious, ladies. Itorea isn't as safe as everyone believes—especially not in the keep. You are right to be wary."

"We aren't ladies," Aely retorted, "and I still don't trust you."

Kat smirked. "I have a task for you both. You must remember Ernon's inability to enter the great hall, but things have changed over the past two days. Lords are not used to living without all the wine and delicacies they can swallow. They need servants to deliver food and drink to them. You will be those servants."

"How are we supposed to do that?" Kaylen asked, lowering her dagger slightly.

"Find Gera in the kitchens. Go now. She is waiting for you." Without another word, Kat left the washroom and disappeared down the corridor.

Kaylen dropped her dagger and threw her arms around Aely, sobbing into her shoulder. "I thought I was dead. She moved so fast."

"I know," Aely said as she returned the hug. "So much for our plan to stand guard."

Kaylen forced herself to stop crying, then sheathed her dagger and led Aely out of the room by her hand. "We need to get to the kitchens."

Aely pulled her hand free. "You're going to trust her?"

"Why shouldn't we? She had Queen Cyra's necklace. She knew about Ernon. She could have easily killed us. I'm seeing this thing through." Kaylen turned and continued down the corridor.

"The kitchens will be sweltering," Aely complained. She blew out her breath and followed.

✻   ✻   ✻   ✻   ✻

By the time Kaylen and Aely reached the kitchens, it was mid-morning. Only one woman was in sight. At first Aely thought she was Lady Netsey, so she pulled Kaylen back behind the wall. Upon further inspection, however, she realized the woman was a lot chubbier than Netsey, and bubblier, too. The woman whistled as she bounced around the kitchen.

Aely rolled her eyes. "There's *no way* that's Lady Netsey." She reentered the kitchen with Kaylen half-hidden behind her.

"Where is everyone else?" Kaylen whispered. "Last time we came here, this place was bustling with people."

Aely shrugged, but realized the danger of their situation. Her hand slipped behind her apron as they closed the distance between themselves and the chubby woman.

"Gera?" Aely asked when only a few feet separated them.

The woman glanced over her shoulder at Aely and Kaylen, then stepped to the side. "Took you long enough," she complained, gesturing to a sizable tray laden with piles of fresh fruit, meat, and a large pewter pitcher full of wine. "Take these to the great hall and deliver them to the council."

Kaylen stepped around Aely and picked up the pitcher of wine. "What should we do when we get there?" she asked, leaning close to Gera.

Gera furrowed her brow at Kaylen. "Are you daft, child? I told you to give the lords their food. Now get out of my kitchen. My help will be back any minute with lunch, and I have more important things to do than stand here and talk with you."

Without argument, Aely picked up the tray and led Kaylen out of the kitchen. Minutes passed in silence as they made their way toward the great hall. "Deliver food?" Aely finally whispered. "Sounds like *really* secretive work." Her voice oozed with sarcasm.

As they navigated the corridors, anxiety continued to build inside Aely. Her imagination consumed her as she thought about what might happen when they reached the great hall. Would they be allowed inside? Would they be forced inside? What would they see? What would happen to them? By the time they finally reached the closed doors, Aely's arms trembled with fatigue and fear. It was all she could do to keep herself from dropping the tray to the stone floor, yet she tried to act confident. If she felt worried, Kaylen would be frantic. She had to remain calm for her friend's sake.

Kaylen hugged the heavy pewter pitcher with one arm and reached for the massive brass knocker with the other. With obvious exertion, she barely lifted it and slammed it back down against the wooden beams. The door cracked open and a man peered through the small space, then his head disappeared again.

"Come," said a low voice as the door was pulled farther open.

Aely returned Kaylen's frightened glance before stepping into the great hall. The enormity of the circular room took her by complete surprise. Every surface gleamed with polished white marble. There was no mortar to be seen, nor trusses or pillars rising up to support the domed roof arching a hundred feet overhead. Twelve deep fireplaces surrounded the room's perimeter, unused because of the summer heat. A sturdy chain hung from the center of the dome, dangling halfway to the floor. At its end was a giant spiked crystal, clear as glass.

A loud thud resonated through the hall when the door was shut and secured, then a man appeared in front of the two women. "Follow me."

Not a speck of sunlight entered the windowless hall, yet the crystal sparkled brilliantly like a diamond. White light glowed from within itself, filling the room with breathtaking radiance. When Aely turned to see if Kaylen had noticed, the crystal's white glow sparkled in Kaylen's wide eyes.

The man led them to the other side of the great hall, where the council sat around a large rectangular table. A dark green satin cloth, with a white halberd head stitched into the middle, covered the entire surface of the table. It draped over the edges and onto the laps of the thirty-four lords seated around it. The great hall was as silent as a tomb as the lords watched the approaching women.

As they drew closer, Aely winced at the two men tied to their chairs at one end of the table, just as Ernon had described. They sagged lifelessly against their bonds, and their faces were bruised, bloody, and swollen.

A man sitting at the head of the table grinned, upright in his upholstered chair. "Ah, what have you brought for us, Sergeant Ched?"

"Lunch," the man escorting Kaylen and Aely replied, "and dessert if you wish it."

Aely's steps faltered at the Sergeant's words. She could see the ravaging hunger in the council members' eyes and lips, especially in the man at the head of the table. He leaned back in his chair, and his mouth curled into a sinister sneer. "A tempting offer, Sergeant Ched, but we can't afford to spoil our reputation. Not yet."

It wasn't until Ched pushed them forward that Aely realized she and Kaylen had stopped moving. She forced one foot in front of the other, afraid of the unspeakable evil any rebellion might ignite in the men. They reached the head of the table, set the tray and pitcher down, then dipped their heads and tried to step back. Ched blocked their way.

"Thank you, ladies," the man at the table spoke with oiled words. "Allow me to introduce myself. My name is Lord Ramik Gunderott, Chamberlain of Itorea and head of this council."

Aely and Kaylen curtsied and spoke together. "Pleased to meet you, my lord."

Ramik's sneer crawled up his cheek. "Would you ladies be so kind as to taste all of the food on this tray? It would be ungracious of me to make you bring it all the way here and not allow you a sample. Of course, you'll want to wash it down with a bit of wine, too."

Aely's eyes widened at the offer. As servants of the keep, her and Kaylen's meals had been limited to bread, beans, vegetables, and water. Scraps of meat occasionally found their way onto their trays, but infrequently and in very small quantities. Fruit was an extremely rare commodity. Although both women had served the keep for many months, neither of them had tasted fruit prepared by the court chefs. To eat their fruit was a mouthwatering proposition.

Kaylen reached for an apple. Its polished red skin sparkled under the hovering crystal's glow. She wrapped her fingers around it and licked her lips.

As her friend brought the apple to her mouth, Aely suddenly realized why Lord Ramik had offered them a taste of the food. Lord Ramik wasn't showing them kindness. He was using them.

Aely took the apple from her friend. "Let me try it first."

Anger flashed across Kaylen's face, but it quickly transformed into recognition. "Don't be silly," she argued as they fought for the apple.

Ramik pounded his fist on the table. His smile had been replaced with a soul-piercing scowl. "You will both eat at the same time, and quickly. My council is hungry. If the chefs were foolish enough to poison this food, you will be the first of many to die."

Aely's mind reeled. Was this why the king and queen wanted their service? Was this the reason for Kat's urgency? For Gera's indifference? Had she and Kaylen become pawns in a grander scheme? Regardless of the reasons, Aely knew they didn't have a choice. Ramik didn't care about their lives. That much was clear.

Aely yanked the apple from Kaylen's grip and took a small bite. It tasted wonderful, but she couldn't enjoy it. She put the apple aside and reached for the next item on the tray while Kaylen peeled back an orange's rind and sampled a small section of its interior. All eyes were on the two women as they made their way through each item in the pile of food and took a few swallows of the wine. Aely felt engorged when they finished, but otherwise perfectly normal.

"There now," Ramik commented. "Wasn't that wonderful? It's not every day that a servant is given the honor to try a nobleman's food. How was it?"

"Excellent, my lord," Kaylen answered. Aely didn't speak. She was worried that the food bobbing in her throat might force its way out if she opened her mouth.

"I'm glad to hear it," Ramik said. "You've both eaten a soldier's share. Sit down and rest until your stomachs settle. Sergeant Ched, grab these two lovely ladies a chair."

Ched retrieved two adorned chairs from the far end of the table and placed them against the wall, a few feet to the right of Ramik.

*　*　*　*　*

When they sat down, Kaylen stared with concern at the two unconscious men across the table.

"That will do," Ramik told Ched. "Keep that door shut, Sergeant." Ched saluted and returned to his post at the entrance.

"As for the rest of us," Ramik continued, "we will wait an hour before we eat. Some poisons take longer to show than others." He regarded Kaylen and Aely with the same sinister sneer. "In the meantime, let's return to more pressing matters. How long have Anton and Haedon been out this time?"

"Two hours, Chamberlain," a man answered. He was one of the older men at the table, with a long face and a pointed chin. His thin, tanned skin was tight against his face, hollowing his eyes and accenting his high cheekbones. He regarded the two unconscious men with a smile. "Shall I continue?"

"Absolutely," Ramik replied. "I'm growing weary of their pride. Be sure to break it this time, Lord Tyram. I want to sleep in my feather bed tonight."

Tyram laughed and stood with a ribbed leather whip in his hand. "My pleasure, Chamberlain."

Kaylen glanced at the other men at the table. A few of them laughed along with Tyram, including the two men at his sides. Most of the other lords sat with resigned faces, neither willing to show their support nor voice their protest. Two men, however, showed obvious disgust at what was being done. One of these men sat to the right of Ramik. He was the first to speak.

"Chamberlain, it has been two days. You cannot break these men. I would rather see them killed than endure more senseless beatings."

"Duly noted," Ramik replied. "I cringe at the sight along with you, Lord Teph, but it must be done. I don't expect you to understand, but it is my responsibility as head of Council to see that we reach a unanimous decision. You see to your responsibilities, Steward, and I'll see to mine."

Teph blew out his breath. "That's hardly possible when you have us locked up in here."

Ramik smiled. "Again, duly noted."

Kaylen watched Tyram approach Haedon and Anton. Haedon was the king's advisor and Anton the queen's chancellor. Kaylen knew they were good men. If nothing else, their blood was proof of that. They would die before yielding to the council's wishes—whatever they were.

Tyram unraveled his whip and stood five paces behind the two men. He whirled the whip around his body, then flicked it above their heads. A fearful crack echoed through the great hall, but neither Haedon nor Anton stirred.

Kaylen's mind raced when she saw Tyram pull a knife from his belt. She couldn't sit still and allow innocent men to be harmed. Her hand slipped under her apron and gripped her hidden dagger. Ramik was leading the council against King Drogan, and undoubtedly the men behind the attempt on his life. There were other good men in the council. If she could kill Ramik, perhaps the others would protect her and Aely. Ramik was only three steps away. She could do it. She *had* to do it.

Just as Kaylen was about to leap from her chair, Aely placed her hand on Kaylen's arm. Aely's body was rigid, and she dug her fingernails into Kaylen's skin.

Kaylen turned her head to look at her friend. Although neither woman spoke, Kaylen knew the look in Aely's eyes. She was terrified. Kaylen placed her free hand reassuringly on Aely's face and tightened her lips. *This has to be stopped*, Kaylen screamed in her mind, hoping Aely would understand. Aely's body shuddered, but she nodded her agreement, and her hand slipped under her own apron.

A tear trickled from Kaylen's eye as she took hold of Aely's free hand. Then, together, they rushed at Ramik.

Chapter 12

Migration

"General Tarek," Dovan called as he finished crossing Justice. Its tip had been reinforced and secured to the southern edge of the Zaga Ravine. Planks had also been layered along its sides to keep livestock and small children from accidentally falling over the edge while crossing the one-hundred-thirty-foot span.

Tarek Ascennor looked up from a large map and smiled. "Well, kick me in the head. Good to see you, Dovan. How goes everything in Taeja? Lon kill himself yet?" A deep belly-laugh erupted as he finished speaking.

Dovan shook his head with amusement as he galloped toward Thorn, the ancient watchtower the first Rayders had built out of the bridge that had once spanned the ravine. When he reached the Rayder general, Dovan dismounted and saluted. Tarek ignored the salute and wrapped his thick arms around Dovan in a tight hug. Dovan gasped as he was lifted off his feet and dropped back to the ground. He paused and eyed his general.

Tarek chuckled and leaned closer to Dovan. "Don't mind me. It's just nice to see a familiar battle-hearty face. Speaking of, what happened to yours? Looks like someone caught you with a mean fingernail. Getting a little too friendly with the ladies?"

Dovan frowned and eyed the other nearby Rayders. "Will you accompany me for a ride, General?"

Tarek nodded, tossing his banter aside, and turned to one of his soldiers. "Don't let anyone cross yet. We need to wait for the rest of the supply wagons first." He mounted a nearby horse and turned back to Dovan. "Lead the way."

The two of them galloped west along the Zaga Ravine for a few minutes before Dovan slowed his horse to a walk. "Things are not going as well as planned."

"They never do," Tarek answered, "not even with Omar. What's the problem?"

"You mean *problems*," Dovan countered. "The most pressing is that Taeja is completely flooded."

Tarek sighed. "Lon been trying his hand at water-wielding?"

"Yes, but not until after the city was already flooded. He is doing a lot to help fix the problem. By the time I left, he had already rerouted thirty miles of river and was starting to drain water out of the city."

"Sounds like he's got it all under control," Tarek said with a smile. "If that's our biggest problem, then I'm not too worried."

Dovan pulled back on the reins and gazed west, toward the Meridina Pass. "I said it was the most pressing, not the biggest."

Tarek's humor disappeared. "Is Appernysia planning another attack?"

"Most likely, but that is not the problem. Danger comes from the west. Our squad was attacked by something ferocious while we escorted Beholder Lon to open the rivers. He and Omar are worried it was a band of kelsh."

Tarek raised an eyebrow. "Worried? Didn't you see what attacked you?"

"No. It was at night and Beholder Lon fought them at a distance with True Sight. The beasts dragged away their dead and wounded, too, so there was nothing left but tracks in the morning."

Tarek let go of his horse's reins and folded his arms across his broad chest. "And what do you think, Dovan?"

Dovan looked at the ground. "I do not know what to think. It sounds ludicrous, I know, but they may be right."

"You were there for the fight, Dovan, and you struggle to believe it. How am I supposed to convince everyone here that the calahein have returned, especially when I don't know if I believe it myself?"

"Our commander does not want anyone to know," Dovan said urgently, looking up at Tarek. "He just wants you to be prepared for an attack."

Tarek shook his head. "I have miles of unarmed Rayder civilians with me. Four thousand soldiers won't be enough."

Dovan nodded. "I hope it does not come to that, General. Our commander and Beholder are doing everything they can to make Taeja defensible by the time you arrive. They just want to ensure you travel safely there with the rest of our people. I will stay and do my part to help make that possible."

Tarek glanced over his shoulder at the Rayders massing near the bridge. "Maybe it would be better to stay in Flagheim. Its walls are already built."

"Perhaps, but it is not just a matter of protection. We have been waiting more than twelve hundred years to return to Taeja. Very few of us could be convinced to stay in the Exile."

Tarek blew out his breath. "I know."

* * * * *

The migrating Rayders continued to gather at Thorn for another seven weeks. They were laden with everything they could haul, carry, or drag, having permanently abandoned their homes. When Tarek finally led them across Justice and started the eighty-five mile trek to Taeja, fall had arrived and, along with it, a refreshing northern breeze.

"At least August is behind us," Tarek mused to Dovan as they rode. "The heat would have made everyone miserable."

"I never took you for an optimist, General," Dovan replied with a smile.

"Don't get used to it." Tarek said, and harrumphed.

Their progress across the Taejan Plains was slow and painstaking. The trail they followed was new and rough, so not a day passed without at least one wagon breaking its wheel on a rock or hole hidden in the tall yellow grass. Then, of course, there was the constant fear of attack hanging over Tarek's head. Trusting Lieutenant Thennek and his men at Three Peaks to signal them of Appernysian troops approaching from the southeast, Tarek placed a long, thin line of his soldiers along the west flank of their supply train—with scattered patrols running even closer to the Tamadoras Mountains.

After five days, the Rayders reached a beautiful sight that bolstered their spirits. Before them was a river stretching as far as they could see to the east and west. On both banks of the river, the dry plains had sprouted lush green grass.

"This is the northern fork of a river that Beholder Lon unblocked," Dovan explained to Tarek. "It is roughly halfway between Thorn and Taeja. The other fork runs straight to Taeja. We will reach it before we reach the city."

"Halfway," Tarek repeated as he observed the excitement raging through the Rayders, "which means another four days in dry plains. We'll stay here the rest of the day and continue tomorrow morning. It will do everyone good to rest and enjoy the fresh water."

Tarek's words quickly spread through the Rayders. By mid-afternoon, wagons were camped in a long line on the north and south banks of the shallow river. The women soaked their feet in the cool water while old men yelled at the children, who laughed as they splashed around and threw mud at each other. Tarek positioned his soldiers in an arch around the western end of the column. He knew the citizens would question the placement of his soldiers, considering the real threat to be from the east, but he didn't care. "Let them think what they want," he grumbled to himself. They had not encountered any trouble yet. He hoped their luck would continue.

By the next morning, the Rayders' morale had lifted significantly. The women and children sang as they continued toward Taeja. From time to time, even the old men would get caught up in the excitement and join in the singing.

Tarek watched the Rayders sadly, fearing what might be waiting for them when they reached Taeja.

"Lon's had almost two months," Tarek mentioned to Dovan as they rode at the front of the column. "Think he did it?"

Dovan shrugged. "It seems impossible that he has already drained Taeja, but perhaps. He is a Beholder, after all. I have seen him perform miracles with his power, General."

"I hope you're right. Living in mud will get really old really fast, even for the children."

Despite the return of dusty plains, the Rayders' attitudes continued to improve with every step they took toward Taeja. None of them had seen the ruins, with the exception of Tarek, Dovan, and the other soldiers. The people began imagining what the city would be like. This added to Tarek's anxiety. Even if the city had been drained, the Rayders were setting themselves up for major disappointment. It would take years for them to finish rebuilding the city.

On the morning of the Rayders' fifth day from the river crossing, an escort arrived from Taeja—led by Acting Commander Omar Brickeden.

"Well met, General Tarek," Omar said with a smile.

"Likewise, my Commander," Tarek responded. "Why do you look so lively?"

Omar's smile grew even bigger. "You will have to be patient, General."

"I hate waiting," Tarek grumbled.

With Omar and his escorts in the lead, the camp quickly assembled and made their way south. They reached the southern fork of the river before midday. As they closed the distance to their new home, whispers poured from the Rayders. A strange vision stretched across the southern horizon.

"What is that?" Dovan asked Tarek as he squinted his keen eyes. Tarek shrugged and passed the question to Omar, but the acting commander didn't answer. He just kept smiling.

By mid-afternoon, the unclear vision had materialized into a long line of raised earth with a deep ravine in front. Omar led the travelers south through green reeds lining the eastern shore of the river.

Tarek turned to Dovan. "I thought you said this place was flooded."

"It was," Dovan uttered with a gaping jaw, "nearly as bad as the Gaurelic Waste."

"Lon's been busy," Tarek added with raised eyebrows. Omar led them across the river by way of a new bridge located at the south end of the city, and continued west around the perimeter wall.

Tarek shook his head as he observed the high mounds of dirt arcing into the city in long segments. "I can't believe what I'm seeing, my Commander. When you showed me your plans to rebuild Taeja, I was impressed, but I thought it would take years to build."

"It is not finished yet," Omar replied, "but as you can see, Lon's skill with True Sight has improved."

Tarek laughed. "Obviously." His eyes followed the curving wall to a large segment that jutted over two miles to the south. "It looks like you kept the shape of the perimeter wall the same as you had planned."

"Two Beholder's Eyes wrapping around each other," Omar answered with a nod. "I am taking you through the south gate."

"Why not the north gate? Hasn't he finished it yet?"

Omar smiled. "Of course he has. He also drained the city, raised the full eighty miles of the perimeter wall, and moved on to Taeja's interior."

Although Tarek was stunned that Lon had accomplished so much in only two months, he returned Omar's smile and winked. "I got it. We're going the *long* way into Taeja so you can show off your city to the new arrivals."

Omar lifted his chin and clicked his heels against Dax. He and his escorts rode ahead of Tarek and the rest of the Rayders.

Tarek laughed and turned to Dovan. "He'll make a great commander, won't he?"

Dovan nodded. "If he wins the tournament."

"He's the obvious choice."

"I agree," Dovan continued, "but the tournament is open to all Rayder men."

"Who would dare fight against Omar?" Tarek questioned. "You?"

"Of course not," Dovan replied, "but some might."

Tarek rolled his eyes. "Give me names, Dovan."

Dovan shifted in his saddle. "I know neither you nor Beholder Lon will join the tournament—as long as Omar enters—but perhaps people who disapprove of his decisions."

"Such as?"

Dovan shook his head. "Forgive me, General, but I refuse to project my impressions of loyalty on my Rayder brothers. I would prefer to wait and see."

Tarek sighed. "I know Braedr's name is bouncing around in your head, along with a bunch of other people Lon angered with his *Unite Appernysia* speech—like Preton."

Dovan's countenance fell.

The Rayders followed Omar another six miles to the south entrance, a long causeway running between the deep gulches. At its outer edge, the causeway was more than seven hundred feet wide, but it narrowed more and more the farther the Rayders pushed in. By the time the Rayders passed over the mile-long causeway, the path had narrowed to twenty feet.

Tarek rode ahead to Omar. "Where's the gate?" They were surrounded on all three sides by the gulches and high walls of raised earth, but no visible entrance into the city existed.

Omar waved his hand at one of his escorts, then interlocked his fingers over his round belly and grinned at Tarek.

"Our commander wishes to enter Taeja," the escort boomed to the men standing atop the dirt wall. "Lower the gate."

"What—?" Tarek started to ask, but before he could finish, the wall of hardened dirt in front of them rumbled and started to collapse. Loose soil poured off the top of the wall and disappeared into the gulch. Before long, the thick wall had disappeared. Lon sat behind it on his horse, with Wade close behind, his hand on his sword hilt. Lon stretched out his hands and a land bridge rose from the depths of the gulch.

Omar leaned over and slapped Tarek under his dropped jaw, then turned to Lon and saluted. "Thank you, Beholder."

Lon returned the salute and nodded. "My Commander."

At Omar's signal, the Rayders began funneling forward. They moved slowly, taking care to keep a safe distance between themselves and the deep gulch.

Once Tarek reached Lon on the opposite side of the bridge, he peered down over the edge. "That has to be at least fifty feet deep, and just as wide," he spoke quietly to Lon. "This place will be a lot easier to defend than Flagheim, especially with you around. I've only been gone two months, and you've built a whole city. Impressive."

"Nice to see you, too," Lon responded with a smirk, then turned Dawes around and rode alongside Tarek as they entered the city. Wade continued to stay a few feet behind them.

"I was watching your approach from the east," Lon continued. "You've gathered quite a crowd. That's even more impressive."

"A hundred thousand civilians," Tarek said, "and massive amounts of food and lumber."

Lon nodded. "Excellent." He paused for a moment before continuing. "How was your journey?"

Tarek scowled at him.

Lon laughed. "That fun?"

Tarek smiled and slapped his friend on the shoulder. "It's good to be back, Lon."

"Agreed."

Chapter 13
For Taeja

As the Rayders entered Taeja, they marched between the six thousand soldiers who had remained to prepare the city. The soldiers stood in a two-column formation, one on either side of the main thoroughfare. Each soldier was dressed ceremoniously in his battle gear—a steel breastplate and helm, shield, glaive, arming sword, longbow, and a quiver of arrows. Their two lines stretched toward the heart of Taeja, which was more than six miles to the north.

Lon didn't need to look to know that both the soldiers and civilians were searching for familiar faces. They moved mostly in revered silence, but on occasion, a child would scream with excitement and rush out of the crowd to wrap his or her arms around one of the soldiers. The children were quickly followed by their mothers and dragged back to the line of marching civilians.

It bothered Lon to see the families treat each other with such formality, but he knew there had to be strict organization to their reunion. If the civilians and soldiers were left to their own terms, all would turn to chaos. It was better to secure the supplies first, escort the civilians to their new homes, then allow the soldiers to seek out their families and friends.

At the center of Taeja, rows of tall stone silos stretched to the west. To the east, just within earshot of a well-projected shout, Lon's squad stood in front of the rescued Appernysians.

"They still aren't fitting in?" Tarek asked.

Lon shook his head.

Tarek tightened his lips. "I'm going to do something about that."

"How?"

"I'll start with teaching them how to fight. If they hope to survive with us, they'll need to know how to defend themselves. Once they're worthy, our new commander can brand them with the Cross." As Tarek finished speaking, he pointed at the women and children amongst the Appernysians. "What's with the extras?"

Lon frowned. "They're some of the Appernysians' families. Omar said they started showing up two weeks after our battle, right after you and I left."

Tarek furrowed his brow. "Why did they come here? And why did Omar let them stay?"

"They don't have anywhere else to go," Lon answered. "As soon as the men joined us, they became traitors to Appernysia. Unfortunately, so did their families. I wasn't going to turn them away, and neither would Omar."

"I'm not saying you should, but their presence is only going to complicate things—especially for you, Lon. Some of our brothers already hate you, and many can't decide how they feel. This might make up their minds."

Lon shrugged. "This isn't about my reputation. This is about people's lives."

"What about your life? You'd be a fool to think you're immune from danger."

"That's why Wade is following me around," Lon replied with a forced smile, which disappeared again just as quickly. "What do you suggest, Tarek? Throw them out?"

Tarek shook his head. "Don't put words in my mouth. I just want to make sure *you* are safe."

"Oh, how sweet," Lon said, batting his eyelashes at Tarek. "I never knew you cared so much."

Tarek swung his fist at the Beholder's head, but Lon pulled Dawes far enough away that Tarek's blow fell short. Tarek grumbled and started to move his own horse closer, but stopped and stared as Lon summoned True Sight.

"You win," Tarek grumbled. "Cheater."

Lon laughed. "It's not fair that you're so huge. I have to keep a safe distance."

Tarek chuckled and reached for his sword, but stopped quickly. Omar was riding toward them.

"I need to speak to our new arrivals," Omar said, looking at Lon. "Would you mind helping me?"

"Not at all," Lon replied. "Here?"

"Yes."

Lon used his power to create a wide platform. It rose ten feet into the air with a ramp spiraling up to its top. Although Tarek had undoubtedly informed the civilians about the Beholder and what he did at the Battle for Taeja, this was the first day any of them had seen him use his power. Lon couldn't help but smile at the continuing gasps and whispers pouring from the crowd.

After Omar moved Dax up the ramp, Lon followed with Dawes and stopped behind the acting commander. Wade and Tarek took position with their horses at the bottom of the ramp.

"Don't forget," Lon whispered as he winked a clouded eye at the acting commander, "use small words."

Omar smiled and faced the miles of people. "My Rayders . . ."

Lon concentrated on the air flowing from Omar's lips. He captured the sound and carried it on a soft stream of wind to the masses. Many gasped and searched around in panic. It took a few minutes for them to calm down enough for Omar to continue his speech, even for those who had just seen Lon raise the platform out of the ground.

". . . As all of you should know by now, First Lieutenant Lon Shaw is a Beholder. Our soldiers fought bravely during our battle for Taeja, but the Appernysians responded as cowards and traitors—launching flaming oil casks into the middle of their own men to stop us. But our Beholder would not have it. He deflected the casks and scared the Appernysian army all the way back to Itorea. It is because of him that Taeja is in our possession. We owe him our victory and our lives."

Cheers erupted from the enormous audience. Soldiers banged glaives on shields while the civilians clapped their hands together and stomped their feet. Although Lon was honored by their support, he felt very uncomfortable receiving so much attention and credit. His face flushed as he looked out at the glowing figures of more than a hundred thousand Rayders.

"Only two months ago," Omar continued, "Taeja was flooded and uninhabitable. Now, because of our Beholder, this city is a stronghold greater even than Flagheim. It is now our responsibility to inherit this city and keep each other alive. It is obvious to me that, while our soldiers were away at war, you have not been idle. Thank you for your efforts to stockpile food and supplies. I have no doubt it will see us through until we can plant and harvest new crops next year . . ."

Lon noticed movement in the center of the crowd. Random people were moving slowly, but steadily toward the platform.

". . . To my right is a long line of silos built from the rubble of ancient Taeja. It will be in these silos that we will store our food for the winter . . ."

Lon clenched his jaw as the advancing people formed into two small groups. They had moved close enough to the platform that their behavior shifted from curious to threatening.

". . . Once you have dropped off your supplies, our soldiers will direct you to where you can set up your shelters. The more organized you remain, the smoother this will flow. Remember, this winter is about survival. Next spring, we will rebuild the beauty of this city . . ."

Lon glanced down at Tarek and Wade. They, too, had noticed the movement and had their hands on their sheathed swords. Lon readied himself for an attack.

". . . There is one important thing that must take place. In three days, a tournament will be held to choose a new commander."

Five javelins shot out of the crowd and whizzed toward the platform. Lon redirected the flying projectiles over their heads, then moved Dawes forward. "Get behind me, Omar!"

Omar ignored the Beholder's request and held his position next to Lon. Wade and Tarek drew their swords, and Lon's squad galloped toward them in a mad rush from the side.

Lon stretched his left hand toward the group of men that had thrown the glaives, but their glowing forms scattered before he could capture them in the dirt. He tried to follow their paths, but soon the whole crowd was bustling with movement. Lon lost track of the attackers.

"This is too dangerous," Lon shouted. "We need to get off this plat—"

Lon's speech cut off as he noticed another cluster of javelins flying at them from the right. He barely had time to lift his right hand and deflect them, then focused on the soil under the attacking men's feet. Just as Lon was about to sink them into the ground, Omar made a quick movement in front of Lon. With a grunt, Omar fell into Lon's lap. A javelin—intended for the Beholder—protruded from the left side of Omar's chest.

"Run, Lon," Omar gasped. "Survive."

"Not without you," Lon shouted back. He could feel himself panicking as he watched a stream of blood ooze from Omar's wound. With all of his power, Lon had been unable to protect the person dearest to him in all of Taeja. He knew the wound was mortal, but he refused to accept defeat. Not with Omar.

With complete disregard for his own safety, Lon pulled the acting commander completely onto Dawes's saddle in front of himself, then turned down the platform. Wade and Tarek joined him as he galloped to the Appernysians, the safest place he could think of amid so much chaos. After all, the attack had come from his own people. From Rayders.

Lon's squad soon joined them and escorted Omar toward the Appernysian crowd. At the front edge of the Appernysians, Lon turned to Thad and Nik. "Stay here and keep watch. No one approaches."

The two saluted and pulled back their reins. Thad removed his glaive from its leather sleeve while Nik strung his bow and nocked an arrow. The rest of Lon's squad followed after him and Tarek.

"Fight, Omar," Lon growled desperately as they forced their way through the Appernysians. "Don't you give up." He could hear the acting commander's rattled breath. There wasn't much time.

Once Lon felt they had traveled far enough into the clustered Appernysians, he dismounted and pulled Omar from the horse. Tarek also slid out of his saddle and helped Lon lower the acting commander to the ground while shouting orders to the other members of Lon's squad. "Make a perimeter."

As Wade and the rest of the squad formed a large circle around them, Lon gripped Tarek's arm. "Keep an eye on him." He indicated at Preton with a distinct nod. The Rayder was part of the protective circle, facing away with no apparent interest in his commander.

Tarek's jaw clenched and he faced the suspicious Rayder. "Now help him, Lon."

Using True Sight, Lon looked into Omar's body. The javelin had penetrated deep into his chest, puncturing a lung and severing the edge of his heart. There was nothing the Beholder could do. Lon released his power and looked at the acting commander's face. His breathing wheezed, and blood trickled from one corner of his mouth.

Omar's eyes fluttered open. He tried to clear his throat, but winced and groaned at the effort. When his face relaxed again, Omar gazed up at the Beholder. "My . . . time has come."

"Not now." Lon ground his teeth and clenched his fists. "We need you, Omar. *I* need you."

"Forget me . . . think of your men . . . for Taeja . . ." Omar's breath caught and his body shook, then a final gasp escaped his lips as he closed his eyes and relaxed.

Lon stared at his mentor's still body. He had seen many people die, but this one touched too close to his heart. Lon's mind was numb, unwilling to and incapable of accepting this death. Not this one. But he lost all hopes of a miracle when Omar's glowing essence shifted out of his motionless body and disappeared.

Tarek placed his hand on Omar's chest and tears filled his eyes. "My Commander."

Chapter 14

Llen

Kutad sat in his wagon at the front of the caravan. They had been traveling along the West River from Humsco for nearly three days, and Roseiri was just coming into sight.

Kutad blew out his breath and glanced over his shoulder. Although the caravan hadn't traveled to Pree, Aron Marcs had stopped them just north of Humsco. Kutad still couldn't push the memory out of his head.

"Is it true?" Aron had asked.

"Is what true?"

"Don't waste my time, Kutad. Did the Rayders retake Taeja?"

"Yes."

"Is the other rumor true, too?"

"About the Beholder? I'm afraid so, my friend."

That had been the end of their brief conversation, but it was the look Aron gave him afterward that made a lasting impression on Kutad's mind. It was the same look Mellai had given him when he delivered Kaylen's letter. Rage and sorrow had battled in Aron's eyes, fighting for dominance. While Kutad sought the right words to comfort his friend, Aron had turned and stormed away toward Pree. He never looked back.

Kutad had watched his friend depart, trying not to imagine Shalán's reaction when her husband confirmed their suspicions. It wouldn't be a pleasant reunion in Pree.

As Roseiri crept closer, Kutad struggled with his own feelings. He didn't know what to tell Mellai. Last time he gave her bad news about her family, Mellai had disappeared into the mountains. Another sad report might be more than she could bear.

The caravan was met with a familiar scene when they reached the village at sunset. Children appeared in the streets and followed the tradesmen all the way to the north clearing, then an excited celebration ensued with a large fire, feasting, music, and dancing. Kutad watched for Mellai and her grandparents, but they never appeared. Determined to share the truth, Kutad left the festivities, crossed the north bridge, then turned onto the small road leading to the north end of the village.

Kutad paused for a moment at the front door of the Ovann home, then tapped lightly on the wood with his knuckles. After only a few seconds, he was surprised to see Theiss Arbogast answer the door.

Before Kutad could speak, Theiss stepped outside and wrapped his arms around the tradesman. Kutad returned the hug, then stepped back to look at Theiss. "What happened?"

"Too much for a doorstep conversation," Theiss answered. "Come in, please."

Kutad searched the room, but nothing caught his attention. Allegna was bustling about the kitchen, while Dhargon smiled from his padded chair, and Mellai sat on the sofa, knitting.

Kutad let out a long sigh. "You had me worried, Theiss. I half-expected one of you to be dead."

Dhargon crossed the room and took Kutad's hand. "It's good to see you."

"Aye," Kutad answered with a smile. "So what's the big news? Is it this?" He gestured toward Mellai, who was still weaving her knitting needles. "Mellai, knitting. I never would have guessed such a thing was possible."

Everyone chuckled as Mellai pushed her knitting aside. "It's a recent development," she said with a glare.

Kutad nodded, then looked around with raised eyebrows. "Is someone going to tell me what's going on?"

Allegna left the kitchen and placed her hands on Mellai's shoulders. "Mellai died the night you left—well, at least we thought she did. She was breathing again by morning, but it gave us a big scare."

"Died, did you?" Kutad asked skeptically as he tilted his head toward Mellai.

Mellai shrugged. "That's what they keep telling me. I don't remember much of it. I guess I became really sick, but I'm fine now."

Kutad smiled. "It must have been something serious, like brain fever, for you to take up knitting."

"Very funny," Mellai replied after rolling her eyes. "Oh, so *very* funny."

"Come now," Kutad continued. "Let me in on your secret."

Dhargon placed a hand on Kutad's shoulder. "My wife is completely serious. We almost lost our granddaughter, and I wouldn't have been far behind. It was the worst night of my life."

Kutad's face sobered. "Please forgive me for my rashness. It pleases my heart to see you've recovered, Mellai."

"Don't you worry about it for one second," Allegna chimed in. "We have great news, too. Mellai's making a wedding present for Theiss."

Kutad turned to Theiss. "You're engaged? I assume to Mellai?"

Theiss's face flushed as he smiled and nodded.

"Congratulations to the both of you. When will you wed?"

"In the spring," Mellai answered. She leaned forward, and Theiss rushed to her side. She took his hand and pulled herself to her feet, leaning on her future husband for support.

Kutad eyed Mellai's flat stomach. "Are you pregnant?"

Dhargon laughed and slapped Kutad on the back. "I better jump in on this one. Mellai vowed she'd claw the eyes out of the next person who asked her that question. She's not pregnant. The sickness just left her a little weak, that's all."

Mellai smirked. "It's a good thing you're the one who asked." With Theiss's help, she crossed the floor and embraced the tradesman. "Thank you for coming to visit. It means a lot to me."

"The pleasure is mine."

Mellai leaned back against Theiss. "Did you make it to Pree this year, Kutad?"

Kutad frowned. "I'm sorry, but no. I wanted to, but I was outvoted by the rest of the caravan. Too many of them still remember last year's blizzard."

"I understand," Mellai replied. "I need to send a message to them about the wedding, anyway."

Kutad's eyebrows rose. "They don't know yet?"

"It's another recent development," Allegna answered.

Theiss's face turned red again from embarrassment.

Kutad laughed. "Why don't you all join me at the clearing? There's a big celebration going on, one I'd like to direct in your honor. I'd gladly carry you, Mellai, if Theiss allows me to."

"Thank you," Mellai answered, "but the chill weather makes things worse for me. I'll come visit tomorrow afternoon when things warm up a little."

"I'll be looking forward to it." Kutad tipped his head. "I should be getting back. Enjoy your evening." He exited the house and began retracing his steps to the clearing, having changed his mind again. In her weakened condition, Mellai didn't need to know about his conversation with Aron. That could wait.

*   *   *   *   *

By the time Mellai cracked open the front door of her grandparents' house and slipped outside, the festivities at the clearing had ended and the villagers had returned home. Everyone was sound asleep. Mellai crept to the road in front of the house and peered down the street. She gazed over the glowing energy of the village through her clouded eyes, but no one was in sight. Satisfied, she turned left and followed the river north. She took care to avoid dry leaves and twigs with her bare feet, but she could have made the journey blindfolded, having followed the same path every night for the previous month. She didn't like deceiving her grandparents with feigned weakness, but she had no choice.

When she was two miles north of the village, Mellai stopped and sat down on the west riverbank. She watched the flowing water, identifying the clusters of condensed energy from the swimming fish. Mellai reached her right hand toward one of the larger fish, captured it with her own essence, then pulled it from the water and into her hand. The fish wriggled in protest, but she gripped it tight with her fingers while she searched its insides. When she located the spinal column, Mellai severed the nerve to end the fish's suffering.

After watching the fish's glowing essence dissipate, Mellai used her power to remove the fish's internal organs and force the fish a foot into the air. While holding it aloft with her right hand's essence, she located a fallen log a few feet away. She cycled the lumber, along with the surrounding air, through her body and out her left hand, compressing the two ingredients until they ignited into a small sphere of fire above her hand.

Smiling, she moved her hands together until the fire rested under the hovering fish. Its scales sizzled. When she was satisfied, Mellai dispelled the fire and extracted a sphere of water from the river with her left hand's essence. While imprisoning the water with her essence, she broke apart the energy into a fine mist, then released it over the fish to cool it. After all of this, she lowered the fish into her right palm. It was still warm, but tolerable on her bare skin.

A low growl broke her concentration. She jumped to her feet and spun around to see a large bear approaching. She hurled the fish at the bear and took a few steps back, her naked feet nearly touching the river water.

While the bear picked up the cooked fish in its teeth, Mellai quickly concentrated the air and moisture floating around her into an angled mirror between herself and the animal. The energy mirror acted as a prism, bending the light around her so that she appeared invisible to the bear. Mellai couldn't help but smile, having finally mastered this difficult task. So many hours studying how water *bent* the submerged section of a stick. She hated that stick; she'd broken it in half and lit it on fire when she was done.

Once the beast consumed its snack, it turned its attention to Mellai. Although the bear couldn't see her, it could obviously smell her. It knew she was there. Mellai extended her essence and carefully penetrated the surface of its mind, taking care not to delve too deep for fear of losing herself in another's mind. She found only raw aggression and hunger in the bear. It was going to attack.

Mellai retreated into the river until the water was lapping at her knees. She pulled two spheres out of the water, one with each hand, and formed them into sharp cones as thick as her arms. She then slowed the internal movement of the water's energy until they became solid icicles.

The bear made threatening lunges in Mellai's direction—two leaps forward and one back—but Mellai held her ground. She knew if she turned and ran, it would chase her down. She had to face the threat and keep the bear where she could see it. Always keep danger where she could see it.

The bear finally lowered its head and charged forward in a powerful sprint. Mellai forced both of the sharpened icicles at the bear's head, stabbing deep into its eye sockets. She barely managed to dive to the side as the bear stumbled through her energy mirror and crashed into the river.

Mellai sat neck deep upriver from the bear, watching it carefully for remaining signs of life. When its glowing essence shifted out of the bear's body and disappeared, Mellai heaved a sigh of relief and pulled herself out of the water.

After she stood on the riverbank, a bright figure appeared in front of her with the outline of a man. "Well done," he said, hovering above the ground.

"Thank you, Llen," Mellai answered. "I thought you might try something like this when you told me to come here and cook myself a fish. It had suspicious written all over it."

"You are very wise," Llen commented sincerely. "Dry yourself."

Mellai created a small cyclone in front of herself to dry out her clothes and hair. When the front half of her body was dry, she moved the cyclone around to dry off the back half of her clothes.

"This would be a lot easier if I could do this without looking," Mellai complained as she strained her neck to keep the cyclone in her vision.

"I have already told you, Mellai. It cannot be done."

"Even so."

Llen hovered to where Mellai could see him. "What part of mastering True Sight has been easy to you?"

"None," Mellai grumbled, then dispersed the cyclone.

"Nor will it ever be so," Llen continued.

Mellai sighed. "I know. You've told me that every day for the last month."

"Follow me," Llen said. "We do not have much time."

Mellai sprinted after Llen to the north end of Roseiri, then Llen pointed to the clearing across the river, where the trading caravan was still camped. "Look, Beholder."

Being called a Beholder still twisted Mellai's stomach, but she had become more used to it since Llen started training her. She obediently focused on the clearing and saw two glowing forms standing off from the rest of the trading caravan. She retracted the sound from the two men to her own ears. ". . . just arrived tonight. You can't expect me to pick up and leave. We still need to finalize our trades with the villagers."

Kutad, Mellai thought.

"He didn't ask for your caravan's presence," the man replied. "He asked for you. You must leave them tonight and come back with me. His life is in danger."

Mellai didn't recognize the voice of the second man.

"His life has always been in danger," Kutad argued. "That's the nature of being king. Besides, if what you're telling me is true, then he's had two months to regain control of Appernysia. How am I supposed to help?"

"He didn't say," the other man replied. "He only said he needs you. Please, Kutad." There was a pause in the conversation, then the man continued. "As a subject of Appernysia, it's your duty to help King Drogan."

"Duty?" Kutad spat. "Have you forgotten what *duty* King Drogan denied me, Jareth?"

"That was almost eleven years ago. A lot has changed since then."

"My daughter is still dead," Kutad growled. "I've made up my mind. You can return and tell him he still needs to earn his position as my king. I made a mistake by trying to help last December. I won't do it again."

Another pause.

"I haven't told you about your friend, Kaylen, have I?"

Kutad's response was icy. "What about Kaylen?"

"She killed the chamberlain. She's a loyal servant of the court. Do you think defying an order from our king will please her?"

Kaylen killed the chamberlain? As Mellai tried to process such an unimaginable feat, Kutad's glowing figure knocked Jareth to the ground, then Kutad unsheathed his scimitar and held it to Jareth's chest.

"Get out of my sight," Kutad ordered, his voice full of anger and hatred.

Jareth stumbled backward, then stood, retreated to his horse, and galloped away.

Kutad sheathed his sword and paced back and forth along the river. Mellai ached to know his thoughts. She reached out for his consciousness.

"Not yet," Llen's voice sounded. "You are not ready, Mellai."

Mellai pulled back and turned to Llen. "Why not?" she whispered. "I was successful with the bear."

"A bear's mind is very different from a human's. You are not ready."

Mellai sighed out her nose, but acquiesced to the Jaed's counsel as she watched Kutad continue his pacing. After a half hour, he finally crossed through the camp and unhitched a donkey from his wagon. He took one final glance over the caravan, then slid onto the donkey and followed after Jareth.

Mellai turned to Llen. "What was that all about?"

"You will know soon enough. Come. I have more to show you."

✳ ✳ ✳ ✳ ✳

Dhargon left Allegna sleeping in their bed and crept out of their room. He closed the door softly, then slipped into the kitchen. Since Mellai's near-death two months earlier, Dhargon had taken a liking to getting out of bed first to prepare their morning tea. It wasn't until after he lit the fire on the warm coals that Dhargon realized it was still the middle of the night.

I'm getting too old, he thought as he shook his head and chuckled, then turned to go back to bed. It was then that he noticed Mellai wasn't on the sofa.

Dhargon searched the room for his granddaughter, then headed for the door. As he reached for the handle, the door cracked open and Mellai stepped inside.

"Grandfather," Mellai started when she saw him standing at the door. "What are you doing awake?"

"What are you doing out of bed?" Dhargon countered. "Please don't tell me this has something to do with Theiss."

"Hardly," Mellai replied, regaining her composure.

Dhargon put his hand on Mellai's shoulder. "How did you get out of bed? You can barely stand by yourself."

"I need to talk to you."

Mellai took Dhargon's hand and made him sit on the sofa with her, then she pulled the blanket around herself. Dhargon prepared himself for a long, painful conversation, guessing that Mellai's pretended lack of energy was a ruse to allow her to sneak out and be with Theiss at night.

"Tell me about Grandmother," Mellai said. "What was she like when she was younger?"

Dhargon furrowed his brow and cocked his head to the side. "I think we have more important things to discuss."

"Please, Grandfather," Mellai responded. Sincerity poured from her softened eyes. "It's important."

Dhargon sighed. "Well, she was exactly the same as she is now, except with more energy and less wrinkles."

Mellai leaned forward. "So she couldn't have children back then, either?"

Dhargon eyed his granddaughter. "That's a big presumption to make, especially when we have a daughter."

"But did Grandmother carry my mother? Did she give birth to her?"

His mind reeled. "Who have you been talking to? Who's been feeding you this garbage?"

"Why won't you answer my question, Grandfather?"

"Because I shouldn't have to, Mellai." Dhargon shifted forward on the sofa and stared at the shuttered window. His eyes flickered in the firelight. "I want to know who you have been talking to. Was it Theiss that put you up to this?"

"Does it make any difference, Grandfather? I just want to know. I have a right to the truth."

Dhargon didn't answer her question directly, but began muttering to himself. "My guess is Gorlon. He's trying to destroy our family because we kept your identity a secret from him. There's no reason to bring up the past because of the present. What's done is done. What a coward."

"So it's true?" Mellai inserted. "Mother was adopted?"

Dhargon froze as he realized what he had revealed.

Mellai's lips went tight, but she said nothing until she had scooted closer on the sofa and taken her grandfather's hand. "For my own peace of mind. I won't tell anyone. I promise."

Dhargon gripped Mellai's hand and stared at the floor. He believed her. "It's true, although I wouldn't say she was adopted. I found her."

Mellai raised her eyebrows. "What do you mean?"

"Our village was hurting for meat that year. I was younger then, twenty-five or so, and foolish enough to lead a hunting party into the Vidarien Mountains. I heard a newborn baby crying while I was stalking through the woods. I followed her cries and found her stashed inside a tree hollow high off the ground. Nobody else was there but her. I couldn't leave her to die, so I brought your mother home."

Mellai laid her head on Dhargon's shoulder, uncharacteristically calm after everything he just told her. "I wonder what happened. What kind of mother would stash her child in a tree and run away?"

"I don't know," Dhargon said as he tilted his head against Mellai's, "but I'm glad I found her. We couldn't have asked for a better daughter. I have to ask, Mellai. How are you receiving all this information so easily? I'd expect you to be screaming at me by now."

Mellai didn't answer her grandfather's question, but sat up with a start. "Do you still remember where you found her? I'd like to see it."

Dhargon frowned. "You've already seen it, twice, I think. It's the same clearing where you found Kaylen last winter, and where Theiss found you a couple months ago. There's something strange about that place—something that pulls travelers to it. Please don't go back there, Mellai. It's not safe. Promise me."

Mellai pulled her blanket tighter around herself and leaned back on the sofa. "I can't make that promise, Grandfather."

Dhargon blew out his breath. "I had a feeling you'd say that." He also leaned back on the sofa and stared up at the ceiling. He knew that if he didn't agree to help his granddaughter, she would take matters into her own hands. "I'll talk with your grandmother. You and I will make for the clearing after breakfast. I'd rather get this idea out of your system before bad weather hits and makes it more dangerous to travel."

Mellai sat forward and kissed him on the cheek. "Thank you, Grandfather."

"I still want to know where you were tonight." Dhargon spoke half-heartedly, already knowing his granddaugher's reply.

Mellai yawned and curled up on the sofa. "I'm really tired."

Within a few seconds, Mellai was fast asleep. Dhargon watched her calm face, heaved a sigh, then stood and returned to his own bed. Despite his many questions and his concern for Mellai, fatigue eventually caught up to Dhargon, too.

Chapter 15

Clawed

"Y our men are hidden and protected, Clawed," Bryst whispered in the flickering torchlight. "Everything is going exactly as you planned."

Clawed crossed his arms and leaned against a nearby wagon. "This would've been a lot easier if Omar hadn't moved in the way. I was so close. But killing the Beholder will never be easy, and my javelin found a good mark for now. Omar needed to die."

"Of course."

"Have you talked with Preton?"

Bryst nodded. "He will persuade the Appernysians to help us, one way or another."

"Good. I want Lon's confidence ripped away one layer at a time. Every man in his squad represents a powerful ally."

"By the end of tomorrow," Bryst said with a chuckle, "his trust will be shaken."

"Don't be so sure—" Clawed began, but stopped mid-sentence at the sound of light footsteps from the other side of the wagon. Clawed questioned Bryst with a furrowed brow, but Bryst only shrugged.

Seconds later, a glaive-wielding man appeared around the wagon. "Identify yourself," the man ordered as he squinted into the torchlight. His eyebrows rose at the sight of Bryst and Clawed. "I am sorry, Lieutenant. I did not know you were here."

"I was just discussing today's events with Bryst," Clawed replied. "Join us. There is one point that keeps puzzling us."

The Rayder lowered his glaive and stepped into the torch's ring of light. "What is it, Lieutenant?"

Faster than a striking serpent, Clawed drew his sword and thrust it through the Rayder's throat. Clawed leaned forward and whispered into the gasping man's ear. "Why is everyone so supportive of Lon? Beholder or not, he's a fool and a coward. You should have joined my true cause."

The Rayder's eyes glazed over and he fell to the ground, dead. Clawed pulled his sword free and wiped it clean on the man's pants. "He seems at a loss for words. What do you think, Bryst?"

"The Beholder's confidence will be his undoing. He does not realize the number of his enemies."

Clawed sheathed his sword and turned to Bryst. "But we can't kill him yet. Unless we defame him first, we'd only make him a martyr. Nobody would listen to us."

"But we need to act fast," Bryst countered. "With every day that passes, the Beholder grows stronger. Soon he might be impossible to kill."

"That'll never happen," Clawed said with a smirk. "You just have to know where to strike. Have you identified other potential targets?"

Bryst nodded. "Flora Baum and her three children, but he hasn't spoken to them in months. Will they hold sway with him?"

Clawed leaned back against the wagon again. "Once we have them, he'll care. I'll make him care." He looked up at the dark sky. The stars and moon were shrouded by a dense layer of threatening clouds. "Better find some shelter. It's going to rain."

Chapter 16

Preparations

Dhargon's eyes flew open. Sunlight had filled the room, illuminating Allegna's face as she stood over her husband and shook him like she was emptying a sack of potatoes.

"What is it?" he asked, his eyes searching the room in panic.

Allegna dropped him to the bed and let out a deep sigh. "Oh, thank the stars. I couldn't get you to wake up, Dhargon. Are you feeling ill?"

After taking a moment to regain his senses, Dhargon sat up in the bed. "Not at all. I was up for hours last night. Is Mellai still asleep?"

"Of course," Allegna replied.

Dhargon nodded with new perspective. If sneaking out at night was a regular habit of hers, it's no wonder that Mellai slept until lunchtime every day. And her supposed lack of physical strength? That was either a complete lie or the result of serious lack of sleep. Whatever the reason, Mellai had no problems moving about the previous night.

What's she hiding? Dhargon thought as he stood and dressed himself for the day.

Allegna stepped in front of her husband. "What is it?"

"What's what?"

"What's troubling you?"

Dhargon frowned as he looked at his wife. "Is the tea still hot?"

Allegna nodded, but held Dhargon's gaze.

He sighed. "Mellai knows about the tree hollow."

Allegna blinked and draped an open hand over her mouth. "About Shalán?"

"Yes."

"How did she find out?"

"I don't know, but she and I are going back into the mountains today. I promised her last night that I'd take her to the clearing."

Allegna's lips tightened, then she dropped her arms and stomped out of the room.

Dhargon slipped into his boots and followed after his wife, seating himself at the table in front of his morning cup of medicated tea. He drained the cup slowly while his wife aggressively reorganized a shelf in the kitchen. The tea was lukewarm, but still relieved his aching joints. Once Dhargon was finished, he stood and took the cup to the sink. "Thank you."

Allegna dropped a stack of plates onto the shelf and glared at her husband. "How could you be so short-sighted? I can think of a wagon full of reasons why now is a terrible time to make such a foolish promise to your granddaughter."

"I know."

"The weather's turning. Even if it doesn't snow, the mountains are freezing. Mellai still hasn't completely recovered, and the cold hurts her, which brings up another point. How do you expect to get Mellai to the clearing? She can barely stand by herself."

"I—"

"And it's harvest time. Who's going to take care of our crops?"

"Well, I—"

"And what about Theiss? He's not going to let you take Mellai without him. Gorlon is already upset. This will only make things worse with his father."

Dhargon placed his hands on his wife's shoulders. "I know, Allegna. I know."

Allegna buried her face in Dhargon's chest. "Then why are you doing it?"

"To rectify a broken promise we made ten months ago," he replied as he stroked Allegna's gray hair. "No more secrets, remember?"

"This isn't a secret," Allegna sniffed. "It's just an unnecessary truth."

Dhargon chuckled. "Perhaps in the past, but not anymore. We can't stop Mellai from doing something once she gets her mind set on it. She's determined to see the clearing again. The best thing we can do is go with her. It's the only way I'll be able to keep her safe."

Allegna wrapped her arms around her husband and sighed. "She isn't the only person I'm worried about. You're an old man."

Mellai's grandparents spent the morning packing two week's worth of supplies and food for the journey. The clearing was three days away at a comfortable pace, but Allegna made sure they were over-prepared. "Mellai is unpredictable," she argued when Dhargon complained about having to carry so much weight. "For all we know, she might build herself a shelter and insist on living in the clearing through the winter."

While they were packing, Dhargon also told Allegna of his conversation with Mellai the previous night. As he was stuffing the last of the lighter-weight clothes into a pack for his granddaughter, Mellai stirred and sat up on the sofa.

"What's all this?" she asked when she saw Dhargon by the front door.

"Just rooting through your personal things," Dhargon answered with a wink.

"Don't listen to him," Allegna called from the kitchen. "Actually, I take that back. I want you to listen to *and obey* every word your grandfather says during your journey."

Mellai turned around and stared with shock at her grandmother. "You agreed?"

"No," Allegna replied, "but at least this way we can keep an eye on you. Are you sure you can't wait until spring?"

Mellai leaned back against the sofa. "I have to see it."

CHAPTER 16: PREPARATIONS ✦ 145

"That's what I told her," Dhargon inserted. "Get yourself dressed, Mellai. Once your grandmother has shoved a hearty meal down your throat, we'll be on our way."

"With extra helpings of hearty," Allegna added as Mellai disappeared into their bedroom. Once the bedroom door was closed, Allegna crossed the room to her husband. "You're right about her," she whispered. "Did you see how quickly she hopped up to get dressed? She seems to have forgotten that she's supposed to be weak and helpless."

Dhargon sighed.

*　　*　　*　　*　　*

Before the two of them finished tying off the packs, Mellai had dressed and sat herself at the table. Dhargon joined her while Allegna brought a steaming pot of stew from the fireplace. She moved with exaggerated slowness, carefully removing one bowl at a time from the shelf and scooping small amounts of stew into each bowl. Mellai asked her to hurry a few times, but Allegna ignored her with a teasing smile.

It wasn't until all three bowls were filled and at the table with chilled milk that Allegna spoke. "There's one matter that needs to be cleared up before you leave. I want to know where you were last night."

Mellai paused with her spoon halfway to her mouth. "I . . . was with the caravan." She quickly jumped into the next sentence to change the subject. "Did you know Kutad was summoned by the king? He left with an embassy in the middle of the night."

"What?" Dhargon asked. "I thought he hated King Drogan."

"I thought so, too," Mellai added.

Allegna was undeterred. "Is there something going on with you and Kutad? Why would you visit him in the middle of the night? Are you being unfaithful to Theiss?"

Mellai dropped her spoon into the bowl of stew and sat back in her chair, scowling at Allegna.

"I'm sorry," Allegna responded, "but you are acting very suspicious. I'm just grabbing at ideas."

"I told Grandfather that last night had nothing to do with Theiss," Mellai growled. "I love him."

Dhargon placed his hand on Mellai's forearm. "Then what was it? Why did you leave?"

Mellai took deep breaths to calm herself, as well as think of a lie. More forced deception, all because of Llen's warning. *If they discover the truth, consequences will ensue far beyond your comprehension.* Although she didn't understand why, Mellai couldn't tell her grandparents the truth about her newfound power. She thought through the previous night's events, through Kutad's conversation with Jareth. Suddenly an idea popped into her head.

"Kutad was hiding something last night. I tried to go to sleep, but I couldn't push the idea aside. I admit my decision to leave was impulsive, but I'm glad I went. I found him wandering around on the road to Réxura, worried out of his wits. He's fallen in love with Kaylen."

There was a lull in their conversation as Mellai's grandparents processed her story. Dhargon was the first to speak. "That explains his urgency to see us last night. I thought he was acting peculiar."

"Did you tell him that Kaylen loves Lon?" Allegna asked.

Mellai winced at the mention of her brother's name. He was a painful subject, one that none of them liked to bring up. "Of course not," she answered. "Kutad already knew that her heart belongs to him. I just confirmed it."

Allegna frowned. "I thought Kaylen was angry with Lon for . . . well, you know."

"That doesn't mean she can't love him," Mellai snapped. "It just makes her heart hurt worse. That's what bothers Kutad so much.

He knows Kaylen is hurting, but he can't do anything about it. Not to mention he still wants her."

"That's a tough spot to be stuck in," Dhargon observed. "I've said it a million times: courting is one of the most agonizing things a person can go through."

Mellai smiled. "Not all relationships are bad."

Dhargon laughed. "You say that now, but only because you're engaged to Theiss. If I had suggested that a year ago—"

"Point taken," Mellai interrupted. "Anyway, so that's why I was out last night. Can we forget about it now?"

Mellai watched her grandparents lock eyes. Unspoken communication passed between them, but she couldn't read it. It was something that only decades of marriage could develop in a couple.

Dhargon breathed in through his nose and sighed. "For now."

Chapter 17

Knitting

"A re you going to say goodbye to Theiss before you leave?" Allegna asked.

Mellai shifted her pack on her shoulders and frowned. "If he knows the truth about Mother, there isn't any need to say goodbye. He'll understand. If I talk to him before we leave, he'll just insist on coming along with us."

"Which is why we need to hurry," Dhargon said. "He could come looking for you at any moment."

After a quick goodbye, Dhargon and Mellai slipped around the back of their house. It appeared the whole village was with the caravan on the other side of the river, busy with negotiations and entertainment. None of the villagers or tradesmen seemed to notice Mellai and Dhargon as they turned north toward the mountains.

They spoke very little during their first day's march. They camped that night near the West River, halfway between the mountains and Roseiri. Mellai waited for an hour after her grandfather had fallen asleep, then climbed out of her bedroll and summoned True Sight. She wandered a half-mile west and sat down on the grass near a fallen oak tree. Moments later, Llen appeared.

"I don't like this," Mellai complained aloud. "I'm deceiving my grandparents."

"It is an essential part of your training," Llen answered.

"How?" Mellai knew she had spoken out of place as soon as the words left her lips. "I'm sorry, Llen. It's just that my grandparents are going to extra lengths to help me. I don't like lying to them, and especially not in situations like this."

"I understand," Llen replied.

"What do you have planned for me tonight?" Mellai asked. She tried to act excited, but her eyes felt heavy, and her body yearned for sleep. What she really wanted was to be back in bed.

"Two small exercises," Llen said. "They shouldn't take you long to learn; nonetheless, they are essential tools for any potentially dangerous situation. You must learn them before you enter the mountains tomorrow."

Mellai raised her eyebrows. "Are we going to be attacked?"

"A Beholder must always be prepared for the worst."

"Right," Mellai said dryly, but not without respect. "What are these tools?"

"One you have already experienced at your brother's hand. The energy blast."

"You mean what he did to throw me off the road?"

"Correct. This is how he knocked down the house he was building for Kaylen. These two scenarios are perfect examples of how an energy blast can work for good or evil. It is a powerful tool that can be used in many applications, but it is also the most dangerous weapon a Beholder can wield. If done incorrectly, it can kill you and everything for miles around you."

Mellai frowned. "I have to collect energy?"

"Yes. The more energy stored, the greater the blast."

"How will I know when I have collected my maximum capacity? How will I know when it's too much?"

Llen hummed his approval. "Excellent question, Beholder. You will learn by trial. Start small. Before we begin, I must point out one important note. The larger the feat, the longer the preparation."

"What do you mean?"

"When Lon threw you from the road, he did so in an instant. Had he spent a longer time preparing himself—"

"By preparing," Mellai interrupted, "you mean pulling energy into himself?"

"Yes. If he had pulled more energy into himself, he could have sent you flying over the tops of the surrounding trees. Also remember that control is not the only component you must consider. Pay attention to where you draw energy from, although manipulating your immediate surroundings can be done quickly. Above all, do not forget that energy blasts take time and careful execution. Do you understand?"

Mellai nodded.

A small pebble lifted from the ground and settled on a branch of the fallen oak tree. "Tonight is about patience and control, Beholder. You will feel like we have fallen back to our first days of training. You must move in small increments so you know the *exact* effect of every ounce of energy you pull into yourself. Patience and control."

"Understood."

"Absorb a small amount into your hand—the smallest quantity possible. The type of energy does not matter. Once you have absorbed the energy, form it into a compressed sphere in the tip of your finger, then move it with your essence until it rests next to the pebble. At that point, do not simply dissolve the energy or it will not create the desired effect. The sphere must be shattered abruptly to create a blast."

Mellai compacted a tiny energy sphere in her finger and pushed it next to the dull glow of the nearby pebble. She then attempted to shatter the energy sphere by slicing at its outer barrier with her essence, but only cracked one side of it. The contained energy drizzled out and the sphere disappeared with no effect on the pebble.

"Again."

Mellai tried once more, but cut the sphere in half instead of along one side. Again, there was no effect on the pebble. "Could you show me once?" she asked. "I'm having a hard time visualizing what you mean by shatter."

Llen nodded, then a small sphere escaped his glowing figure and stopped next to the pebble. "Shatter," Llen boomed. In an instant, the entire lining of the sphere cracked and combusted in a tiny burst of light. The small pebble whipped off the branch and fell to the ground. Llen moved it back to the branch and turned to Mellai. "Your turn."

"Do I need to say the word shatter?"

"Only if giving the command will help you to actualize the reaction in the sphere."

Mellai nodded, then made a third attempt. She moved the small sphere next to the pebble, wrapped it in her essence, then shouted "Shatter." The sphere exploded in a burst of light, but Mellai accidentally poured extra energy into it. The pebble shot from the branch and landed twenty feet away.

Llen extended his glowing essence and pulled the pebble back onto the branch. "Do you realize your mistake?"

"Of course I do. Let me try again, less excited this time." On her fourth attempt, she successfully copied what the Jaed had accomplished.

Llen hummed more approval. "That was the hardest part of the whole exercise. As always, you astound me with your ability to learn so quickly."

The Jaed continued tutoring Mellai. They moved forward in small increments, testing the blasts' effects on objects of various sizes. She moved from using her finger to her hand, then to both hands. After fifteen minutes, Mellai successfully shattered a sphere the size of her head next to the fallen oak tree. The tree flew through the air and landed fifty yards away.

"How did that feel?" Llen asked.

Mellai shuddered, pleased at what she had accomplished but weary of the power she felt pour through her. "A little strange. I was still in control, but I could feel its instability."

"And so you have answered your own question. You are approaching your maximum capacity. As your experience and knowledge of True Sight increases, your capacity will also increase. However, do not push your limits. Never try to control more than you are able. If you start to feel the instability, you must stop."

Mellai sat on the grass and laughed. "It's invigorating to do, especially when I know that no one else can see what I'm doing."

Llen hovered next to Mellai. "Except for another Beholder."

Mellai sighed and looked north. On the far side of the mountains was Taeja, reclaimed by the Rayders. "Has Lon learned how to control energy blasts?"

Llen's glowing eyes narrowed. "I will not speak of Lon or of his abilities. You know this. Do not ask me this question again."

"I know," Mellai continued. "It's just that when I reach out for him lately, he feels . . . *different*. He feels endowed with power."

"You are a Beholder now, Mellai, and feeling what you could not recognize before."

Mellai nodded. "But I can't help myself, Llen. What am I expected to do when I master True Sight? All I know is that the world's balance of energy is in danger—that Appernysia needs me. I'm terrified of what that means."

Llen's eyes softened. "I know it is frustrating, but when a person has wandered in the dark for their whole life, they must be gradually introduced to the light. Be patient, Mellai. Soon your sun will rise."

Mellai chuckled. "You're oozing with obscured wisdom, Llen."

"As will you, when you have been around as long as I have."

Mellai sat forward. "I would give anything to know what you know—to see what you've seen. I get chills every time I think about your story. To be the first Beholder in the history of Appernysia . . . that would be amazing."

"It is not all you imagine it to be. I have experienced more sorrow than anyone to step foot on this soil."

Mellai didn't respond, but thought instead of the many trials she had experienced in her own life and tried to imagine them multiplied by millions. She shook her head, overwhelmed by the Jaed's words. He had lived and fought during the First Age, the most dangerous and bloody time in Appernysia's history. Calahein and rebelling Rayders had murdered or corrupted everyone and everything he loved. Suddenly, being a First Age Beholder didn't sound nearly as amazing.

And what of the Second Age? Mellai thought apprehensively. *What sorrows will come my way? Who will I watch die? Who will I have to kill?*

Llen drifted a short distance away. "Join me. It is time for you to learn the second tool. It is not as dangerous as energy blasts, but it still requires skill and concentration."

Mellai followed Llen until he pointed to a large boulder pushing out of the ground.

"What do you see in this stone?" he said.

"The same thing I see in all other rocks. Dull energy with very little movement."

"What would happen to this boulder if we sped up its energy?"

Mellai shrugged. "Burst into flame."

"A good assessment," Llen said, "but what if you sped up the energy even faster?"

"Faster than fire?" Mellai said, raising her eyebrows. "I would imagine the object would get hot, but the energy would become impossible to contain. It might even explode."

Llen's eyes brightened. "Exactly, although many other options are possible if you are capable of containing the object's energy. It is also possible to crystallize an object or bond it to another."

"Like packing dirt together?"

Llen shook his head. "Think deeper. No matter how much dirt you pack together, it will still turn to mud when gets wet. I am talking about changing the actual makeup of the object—processes that would take nature thousands of years to accomplish."

"What do you mean?"

"It is possible to create crystals that are impervious to damage, or bond objects permanently together. Take a ghraef's tail, for example. Do you think the crystal on the tip of their tail just grew there naturally?"

Mellai raised a questioning eyebrow. "I've never seen a ghraef before."

Llen nodded. "Fair enough. Another example would be the giant crystals embedded in the perimeter wall of Itorea. I know you have not seen Itorea, but your friend Kaylen has written you about it."

Mellai frowned. She hadn't heard from Kaylen in months. Now, after the conversation she overheard between Kutad and Jareth, she didn't know what to think. Jareth had to have mistaken her for someone else. Either way, she hoped her friend was alive and safe.

"I am telling you all of this so you know what is possible when you speed up energy," Llen continued, interrupting her thoughts, "but for now, I will teach you only to heat, melt, and create explosions. We will proceed in the same way you learned to create energy blasts. Pick a small stone, then increase the speed of its energy. When you advance in your skill, move to larger objects."

Mellai pushed her thoughts of Kaylen aside and found a nearby stone, penetrating it with her own energy. When she had created ice the previous night, Mellai had soothed and gently stroked the water's energy with her own essence to get it to slow and freeze. With the rock, she jabbed and whipped at its energy. It became angry, racing around itself in an attempt to escape. In less than a minute, the stone turned bright red and exploded, propelling tiny shards of hot stone through the air.

Mellai screamed when a shard stuck into the palm of her outstretched hand. She fell to her knees, lifted her palm upward, and pushed the painful projectile out of her skin with True Sight. In its place was a charred hole about a half-inch wide, permanently branded into her flesh. She looked up accusingly at Llen with tear-filled eyes.

Llen nodded toward her hand. "Practice your knitting."

With a clenched jaw, Mellai turned her attention to her right hand. The pain was excruciating. It took all the concentration she had to focus on the energy whirling around her wound. She closed her eyes and took a deep breath, then reopened them and focused. Using her left hand, she probed at the jagged flesh. When she touched the seared skin with her finger, pain coursed up her arm and shook her shoulder.

"It hurts too much," she cried.

"The pain will not stop until the injury is repaired. If you can concentrate enough to repair your own wound, then healing others will be an easy task for you. This is an opportunity for growth, Beholder."

"I can't," she argued, her body trembling and glistening with chilled sweat. "It's impossible."

Llen floated in front of her, his eyes bright and piercing. "What satisfaction comes from tasks that are accomplished without effort? It is not a matter of possibility, but of courage. How great is yours?"

Mellai cringed as she placed her left hand over the wound in her right, battling with herself to keep her eyes open. After taking a deep breath, she forced her essence to grab hold of the fibers of her skin. She stretched them across the wound, weaving them together until the charred flesh was replaced by the surrounding skin. It felt nothing like the knitting she had been doing at her grandparents' home, but the method was similar in effect. By the time she finished, Mellai collapsed to the ground and danced on the edge of consciousness.

When she finally gained enough control to sit up, Mellai was surprised by the look on Llen's face. Although his eyes were just bright holes in a glowing mass, Mellai was captured by their intensity. His gaze held her . . . lifted her . . . comforted her. His energy was inescapable.

"What is it, Llen?" she asked with a slackened jaw.

The Jaed's eyes flared bright, then loosed their hold on Mellai. "I have witnessed the rise and fall of countless Beholders through thousands of years." He spoke with revered authority. "A scar will remain where you repaired your wound, but know this. Only two others have been capable of such feats. You have more skill than you realize, Mellai—more than anyone I have ever met."

Mellai's head swam at the Jaed's words. "Could most Beholders heal others?"

Llen nodded. "During battle, the placement of Beholders was methodically planned. Healers were always positioned in the rear to save those with lesser wounds. It was unheard of for a Beholder to heal himself. The pain was too intense and overpowered his concentration."

Although grateful for Llen's approval, Mellai squirmed uncomfortably. She had never been very good at accepting compliments, and this circumstance was no different. She grasped for a change of subject. "That rock only exploded. How do I melt it?"

"Only certain types of rocks will melt, and only in certain conditions. That rock was wet and porous, which will almost always explode when heated quickly. In contrast, solid and dry rocks will melt with intense heat or pressure, along with mineral clusters like iron or copper. It is very simple to determine. Just think of what would happen to the object if you stuck it in a blacksmith's furnace. Take wood, for example. Could you melt wood?"

"No," Mellai replied. "It only burns and turns to ash."

"So it is with everything you might place in a fire. As a Beholder, you are still bound by nature's laws. You just have insight into rules that baffle those without True Sight."

Mellai licked her dry lips and pushed her long, curly hair behind her ears. "Are you telling me that if I was battling a knight, I could melt his own armor onto his body? What a gruesome way to die."

Llen's eyes became very serious. "Everything about forced death is gruesome. As a Beholder, you are capable of torturing a man beyond mortal comprehension. Is that a talent you desire?"

Mellai's face contorted with disgust. "Not at all."

Llen nodded. "Good. We have discussed enough for tonight. Return to your grandfather, Mellai. We will meet again tomorrow night."

Chapter 18
Farewells

Dawes carried Lon easily from the north blade of Taeja. The blade was a refuge for the Appernysians, protecting them from the normal Rayder dwellings. Because of its migrating inhabitants, the north blade of Taeja had been dubbed the Swallows by the rest of the Rayders. Lon's squad had slept in the Swallows the previous night to keep the Beholder safe from another attack.

"Slow down," Lon ordered Preton, who was leading the way toward the heart of Taeja. Preton pulled back on his horse's reins and slowed their pace to a walk.

"This is ridiculous," Lon spat. He was surrounded on all sides by his squad. "No one should need an escort through his own people. What happened to Rayder honor?"

Wade rode to the right of Lon. "I understand your frustration, Beholder, but this is the way it has always been among our people. We became too relaxed."

Lon looked forward, guilt pressing down on him. "We both know it was my fault that Omar died."

Wade did not respond, a readily welcomed silence. He had been pushing the same point nonstop since Omar's death the previous day, insisting that if he had kept his oath, Omar wouldn't have needed to lunge in front of the javelin. Wade would have been the one to die, and it would have been with honor. Lon didn't see the point in arguing about acts of honor with Wade, or over what could have happened. The past was just that. Past. Nothing they said would change what really happened.

The recent change in weather only made Lon's mood worse. Rain had started to fall on Taeja during the night and continued through morning. The city was covered with grassy mud, and the rain continued to pour down. Until the rain stopped, Taeja would stay covered in mud—unless Lon figured out a way to create a fifteen-mile-wide dome over the entire city. He had no interest in such a task. The weather would have this victory.

An enclosed canvas tent was set up in the middle of Taeja where the keep would eventually be built. The tent was the largest in Taeja, big enough to hold a hundred Rayders. Lon crossed into the tent with his squad, grateful to escape the rain.

Omar's body was inside, protected by Tarek from abduction or mutilation. He had sat over his commander's body all night with a drawn sword.

"News?" Lon asked, disheartened by the obvious tearstains running down his friend's face.

"Not one attempt," Tarek growled, followed by a string of curses.

Lon understood his frustration. Tarek had hoped someone would try to steal or desecrate the corpse, allowing him to vent his anger on a deserving person.

"Good morning, my Commander," Wade greeted with a salute.

"Don't call me that," Tarek spat. "Omar is your commander until the tournament."

Wade only nodded, a wise response in Lon's eyes. Tarek was looking for any excuse to start a fight. The fury burning in his bloodshot eyes was frightening enough without knowing his unmatched martial skill. Wade was usually insistent upon following Rayder procedure, but he wasn't a fool.

Tarek nodded at Lon. "How are you?"

Lon shrugged, still numb over Omar's death. "Not one of my better days."

Tarek lifted a jar of oil and poured it over Omar's body, which he had placed on a large pyre. "Let's get this over with so I can start searching for his killer." He walked to the front of Lon's squad and extended the torch. "I think this responsibility is best suited for Preton. It's the least you can do."

Lon watched anxiously, wondering how Preton would react to Tarek's test of loyalty. Preton hesitated, but eventually took the torch. He moved his horse next to Omar, placed the flame in the oiled wood, and moved away. The flames spread quickly and soon engulfed the acting commander's body. Smoke billowed into the air and escaped out a hole in the top of the tent.

Lon's heart ached, nearly too much to bear. He had spent countless hours in Omar's quarters, gleaning insight as his mentor patiently tutored him. But their relationship had progressed far beyond simple academics. Omar had become a guardian, an understanding father figure he could always turn to for advice and comfort. Above all, Omar had saved his life, time and time again. Lon owed him everything. A thick lump formed in his throat.

"For Taeja," Lon whispered. "This city will regain its former glory, Omar. Your dream will be realized. I promise."

"For Taeja," Tarek echoed softly.

"For Taeja!" the squad shouted.

After the roaring bonfire died down, Tarek clenched his jaw. "Spread the word, Lon. I'm not waiting another two days. The tournament starts tomorrow at sunrise. I'll fight in the first round. I dare his assassins to challenge me." Without another word, Tarek stormed out of the tent.

After Tarek's horse splashed away, Lon covered the smoldering ashes with a white linen banner stitched with the blue King's Cross, then he and his squad exited the tent. Omar's horse, Dax, was tethered outside. Lon took hold of Dax's lead rope and rode six miles to the south gate with his squad. Once outside the city's border, Lon dismounted and stood in front of Dax.

"Your master has passed from this life," Lon said, caressing the horse on his long snout. Rayder tradition required that the horse of a fallen soldier be released to the wild, but Lon feared for Dax's safety. As Lon anguished over the death of Omar, a fate that would most certainly befall a horse sent into the Taejan plains, the second half of *The Song of the Dead* entered his mind. He sang softly as he moved along Dax's side to remove his saddle.

> *I free you now from world-bound strife,*
> *And wish for you a better life;*
> *Release your pain, forget remorse,*
> *Continue on your ordained course.*

Lon unhooked Dax's bridle and removed it. The horse returned his gaze, calm and reassuring. He touched his forehead against Dax's snout and continued singing.

> *Go and find your resting place,*
> *Embrace no more this mortal race;*
> *Where pain and sorrow took their toll,*
> *Let joy and peace encase your soul.*
> *I will be watching for the day*
> *When my pains, too, are washed away;*
> *But 'til that time doth find me here,*
> *I bid goodbye, I'll shed no tear.*

He stepped to the side and gave Dax a soft swat on his flank. Dax trotted forward with a lengthened gait, head high and proud. Lon's chest ached as he watched his mentor's horse wander the Taejan Plains, but both master and horse had lived long, full lives. Omar wouldn't have it any other way.

Lon brought his two fingers to his King's Cross brand, dipping his head in the horse's direction. The closing line of *The Song of the Dead* crept from his lips in a whisper.

> *Farewell, my friends, my time draws near.*

Chapter 19

Shelter

When his squad reached the closest cluster of tents and shelters, Lon projected Tarek's announcement to all of the civilians and soldiers in Taeja. Wade suggested they take the proclamation to the Swallows, but Lon had something else in mind. Omar's funeral had forced Lon's mind into the past. He wasn't the only Rayder who had lost someone close. Some Rayders died before Lon even made it to the Exile. Rayders like Gil Baum.

Lon kicked Dawes into a trot down the nearest pathway. His squad closed in around him as a protective barrier. "Continue through the shelters," Lon ordered Preton. "I'll tell you when to stop."

They explored for most of the morning until Lon finally found who he was looking for. Flora Baum was huddled under a small canvas roof with her daughter in her arms and two sons beside her. She smiled up at Lon as he dismounted and stepped out of the rain. Wade followed while the rest of the squad formed an arc around them.

"I'm sorry," Lon apologized. "I've been so caught up with the past few months that I forgot my oath to your family."

A sincere smile formed on Flora's careworn face. "You have had greater responsibilities than caring for my family, Beholder. I hold no grudge."

"I have a name, Flora. Please use it."

Flora nodded. "You are a remarkable man, Lon Shaw. Despite all the trials and dangers surrounding you, you appear at my tent to apologize for our poverty. The Jaeds have blessed us with your gift. No better man could have been chosen among all the Rayders."

Lon returned her smile. "How is your supply of food?"

"Limited, but enough to get by."

Lon searched her shelter. They had only one small cask, which Flora was using as a chair. Her two boys were standing tall and proud, but the family's desperate situation was readily apparent in Flora's daughter, Cortney. In Flagheim, Cortney had been sweet and bashful, with full rosy cheeks and nonstop energy—everything a parent could hope for in a healthy daughter. All of that had disappeared. She hung limply in Flora's arms, drifting in and out of sleep. Her face was drawn, and her eyes were sunken. Worst of all, she seemed completely unaware of Lon's presence. Her joy for life had vanished.

Another pang of guilt racked Lon's conscience. He took Cortney and insisted Flora get onto his horse. After Flora climbed into the saddle, Lon handed Cortney to her mother and pulled Dawes's reins over the horse's head. "You deserve a better dwelling, Flora."

Wade offered his horse to Flora's two sons. They eagerly mounted the horse and rode next to their mother and sister. Wade walked alongside Lon while the rest of the squad remained in their saddles, formed in a protective circle. As they made their way down the muddy path, Lon realized many of the Rayder civilians were living in circumstances similar to Flora's. Most of their shelters were inadequate, their possessions limited, and their food supplies poor.

Lon's gaze shifted to the tall stone silos he had helped create from rubble near the center of the city. "Did we move too fast?"

Wade turned to Lon. "What was that, Beholder?"

Lon gestured toward the silos. "Food isn't enough to keep a man alive. Look around you, Wade. How many of these people do you think will survive the winter?"

The lieutenant kept his eyes locked on Lon. "Do not question yourself, Beholder. Everyone knew what they were up against when they decided to come here. Yes, some will die, but look at what we have accomplished thus far, with minimal casualties. Taeja is well-provisioned and our army is strong. It would be foolish for the Appernysians to attack us now."

Lon shook his head. "Thousands of us won't survive to see spring's blossom. Is it better for civilians to die of exposure rather than soldiers in battle?"

"Yes."

Lon sighed as he trudged forward. As usual, Wade's answer had been quick and to the point. It was a fitting answer for any typical Rayder. Although Lon knew it made sense to keep soldiers alive to ensure the protection of Taeja, the civilians they protected also had responsibilities and loved ones. They deserved to live as much as anyone.

"Something has to be done about this," Lon uttered. "I can't stand by and watch our people waste away."

"What can you do, Beholder?"

Lon peered upwards into the darkened sky. "Until this rain stops, not much, but I have an idea. I'll show you once we're inside the main tent." Lon brought his head back down. "Preton, fetch me a wagon full of clay from the old riverbed."

Preton saluted, then kicked his horse into a gallop toward the eastern region of Taeja.

Wade leaned close to Lon. "Can you trust him?"

Lon sighed. "I don't have a choice. I won't risk sending any of my other men out by themselves."

Wade's lips tightened as he watched Preton gallop away. "I am not so sure, Beholder. Sending Preton off by himself could be more dangerous than you realize."

*   *   *   *   *

Once Lon's squad was out of sight, Preton slowed his pace to a trot. He made his way through the Rayder camp until he reached the eastern edge, about a mile south of the center of Taeja. A large group of open wagons were clustered there, along with a small stash of tar-treated canvas tarps.

"Well, well," a man said as he stepped out from the midst of the wagons. "Look who finally decided to pay us a visit."

"Shut your mouth, Bryst," Preton growled. "Getting away from Lon wasn't easy, especially after your sloppy attempt on his life."

"Sloppy?" Bryst laughed. "I would hardly call it sloppy. It served its purpose."

Preton shook his head. "Perhaps, but I feel sorry for those who decide to fight against Tarek tomorrow. He is as angry as a bear caught in a bee's nest."

Bryst smiled. "Good. The angrier he is, the quicker he will exhaust his energy. What do you want, Preton?"

"I need a team-drawn wagon lined with a canvas tarp. Lon wants me to bring him a stash of clay from the old riverbed."

"Why?"

Preton shrugged. "He is up to something."

Bryst cursed and spat on the muddy ground.

"Do not act so surprised," Preton said. "Killing Omar was a fool-hardy attempt to stifle Lon's ability to use True Sight. He is still young and curious."

"Be careful of what you say," Bryst said with a glare. "You are starting to sound like you doubt Clawed and his plan. He might take it personally."

Preton's eyebrows softened with worry. "He killed Omar?"

"Of course," Bryst replied. "Who else would have done it?"

"He knows where my loyalty lies," Preton said, fidgeting with the pommel of his sheathed sword.

"Start acting more like it," Bryst replied. "You know as well as anyone that hiding in the Swallows will not keep you safe if Clawed decides your time is up."

"I understand," Preton said with a nod. "How about that wagon? I will need a shovel, too."

"Of course," Bryst said with a sneer. "Right this way."

*   *   *   *   *

"If you can do it," Wade commented with wide eyes, "that will be a glorious solution."

"Blast this rain," Lon said as he removed his soaked wool cloak. "Will it ever stop?"

Wade glanced around. They were inside the main tent where Omar had been burned. His covered ashes were still there, surrounded by a ring of large stones. "The soil is still dry under this canopy. Could you attempt it now?"

Lon nodded. "That's why I sent Preton for clay. Once he returns, I'll show you what I mean. Until then, help me create the rest of the mixture." Lon turned to Flora, who was still sitting on Dawes's back with Cortney in her lap. "May I help you down?"

"I would prefer to remain in the saddle," Flora replied. She patted Dawes's side with her free hand. "I have missed this horse."

Lon nodded with understanding. Dawes hadn't always belonged to him. His old master was Flora's deceased husband.

Dawes nickered and tossed his mane, bringing life back into Cortney's eyes. She reached forward and touched the coarse black hair on the back of Dawes's strong neck. "Horsey."

Flora hugged her daughter and smiled. "That is right. Father's horsey."

Lon fought off painful memories of Pree as he pulled his own canvas tarp from one of Dawes's saddlebags and opened it up on the ground. If Flora knew he had killed her husband, what would she say? Would she understand it had been an impossible contest between her duty-bound husband and an innocent peasant fighting for his life? Lon shook his head to clear his mind.

"The trick is finding the right mixture of sand," he said to Wade as he summoned True Sight.

"We will gather the dry reeds before you collect the sand," Wade inserted, then whistled to the rest of his squad. They all dismounted and wandered over the dry earth, cutting the tall reeds of yellow grass with their swords.

Once all grass under the tent had been removed and piled next to the canvas tarp, Lon used True Sight to comb through the dry soil. He sifted the sand from the rest of the dirt and placed the sand on the tarp. In less than a minute, he had created an arching pile as high as his waist.

"Amazing," Flora commented while her two sons gaped. Lon couldn't help but smile. This was the first time they had witnessed a Beholder's power up close.

Lon released True Sight, reached his hand into the pile, pulled out a handful, then let the dry grains of sand sift through his fingers. "That was a lot easier than it used to be."

A short time later, Preton arrived and led the wagon inside the tent. Lon summoned True Sight, hoisted the entire stash of wet clay from the wagon, and placed it on the tarp next to the sand. "Take the wagon back to the riverbed and fill it with more clay."

Preton breathed out through his nose. "I would appreciate a little help," he muttered as he disappeared outside of the tent.

As Lon expected, Wade ordered the cousins, Channer and Keene, to go with Preton. *Of course he'd send the cripples,* Lon thought. Channer's ankle had mostly healed, but it still presented a vulnerability, and Keene's broken arm hadn't fully healed.

Despite their injuries, both men replied with a salute, then mounted and rode out.

Nik stood in front of Wade and saluted. "Should I go with them, Lieutenant?"

Lon intervened before Wade could answer. "Yes, Nik. Leave immediately."

Wade turned to Lon. "Beholder, we should keep as many men as possible here for your protection."

Lon shook his head. "Your lives are as important as mine. Now go, Nik. Keep your distance, but string your bow and stay within range. They are not as fit for an attack as usual. They will need your sharp aim. Is your shoulder capable of operating a bow?"

"Yes, Beholder," Nik answered, then galloped after his fellow Rayders.

"I disagree with this order," Wade argued. "Your life is much more valuable than ours. You know this."

"I am of little value if I don't protect those around me," Lon retorted, "which is why I'm building these huts. Besides, Tarek will be the next commander, not me. I don't see any of you chasing around after him."

Wade sighed. "Tarek refuses to be found."

"Forget about it, Wade," Lon said. "I need to concentrate."

Without waiting for an answer, Lon drew on his power and began mixing the three ingredients together with water—half sand, one-third clay, and one-sixth grass. He hoisted a sphere of sand into the air and pulled the other two ingredients into it, carefully managing each task with his essence extending from his outstretched hands. When Lon felt the mixture was satisfactory, he walked to the altar, created a dome of air over Omar's ashes, and spread the mixture over the dome. Once it was evenly spread, Lon took a deep breath. "This is where it gets difficult."

Lon was already maintaining an air dome with his right hand and the mixture with his left, yet he also needed to pull the moisture from the mud to harden it. He couldn't release either of the other two tasks or else the mud-dome would collapse. To solve this problem, Lon used the hand already maintaining the dome to create another layer of air on the outside of mud. While the two layers held the mud in place, Lon carefully released his control of the mud with his left hand, extracted the moisture, and threw the collected water aside.

To Lon, the process was methodical and scientific, but he knew that to everyone in the tent, it looked like magic. They couldn't see Lon's essence or the glowing trails of energy he manipulated. To them, it would appear as though water, sand, clay and grass were dancing inexplicably in the air. Repeated gasps from Flora's children confirmed his assumptions.

"And for the test," Lon said after pulling the last drops of moisture from the mud. He took another deep breath, then closed his eyes—severing all control of True Sight. He paused, waiting for the sound of crumbling soil, but only the constant drumming of raindrops on the canvas tent reached his ears. When he cracked one eye open to peer at the earthen dome, it stood solid and intact.

Lon blew out his breath. "I have to admit, I had my doubts that would work."

"What have you done?" Flora asked. "Is he buried in dirt?"

"I'll show you," Lon answered. He grabbed hold of the dome with his essence and lifted it into the air, revealing Omar's undisturbed grave.

Flora gawked as Lon lowered the hollow dome over Omar's ashes again.

Elja stepped up to the dome and tapped it with the back of his knuckles. "Hard as wood. Did you turn this to brick? I did not see fire."

"Yes," Lon replied as he released True Sight, "but this kind of brick doesn't require fire." He didn't mention it, but he had learned to create the unfired brick in Pree. It was the same strong mixture they used to daub the cracks in their log homes. Tarek would know the same recipe, and would have certainly provided the same solution if he had not been so deeply impacted by Omar's death.

"Normally," Lon continued, "you would create the mixture and let it dry naturally under the sun—which takes more than a month. Because it's not fired, it's less brittle, too. It should be sturdy enough to create much larger domes."

But not strong enough, Lon thought, his memory drifting deeper into his past—how easily he had blown apart his partially built home in Pree. Hurling logs. Kaylen's helpless figure. Her cry of pain. How could he have been so selfish? So short-sighted? Why had he left without saying goodbye? His heart rent with pain as he sifted through his memories. He had never imagined he could love someone so intensely. He hadn't seen her for nearly a year, but still missed her and longed for her presence. Her calming influence. Her soothing words. Her gentle touch. Beautiful blond hair that would flutter in a warm breeze. But her green eyes. How they sparkled. Pulled at him. Made him want to better himself. And he'd never forget that dress she wore at his coming of age celebration. The warmth of her body when they had danced. Her full lips. What a perfect night to become engaged.

Lon smiled as he thought of her father, Scut, asking him to marry his daughter. Tall. Awkward. Fumbling over his words. The exact opposite of his daughter.

His mind continued through the other villagers in Pree, ending with his parents and sister. He missed them terribly. They had sacrificed so much, all to protect him and his identity. What was happening in Pree? Why was his sister in so much pain?

Lon closed his eyes and reached for Mellai, but the voice of Flora's older son interrupted his concentration before he could connect. "Shelters."

Lon opened his eyes and wiped his forehead, pulling his thoughts back into the moment. He smiled reassuringly at the young man. "Exactly, Gavin. You're very insightful. I'm going to create these domes for all the civilians in Taeja. If everything goes as planned, they will be large enough to hold many families."

Flora cleared her throat. "It is a brilliant idea, Beholder, but how will we get inside the shelters?"

"I'll dig tunnels that dip under the outer wall and come up inside the dome. That should help keep warmth inside the dome. Of course, I'll cut a hole or two in the top of the domes to vent the fire smoke."

"The tunnels will fill with mud during our first rainstorm," Flora argued. "Shouldn't you line them with something like stone?"

"I hadn't thought of that," Lon replied. "Thanks for the suggestion. It is a perfect solution."

"And what about light?" Flora continued. "These domes will be very dark inside, even with a hole in the top."

"Firelight and candles should provide enough," Wade interjected. "The domes won't be permanent. They are only meant to get our people through this winter.

Lon nodded. "Excellent point. As soon as I've created the domes, we'll start working on permanent residences."

"With what?" Flora asked again with unguarded cynicism. "There are only a few scattered clusters of trees for fifty miles in every direction. Do you plan to fill Taeja with mud huts?"

Awkward silence overtook the tent. Flora had spoken hard truths that bordered disrespect for the Beholder. Lon knew everyone was watching him, wondering how he would respond.

Lon moved to Flora's side and extended a hand to help her from the saddle. She handed Cortney to him, then dismounted without his assistance and took back her daughter. Her lips were pulled tight in a flat line.

"I understand," Lon said with a frown. She wasn't making this easy for him. "The truth is, I expected this reaction when I found you earlier today."

"It is desperate," Flora said as tears filled her eyes. "So many of us had high hopes for our new lives in Taeja. Our songs spoke of beauty and grace, not mud and . . . mud. On our way here, we crossed two rivers that had turned the surrounding soil to heaven. Why hasn't that happened here? Is Taeja cursed?"

Lon embraced Flora and Cortney. "Be patient, Flora. Taeja isn't cursed. It's just stubborn. By the time spring comes, everything will be repaired and Taeja will transform into the land you have dreamed of."

Flora buried her face in Lon's shoulder. "I do not understand. What needs to be fixed?"

Lon frowned. "The Beholders of the First Age created Taeja with a complex underground water system running through stone pipes. Most of those pipes have been damaged over the years by plants and rodents. When we first opened the rivers to Taeja, the city flooded. I was able to drain the water out of the city, but we have to keep the water out until I repair the pipes. That's why Taeja isn't what you had imagined. Little water means little vegetation." Lon leaned back and lifted Flora's chin with his hand. "Do you understand now?"

Flora nodded and sniffed back her tears. "I am sorry, Beholder. I spoke ignorantly. I have tried my best to remain positive."

"And you've done an excellent job at it. Don't be discouraged. It will take time, but Taeja will become greater than it ever was in the First Age. You have my word."

As Flora searched Lon's eyes, he saw confidence replace her despair. She closed her eyes and leaned forward on her tiptoes, brushing Lon's lips with her own.

Lon stepped back in shock. He studied Flora and her daughter, Cortney, then glanced up at the two young men sitting proudly on Wade's horse. Lon knew in that moment that he cared for Flora— that his heart longed for her family's safety and well-being—but a kiss felt wrong. So completely wrong. Romance was a separate emotion, one which he could never feel toward anyone but Kaylen. He stammered for something to say, trying not to hurt Flora's feelings, but only babbled like a fool.

Flora smiled. "No need for words, Beholder. I know I have surprised you. Show us to our new quarters, and we will leave you to your thoughts."

Lon nodded awkwardly and turned back to the piles of sand, clay, and yellow grass. He knew his squad was watching him closely, but he ignored their stares. He summoned True Sight, then carefully mixed another sphere together and created a larger dome for Flora and her family, making sure to remove a four-foot doorway before the dome hardened.

Lon released True Sight and turned to Flora. "You can stay here until I build you a proper home. My squad will remain here to look after you." Lon redirected his attention to Wade. "Make sure that Preton continues to bring more clay from the riverbeds. I'm going to need all of it to build the shelters."

Without another word, Lon mounted Dawes and disappeared out of the tent in search of Tarek.

Chapter 20
Shield

Dhargon hunched over a small cooking fire, watching his granddaughter as he prepared breakfast. It was an hour past sunrise, but Mellai showed no signs of stirring. It wasn't until Dhargon flipped a piece of bacon on the skillet that Mellai sat up, startled by the burst of sizzling. After eyeing the bacon, Mellai flopped back down on her bedroll.

"Good morning," Dhargon boomed. "Ready for breakfast?"

Mellai groaned. "I'm ready for another four hours of sleep."

"When did you get back?"

Mellai leaned to the side and looked at Dhargon. "What do you mean?"

Dhargon frowned. Through many frustrating experiences, he knew that arguing with his granddaughter would be pointless and counterproductive, just as chasing after her the previous night would have been. He had to approach this conversation carefully, spearheading with love rather than authority. "I heard you leave last night, but I wasn't awake when you returned. How long were you gone?"

Mellai sat up and ran her fingers through her tangled hair. "Maybe two hours, but I couldn't get to sleep for hours after I came back."

"A lot on your mind?"

"You could say that."

Dhargon stood and brought the sizzling bacon to his granddaughter. "I understand. Really, I do. I can't tell you how many times I've lain awake at night wishing for sleep, but you have to realize it's not safe to wander off by yourself. We'll be in the mountains by tonight. Promise me you'll stay by my side."

"Grandfather, I'm a big girl," Mellai complained. "I can make my own decisions."

"You're absolutely right," Dhargon replied, trying to reassure her. "I just want to make sure you're safe."

"I'll be fine," Mellai said, looking at her grandfather. "That much I can promise."

Dhargon nodded and sat on the ground to sip his medicated tea. "I want to talk with you about something, but I need you to put your defensiveness aside."

Mellai furrowed her brow, obviously throwing mental walls around herself. "What?"

"I should've known that wouldn't work," Dhargon chuckled. "Listen, I still don't know how you heard about your mother. I also don't know why you pretended to be so weak. I'm not going to try to force answers out of you. I just hope that by the time we get back to Roseiri, you'll decide I'm worth trusting."

"It's not about that," Mellai argued. "I trust you completely."

"I'm glad to hear that," Dhargon said with a smile. "Finish your breakfast and we'll get moving."

* * * * *

Mellai watched her grandfather sip his tea. She knew he hadn't let the subject go. He wanted answers. Dhargon was taking the nice approach, but pointlessly. Llen had forbidden her honesty. She had asked many times what consequences were hanging on her secrecy, but the Jaed refused to answer.

Mellai sighed. Dhargon wasn't the only person being kept from the full truth.

It wasn't until after the two of them finished breakfast and started north that Mellai spoke to her grandfather. "What was it like for Grandmother, not being able to bear children?"

Dhargon eyed his granddaughter. "Difficult, for both of us. It's not easy seeing your life slowly waste away without somebody else around to take it over. I had convinced myself that my life was complete, but I was proven wrong when I found your mother. She became the greatest joy in our lives. Then she married and gave birth to you and Lon. It was then that I realized life is a culmination of continuing joys that can only be silenced by death. Few things in life are more satisfying than seeing your children and grandchildren grow. I suppose that's what made the years after your family left so difficult for your grandmother and me. Everything most dear to us was taken away in an instant. We came home to see thirty-two of the most important years of our lives gone. I nearly gave up hope that we'd ever see you again."

"I can't believe Mother is thirty-seven . . ." Mellai said, mostly to herself, then wrapped her arms around Dhargon's arm and leaned her head against his shoulder. "I'm glad you didn't give up hope, Grandfather. I don't know what I would've done without you and Grandmother the last ten months."

Dhargon smiled. "Just wait until you marry Theiss. You'll forget all about us, and I won't blame you. Theiss is a good man, and he loves you fiercely. Don't ever take him for granted."

"I won't."

Mellai drifted into her memories. So much had happened since Lon left Pree—most of which tore at her heart. Yet amid all the pain and trials, Mellai had found an unexpected source of overwhelming happiness. Theiss was the kind of man women dreamed about. Everything he did was centered around Mellai and her happiness, so much that it would have been easy for Mellai to manipulate and take advantage of him. But she never would—because she felt the same way about him, which only complicated things.

When Llen had first appeared, he had endowed Mellai with True Sight. The month following was torture. Pain had constantly racked Mellai's mind and body as the power bonded itself with her essence. She drifted in and out of consciousness, but every time she opened her eyes, Theiss was there. His presence had given her the strength to endure the torment, which had ended as abruptly as it had come. Mellai woke one morning completely whole. Her mind was clearer than ever before, which enhanced her understanding of Theiss's love for her. It also strengthened her love for him.

Mellai was overjoyed at the change, but it was short-lived. Llen had appeared to her again that evening—and every night since—tutoring her on how to wield True Sight. In one short month, Mellai had learned to do unimaginable things, yet the experience remained bittersweet. Above all else, her forced deceit nagged at her the most. If anyone deserved to know the truth about her, it was Theiss. She despised keeping him in the dark, but she had no choice. Llen had forbidden it.

"Everything alright?" Dhargon asked.

Mellai realized she had slowed to a stop. "I'm fine," she said as she resumed walking. "I was just thinking."

"About what?"

Mellai looked up at her grandfather and frowned. "Everything."

Dhargon gave her a reassuring hug. "I understand."

Mellai's gaze fell to the ground in front of her feet. *I wish you did, Grandfather,* she thought. *There's so much I want to tell you.*

The two of them drifted in and out of conversation as they continued north, stopping briefly for lunch and dinner. Dhargon suggested setting up camp at dinner, but Mellai refused to stop, anxious to reach the clearing as soon as possible. They were deep in the dense woods of the mountains by the time Dhargon demanded they make camp.

As with the previous night, Mellai waited until she thought Dhargon was asleep, then slipped out of her bedroll and walked a few hundred yards away in the darkness with the aid of True Sight. She sat on a large boulder and wrung her hands together, anxious to speak with Llen. He appeared moments later.

"Good evening, Beholder," Llen greeted.

"I don't know if I can do this anymore."

Llen's glowing eyes narrowed. "If you knew what was at stake, you would not speak so foolishly. Beholders are never chosen out of convenience, Mellai. Every one of them has a purpose."

"What's mine?" Mellai asked. "I mean no disrespect, but I'm tired of the secrets. Everyone has something to hide, including me. I hate it."

"If there is one inherent trait that radiates from your core, it is unguarded honesty. This is one reason why I ask for your complete secrecy. You are not only honing your ability to use True Sight. You must also master your tongue."

Mellai breathed out with frustration. "I know, but you avoided my question. When do I find out my purpose?"

"When it is time," Llen answered. "There are still a few things you must learn. Everything has its season, Beholder. Be patient for yours."

Mellai slouched and grumbled under her breath, but she didn't argue.

"You have learned to speed up energy in objects," Llen continued from the previous night. "When you shattered the rock, it sent pieces flying in all directions. Melting objects will produce a similar effect, so you must learn to control the result. This can be done using energy shields." Llen floated a short distance away. "When you create an energy blast, you collect the energy into a sphere, then shatter the lining. Energy shields are created in a similar way, but their effect is more complicated—and taxing. Pick up a rock and throw it at me."

Mellai used her essence to grab a rock from the ground and fling it at Llen. A translucent wall formed in front of the Jaed. When the rock struck the wall, it ricocheted away.

"There are two very important rules to an energy shield," Llen continued, removing the translucent wall. "First, they are as temperamental as the spheres you make to create energy blasts. If shattered suddenly, the shield will explode. Secondly, the shields weaken when deflecting objects. They must be supplied with new energy to remain intact."

"So energy shields can be used to protect people?" Mellai asked.

"Yes, but at a cost. Let me pose a scenario. Suppose you were living in the First Age with other Beholders. If you were assigned to capture one of your fellow Beholders, how would you neutralize his power?"

"The only way possible," Mellai answered, hoping she'd never have to do such a thing. "I'd cut out his eyes."

"Yes, but suppose he knew you were coming and wouldn't let you get close enough to do so."

Mellai stared at the ground as she contemplated the Jaed's question. "True Sight draws on the Beholder's surrounding energy, so I'd have to find a way to cut off their access to it . . ." Mellai's eyebrows rose. "Could that be done with an energy shield?"

Llen nodded. "Yes, but remember, the other Beholder will also be able to see the shield—and fight against it. It will become a battle of his energy versus yours."

"But I'd have the advantage," Mellai argued. "I'd be able to draw on the energy surrounding me, but he'd be trapped inside my energy pocket."

Llen hovered back to position himself directly in front of Mellai. "Exactly, but as I said before, it will come at a cost. The energy has to be pulled from somewhere. What would happen if you pulled too much energy out of yourself?"

"I'd die."

"Is that different for anything else surrounding you?"

Mellai sat back and let out a slow breath. "No."

Llen spoke pointedly, more serious than Mellai had ever witnessed before. "If you pull too much energy from anything, it will be destroyed—whether living or inanimate. But an even worse outcome is possible. Observe."

A tiny pebble lifted from the ground and hovered between Mellai and the Jaed. It pulsed as Llen began extracting its energy.

"Release True Sight," the Jaed said, "and see what happens to the rock in the eyes of a normal human."

Mellai did as the Jaed asked, losing sight of Llen and his manipulation of the rock. It was surreal for Mellai to watch a rock hovering in the air without the help of True Sight. If she didn't know what was happening, it would have terrified her. She watched the rock carefully, waiting to view a change as Llen removed its energy, but nothing happened. Just when Mellai was about to give up waiting, the rock disappeared abruptly after a quick flash of light. No signs of the rock's existence remained.

Mellai summoned True Sight and was surprised at what she saw. Llen was still hovering in the same spot, but with a tiny sphere of swirling energy in front of himself.

"Is that the rock?" Mellai asked.

"Yes," Llen answered, "but as you can see, it is no longer a rock. It has transformed into raw energy. It is driven to bond itself with something new, which is why it is so explosive in an energy blast. To the regular human eye, this rock ceased to exist, but as you can see, such is not the case. Energy will take new forms, but it never stops. You cannot destroy energy."

Mellai furrowed her brow. "I understand, but what does this have to do with energy shields?"

Llen's voice softened to a resonating whisper. "Listen to me very carefully, Mellai. If you use an energy shield, you need to be aware of its effect on the world. When an object strikes the shield, part of the shield bonds itself with the object before it is deflected. Every impact will weaken the shield, so it will require your constant care to maintain its strength. Should a situation arise where you must pour massive amounts of energy into the shield to keep it strong, you could obliterate the world surrounding you without even realizing it. Aside from that fact, the people surrounding you will panic when things start disappearing. In that circumstance, it is usually better to release the shield and resort to other means."

Mellai stood and rubbed her sweaty palms together, struck by the implication of the Jaed's words. "So the cost of creating and maintaining an energy shield could be the destruction of the world?"

"Ultimately, yes, but the thought is impractical. You would destroy yourself and the land around you long before the world's destruction."

As Llen finished speaking, he released his hold on the sphere of energy. Its glowing mass combusted into a fine mist, each particle fleeing to bond itself with the closest entity. "Remember this. You cannot replace something that has been completely absorbed. In most cases, it comes at a terrible cost."

"I understand what you mean on a large scale, by why is it so terrible in a circumstance like this?" Mellai wandered between the surrounding trees, pondering the value of each entity. "It was just a rock."

"Everything surrounding you has an important role in the balance of Appernysia's energy. In the case of living matter like plants and trees, their role has more significance than you realize. As long as they are living, they retain memories of everything that happens to them. With patience, a Beholder can sift through these memories to learn things that happened hundreds of years earlier."

Mellai regarded Llen with a slacked jaw, having finally pieced together the significance of the clearing where Llen first visited her. "That's why I'm going to the clearing, isn't it? I'm going to learn where my mother came from and what happened to her real parents."

Llen's eyes brightened. "Correct. Penetrating the memories of the clearing will be one of the final steps in your training. Once you are able to do this, there will be little left that I must teach you.

182 ◆ TERRON JAMES

When you have learned this skill, your purpose as a Beholder will be made known to you."

Mellai smiled to mask her churning stomach. The thought of learning her full purpose was both exciting and terrifying. As impatient as she felt, Mellai wasn't sure she wanted to know.

Llen hovered a few feet away. "Review our conversation tonight. Now that you understand how to create an energy shield, how do you think it could assist you when speeding up energy in objects?"

"Energy shields would create a protective barrier around the object."

Llen nodded. "Now test your theory. Create a sphere of energy, then mold it into a thin wall around a moist rock on the ground." After Mellai had done as he instructed, Llen continued. "Now speed up the energy of the protected rock."

Mellai licked her dry lips, wary to comply. She hadn't forgotten the pain she endured the previous night. Blowing up another rock was the last thing she wanted to do.

"Trust me, Mellai," Llen said. "The barrier will protect you."

Mellai took a deep breath as she maintained the energy shield with her left hand, then used the essence of her right to pierce the shield and speed up the energy in the rock. Seconds later, the rock shattered violently, but all shards were kept safely inside of the shield.

"Well done," Llen commented as he extracted an oddly colored rock from the soil and placed it next to the energy shield. "Now try the same thing, but this time use the energy shield as a bowl rather than a barrier. Make sure to leave the top open. It will need air to melt."

"It won't explode?"

"No," Llen replied. "This is raw iron ore, the same material blacksmiths mold."

Mellai moved the energy shield under the new rock and proceeded to speed up its contained energy. She was awestruck at what happened. At nearly the same point the previous rock had exploded, the iron ore turned bright orange and morphed into a spongy mass.

She looked to Llen for guidance, but he encouraged her to continue. It took significant concentration to heat the rock further. The spongy mass melted and turned molten. The glowing liquid pooled at the bottom of the energy shield.

"Release your influence on the iron," Llen instructed, "and allow it to cool inside the energy shield."

Mellai obeyed. The orange fluid slowly cooled and hardened into a solid dome of iron.

"You are now a blacksmith," Llen said with smiling eyes. "Take it with you as a token of your hard work."

"I've never been in a blacksmith shop before," Mellai commented as she picked up the fist-sized steel with her hand. "I've always wondered how armor and weapons are made."

"Realize that this is not the normal way to smelt iron. A blacksmith has to use coal to heat the iron enough that it becomes malleable, but the process introduces impurities into the metal. Blacksmiths will spend hours hammering the heated iron to remove those impurities and molding it into their desired shape. For a Beholder, it is as simple as creating the energy shield encasing, then heating the iron to its melting point and allowing it to cool in the mold. What you just accomplished would take a blacksmith a whole day to create, yet the quality of his product would be significantly inferior."

"I enjoy learning new things, but why couldn't I use air to mold the melted iron? Why use an energy shield?"

Llen nodded. "Important question, Beholder, and it comes with an equally important answer. As you heated the iron, it was absorbing small portions of the shield's raw energy. Unlike the coke used to heat iron in a blacksmith's shop, the raw energy in your shield strengthens the iron as it cools and hardens. It purifies the raw iron, if you can grasp that concept. Air would not strengthen the steel, but weaken it, and struggle to maintain the barrier. Remember that fire burns from elements in the air. The iron would burn through an air pocket much quicker than an energy shield."

Mellai dipped her head at the Jaed. "Thank you, Llen. I know I'm not an easy person to work with, but I'm grateful for what I've learned so far."

Llen's eyes softened. "Do not thank me yet, Beholder. You have only a few more essential skills to learn, but they are the most difficult. Once you have returned to Roseiri, I will teach them to you. Until then, focus on reading the memories of the clearing where your mother was found. I will not visit you again until you are successful."

"I have to do this by myself?" Mellai complained.

"Yes, but you have already learned the skills. You will penetrate the memories of plants and trees in the same way you read the thoughts of animals, but the memories will require prolonged concentration. Be patient, Mellai, and do not expect to master this skill quickly. It will take you more than one night before you find what you are looking for in the clearing."

Mellai frowned. "That won't make Grandfather happy."

Chapter 21
Ambushed

Although Tarek had claimed he was searching for the assassins, Lon knew where Tarek would be. He found Tarek three miles to the west, in the center of what would become the grand arena of Taeja. Omar had completed specific plans on the arena's construction before he died, but Lon hadn't found the time to build it yet. Its construction—a magnificent amphitheater designed in the shape of the King's Cross—wouldn't begin until after Lon finished the shelters.

As Lon approached Tarek, the general stood and turned with a drawn sword. His grim face and tense body were streaked with mud. Tarek eyed Lon for a moment, then sheathed his sword and returned to his seat in the mud.

"I realized today that most of our people won't survive the winter," Tarek said as Lon rode up and dismounted. "Have you seen their pitiful shelters, Lon? It was my responsibility to bring them here. Their deaths are going to be on my head."

Lon sat in the mud next to his best friend. "Don't worry. I have it covered."

"How so?"

"With a mixture of sand, clay, and grass, like the daubing they use in Pree. It's a lot stronger than fired bricks and will make perfect dome shelters to get us through the winter."

Tarek smirked. "You have it *covered*? Did you say that on purpose?"

"No," Lon said with a laugh, "but witty, wasn't it?"

"A regular Omar," Tarek said, then his smile disappeared. "We're in trouble, Lon. You realize that, don't you? Omar was the obvious choice as commander. Who are we to try and fill his shoes?"

"Everyone rules in their own way. Don't try to replace Omar. Just take your own position and do the best you can."

"Sometimes I wonder if you'd make a better commander than me, Lon. Experience aside, you'd keep our people safe. Are you entering the tournament?"

Lon shook his head. He had known Tarek long enough to understand what really bothered him. He was apprehensive of becoming the new Rayder commander—worried he would dishonor the position's legacy. They both knew Tarek would fill the role exponentially better than Lon. "So would you. The Rayders respect you."

"Perhaps," Tarek said with a shrug, "but that doesn't make me the best leader. I couldn't even protect Omar. Who am I to think I can protect Taeja?"

"Stop focusing on Omar," Lon argued. "He was a remarkable man, but neither of us can afford to sit in his shadow. Make your own name, Tarek Ascennor. We kept Taeja safe once already and against impossible odds. We'll do it again if the need arises. You know I'll always be at your side." Lon paused to elbow his friend. "You'll be the one responsible, though, so don't foul things up."

Tarek chuckled and tried to smack him, but Lon rolled out of the way. The two men stood and grappled in the mud. Tarek had the dual advantages of size and strength, but Lon was surer on his feet in the slippery terrain. They flung each other to the ground repeatedly until they were both covered in mud.

"You look ridiculous," Lon laughed when he sat down to catch his breath. "The true makings of a Rayder commander."

"You don't look so good yourself, Beholder," Tarek countered. He tried to wipe the grime from his face with a muddy hand, which only made Lon laugh harder.

"This feels good," Lon said, leaning back to let the rain pour down on his body. "It's nice to act like a child again, even if it's only for a few seconds. I grew up too fast."

"You didn't have a choice," Tarek replied, flinging a glob of mud at the Beholder's face. "Life likes to order us around sometimes, doesn't he? Sometimes I'd like to find him and kiss his face with my gauntlet."

"I'd travel to the ends of the earth to see that."

Tarek snorted. "You made half that trip, and for a lot less, too. Or a lot more, however you want to look at it. Right now, it's hard to say."

Lon had nothing more to add. They sat in silence, the rain splattering over the mud, until Tarek finally stood. "We better clean ourselves up before someone sees us."

"Hold still," Lon said as his eyes clouded over. In less than a minute, he had removed the muck from Tarek's clothes. "You're free to go, my Commander. I'll wait for the rain to wash me clean." Lon ran his fingers through his short hair, grateful that he no longer had the unruly curls that used to cover his head in Pree.

"Don't call me that," Tarek said, his voice turning grim again. "Not yet, at least. That title needs to be earned."

"Stop worrying you'll fail. You earned our respect and loyalty a long time ago. This tournament will just remind everyone of that fact."

Tarek tried to argue, but Lon cut him off with a new subject. "Remember Flora Baum?"

"Gil's wife, right?"

"Yes," Lon answered. "She just kissed me."

Tarek burst into laughter. "Looking like that?"

Lon stood and clenched his jaw. "I'm serious, Tarek. This is a big deal."

Tarek stopped laughing and placed his thick hand on Lon's shoulder. "I know. The question is, did you kiss her back?"

Lon folded his arms. "No."

"Sounds like you've kicked over an anthill. Not giving up on Kaylen yet?"

"Never," Lon replied. "She's everything to me."

Tarek raised an eyebrow. "Who are you trying to convince?"

Before Lon could answer, a man caught his attention. He was galloping hard toward them from the east. Tarek drew his sword and Lon maintained his power, both ready for an attack, until Lon finally recognized the man.

"It's Wade," Lon said as he swung up onto Dawes.

Tarek smiled. "He doesn't look too happy that you got away from him."

Lon would have normally agreed with him, but Wade's urgency looked more pressing. The last time he had pushed his horse that hard was during their ride from Three Peaks to Thorn. "Something's wrong."

"Then go find out what it is," Tarek ordered. "I'll be right behind you."

"Yes, my Commander," Lon replied with a smirk, then kicked Dawes into a gallop. He heard Tarek cursing at him, but the rain and splashing of Dawes's hooves drowned out the words.

The closer Lon drew to Wade, the more worried Lon became. Anxiety covered Wade's face. Lon recognized the urgency and pushed Dawes faster to close the gap between them.

"There was another attack," Wade shouted.

"Where?" Lon shouted back.

"At the river. We must hurry."

Lon glanced over his shoulder at Tarek, who was already on his mount and galloping in their direction, then turned back to Wade. "Ride with Tarek. Where am I going?"

"To the keep. Hurry, Beholder."

The two men crossed paths as Lon urged Dawes into a dangerous gallop over the muddy terrain. Despite their urgency, Wade still took the time to salute, but Lon ignored the gesture. His thoughts were focused on what waited for him at the keep.

In just a few minutes, Lon and Dawes burst through the opening into the large tent. Five glowing figures converged on Lon, but he ignored them. He released True Sight and peered past his squad at Preton, who was lying facedown on the dirt. His hands and feet were lashed together behind his back with a leather strap.

Lon looked over his squad, not terribly surprised to see Preton bound. "What happened? Where's Channer and Keene?"

Dovan saluted, then pointed to the shelter Lon had created for Flora. "In there, Beholder."

Lon hurried into the shelter and waited for his eyes to adjust to the darkness. Flora's younger son, Nellád, was standing in the center with a torch in his hand. Gavin and Cortney were sitting on the ground behind him. Keene was illuminated by the torch, lying on a bedroll with Channer and Flora at his sides. Keene's face was covered in sweat and he pulled absently at a blood-soaked dressing that wrapped his abdomen.

"Easy, Cousin," Channer said as he grabbed Keene's arms and restrained him.

Lon inched forward and summoned his power to evaluate the wound. Bile immediately filled his throat. Yet again, an invaluable member of his squad had received a mortal wound and there was nothing he could do to help. Keene would die, and all Lon could do was watch.

"We were ambushed," Channer said without looking at the Beholder.

"By Preton?" He felt his anger rising, burning his cheeks.

"Not directly."

"Then who was it?"

"Appernysians," Channer said, then heaved a deep sigh.

Lon stared blankly, his fury somewhat quelled by his confusion. "*Our* Appernysians?"

Channer nodded. "I didn't recognize their faces, but none of them were branded with the Cross."

Lon crouched next to the bedroll. "Tell me."

Channer licked his dry lips and breathed deeply. "We were filling the wagon with clay and five of them appeared, riding donkeys toward us from the Swallows. Their pace was casual. We had no reason for alarm. It wasn't until they had crossed the old riverbed that I noticed they were hiding swords under their cloaks, but by then it was too late. The closest man slid from his donkey and slashed Keene with a kill stroke. I bashed the man with my shovel while the other four 'Nysians drew their swords and grouped behind me. Before they were able to attack, they were brought down by arrows. If Nik hadn't been watching, I might be lying next to Keene on my own deathbed." The last word caught in Channer's throat.

Lon sat on his heels and fingered the muddy stubble on his chin, lost in his thoughts. His gut told him that the Appernysians were victims in this attack, too. Perhaps their own lives had been threatened. Or maybe their families'. They had used a kill stroke, after all. They must have been tutored—no, blackmailed—by a Rayder. And not just any Rayder. A talented swordsman, interconnected with the movements of Lon and his squad.

His fists tightened, his suppressed fury returning with doubled force. "Where was Preton during all of this?"

"Sitting safely on the wagon," Channer spat. His jaw clenched as he shook his head. "Keene was foolish enough to allow him to rest." He let go of Keene's limp arms and wiped the sweat from his cousin's brow. "Preton jumped down from the wagon to help, but not until after the five Swallows were—"

"Don't call them that," Lon interrupted. He spoke with authority, tired of the disrespect constantly thrown at the Appernysian refugees. "They don't deserve that title."

Channer nodded. "I apologize. I feel bad for them, really. When they attacked, it was not out of anger—rather, I saw fear in their eyes. Someone made them do it, and it cost them their lives." Channer touched the blood-soaked cloth on Keene's stomach and looked at Lon. "Can you heal him, Beholder?"

"No," Lon replied abruptly, his fingers itching to draw his sword. Preton had caused this.

At that moment, Tarek entered the shelter and paused in the doorway. "What happened?"

"An ambush," Lon interceded before Channer had to repeat his answer.

Tarek's lips tightened. "Keene won't survive?"

Heavy silence fell on those who heard the question. Lon had been fighting his malevolence, but the hostility bursting from Tarek subdued his own bloodlust. Preton needed to be punished—and he would be—but they needed information first. Killing him wasn't the answer. Not yet. Lon stood and placed his hand on Tarek's shoulder and spoke as passively as possible. "I'm sorry."

"Coward," Tarek growled through his teeth, then drew his sword and exited the shelter.

Lon hurried after him and emerged just in time to see Tarek kick Preton hard in the face. There was a loud pop and blood splattered from Preton's broken nose. Tarek followed up with a boot to his side. Preton screamed as his ribs cracked. He rolled onto his side, gasping for air.

"Don't turn your back on me," Tarek roared. He lifted his sword arm and swung at the helpless Rayder. Lon summoned True Sight and stiffened the air around Preton, and the sword stopped a foot away from Preton's body. Tarek's face contorted with rage, but he remained motionless.

Lon crossed the room and stood in front of Tarek. "Wait."

"Get your creepy eyes out of my face," Tarek barked. "Let me go."

"Not yet," Lon answered, tears filling his eyes. He wanted to join with Tarek, bleed Preton until there was nothing left to bleed. It took every ounce of control not to, and even more to stand in the way of Tarek.

"You talk too much. He deserves to die." Tarek's muscles bulged as he fought against his restraints, then he became dangerously still and looked Lon in the face. "If you don't release me right now, I'll kill you next."

Lon frowned, knowing the threat was empty, but respecting the rage that overpowered his friend. "We need to talk first." He brought his other hand forward, preparing to lift Tarek and move him out of the tent.

"Don't you dare," Tarek whispered, obviously reading the intentions in Lon's eyes.

"I'll give you your legs, but only if you leave. This isn't the right move, Tarek. Trust me."

Tarek turned his head and looked over the other Rayders. "I'll give you thirty seconds."

Lon nodded. That was all he'd need. He removed the pocket of air from Tarek's sword hand, took the weapon, then released True Sight completely.

The acting commander stumbled from his sudden freedom, then straightened his back and stalked out of the tent with Lon following behind. They sloshed through the deafening rain and mud until they were out of earshot of the tent.

Tarek turned with clenched fists. "You humiliated me, Lon, and I'm the acting commander."

Lon shook his head. "You saw my men's faces. Your humiliation was the last thing on their minds."

Tarek blew out his breath. "What do you want?"

"Channer told me something that caught my attention. They were attacked by Appernysians, but one of them used a kill stroke on Keene."

Tarek's eyes narrowed. "Appernysians don't even know what a kill stroke is, let alone how to execute one."

Lon nodded. "Unless someone taught them."

Tarek's eyes widened and his nostrils flared. "It *was* Preton"

"I think this is a lot bigger than Preton," Lon replied. "He's a skilled and experienced fighter, but not much of a leader. Someone else is behind these attacks, someone with a much larger sphere of influence." Lon offered Tarek his sword. "I want justice as much as you, but we need Preton alive to help us find out who. If you kill him, the truth dies with him."

Tarek ripped the sword from Lon's hand and sheathed it. "Then let me back in there to beat the truth out of him."

Lon stepped to the side and gestured back at the tent with his hand. "Violence won't get him to tell you what you need to know."

"Even if he doesn't," Tarek said as he shouldered past Lon, "it'll make me feel better."

"Just don't kill him."

When they reentered the tent, Channer was out of the small shelter. Dovan, Thad, and Elja were holding him back while Wade knelt over Preton. Nik stood off to the side, obviously torn with strong emotions as he glanced between Channer and Preton.

"You broke your oath and betrayed us," Channer shouted with tears running down his face. "He was the only family I had left!"

Lon summoned True Sight and glanced through the opening in the shelter. The glowing forms of Flora and her three children were still inside, surrounding Keene's motionless body. The essence that used to fill his body was no longer present. Lon released True Sight and nodded at Tarek.

Tarek and Lon crossed the room to Wade's side and were met with a gruesome sight. Preton's face was beaten beyond recognition, and the rest of his body was deformed and disfigured in various ways.

"Did he try to escape?" Lon asked after noticing that the leather straps, which had been binding his hands and feet, had been cut.

Wade shook his head. "Channer cut him free, then threw down his sword and challenged him. Preton did not fight back, so Channer easily won."

"To cause him the same pain he has caused me," Channer roared.

Lon knelt over Preton and lifted his head from the ground. "Has he said anything?"

"Not a word, Beholder," Wade replied.

One of Preton's eyes opened slightly and peered at Lon.

Lon leaned close to Preton, knowing there was little time left for him. "Who was behind these attacks?"

Preton started to speak, but his voice caught and he violently coughed up blood.

"Please," Lon urged, wanting to shake it out of him. "Who?"

"Clawed," Preton replied in a half-cough. Most of his teeth were missing and his voice rattled from the blood in his lungs.

"Who's Claude?"

Preton's tongue lifted and touched the back of his teeth, trying to form a word, but none escaped his lips. He tried again, but unsuccessfully. His body shook with frustration.

Lon frowned. He didn't need his power to know that Preton's essence was moments away from departing. If only he could read minds. If only he could do a lot of things.

Preton's lips tightened with concentration. With his last reserve of energy, he brought his right hand up next to his head. A tear escaped his open eye as he placed his first two fingers on his King's Cross brand and nodded in the Beholder's direction. Lon couldn't help but return the salute, then Preton's hand dropped, and a final gasp of air escaped his mouth.

Channer pulled himself free. "Let me go," he shouted, then returned to his cousin's side inside the small shelter.

Lon released a few calming breaths, then stood and faced Tarek. "Know any Rayders named Claude?"

Tarek shook his head. "No Appernysians, either."

Lon glanced back at Preton's lifeless body and sighed. "Tomorrow's tournament could offer a perfect chance to find him, but I'm worried about you. You'll be completely surrounded by thousands of our people. If there's another attack, you won't be able to escape."

"I'll be fine," Tarek replied, then walked to Flora's shelter and disappeared inside.

I hope so, Lon thought as he glanced over the remaining members of his squad, *for the sake of Taeja.*

Chapter 22

Dissenters

The nights were growing colder as September was drawing to a close. Lon stared through the crowd at the rising sun, basking in its warmth. The rain had finally stopped after dusk, giving Lon an opportunity to prepare a temporary tournament ring at the site where the grand arena would be built. After pulling the water from the soil, he had created a ring of chest-high dirt a hundred yards in diameter to separate the standing spectators from the competitors. He had worked through most of the night.

Tarek stood in the middle of the ring, alone and confident. His long red hair was pulled back in a low ponytail, and his body was covered in polished plate armor. Nearby was a rack of assorted weapons. Lon absently rubbed the scar carved into his right forearm as he thought of his own weapons trial. That was only ten months earlier, but so much had changed since then.

Wade's voice pierced Lon's thoughts. "Should we begin, Beholder?"

Lon acknowledged his lieutenant, who stood next to him amid the other six surviving members of his squad.

Lon's eyes clouded over and his voice boomed through the crowd. "First contestant."

Silence fell over the crowd as they waited for someone to leap over the wall. Minutes passed without a response. Lon knew it was impractical to think no one would challenge Tarek, but hope still fluttered in his stomach. If an hour passed without anyone entering the fighting ring, Tarek would be named tournament champion and thereby commander of the Rayders.

After about fifteen minutes, a man clothed in ragged linen finally crossed the wall. Angry shouts followed after him as he walked toward Tarek.

"Go home."

"Fly away, little bird."

"Back to the Swallows."

"You've got a worm stuck in your beak."

When the Appernysian reached the center of the ring, he looked over the weapons and pulled a long warhammer from the rack. He kept the weapon at his side and turned to face the acting commander. Tarek brought his two gauntleted fists together in front of his chest, signaling that he chose no weapon.

Lon projected his voice over the crowd. "Begin."

The Appernysian gripped the warhammer with both hands and swung it sideways at his opponent's waist. Tarek stepped back to avoid the blow, then lunged forward and punched the man in the face. The steel covering Tarek's fist rang as the man flew back and landed motionless on his back.

"Winner," Lon announced, then shook his head. *What was that man thinking?*

Two Rayder soldiers slipped over the wall, hurried to the center of the clearing, then dragged the unconscious Appernysian back to his people.

"Next contestant."

Another Rayder soldier hopped into the ring. Lon recognized him as Warley Chatterton, the lieutenant of siege weapons. He was a good twenty years older than Tarek, but he was tall with broad, powerful shoulders. He retrieved a two-foot morning star from the rack, and Tarek chose a quarterstaff. The two faced each other, then Warley saluted his general and acting commander.

"Begin."

Warley reared back and flung the mace at Tarek's head. Tarek barely managed to dodge the flying projectile, then rushed forward at his opponent. Before the counterattack, Warley dropped down to one knee and saluted again.

Lon breathed in sharply. By surrendering, Warley had placed Tarek in a conflicting circumstance. If he chose mercy, Tarek would be thought of as weak. If he chose to attack, his brutality would be no different than the previous Rayder commanders. He would rule by fear rather than respect.

Tarek halted his attack and held the quarterstaff defensively. "Retrieve your weapon, Lieutenant."

Warley hesitated briefly, glancing to one side before he finally stood and crossed the soil to the spiked mace. Tarek pivoted around to keep his opponent at bay. When Tarek had turned completely around, a slight movement at the edge of the fighting ring caught Lon's attention—amid the glowing forms of the Rayders standing behind Tarek. Energy pulsed in Lon's vision as his worry and concentration increased. There was a loud crossbow snap and a bolt whizzed into the ring, directed at Tarek's back. Lon reacted quickly, refusing to allow another death, nor escaped assassins. He stopped the bolt with his right hand and formed an impenetrable pocket of air over the offending group of men with his left. He gave the attackers no time to react. Lon knew he had trapped them.

"Follow me," he shouted to his squad as he leaped over the wall and sprinted toward the group.

* * * * *

Tarek knew what had happened. He glanced over his shoulder at Lon crossing the fighting ring with his escorts, then turned back to his wide-eyed opponent. "Foolish move, Lieutenant."

Warley's lips tightened as he picked up the spiked mace. "It is all relative, *General*. Some believe it is foolish to attack you or the Beholder, while others believe it is foolish to accept 'Nysian lovers."

Tarek smirked. "I'm glad to know where you stand."

The two circled around each other, then Warley leaped forward to attack. Tarek parried the blow, swept the lieutenants legs with one end of the quarterstaff, then brought the other end down on his falling head with a loud crack. Tarek aimed a jab at the unconscious Rayder's neck, but couldn't help but think of Lon. *I know, I know,* he thought as he glanced up at his friend. *You want him alive.*

Tarek dropped the quarterstaff, threw Warley over his shoulder, then sprinted toward the captured group of men—making sure to grab an arming sword from the weapons rack on his way.

* * * * *

When Lon and his squad reached the captured men, many of them had collapsed on the ground gasping for air, while others stood at its edge pounding on the invisible barrier. Those surrounding the men had backed away in fear. Lon approached the area cautiously, hoping that he had captured the offender and his protectors, but knowing that some might have escaped. Anger welled up inside of him, threatening to overpower his concentration. With strained focus, he watched the faces of the spectators, searching for signs of anger or contempt. Finding none, he returned his attention to the pocket of air, tempted to allow those inside to pass out of existence. After all, their deaths would eliminate a significant number of mutineers. Lon's moral side eventually took control, though, and he created scattered holes in the pocket of air. The men trapped inside were breathing normally again by the time Tarek arrived with the unconscious lieutenant.

"Throw him in," Lon ordered.

"With pleasure," Tarek said as he brought Warley down and hurled him at the others.

Lon removed a portion of the air pocket so the body could enter, then sealed it again with a smile as the unconscious lieutenant knocked three other men to the ground. Tarek walked up to the edge of the barrier and looked over the men inside. The remains of a crossbow were on the side closest to the fighting ring, stomped to pieces.

"Tsk, tsk," Tarek said. "Looks like we caught a whole crowd of conspirators, and using Appernysian weaponry, no less. I'd hate to kill you all, so maybe one of you could tell me who loosed the bolt at me."

One of the prisoners stood and pulled back the hood of a heavy cloak. Long red hair poured out of the hood and wrapped around the face of a beautiful woman. On her right temple was the King's Cross brand.

"I did," the woman said. "What can I do for you, my Commander?"

Tarek eyed the woman for a moment, then snorted. "We'll start with your name."

"Elie Swasey, my Commander."

"You're awfully brazen for a woman, Elie."

"You are overly dense for a general, *my Commander*." The last two words slithered from her tongue. "And what about you, Beholder?" She looked at Lon. "Do you really think this silly wall can save your lives?"

A group of ten men charged from outside the barrier. Tarek and the rest of Lon's squad formed up to meet the attack. The assault broke on their formation, dissolving into a brawl. As Lon dueled three men, Channer rushed in from one side. He slaughtered all three before they even knew he was there, freeing Lon to turn his powers on the other attackers. Channer stopped and glared at the dead bodies, his chest rising and falling with rage. Every one of them was branded with the Cross.

Elie's eyes widened as she fingered the barrier still holding her captive.

"You're overly confident for an assassin," Lon growled. He clenched his jaw and stepped forward until only a few inches of air separated them. "Where's Claude."

Worry flickered across the woman's face before it was quickly replaced with calm. "Claude who?"

"The man who pretended to care for you," Lon spat, "then sent you to your death. Where is he?"

Elie recoiled under Lon's piercing stare. She stepped back and brought her hand to her chest. "Can you read my mind?" she whispered.

Lon smirked. He couldn't read minds; he didn't even know if it was possible for a Beholder. But he had guessed correctly. He had seen pain radiate from a woman's eyes before, even when she was doing her best to hide it. He knew Elie's relationship with Claude was personal.

Lon took another step forward, moving the invisible barrier forward with him. "Where is he?"

Elie's breathing quickened as the barrier knocked her back. "My silence is the only thing keeping me alive. If I tell you, he will kill me."

Tarek tapped the air barrier with his sword. "If you don't tell us, we'll kill you anyway."

"Perhaps," Elie said, shaking her head, "but Clawed will not stop there. He will come after my family and everyone I care about."

"We'll protect you and your family," Lon said.

"Like you protected Omar?"

Her words cut into Lon. His eyebrows slanted as he scowled at her.

Elie smiled again. "I am not the only one with demons in my past. I am sorry, Beholder, but you will have to find him on your own. You cannot protect me."

With a shout of frustration, Lon clenched his outstretched hand, collapsing the pocket of air around Elie. Her eyebrows raised in fear as her supply of air was cut off. Lon tightened his fist to compress the air, his fingernails cutting into the palm of his clenched hand. Elie's body shook under the pressure. She opened her mouth to scream, but no sound emerged.

Lon leaned forward, his hazy eyes roaring with intensity. "I'll ask you one more time. Where is Claude?"

Elie blinked and her lips moved quickly, but there was still no sound coming from her. Lon was so enveloped in anger that he had not opened a hole to allow her to speak. Before he realized it, her eyes unfocused and her body went limp in its crushing prison. Lon released his hold on Elie, and her body fell to the ground.

Lon watched her closely, grateful to see her chest rising and falling. He needed the secrets that would have died with her. She would break; her anger for Claude would be her undoing. If anyone was going to reveal Claude's whereabouts, it would be her. But the rest of the crowd needed to be controlled, and their fellow Rayders needed to see him and Tarek as men of action, swift to assist or punish accordingly.

Lon took a few steps back and addressed the crowd of people surrounding Elie. "Unless you all wish for a similar fate, then you will do exactly what I say. Each of you will be detained. You will be released after the tournament ends and your new commander has questioned you. If you have done nothing wrong, you have nothing to fear."

"Throw us your weapons," Tarek ordered. "Slowly."

Despite murmurs and complaints, everyone nodded. Soon a small pile of swords and daggers were piled together. After sending Channer to search for hidden weapons, Lon focused on the ground below the prisoners and lifted them forty feet high on a pillar of earth. A few heads peered over the sides, but Lon guessed that most of them were cowering in the middle.

"Stay."

Lon leaned close to Tarek. "The tournament has to continue. This kind of lawlessness will keep getting worse until a commander is chosen."

"Agreed," Tarek said. "Thank you for protecting me. If you hadn't intervened, I'd be dead and you'd have an even bigger mess on your hands. Now make a safe place for yourself and I'll finish this."

While Tarek returned to the center of the fighting grounds, Lon formed a half dome of earth at the perimeter, thick enough to thwart a projectile, then stood underneath it with his squad. He knew the wall of dirt would hinder his situational awareness, but he had no choice. He couldn't focus on everything at once.

"We need to build a fortress of stone for you and our commander," Wade commented. "Your ability to manipulate the ground is unmatched, but even this dome will not stop a boulder or oil cask."

"I know," Lon replied, "but let's get through this day first."

Chapter 23
Rise of a Commander

The tournament for Rayder commander lasted most of the day. At first, it appeared that nobody would follow the first two contestants, but a man finally emerged just before an hour had passed. His fight with Tarek, like most following it, ended quickly with an abrupt blow to his head. Tarek had no interest in coddling the weak or inexperienced, as he proved with his first fight with the Appernysian. Even those with greater skill didn't last long against him. Tarek battled fiercely with every opponent, determined to secure his role as commander.

Tarek remained focused during each fight, but his thoughts wandered during the lulls between contestants. At the forefront of his mind was Claude. Who was this man? Was he a Rayder? Did he live in Taeja? How had he managed to gain such a large and passionate following? His people were willing to sacrifice their lives for his cause, which was what? Obviously they wanted to kill Tarek and Lon, which may have been the reason behind the ambush on Channer and Keene. With the death of each member of Lon's squad, the less protected the Beholder became.

But was there more? What would Claude do once Tarek and Lon were out of the way? Was he seeking control of the Rayders? Did he desire to become commander?

The last question lingered in Tarek's mind, fueling his resolve to win the tournament. It wasn't so much that he wanted to be commander, but that he couldn't trust anyone else with the role. Of course Lon and his squad would do fine, but they would never join the tournament as long as Tarek was standing.

When sunset drew near, Tarek's puzzled thoughts began fitting themselves together. The first piece emerged when his next contestant stepped into the tournament ring. He squinted into the sun's glare reflecting off the man's steel plate armor. It wasn't until the man reached the center of the ring that Tarek realized who it was. Most of the man's face was hidden by a steel helm, but his suit of armor gave his identity away. It was similar to other Rayder lieutenant armor, with the exception of the left arm. The steel ended halfway down the forearm, and a small buckler was secured at its tip. There was no gauntlet on the left arm because it was unnecessary. The man didn't have a left hand.

Tarek nodded at his opponent. "I've been wondering if you'd participate in this tournament, Lieutenant."

Braedr removed his helm and saluted. "It will be an honor to fight you, my Commander."

Long, deep scars covered the lieutenant's face, running down from his forehead to his chin. Aside from Lon and Braedr, Tarek was the only other person living in Taeja who knew the truth behind those scars. Braedr had attacked Mellai in Pree, but she had fought back ferociously. Even after he had fallen to the ground, she had kicked him and clawed his face.

Clawed his face, Tarek thought again, then raised his eyebrows with new understanding. *We aren't looking for Claude. We're looking for Clawed!*

"Everything alright, my Commander?"

Tarek wanted to incapacitate Braedr, even kill him, but he knew the repercussions. He had no proof behind his suspicions, and Braedr—or Clawed—had a sizable following of insurgents. If he killed Braedr, they would condemn his actions and plunge the Rayders into a bloody civil war.

"Choose your weapon," Tarek ordered. "I have a tournament to win."

Braedr replaced his helm. "As you wish. I just thought you might want a little break. You look tired." The corners of Braedr's mouth turned up slightly as he finished speaking.

Tarek clenched his jaw at the subtle insult. "Pick your weapon, Lieutenant."

"Patience." Braedr started circling the weapons. "I'm new to this, my Commander, so let me verify the rules. I can choose any weapon housed by this rack?"

"Yes."

"And once you choose your weapon, the fight doesn't begin until we're both ready?"

Tarek glanced at the lowering sun. "Yes."

"Hmm . . ." Braedr made another full circle around the rack. "There are many good choices . . . but I think I'll go with this." He slid his fingers into the hollowed out section of one of the crossbeams and pulled out a composite bow and an arrow.

Murmurs poured from the surrounding crowd. Tarek noticed Nik making his way toward Braedr, but Tarek waved him off.

"You're a cunning man, Lieutenant, to slip that bow and arrow into the rack. I don't even care how you managed it. I'll allow you to use it, but are you sure it's the best choice? I don't know if you noticed, but you're missing a hand."

Braedr's eyes narrowed. "I'll make it work."

While Braedr struggled to nock an arrow onto the bowstring, Tarek searched the weapons and chose a two-handed battle-ax with a broad double blade. Although he didn't know how, Tarek was certain Braedr had a method for shooting the arrow at him. The thick steel of the ax would offer valuable protection against a projectile. By the time Tarek returned to his position, Braedr had managed to nock the arrow onto his bowstring.

"Ready?" Tarek taunted.

"One moment." A small steel rod with a groove in its center had been attached to the edge of Braedr's buckler. After moving the bow into his right hand, he hooked the rod around the bowstring—just below the nocked arrow—and pulled it back. "Now I'm ready," he said icily as he aimed the steel-tipped arrow at the acting commander.

Tarek moved the ax in front of his chest to protect his vital organs. "Last chance to back down, Lieutenant. You only have one shot."

"Then I better make it count," Braedr sneered.

Stillness hovered over the tournament grounds as the two men faced each other. Tarek gauged the distance between them and planned his counterattack. The arrow only had to travel a short distance of twenty feet, which didn't allow for much reaction time. He would have to trust his survival to luck.

Tarek looked in the direction of Lon, pouring his thoughts at the Beholder. *Don't you dare intervene! This is my fight. My trial. My honor.* He turned back to Braedr and nodded. "I'm ready."

Lon's voice echoed over the grounds. "Begin."

Tarek crouched low behind his ax, but Braedr didn't shoot. He stood there smiling at the acting commander.

"Lose your nerve?" Tarek growled.

"Hardly," Braedr replied with a smile. "I'm just savoring this moment. Look at you, cowering behind your makeshift shield. How embarrassing."

Tarek chuckled from behind his ax. "You know what's really embarrassing? Your face. How can you live with yourself, looking that way? Seems like Mellai was too much of a woman for you to handle, *Clawed*."

Braedr's lips tightened. He flicked his left forearm, and the arrow whistled from its bow.

The arrow was aimed directly for Tarek's head. He jerked to the side and the arrow pierced through his armor, sinking deep into his left shoulder. Tarek shouted and winced in pain, then looked up just in time to see Braedr leap at him. The two men crashed together and rolled across the ground away from the battle-ax.

"There," Braedr said breathlessly as he stood. "That ought to even things up."

"It'll take a lot more than an arrow to even things up between us," Tarek replied. He pushed himself to his feet, then deliberately reached up with his right hand and broke off the arrow mid-shaft and tossed it aside. "My turn."

Tarek rushed at his opponent, and Braedr swung at his head with his buckler. Tarek ducked the blow, slipped behind him, and wrapped his thick arms around Braedr's chest. Tarek growled as he locked his hands together and squeezed. Despite his injured shoulder, their armor groaned under his crushing grip.

Braedr gasped and squirmed, desperately trying to free himself, but Tarek held fast. It wasn't until Braedr whipped his head back and caught Tarek in the nose that Tarek let go and staggered back, blinded from the blow. Braedr turned and threw himself at Tarek. Air gushed from Tarek's lungs as the weight of Braedr's armored body smashed him against the ground.

"Funny how quickly things can change," Braedr scoffed as he reared back to knock Tarek unconscious with his buckler.

Despite his blurred vision, Tarek was far from incapacitated. He blocked Braedr's blow with his vambrace, then grabbed Braedr's forearm and hurled him to the side. As Braedr fell onto his face, Tarek rolled over and pinned Braedr's right arm behind his back.

"Surrender," Tarek shouted, "or I'll break the one good arm you have left."

Braedr's nostrils flared. "Never."

Tarek wrenched the lieutenant's arm upward and dislocated his shoulder. Braedr screamed in pain.

"You scream like a girl," Tarek spat through his blood-soaked beard, then bashed the back of Braedr's head with his elbow. Braedr's squealing was instantly silenced.

Tarek stood and raised a closed fist at Lon, indicating that his opponent was alive, but unconscious.

"Winner," the Beholder's voice announced to the crowd. Two soldiers ran out to move Braedr. Tarek held up his palm in their direction, sending them away, then waved Lon and his squad forward.

Lon moved out from under his half-dome of dirt and into the ring. His men followed behind, walking backward to protect the Beholder's blind side.

"What is it?" Lon asked when they reached the acting commander.

Tarek reached down and removed Braedr's helm, revealing his heavily scarred face. "May I introduce Clawed. C-L-A-W-E-D."

Channer jumped forward with his fist around his sheathed sword, but Tarek moved between him and Braedr. "No one wants this man dead more than Lon and I, but we can't kill him. Trust me. I've thought it through many times."

"He deserves to die," Channer shouted through hot tears.

"I know," Tarek replied, "but killing him will only strengthen his followers—our enemies. They're too radical. Too irrational. We already have to defend Taeja against the Appernysians, and maybe even the calahein. We can't afford to start a war among ourselves."

"Did he confess?" Lon asked.

"Not directly, but I read it in his face. He's behind everything. Omar's assassination, Preton's treachery, Keene's death, this tournament . . . Braedr crafted it all to make himself the new commander. He wants control of our people."

"So what should we do, if we can't kill him?" Lon asked. "We don't have a place to hold him prisoner where he can't be rescued by his men."

"On the contrary," Tarek said as he pointed at the high pillar. "Just make a permanent pillar out of the mud you used to create Flora's shelter. You could even surround it with an impassible trench to discourage rescue attempts.

Lon nodded. "It'll have to do for now, until we collect enough stone to construct the keep. In the meantime . . ." He forced a narrow pillar of dirt out of the ground and raised Braedr fifty feet in the air.

Tarek chuckled. "That'll be a nasty shock for him to wake up to. Or better yet, maybe he's a restless sleeper. That would solve a few problems for us."

Wade cleared his throat and saluted Tarek. "My Commander, we still need to finish this tournament. Should we escort Lon back to his stronghold?"

"No, Lieutenant," Tarek replied, resetting his broken nose with a stifled grunt. "I want all of you here to guard Braedr, but step aside to make room for more contestants."

*   *   *   *   *

No other men entered the fighting ring. After an hour had passed, Lon hoisted Tarek on a pocket of air, named him tournament champion, and declared him the new Rayder commander.

A deafening cheer erupted from the crowd, overwhelming the cries of protest from Braedr's supporters. Lon created a narrow staircase leading up to and underneath Tarek, then climbed the steps and stood next to his best friend. He raised his hands for silence, then pulled a silver coronet from his belt.

"You will bring honor to our people," Lon spoke solemnly as he placed the coronet on Tarek's head. "I pledge my life to your will and protection, my Commander. May the Jaeds watch over you."

After speaking, Lon dropped to one knee and saluted Tarek with a bowed head. His example was followed by everyone in the arena—including the dissenters, who apparently weren't so foolish as to disrespect the newly-crowned commander. The crowd remained motionless for several minutes, then Lon stood and placed his hand on Tarek's shoulder. "For Omar."

"For Taeja," Tarek said and returned the gesture. He glanced around, then looked up at Braedr, who sat conscious on his pillar with a pained, pitiful expression on his face. "Speaking of Taeja, if you keep throwing these columns up everywhere, you're going to turn our city into a dirt forest."

Lon chuckled. "Let's get your wounds looked at, my Commander."

"For you, my name stays Tarek."

"Agreed," Lon said, "as long as you don't call me Beholder."

Chapter 24

Clearing

"There's not much to tell," Dhargon said, stepping past the outer rim of trees and into the clearing. "I found your mother there." He pointed to a large hollow in the aged oak tree where Kaylen had been tied. "This place looks different than it did back then, but I'd recognize that tree anywhere. Has a unique look to it, doesn't it? Enough to make me squirm."

Mellai stepped through the dry leaves and pine needles and stood next to the tree. She had to stretch on her tiptoes to see into the hollow, but it was too dark inside to see anything. She glanced back at her grandfather, who sat on a large boulder at the edge of the clearing, then turned and summoned True Sight to peer inside. The hole was shallow, but large enough to hide an infant. The floor of the hollow was filled with a nest of dry grass and sticks covered with white bird droppings.

"This hole has raised more babies than Mother," Mellai said. She removed the empty nest and tossed it aside as she resumed her search of the hollow, making sure to keep her eyes hidden from her grandfather. She could see nothing else in the hole besides pine needles filling the bottom, so she released True Sight and circled around the tree, kicking aside dry leaves and pine needles to look for clues about her mother's origin.

"I'm sorry," Dhargon said as Mellai moved around the rest of the clearing, "but I searched this whole area when I found your mother. I didn't find anything then, so what would change now?"

Mellai wandered around the area, pausing for a moment at the river rushing past the edge of the clearing. Her thoughts drifted back to Kaylen's kidnapping. She stared downriver, wondering where Braedr's body finally stopped before it was ravaged by wild animals. "I haven't heard from Kaylen in over two months. Do you think she's alright?"

"I'm sure she's fine," Dhargon reassured her as he sat on a boulder. "Have you written her lately?"

"No."

"Then she might be just as worried about you, which wouldn't be unfounded. I'm surprised you haven't written her yet. She's your best friend."

Mellai frowned. "She doesn't need to know what happened to me. She has enough to worry about already." Again, she thought of Jareth's news. *She killed the chamberlain?*

Dhargon didn't visibly falter, but he changed the subject. "Have you seen enough?"

Mellai turned away from the river and sat down next to her grandfather. "Not yet. I want to spend a couple days here. I need time to think, without distractions."

"Exactly why your grandmother packed so much food. She's a smart woman, you know." Dhargon glanced up through the colored leaves still clinging to the branches overhead. "Sunset is only an hour or two away. Would you like dinner?"

"Mm-hmm," Mellai responded absently. Her gaze was fixed on the hollowed oak.

* * * * *

Stars danced in and out of view as feathery clouds drifted across the night sky. Mellai stared up from her back and listened to the soft crackle of the dying fire. Her grandfather had fallen asleep hours earlier, but Mellai stayed on her bedroll, reluctant to abandon its warmth.

What will I learn, she thought to herself, *if I learn anything at all? I'm not so sure I want to know Mother's history. I like it as it is.*

These thoughts were only distractions from her true concern. After weeks of refusal, Llen had finally agreed to reveal her purpose as a Beholder, once Mellai successfully read the memories of the clearing. The thought frightened and overwhelmed her. Her fate would be intertwined with Lon's—there was no doubt about that—but what would their roles be? She hoped for a pleasant reunion, but such an idea was highly unlikely. They were both Beholders, but loyal to warring nations. How could their reunion possibly be pleasant?

Mellai closed her eyes and relaxed, searching for her brother's mind. She felt him quicker than normal, but it came as no surprise. After all, she was deep in the Vidarien Mountains and Lon was just north of her in Taeja. They were closer now than they had been since Lon left Pree ten months earlier—except for the last time Mellai ran away to the clearing. But she hadn't felt for him then. She had been too distraught by his betrayal.

Lon's mind was calm, but weary. He also surged with power, a feeling Mellai had gotten used to. She reached out to him, knowing it was pointless, but desperate to help her brother understand the errors of his decisions. She strained at the connection, but it was like trying to force a dream; the harder she tried, the more it slipped away, until his connection disappeared completely.

Mellai sighed and sat up, staring at the hollowed oak nearby. She eyed her grandfather. He was snoring soundly, so she stood and tiptoed through the dry leaves covering the ground, enjoying the feel of the soil between her toes. Wearing shoes didn't weaken her ability to use her power, but she felt more connected to the world without them. It wasn't until she was a foot away from the tree that she summoned True Sight. She searched the surrounding forest for danger. A few curious squirrels watched her from the branches above, but she found no other signs of life. She focused her attention on the oak in front of her. It looked the same as any other tree, a blanket of energy waving back and forth as if caught in a subtle breeze. It was calm and soothing, heedless of what happened around it.

This is ridiculous, Mellai thought as she extended her essence to connect with the tree's. *What memories can something like this hold?*

Mellai stroked the oak, soothing it with her essence while she searched for some source of knowledge or understanding. It was easy to perceive the thoughts and memories of animals because they came from the animal's brain, but the tree had nothing but fibers that pulled water up from its roots. She had no idea where to look for the memories.

At first, her attempts seemed a complete waste of time, yet the more she connected with the tree's essence, the more Mellai became familiar with its composition. Near the tips of its branches, the oak was young and vibrant, constantly striving for growth and survival. The few remaining leaves were lifeless and disconnected, but Mellai suspected they would feel like appendages of the branches during spring or summer.

The further in Mellai moved, the more the tree increased in complexity. In contrast to the small twigs, thicker branches seemed more conscious of their existence and the need for survival. By the time Mellai moved to the trunk, she could sense its density and awareness. It was the source from which everything else stemmed. Unlike an animal's brain, which protested the invasion of something foreign, the trunk welcomed the Beholder. Mellai enjoyed the response and moved further down the trunk.

Maybe the roots are its brain, Mellai thought as she reached the base of the trunk. *They feed it and keep it alive.*

Just as Mellai was about to leave the trunk, a faint consciousness drifted into her mind. She paused and focused on the new presence, which pulsed with a hint of amusement.

Is it laughing at me? Mellai thought.

Almost immediately, a thought entered the Beholder's mind. *Mouth brain.*

Mellai cocked her head to the side and redoubled her focus on the trunk. *I'm sorry?*

The swelling amusement returned. *Mouths feed.*

Finally Mellai understood. The oak was making fun of her for thinking the tree's roots were its brain. She smiled, in spite of the surreal interaction she was having with a tree. *What's your name?*

Tree.

No, I mean your identity.

Oak.

Mellai frowned. For a moment, she had believed the tree was intelligent. Obviously she was wrong.

Immediately, the welcoming atmosphere of the trunk changed to hostile rejection. Mellai's connection was severed. She didn't dare to force entry, fearing it would anger the tree further, so she moved to the branches.

I'm sorry, she emphasized. *I spoke ignorantly . . . or thought . . . or whatever.*

At first, the oak didn't respond, but eventually the moving laughter returned through the branches. *Child.* The comment wasn't an insult—just an honest observation.

Mellai nodded. *Very much so. Forgive me.*

Come.

Mellai returned from the branches to the trunk. She was welcomed as readily as before. *Thank you. I'm new at this.*

Child.

Mellai smiled, refreshed by the tree's pointed honesty. *Yes.*

The tree didn't respond. It seemed complacent to enjoy the presence of another entity without conversation. At first, the silence irritated Mellai. She furrowed her brow, wondering why the oak hadn't responded. Then her frustration changed to worry, knowing the tree could read her thoughts. She didn't want to offend it again.

After a while, once her anxieties had settled, Mellai learned to appreciate the quiet connection. It soothed her, like staring into a fire or listening to a gurgling brook. She lost herself in the calm, and her mind wandered back to her childhood in Roseiri. Life had been so simple then. Peaceful.

Mellai couldn't keep her thoughts from turning to her twin brother. His inability to control True Sight. His desperation. His choice to join the Rayders. A tear crept from Mellai's eye.

Pain.

The worst kind, Mellai replied as she wiped away the tear. *Betrayal.*

The tree pulled Mellai's essence into its midst, wrapping her in its soothing tendrils. Her mind drifted again, but to her first encounter with Llen. It had been in the same clearing.

Memory, the oak echoed.

Mellai sat at the foot of the tree. *Do you remember that day?*

Yes.

Mellai thought of her nearby grandfather, but didn't look at him for fear of breaking her connection with the tree. *Do you remember Grandfather?*

Yes.

Mellai filled with excitement. *Do you remember when he found my mother?*

Confusion radiated from the oak. *Mother?*

Yes, Mellai continued. *He found her as a baby in your hollow about thirty-seven years ago.*

The tree distanced itself. Mellai sat forward, thinking it was searching its memories, but the minutes continued to pass. She sat back and sighed when the oak never replied.

Did I offend you? Mellai asked.

No.

Mellai frowned, unsure of what to do. She desperately wanted to know what the tree was thinking—if it remembered her mother.

The oak's branches creaked. *Pain.*

Mellai leaned forward again. *So you do remember? May I see?*

Pain.

I have to know, Mellai urged.

After another long pause, the tree finally replied. *Search.*

Mellai's stomach nearly leaped out of her mouth. *Your memories?* she asked, just to make sure she understood correctly.

Yes.

Thank you, she emphasized, then took a deep breath and pressed into the consciousness of the tree. She saw herself sitting in front of the oak. Her eyes were clouded. *That's me,* Mellai thought and another tear fell from her eye. She felt the tear on her skin, but also saw it through the tree's memories.

While she tried to process this live feed of information she was receiving from the oak, Mellai became aware that the vision of the tree wasn't only in her direction, but in all directions. By connecting with the thoughts of the oak, Mellai was capable of seeing out from the tree—in all directions—all at the same time.

Strange, Mellai thought as she searched around the clearing. The oak's vision wasn't like normal eyesight, but it wasn't like seeing with True Sight either. It was more of a feeling than anything. The tree could sense what was happening around it and processed its senses into images. As Mellai stared at herself again, she was surprised at the accuracy of the oak's sensory vision. She looked exactly the same as she did in her grandparents' looking glass back in Roseiri, only lacking any color.

A deer entered the opposite side of the clearing, catching Mellai's attention. It paused to nose through the dry leaves for grass, then tensed and leaped away in a hurry.

"Mellai?"

She wrenched out of the oak's memories and shut her eyes. "What, Grandfather?"

Dhargon sat down behind his granddaughter and placed his hand on her shoulder. "Have you been up all night?"

Mellai opened her eyes, balanced her essence, then released True Sight. It was then that she realized the clearing was filled with sunlight. "I . . . I don't know, Grandfather." Her voice trembled.

"Let me make you some breakfast. That'll help you feel better. I just need to collect some firewood. I'll be right back."

Mellai watched her grandfather leave, then turned to the fire pit and noticed that the logs had burned to cool ash.

"All night?" Mellai said aloud. "How's that even possible?" She eyed the nearby tree and shook her head. *I've only been talking to the oak for an hour,* she thought. *No wonder Llen said this would take so long.*

Chapter 25

Memories

By the time Dhargon returned with the firewood, Mellai had curled up on her bedroll in a deep slumber. He let her sleep most of the day until he had prepared dinner.

"You have to stop staying up so late," Dhargon told her after she was up and eating. "We still need to make it back down the mountain, so you have to keep up your strength. Skipping meals isn't helping."

"It's not like I'm starving," Mellai countered as she chewed an oversized bite of salted pork, "or that I have responsibilities during daylight. I'll be just fine."

Dhargon raised an eyebrow at his granddaughter and shook his head. "Look at yourself. You're gnawing on that meat like it's the last scrap of food left in Appernysia. This isn't healthy."

Mellai slowed her chewing and swallowed. "I said I'm fine, Grandfather. I wish I could sleep at night, but it's not really my choice. I'm doing the best I can."

"Your grandmother packed a few herbs I could put in your tea to help you sleep."

Mellai shook her head. "It's not that simple."

Dhargon sighed. "It never is."

"What's that supposed to mean?"

"It means that I hardly recognize my granddaughter anymore," Dhargon said softly. "You've changed so much over the last two months. You won't tell me what you're doing in the middle of the night. What are you hiding?"

Mellai stood to leave, but Dhargon grabbed her arm. "Not this time. Stay here and talk to me. I've tried being nice, but it's only making things worse. No more secrets."

"That's easy for you to say," Mellai spat as she pulled her arm free, "now that you've finally come clean. What about the last thirty-seven years?"

"What about them?"

"Secrets weren't such a big deal to you then."

Dhargon frowned. "That isn't fair."

"Neither is this," Mellai said. "You can't just put your foot down and demand to hear what you wouldn't understand."

Dhargon's softened his voice. "Please, Mellai. Talk to me."

Mellai stepped back with pain in her eyes. He knew that look. She wanted to tell him, but for whatever reason, refused to confide in him.

"You wouldn't understand," Mellai repeated, her voice catching on the last word, then she turned and disappeared into the woods.

Dhargon stood to follow her into the dark forest, but changed his mind. If he chased after Mellai, she'd run, and they would both get lost in the woods without supplies. *She won't go far if I don't chase her,* he told himself. He stooped down to place three more logs on the fire, then went in search of more wood in the opposite direction.

* * * * *

Mellai hadn't gone far, just out of earshot from her grandfather, before she stopped and sobbed. She knew she could trust him, as much as her own parents, so why had Llen demanded her silenced tongue? It didn't make sense. So many things didn't make sense. She was tempted to call out for Llen, demanding that he explain himself, but she knew the act would be pointless. Llen was more resolute in his decisions than anyone she had ever met, probably even more so than a Rayder. There was nothing she could do except vent her irritation through hot tears.

It wasn't until Mellai had mastered her emotions and breathing that she returned to the clearing. She hid on the opposite side of the hollowed oak, watching her grandfather from the deepening shadows, wondering how she could find a way around Llen's restriction. Dhargon was sitting at the fire, poking it with a long stick, but his gaze kept shifting toward the woods where Mellai had disappeared. She agonized that he had to deal with her impudence, but what choice did she have? How could she show her love for him without defying the Jaed's warning?

As the minutes passed, Dhargon's face became more and more worn with concern. After an hour, he finally stood to follow after his granddaughter. It was then that Mellai finalized her solution. She stepped out from behind the tree, startling him.

Dhargon stopped midstride. "Are you purposefully trying to kill me with worry?"

Mellai crossed the clearing and wrapped her arms around her grandfather. "No."

Dhargon sighed and stroked Mellai's hair. "I love you, little girl, but I don't know how much more of this I can take. I'm getting too old."

"I know." Mellai hugged him tighter, fighting back another threatening wave of tears. "I'll answer your two questions, but please don't press me for more information."

"Fair enough."

"I heard about Mother through a friend. That's all I can say."

"Was it Kutad?" Dhargon asked.

Mellai looked up at him with a pained expression.

"I'm sorry. I said I wouldn't ask."

Mellai lowered her gaze. "To answer your other question, I've been acting weak during the day because I haven't been sleeping at night, but it wasn't a complete lie. I've been so exhausted that I really didn't feel like doing much. Sorry. I just didn't want you or Grandmother to worry."

Dhargon kissed his granddaughter on the crown of her head. "What worries us is when we don't know the truth. We're family, Mellai. You don't have to keep anything from us."

Mellai's remaining control ebbed away. She buried her face in Dhargon's chest and wept. *I wish that were true,* she thought bitterly. *You don't know how much.*

✳   ✳   ✳   ✳   ✳

After Dhargon had fallen asleep, Mellai sat in front of the hollowed oak again and summoned True Sight.

Sorrow, the tree responded through their connection.

Yes, Mellai answered in her mind. *More than I'd even wish on Braedr, if he were still alive.*

Braedr, the oak echoed. *Cruel.*

Exactly, but he's dead now.

Ghraef.

Mellai paused at the tree's mention of the historical creature. *Are you sure? They haven't been seen since the First Age.*

The oak's essence reassured Mellai. *Ghraef.*

Wow, Mellai exclaimed. *Not even Llen has told me that.*

As with the previous night, the tree grew passive again. Mellai enjoyed their bond for a while before posing another question. *Can I search again?*

Mother. Yes.

Mellai thanked the oak, then probed its consciousness. Once again, she immediately saw an image in her mind of the tree's complete surroundings. She shook her head at the strangeness, then pushed deeper into the oak's essence. She broke through what she could only describe as a layer of memory and was flooded with the oak's memories of its previous year. Amid the memories were images of Braedr leading Kaylen into the clearing. Mellai's lips tightened as Braedr tied her best friend to the tree and sat across the clearing. She could hear Kaylen's gasps and feel the tree's sorrow as Braedr nodded off. Then Mellai saw what Kaylen and Braedr couldn't. A beast appeared outside the clearing. Although its size was massive, the creature fluttered down from the sky with feathered wings and landed on its four enormous paws without a sound. Its dark hair was long and shaggy, and hung partially over its bright, intelligent eyes. As it crept forward, the beast swept its tail back and forth to hide its tracks. Mellai focused on the tail. Hair jutted between its layers of bone armor before it reached its tip—a heavy sphere of hairless bone.

Mellai was unable to comprehend the size of the ghraef until it stopped next to Braedr and the tree he was sitting against. Braedr was a tall broad-shouldered man, but even if he had been standing, the ghraef's head would have towered over him. Mellai saw Kaylen search around the clearing, then lock eyes with the ghraef. Although the image lacked color, Mellai imagined the beast with blue eyes—as Kaylen had described it. It looked back at Kaylen, then peeled back its lips and flashed a frightening row of sharp teeth. A low growl erupted from the ghraef's throat, then it swung its huge foreleg, knocking Braedr and the tree across the clearing. Kaylen screamed as Braedr flew through the air and broke through the ice-covered river. Before Braedr even hit the ice, however, the ghraef reared back on its hind legs and leaped into the air with a powerful flap of its wings. As it lifted off the ground, the ghraef swept its remaining tracks away with its tail before disappearing into the sky. Seconds later, Mellai saw Kutad burst into the clearing with herself and four other tradesmen.

Mellai pulled out of the oak's memories and smiled. She had just seen a ghraef. Not only that, but she had seen how it protected its identity. It was an unimaginably powerful and intelligent creature.

Ghraef, the oak said, still connected to Mellai.

Yes, Mellai breathed. *No wonder they've been able to keep their presence a secret for so long. They're smart.*

There was a brief pause, then the oak spoke to Mellai again. *Mother?*

Mellai nodded. *Give me a moment to process what I just saw.* She took slow breaths to calm her rushing enthusiasm. Amid the excitement was also a hint of sympathy for Braedr. The vision of his flying body replayed over and over in her mind. It wasn't until the third or fourth time she thought it through that Mellai realized a more subtle detail of the oak's memory. Although Braedr and the tree landed in the river, something else landed on the opposite bank. A hand. The ghraef had severed it from Braedr's arm with sharp claws.

Sad, Mellai thought, but ended her sympathies there. Braedr deserved to die.

Mellai focused and regained control of herself. *Alright, let's try this again.* She pushed into the tree's memories. For a third time, she saw herself sitting in front of the oak. She probed through the hidden layer separating the trees memories and witnessed the same memories that had just flooded her mind. She pushed even further and broke through into another section of memories. Animals came and went from the clearing, but nothing eventful happened. As Mellai eased into another layer of memories, she realized that every group of memories began at the start of spring and finished at the end of winter.

Are these seasons? Mellai asked.

Years, the oak responded.

Like the rings in your trunk, Mellai added.

Wise Beholder, the oak complimented.

Mellai bubbled with excitement. She finally understood how to sift through a tree's memories to find an exact moment in time. For every layer of memory she penetrated, that year's events filled her mind. Her only limitation was the age of the tree.

How old are you? Mellai asked.

Four hundred fifty-three, the oak answered, full of pride.

I didn't know trees lived that long. I bet you're full of important memories. I'd love to see them all, but my grandfather is in a hurry to get back home.

The oak expressed its understanding. *Search.*

Mellai glanced to the east, checking the sky for sunlight, but it was still dark. *I should have time,* she thought, then returned her gaze to the oak and pushed into its consciousness. Rather than wading through the memories, Mellai bounced through them like hopping between stones protruding out of a river. She counted carefully until she breached the thirty-sixth barrier, then she pulled back and allowed the memories of the next year to fill her mind.

A specific memory rose above the rest. Mellai didn't have to see the rest of the tree's memories to know it was one of the oak's most treasured experiences. A young couple entered the clearing. They were about Mellai's age. The man supported the woman, who was pregnant and in terrible pain. They finally stopped at the base of the oak, and the woman sat back against its trunk.

"I cannot go another step, Sévart. The baby is coming."

The man's face filled with worry as he glanced in the direction they had come from, then he sighed and turned back to the woman. "We will rest here."

The woman tried for hours, but couldn't birth her child. "Take it," she begged Sévart. "If one of us must die, let it be me."

Sévart recoiled. "I cannot hurt you. I love you, Geila."

"If you love me, then save our child." Geila pulled a dagger from her belt and held it out.

Tears filled Sévart's eyes, and his jaw quivered as he took the dagger.

Geila's face calmed. "Save our child," she spoke softly.

Sévart cried out in anguish and kissed Geila. "I am sorry." He cut open Geila's belly, pulled out the baby, and handed it to her. "It is a girl." The child wailed and wriggled with life, but calmed when she locked eyes with her mother.

"Hello," Geila whispered, then smiled up at Sévart. "She is beautiful."

Sévart nodded, but his expression hung with sadness. "You should try to feed her."

Geila began to comply, but a noise in the distance distracted her. She looked up at Sévart with horror. "Have they found us?"

The young man didn't answer. Instead, he tore a large section of cloth from Geila's dress and wrapped it around the newborn child. Then he cut a narrow leather strap from his belt, tied it around the birth cord close to his daughter's belly, and severed the cord. With one final kiss on her forehead, he gently laid her in the hollow of the oak tree.

"Be still," he whispered to his daughter, then removed a medallion from his neck and placed it in the hollow with her. Sévart then picked up the afterbirth, made an obvious trail to the river, and threw it into the water. Once complete, he returned to Geila's side.

"She will not survive if we are taken!" Geila cried. She tried to sit up, oblivious to her own pain. "I will not sacrifice my daughter to wild beasts!"

"She has a better chance there than she does with us." Sévart sobbed and kissed Geila fiercely, holding her down.

Just then, a man rushed into the clearing with a drawn sword. "Where is the child?" he shouted when he saw Geila's cut abdomen.

"I threw it in the river," Sévart answered.

The man surveyed the surrounding forest, then returned his attention to the young couple. "That will not save you," he replied, then shouted, "I found them. Bring a healer."

Soon the clearing was full of men. One tended to Geila until she was no longer bleeding, while the others took turns beating Sévart. Both Geila and Sévart glanced at the nearby tree many times, perhaps from concern over the newborn babe's silence. It hadn't made a sound since Sévart placed it in the oak's hollow.

When the healer finished binding Geila's wounds, the first man pointed to the young couple. "Put them on horses. We must return to the Exile. Our Commander will want to see them before they are executed."

Moments later, the clearing was empty and still.

Mellai was weeping openly by then, but didn't stop the memory. She wanted to see her mother's rescue. She had to.

What the young couple hadn't seen was that as soon as Sévart placed their child in the tree hollow, she fell asleep. Hours passed before the newborn baby began to stir. It squeaked at first, as it had in Geila's arms, but soon she found her voice and filled the forest with a piercing cry. A short time later, two men entered the clearing with bows and quivers slung across their backs. Even though Mellai knew who they were, it took her a moment before she recognized them. Her grandfather pulled the baby from the hollow, soothing it as he joined Gorlon in a lengthy search of the clearing. An hour or so later, they finally departed.

Mother, the oak said reverently.

Mellai released True Sight and fell to the forest floor. Tears flooded her face as she wept and clawed at the dirt. The memory had been too much to bear. Shalán's birth parents had sacrificed everything to keep her alive. *What had they done? Why were Rayders hunting them?* As she toiled over these questions, a part of the oak's memory stood out in her mind. Sévart had placed something in the hollow with the baby. A medallion.

Mellai stood and summoned True Sight again. She stood on her tiptoes and searched in the hollow, but it appeared as empty as it had two days earlier. Mellai stuck her hand in the hollow and felt around. Her fingers touched something cool and hard, hidden under the deep layer of pine needles. She grabbed it and pulled it free, then stared in shock at what she held. In her hand was a steel medallion of the King's Cross.

The young Beholder dropped to her knees. *Were the mother and father Rayders, too?*

Suddenly she had an idea. Mellai reconnected with the oak and hurried through the memories to the year Shalán was born. When Geila and Sévart entered the clearing, Mellai searched the young couple's faces. Both were branded with the King's Cross on their right temple.

How did I miss that? Mellai thought.

"We choose to see what we want," a deep voice resonated in response, "even in memories."

Mellai looked up. Llen was standing in front of her, his bright eyes soft with understanding. He placed his hand on the tree. "Thank you."

Jaed, the oak responded, then pulled within itself and closed off its connection to Mellai.

Why show me this now? Mellai asked in her mind as she sat up. *If you knew this whole time, why wait until now to tell me my mother's real parents were Rayders?*

"Know this, Mellai," Llen answered. "When the Beholders were murdered at the end of the First Age, a crucial truth died with them. Two characteristics are present in every Beholder's lineage—pure blood and pure hearts. To become a Beholder, a person must come from a pure line of Taejans. Only their unmixed blood carries the ability to harness True Sight."

And what did you mean by pure hearts?

"If a Beholder's heart becomes corrupt, their power will be silenced. The same must be said for their parents."

I don't understand, Mellai replied, full of fatigue.

Llen nodded. "Only a pureblood Taejan with a pure heart, with parents who also possess pure hearts, can be a Beholder."

Mellai pondered the statement before responding. *So both of my parents come from a line of pureblood Taejans?*

"Yes."

Mellai shook her head. *But it's been over a thousand years since the last Beholder was born. There has to have been Taejans with pure hearts since the First Age.*

Llen's eyes saddened. "Even before the Taejans were banished to the Exile, their hearts became corrupt. The Rayder society today is very different than the Taejan society that existed in the First Age. Your father realized this and fled. Your brother is experiencing it firsthand."

Mellai flinched at the Jaed's mention of Lon. Cautiously, she approached the subject again. *What is happening with my brother?*

"He is . . . struggling," Llen answered, then his eyes brightened with intensity. "I must go, but remember, Mellai. The qualities of a Beholder are a heavily guarded secret. If humanity discovers the truth, all chances of becoming a Beholder will be destroyed. People will become so obsessed with developing pure hearts that the very act will counteract their efforts. Now return home. I will come to you on your first night in Roseiri."

Llen disappeared as he finished speaking. Mellai released True Sight and sat still, having come to a confusing, yet potentially reassuring conclusion. Even though he sided with the Rayders, Mellai hoped her brother was still a Beholder. If he could channel True Sight, he would be pure of heart. He wouldn't be completely lost to their family. He could still be reasoned with.

With that encouraging thought, Mellai returned to her bedroll. Her grandfather was sitting up, watching her in the dim morning light.

"I don't know what you expect to learn, staying up all night staring at that tree," Dhargon said.

Mellai hid the King's Cross medallion in her fist and fell onto her bedroll. "I'm ready to go home, Grandfather. Just let me rest first."

Chapter 26

Terror

Mellai awoke in mid-afternoon and coaxed her grandfather to start down the mountain with her, but only after she ate a full meal. While Dhargon was busy packing, Mellai slipped the medallion's chain over her neck and hid the King's Cross under her dress. She would never tell her grandparents what she had discovered about Shalán's birth parents. They probably wouldn't care that their daughter was birthed by Rayders, but some things were better left unsaid.

By sunset, Dhargon and Mellai were many hours away from the clearing.

"I'm surprised you wanted to leave so soon," Dhargon said. "What changed your mind?"

"I saw enough," Mellai answered, "and now I have closure. Thank you for taking me, Grandfather. I needed it."

"Glad I could help."

They laid out their bedrolls under a thick cluster of birch trees, next to a spring of clean water. Mellai knelt at the deep pool and splashed the cold water on her face. It felt good to wash the mountain grime from her skin, and the chill of the water was refreshing. When she reopened her eyes, she noticed her grandfather watching her out of the corner of his eye.

"What is it?"

"Will you sleep tonight?" Dhargon asked carefully.

"Absolutely," Mellai answered with confidence. She relished in the thought. She hadn't slept through an entire night in more than a month, since she first started training with Llen. She laid down on her bedroll and closed her eyes. "Goodnight, Grandfather."

✳   ✳   ✳   ✳   ✳

Mellai jolted upright and searched the dark forest with True Sight. Her skin was covered in cold sweat, and the hair on her arms stood on end. Something had startled her out of sleep—something dangerous.

After checking on her grandfather, Mellai rose to her feet and placed her hand on a nearby tree. She reached out to its essence and slid into its memory to get a live view of the entire surrounding forest. It was deathly quiet.

Danger, the birch sounded in the Beholder's mind.

I know, she replied, searching the ground and surrounding trees, *but where?*

Branches.

Mellai shifted her focus from the tree's ground view to its vision of the forest canopy. A strange animal was moving toward them. It moved quickly, skirting through the high branches of the clustered trees.

Danger, the birch repeated, but with more emphasis. The creature was only a few trunks away.

Mellai stepped away from the tree and peered up at the approaching animal with her empowered sight. It was clearly visible through the bare branches of the neighboring tree. The creature was the size of a large wolf and covered in short fur. It held onto its perch with large padded feet. A row of short bone spikes protruded along its spine from its head to the base of its long tail.

What are you? Mellai wondered, her hands up defensively.

The creature hissed and flashed its teeth at her. A strange noise sounded in its vibrating chest, then it opened its jaws and spat a wad of red phlegm at her. Mellai stopped the phlegm midflight and dropped it to the ground. Everything it touched—leaves, pine cones, plants—sizzled and dissolved.

Poison, Mellai worried, then doubled her focus on the creature. *I dare you to try that again.*

The beast's chest vibrated, and it opened its jaws, but it didn't spit. It seemed to smile as it stared at her.

What are you waiting for? Mellai thought. *Come on.*

Another attack came—not from the animal in front of her, but from two additional creatures. They leaped out of the trees on each side of Mellai, hissing with their front paws outstretched and sharp claws aimed at her throat. Mellai jumped back to bring both creatures into her view, then redirected their path at each other. But their ambush had startled her and disturbed her concentration. Instead of smashing against each other as she had intended, they hurtled away in opposite directions and disappeared into the trees.

Mellai cursed in frustration as she tried to protect herself from three directions at once. In her error, she had neglected her greatest weakness. No matter which way she defended, her flank would always be unguarded from either ranged or melee attacks.

Unless I create a permanent shield for myself, Mellai thought, grateful for the revelation. She quickly scanned the surrounding forest for a solution, and her eyes rested on the pool of spring water. She captured it with her essence and formed it into a hollow dome, six inches thick and large enough to wrap around herself. She worked as fast as possible, chilling most of it into solid ice. As she stepped into the dome, she heard one of the beasts spit another wad of phlegm. She turned just in time to see it splatter the ground where she had been standing, then she closed and froze the dome's opening.

With the protection of her clear shield, Mellai pivoted about in search of danger, always keeping an eye on the creature in the branches. It seemed content to watch from its perch. Eternities seem to pass, but with no attack. *Where are they?* she thought, then cursed again when she noticed her grandfather's unprotected body, still sleeping peacefully on his bedroll. Why hadn't she thought of him? Was she really that self-absorbed?

Before she could craft another dome of ice for her grandfather, another attack came, directed at him from the tree branches high above. At the same time, the third creature sprung at her dome from the back. She could hear it clawing at the ice barrier, tearing clouds of snow with its sharp and speedy claws, but she wouldn't make the same mistake again. Clever tactic, making her choose between her own safety and her grandfather's, but she would not be deterred. Her own barrier would hold. It had to.

Not wanting to risk another mistake by some extreme show of force, Mellai reached into the falling beast's essence with her own and snapped its spine before it touched her grandfather. It silently fell limp, but stayed suspended by Mellai's control. She hurled the dead creature at the alpha in the trees, then turned on her own attacker. Just in time, too. It had torn a hole large enough for its snout and was regurgitating its own poison.

Abandoning her power for a moment, Mellai reached forward and forced the beast's jaws closed with her bare hands. Its eyes widened in protest and it jerked its head back to escape her grip. It lost its hold on the ice in the process, but surprised Mellai by springing backward, twisting in the air, and landing spryly on its padded paws.

"What's wrong with you?" Mellai shouted, her frustration growing, her voice strange and muffled in the ice dome. What kind of animal looked like a dog, but moved like a cat? And spits poison? It didn't even matter. It needed to die. Mellai used her power to shatter her dome and stab the prowling creature with twenty shards of ice. A tiny yelp was all that escaped its lips as it fell dead.

The creature in the trees spat a third wad of poison. Mellai barely managed to stop it, then hurled it back at the beast. It splattered around the beast's head, burning its eyes and flesh. The creature yelped madly and fell from the top of the tree, skewering itself on a small pine sapling.

Chilling cries filled the clearing, finally penetrating Dhargon's aging ears and startling him out of sleep. He jumped up from his bedroll and stared at the outline of the thrashing creature. "Maggots and plague! What is that thing?"

Under the cover of darkness, Mellai melted the remaining ice dome and hurled the two other dead beasts away—over the tops of the trees. "I don't know, Grandfather. It just fell out of the branches." The lie felt pathetic and forced, but it seemed to satisfy her distracted grandfather.

Dhargon moved closer to the creature. "It's the ugliest thing I've ever seen." Most of the flesh on the creature's face was gone, and one of its half-dissolved eyes had fallen out of its socket, whipping around by a thin strand of flesh connected to its thrashing skull. Knowing the darkness hid her eyes from her grandfather, Mellai reached for the creature's consciousness, anxious to know its mind. A solid barrier blocked her, thwarting all attempts to read its memories. The barrier unnerved Mellai. Only entities of high intelligence were supposed to be able to do such a thing, and only with focused concentration. How was it possible that this tortured beast could maintain its barrier, even on the edge of death?

Dhargon picked up a thick branch. "It shouldn't have to suffer. Turn your head."

Mellai rolled her eyes and looked the other direction, releasing True Sight while her grandfather swung the branch at the critter, finished off what she had started. Dhargon stood over the dead animal for a moment, then returned to his bedroll.

"I know you're tired," he said as he rolled up the pad, "but can you muster the strength to walk?"

Mellai nodded. "I've been up every night. This won't be any different for me."

She helped pack their supplies, then they hurried down the mountain as quickly as Dhargon could move. Mellai was just as anxious to leave as her grandfather, but for a different reason. Even without sifting through the creature's thoughts, Mellai knew the attack had been carefully executed. Those creatures weren't just wild animals looking for a meal. They had hunted her.

"I need a rest," Mellai said after traveling a mile or so. She moved by a birch tree and sent her essence into it, making sure to hide her eyes from her grandfather.

Danger? she asked the tree.

Safe, it replied.

Mellai closed her eyes and leaned her forehead against the trunk. "Thank you," she whispered.

"If you need to stop for the night," Dhargon replied, "I can stay up and keep an eye out for danger."

"No," Mellai said, amused with her grandfather's ignorance. "Let's keep moving."

At sunrise, Dhargon and Mellai finally escaped the mountains. Dhargon again suggested that they stop, but Mellai insisted they continue. It wasn't until they were five miles farther south that she finally consented. They dropped to the ground and fell asleep on the grass without bothering to unbundle their bedrolls.

✳   ✳   ✳   ✳   ✳

Mellai was the first to wake. She sat up and stretched, glad to be free of the congested mountains. She eyed the sun disappearing behind the western peaks, then stood and wandered around their impromptu campsite, gathering scattered logs and twigs, then piled them together and ignited them with her power. She watched the fire for a few minutes, then dug through her grandfather's pack and removed the tinderbox, a skillet, and their remaining supply of salted pork.

Dhargon stirred, then sat next to his granddaughter. Mellai fiddled with the tinderbox, ensuring that it looked like she had started the fire with it.

"Did you sleep long?" Dhargon said.

"Yes," Mellai answered. "We'll be back in Roseiri by morning, so I'm cooking the rest of our food. I'm sick of cold meat."

Dhargon nodded his assent. "I look forward to my soft bed again, and I miss your grandmother."

"Me, too." Mellai stared at her open palms, eyeing the scar left behind from her mishap with the exploding rock. "What do you think those creatures were last night?"

"*Those* creatures?" Dhargon asked. "I only saw one."

"As did I," Mellai quickly replied. "I just assumed there were more. After all, that's why we left."

"I don't know what it was," Dhargon said with a shrug, "but there must be hundreds of different kinds of animals hidden in the mountains. People rarely venture there, and I'm not surprised we haven't heard of that species. Don't worry, though. You're safe now."

Mellai's mind filled with doubt. At the forefront was her unconscious response to the attack. Dhargon was right. The woods had to be full of dangerous creatures, but of three journeys to the mountain clearing, it was the only time she had awoken in a panic. Deep in her heart, she knew those creatures had singled her out specifically. They had even tried to trick her, like they knew she was dangerous.

Mellai flipped the salted pork one more time on the skillet, then jabbed a fork into it and handed it to Dhargon. "Pork on a fork."

Dhargon took the meat and winked. "Perfect."

Chapter 27

Unveiled

Allegna woke with a start. Someone was rattling the locked door. She slipped out of bed and crept through the dark house, retrieving a large knife from the kitchen before moving into the sitting room. She stepped to the side of the covered window, pulled back the shutter ever so slightly, and peered outside. Two dark figures stood outside the door. Their outlines were unmistakable. Allegna dropped the knife, rushed to the door, unlocked it, and flung it open.

"You're back." She leaped into her husband's arms and pulled Mellai into the embrace. "You don't know how much I've missed you."

"We've missed you, too," Dhargon responded with a quick kiss, then moved everyone inside and shut the door. "Had any trouble?"

"Not really, apart from Theiss's constant pestering. Why?"

"You never lock the door," Dhargon replied.

"You left me alone in this house for five days," Allegna countered, "although I should be getting used to this sort of thing by now. No more journeys."

"Agreed," Dhargon said. "Right, Mellai?"

Mellai frowned. "I'll be right back."

* * * * *

As Mellai stepped outside and closed the door, Allegna's voice poured through it. "Don't go waking Theiss in the middle of the night. Gorlon will have your head."

Mellai glanced down the road toward Theiss's house, then summoned True Sight and sprinted north of the village. She stopped after a half-mile and paced in a wide circle around a mature oak.

Llen appeared in the center of Mellai's circular path. "You look troubled, Beholder."

"I'm not sure if I want to know my purpose," Mellai replied aloud, but she already had her suspicions. In what other position would a Beholder be placed than a position of power? It only made sense, along with her destination. She wouldn't be joining the Rayders. She'd give up her gift before she agreed to that. No, she'd be joining the Appernysian army, which was exactly what she dreaded the most.

"Life without purpose is not a life worth living. Everyone has a role, some with greater weight than others. As a Beholder, you cannot hide from your fate."

"I know," Mellai grumbled. "You just asked me how I was doing, so I told you."

"I did not ask," the Jaed countered. "I observed."

Mellai blew out her breath and sat on the grass in front of Llen. "Just tell me what I'm supposed to do."

Llen's eyes brightened with intensity. "War is coming. Appernysia is divided and unprepared. You must travel to Itorea and unite the king with his council, then lead his army in the approaching conflict. This is your purpose, Beholder. Without you, Appernysia will fall."

Mellai felt as though someone had kicked her in the stomach. All of her fears and suspicions were suddenly confirmed and wrapped into an overwhelming burden. "I can't fight against my brother. I can't do it."

"I have said nothing about your brother."

"No," Mellai scoffed, "but are you saying that he won't fight with the Rayders?"

"Beholders do not flee and leave their people stranded," Llen replied, "no matter the opponent. Protect Appernysia. That is your primary focus."

Mellai ground her teeth and shook her head. "Why are you avoiding the question? Why are your answers always so guarded?"

The Jaed's eyes flashed with anger. "You would drown under the depth of my knowledge and experience."

Mellai slumped and hung her head. Her brown curls pooled over the sides of her face. "You have to know what this means to me," she said, her voice thick with desperation. "The thought of fighting against Lon . . . it's like throwing myself in front of an executioner's blade. I can't . . . Even if I survive, I know I'm going to come away with a part of myself missing. I'll never be the same again."

"I do understand, Mellai, which is why you were chosen for this task. Your survival is dependent upon your ability to adapt and improvise. For you, change is essential." Llen's eyes brightened as he reached out to touch the trunk of the nearby tree. He continued with a powerful calm that commanded Mellai's attention. "Even the mightiest oak must adapt with the seasons."

A long sigh escaped Mellai's lips, knowing any further argument with the Jaed to be futile. She fought her anxieties, plucking a blade of grass from the ground and slowly tearing it with her fingers. "May I ask you one more question?"

"Yes."

"I could've used your help last night when those creatures attacked me and Grandfather. You're a master of True Sight. Why didn't you help?"

"It is not a Jaed's place to intervene in the physical affairs of Appernysia. Our responsibility is to prepare other Beholders for that which is to come. You must never expect my help or protection in a fight, because you will not receive it."

"I was afraid of that."

"Do not allow fear to distort your perspective, Mellai. You are a very powerful Beholder. You did not need my help last night."

Mellai tossed the shredded mass of green aside and grabbed three more blades of grass, braiding them methodically. "When do I need to leave?"

"Tomorrow. I have one more lesson to teach you, and then you must go."

Mellai nodded, too afraid to speak. She feared this would be a final farewell. Her grandparents, Theiss, the whole village—she might never see them again.

"You now understand the importance of patience and control when probing the minds of other living things," Llen continued. "You are ready to enter the thoughts of human beings, but do not forget these two important lessons. Human minds are more dense and complex than any other being. If you attempt to read them quickly or linger too long, you will be the one who suffers."

Mellai furrowed her brow at the Jaed. "Suffer how?"

"You will lose yourself in their consciousness and remain there until you die of thirst or starvation."

Mellai nodded. "Go slow, but not too slow. Lesson two?"

Llen's eyes narrowed. "Do not attempt to control the mind of another living thing. You cannot alter their perspective, change their memories, or control their actions. You will be tempted to try, but do not. The result will be as devastating as pulling too much energy into yourself."

Mellai nodded, remembering the adverse effects of True Sight upon her brother. "It would destroy me."

"Well said," the Jaed confirmed. "Now return home and rest, Beholder. In the morning, you must leave for Itorea and seek out your friend, Kaylen. Once you find her, the rest of your path will unfold itself before you."

Mellai tossed the braided grass aside, then stood and turned to leave.

"One more thing," Llen said as he hovered in front of Mellai. "Your departure comes with good news. The time for secrecy has passed. Reveal your gift, Beholder, but only to your family and betrothed. The rest of Appernysia must wait until you reach Itorea."

Despite her burden, Mellai's heart leaped with excitement. After years of deceit, ever since fleeing from Roseiri with her family, she would finally be able to tell the truth. The *entire* truth. It was such a relief, but she couldn't help but wonder why Llen had forbidden her to say anything in the first place. "But why now? What was the danger before?"

"Your departure will fall harder upon them than it has upon you. They may try to keep you from going. Had this happened while you were burdened with the frustrations of learning True Sight, you could have been swayed."

"Who's to say I won't be swayed now?" Mellai asked.

Llen's voice lowered. "Search their minds, Beholder," he spoke with emphasis. "A person's thoughts often contradict their words."

She pondered his counsel. "Will they go with me?"

"Your grandparents will not leave Roseiri. You know this."

Mellai frowned. "What about Theiss?"

Llen's eyes softened. "Herein lies your first test. Do not attempt to alter his thoughts." When he finished speaking, the Jaed disappeared.

Mellai trudged toward Roseiri, but rather than entering her grandparents' house, she continued down the street and across the north bridge. To her left was the empty clearing where the trades-men had stopped just a week earlier. Mellai wandered across the field, lost in her thoughts. She knew what awaited her in Itorea, and she hated to abandon Roseiri and Pree. So many memories were caught up in those two villages.

Mellai paused under the large oak tree where she and Lon had played together as children. She thought back on the events of the last time they'd played there—the terrible windstorm, their sudden departure. Her mother had mentioned that a bale of hay was obliterated by an invisible dome over the twins. Mellai now understood that it was most likely a pocket of air that protected them—both of them. Her eyes widened with new understanding. Ever since that day, their parents had believed it was Lon that had created the protective barrier over them, but that would have been impossible. Beholders can only wield what they can see. The barrier had been created by both of them, unknowingly working together while competing against each other.

All this time, I've been a Beholder, too, Mellai thought. *But why has my power been silenced until now?* She reflected back on the previous six years. Her mind and heart had brimmed with hatred toward her parents for tearing her away from Roseiri. *Of course,* she thought. *My heart was anything but pure in Pree. I'm far from perfect, but at least I'm finally thinking of other people besides myself.*

Her mind shifted to her purpose and the irony behind it. After nearly six years, she'd have to face her brother in another silly contest—only this one would cost lives, and the twins wouldn't be working together. They'd be doing everything possible to conquer each other.

✳   ✳   ✳   ✳   ✳

Mellai opened her eyes and smiled, still half-asleep. Theiss was sitting next to her, stroking her hair.

"Hi," he said, then leaned forward and kissed her on the forehead. "Sorry to wake you, but your grandparents said I should. Aside from that, they won't talk to me. Where have you been all week?"

Mellai shut her eyes and reality rushed back into her mind. "What time is it?" she asked as she stretched her arms above her head.

"Midday," Theiss replied. "It's past lunch, but Allegna saved some for you."

"I'm sure she did." Mellai sat up on the sofa and looked around. Her grandparents were sitting at the table, quietly sipping tea together.

They both smiled at their granddaughter, but their demeanors were crestfallen.

Allegna stood and brought Mellai a tray with jam, bread, cheese, and cold chicken. "You should eat," she said as she placed the tray on Mellai's lap, then returned to the table.

"What's going on with you two?" Mellai asked. Allegna and Dhargon didn't respond, so she raised her eyebrows at Theiss.

"I told you they won't talk to me," he responded.

Mellai handed the tray of food to Theiss, then turned and folded her arms over the back of the sofa and looked at her grandparents. "What is it?"

"Nothing we need to discuss right now," Dhargon said. "Eat."

Mellai frowned and breathed slowly through her nose, trying to control her emotions. "You know, don't you?"

Tears filled Allegna's eyes. "I'm not sure what we know," she said with a shaky voice.

Dhargon reached across the table and placed his hand over his wife's, then looked at Mellai. "You talked in your sleep this morning, Mellai. A lot of it didn't make sense to us, but a few words stood out because you kept repeating them."

"What words?" Theiss asked.

"True Sight, Beholder, and a lot of Llens," Dhargon replied. "She also mentioned Itorea a few times, along with war."

Allegna sniffed. "Do I want to know what you were dreaming?"

Mellai's gaze shifted to the floor. *Llen said to tell them,* she thought as she continued to breathe slowly. She summoned True Sight, then lifted her eyes. Both grandparents jerked back when they saw her clouded brown eyes. Allegna gasped and Dhargon shifted uneasily in his chair.

"How long?" Dhargon asked, failing in his attempt to keep himself calm.

"Over two months," Mellai answered, "since the night I almost died." She felt Theiss's hand slip over her shoulder.

"What's going on?" he asked.

She turned and looked at her betrothed. At the sight of her eyes, Theiss pulled his hand away and flailed back. His chin squished into his neck as he tried to retreat further into his chair. "What's wrong with your eyes?"

Mellai tried to reach forward to reassure him, but Theiss kept his distance. "I never told you what happened when Lon used his powers," Mellai finally answered. "Now you know."

"That's True Sight?"

Mellai nodded and released her power. "It's the only way to identify us."

"Us . . ." Theiss repeated. His body relaxed slightly as Mellai's eyes returned to their normal color. "You're a Beholder?"

Mellai nodded again. "The first female Beholder."

Theiss' expression changed. Wary. Suspicious. "What does this mean?"

"I have to go to Itorea."

"When?"

"Today. Now."

Theiss didn't respond. He sat motionless on his chair, his face torn with emotion. Mellai's grandparents stood. Dhargon left the room while Allegna sat on the sofa beside her granddaughter.

When Allegna took Mellai's hand, she could fill her grandmother trembling. "It nearly killed Lon."

"But he didn't know how to control it," Mellai answered. "I do."

"How?" Allegna asked.

"A Jaed has been teaching me every night for over a month. That's why I've been sneaking out."

"Sneaking out?" Theiss said. "Jaed?"

"Yes." Mellai stared at him. "Do you believe me?"

"What do you want me to say?" Theiss replied. "I just learned that you've been sneaking out at night—which explains why you sleep half the day away—then you leave on a secret journey for a week without telling me. Now you suddenly have to move to Itorea. I've trusted you, Mellai, but I can't remain a fool."

Allegna let go of Mellai's hand and started to rise from the sofa. "If you're suggesting that my granddaughter has been unfaithful, Thiess, I'll—"

"Calm down, Grandmother," Mellai interrupted. "If I were him, I would've stormed out already and thrown rocks through the window."

Allegna relaxed, but kept her eyes locked on Theiss. He squirmed under her piercing stare.

"I'll prove it to you, Thiess." She summoned True Sight, then created a fist-sized ball of fire above her right hand.

"Slap me with a mutton chop," Dhargon shouted from behind, followed by a loud metal clang.

Mellai released the fire and whipped around, instinctively expecting some sort of attack, but her reaction was unnecessary. Only Dhargon stood behind her, with two full travel packs in one hand.

He gaped at his granddaughter as he retrieved a skillet from the floor. "How'd you do that?"

"It's complicated," Mellai answered.

Dhargon crossed the room to sit on the sofa's arm next to Mellai. "What else can you do?" His eyes shined like a little boy on his birthday.

Despite the tension in the room, Mellai smiled and released True Sight. "Plenty."

"Did you do this?" Dhargon continued as he pulled a half-sphere of shining iron from one of the packs.

Mellai's smile disappeared. "So you were digging through my stuff?"

"Don't let him ruffle your feathers," Allegna interceded. "Dhargon figured you'd be going to Itorea—from your dream-talking this morning—so he packed a couple bags, just in case."

"Thank you, Grandfather, but I only need one pack."

Dhargon returned the iron to one of the bags and set them on the floor. "The other one's for me. I'm taking you there."

Mellai glanced at Theiss, half-expecting him to join in the offer, but her betrothed said nothing. He just sat quietly with a bleak face.

"No one's asking me," Allegna said, "but I'm going to say it anyway. You can't leave, Mellai, and neither can Dhargon or Theiss, for that matter. You've already taken two weeks off and it's past harvest time again. I'm not going through another miserable winter like last year. I want my food picked and stored, and I want it done now. Why do you have to leave anyway? What's in Itorea?" By the time she finished speaking, Allegna's face was flushed bright red.

"I'll be alright," Mellai said as she reached out to take her grand-mother's hand.

Allegna pulled back her arm. "I'm not giving in. It's all fine and dandy that you're a Beholder, but you can't leave. I won't allow it. Not this time."

Mellai sighed. "I want to show you another trick, Grandfather." She summoned True Sight, pulled the remaining tea from their cups on the table, then moved it in front of herself in a swirling sphere.

"Serve me a platter of bacon," Dhargon exclaimed. "Look at that."

While Mellai held their attention with the tea, she took the opportunity to search everyone's minds, starting with Dhargon. She extended her essence to his and gently probed at the edges of his consciousness. His mind was easy to enter, unguarded in his excitement and anticipation. He knew why Mellai had to go to Itorea. He expected Lon and Mellai to oppose each other in battle. Although he worried over the safety of his grandchildren, he thought it a necessary sacrifice for the good of Appernysia. Lon and the rest of the Rayders needed to be stopped and driven back to the Exile. One of his grandchildren had been led astray, but he refused to focus on that. Mellai would fix everything.

Mellai moved to her grandmother. Allegna's mind was more guarded than her husband's, but Mellai was still able to read it. At the forefront of Allegna's consciousness was a sense of overwhelming love and loss. Allegna was burdened by the absence of her family and her lack of control over what might befall them. Mellai's imminent journey to Itorea and the forecasted battle with Lon pushed her to the very edge of sanity. Even the death of her own husband wouldn't hurt her as much. Yet, as Mellai probed further, she found an underlying foundation of pride over having two Beholders as her grandchildren. Lon wasn't wrong, and Mellai wasn't right. Allegna believed they were both doing what they thought was best, and that was good enough for her. She would support and love them no matter what, even if it drove her to her grave.

After removing herself from Allegna's mind, Mellai looked at Theiss—and he looked right back at her. She didn't need to read his mind to know that he didn't care about the floating ball of tea. His lips were pulled tight, and his brow was furrowed. When Mellai connected with his essence, she found a hard barrier protecting his thoughts. Every angle of entrance into his mind was closed.

Mellai smiled warmly at him. "I love you, Theiss."

It was just enough. Theiss's face softened, as did the barrier guarding his mind. She slipped inside, and although his defenses quickly returned, he couldn't stop her from sorting through his feelings. Mellai flinched at the hatred radiating from her betrothed. He wouldn't go with her to Itorea. His responsibility to his family and need to please his father was too great. Because of that, Theiss hated Mellai for abandoning him. Shadows of his love for her were still present, but rapidly disappearing. Mellai watched with horror as they were squashed one by one, like annoying bugs that deserved to die.

Please, Theiss, Mellai plead with his consciousness, but he didn't respond. *Please!* Mellai grabbed for the few remaining memories of love.

Llen appeared beside him, his eyes blazing. "Stop, Beholder. I warned you of this."

I can't, Mellai answered back.

"You cannot prevent this. If you keep trying, you will obliterate yourself with the rest of this village."

Mellai sobbed and closed her eyes. She felt the tea splash onto her lap, but she didn't care.

"What is it?" Allegna asked. "Are you hurt?"

Mellai only shook her head until she heard Theiss's chair shift. Mellai released True Sight and looked up at him in agony.

"Stay here with me," Theiss said, standing near their front door. It was neither a fervent request nor an angry demand. It was only a statement, void of emotion.

"I want to so badly, but I can't," Mellai cried. She stood and rushed to him, clinging to the front of his tunic. "Please don't do this."

"I haven't done *anything*," he growled. He pushed her hands away, then spun around and stormed out of the house.

Dhargon and Allegna wrapped their arms around Mellai and held her. She rocked back and forth, racked with torment, haunted by the look on her betrothed's face. No, not her betrothed. Even if she stayed, he would never agree to marry her, nor would she want him to. He didn't love her anymore. He never would again.

Chapter 28

Réxura

Four days later and a hundred miles east of Roseiri, Dhargon and Mellai entered the large trade city, Réxura. As their donkey-drawn wagon crossed the granite bridge arching over the wide Pearl River, she made her grandfather stop so she could absorb her surroundings.

"Quite a sight, isn't it?" Dhargon said.

Mellai shook her head with wide eyes and pulled her cloak tighter around herself. The temperature had dropped overnight, bringing with it a warning of snow. "I've never seen so many people clustered together."

Men buzzed around rows of docks along the banks of the river, unloading crates from long barges and placing them in horse-drawn wagons. When each wagon was filled, an escort of armored soldiers wearing dark green cloaks accompanied it into Réxura.

"What's in the crates?" Mellai asked as she looked down from the stone bridge.

"Mostly iron, but judging by the horses and soldiers, this shipment probably contains some gold and silver. Maybe even diamonds. If I'm right, they'll transfer this shipment to other barges in the Prime River, which will carry the crates another one hundred thirty miles to Itorea."

Mellai watched more barges being pulled upriver by horses walking along the west riverbank. "Where are they hauling it from?"

"Draege," Dhargon answered. When Mellai gave him a confused look, Dhargon continued. "It's a mining city in the Kerod Cluster, a range of mountains two hundred miles south of here. That's a long distance to haul supplies, but it's worth the extra effort. Those mountains are brimming with resources."

Mellai returned her attention to Réxura and watched the lead wagon enter the city and disappear behind clusters of tall buildings and houses. "How can people stand living so close to each other? They couldn't even walk out their front door without bumping into someone."

"Some people, like Kaylen, prefer city life to quiet villages. I'm looking forward to meeting her, you know? I only had a brief glance at her before the tradesmen carted her out of Roseiri, but she seemed like a nice girl. No wonder Lon fell for her."

"She's gorgeous," Mellai replied, directing the conversation away from Lon, "which can get annoying."

Dhargon placed his hand on Mellai's shoulder. "Itorea is even busier than Réxura. If you plan on staying there with her, you better get used to congested places like this."

Mellai's stomach lurched, but she kept her reservations to herself, masking them with a simple nod. "I just can't understand what people do in places like this. In Pree and Roseiri, every person pulls their own weight to help the village survive. That can't be the case here. Are there lots of beggars?"

"Some," Dhargon replied, "but that's typical of any city." He watched his granddaughter for a moment before continuing. "It's amusing to see you react this way, Mellai, after all you've been through."

"Quiet, Grandfather," Mellai whispered. "Llen said to keep it secret until I find Kaylen."

"But that's not until we reach Itorea," Dhargon complained. "What about Kutad? He took you and Kaylen in, kept your secrets, and saved your lives. He's like family."

Mellai smiled. "Just dying to tell someone, aren't you?"

Dhargon didn't speak, but his expression told it all. His eyes were wide with anticipation, and his right eyebrow twitched sporadically as he searched around for familiar faces. Mellai reached up and smoothed out his mess of wiry gray hairs.

"Kutad won't be here, remember? He left the caravan to answer King Drogan's summons."

"But maybe he came back," Dhargon replied, his shoulders slumped with discouragement. He flicked the reins, and their donkeys pulled the wagon forward.

"About time," a man yelled from behind. "Some of us have a schedule to keep around here."

Mellai turned around and realized that five other wagons were behind them, unable to cross the narrow bridge until Dhargon moved out of the way.

"Ooooo," the same man continued as his wagon moved onto the bridge. "You're a pretty little thing."

Mellai's eyes narrowed to tiny slits. She summoned True Sight and shattered the wheels on one side of his wagon. The man toppled sideways into the deep river as his wagon bed crashed down. He hit the water with a loud splash. Moments later, his head popped up with a gasp, and he stared at Mellai with bulging eyes.

"Oh, come on!" another man shouted from further behind.

Mellai snickered and turned back around.

"You call that keeping it secret?" Dhargon commented.

"He deserved it."

Dhargon chuckled. "That he did. Now, how about a tour of the city?"

Réxura stood at the very tip of the Vidarien Mountains. The last, solitary peak loomed over the city's western edge, blocking out the late afternoon sun as Dhargon and Mellai moved into the city. For being so close to the mountains, Mellai was surprised to find Réxura practically undefended. It seemed thrown together without any planning beforehand. The dirt roadways weaved around each other like worms wrestling in the mud. Many buildings looked so unstable that a simple gust of wind might knock them over. There wasn't even a perimeter wall protecting the city.

"Despite the population, there's not much to defend here," Dhargon responded when Mellai asked him about it. "Nothing worth keeping stays long in Réxura. Actually, the more valuable the shipment, the faster it moves through the city. Those crates will be on barges headed for Itorea before nightfall."

"That doesn't make any sense," Mellai countered. "Maybe nothing valuable stays in the city, but the city itself is valuable. Whoever controls Réxura controls the shipments from Draege and Jaul. The Rayders are straight north of here. If they decide to take this city, it would cripple Itorea's supply chain."

Dhargon eyed his granddaughter. "Since when did you learn to think so tactically?"

Mellai slouched on the bench, exhausted by her ever-changing life. "I don't know."

"Don't be ashamed of it," Dhargon continued. "If anything, be grateful for your ability to see things so clearly. King Drogan could use a person like you at his side."

"Not everyone who needs help accepts it," Mellai argued.

"You're right, but I guarantee our king will welcome a Beholder."

Nothing more was said between the two as they continued their search for the trading caravan, but Mellai had to agree with her grandfather; King Drogan would do anything for the allegiance of a Beholder because it would allow him to overpower Lon and the Rayders.

They found the tradesmen camp at the north end of the city, near the north bridge over the Prime River. Despite Dhargon's pestering questions, no one seemed to know where Kutad was. They didn't even seem to know about the messenger that had visited their camp in Roseiri. A man named Rypla, one of the tradesmen who had helped save Kaylen, had taken over as head of the caravan.

"How are you, Mellai?" Rypla greeted. "I was told you weren't feeling well while we were in Roseiri, so I'm glad to see you're on your feet again. What brings you both here so late in the season?"

Dhargon answered for his granddaughter. "Mellai has been trapped in our house for so long that she had to stretch her legs. You know how she is. Once she decides to do something . . ."

Rypla laughed. "She's one of the most independently minded women I've ever met, but some of my younger men admire that about her."

Mellai smiled. "Thank you, Rypla, but I'm not here to find a husband. I already have Theiss." The words stung as she spoke them.

Dhargon reached over and placed his arm around his granddaughter. "They are engaged to be married in the spring." He gave her an encouraging squeeze.

"Congratulations," Rypla boomed. "We'll have to make a special journey in the spring to . . . Roseiri or Pree?"

"We haven't decided," Dhargon answered. "Her parents don't know yet, so please keep the good news to yourself."

"Of course."

"We need to get going," Dhargon continued. "Tell Kutad we came to visit if you hear from him." He then turned their wagon away from the tradesmen camp.

Mellai examined Réxura in the failing light. The mountains loomed dangerously close to the city. "Head toward Itorea, Grandfather. I'd rather be on the road than stuck here overnight."

Chapter 29

History

I t took another five days for Mellai and Dhargon to reach
Itorea. Instead of the snow that everyone knew should be
coming, the weather actually warmed as they travelled. Mellai
barely noticed the change in climate, nor did she acknowledge
the enormity of the Furwen Trees within the Perbeisea Forest.
When they reached Sylbie, she ignored how its size dwarfed
the population of Réxura. She missed Theiss. After their conversation with Rypla, her mood had continually deteriorated
as they neared Itorea. Talking to Kaylen would be the worst.
She'd want to hear every detail of their courtship—and breakup.

"Stop pouting and look at this," Dhargon gasped.

Mellai glanced up and realized they were on a stone bridge crossing over a half-mile of river. To the east was a wall three hundred
feet high constructed of white stone and embedded with colossal
crystals. Their colors sparkled as the afternoon sun poured down
from behind her.

"It doesn't matter how many times you see it," Dhargon droned.

Even in her foul mood, Mellai couldn't stop herself from reeling
at the sight of Itorea's perimeter wall. She gaped at the colored crystals. Even without Llen's descriptions, she would have known they
were made by Beholders. But she couldn't figure out how. *Someday,
I'll have to get a closer look,* she thought.

At the entrance into the city, Mellai and Dhargon were stopped by Appernysian soldiers who checked their temples before allowing them into the city.

"Happy eighteenth birthday," Dhargon said as they were crossing through the fifty-foot thick wall. He pulled a small parchment package out of his pocket and handed it to Mellai. "I've been waiting for the right time to give it to you. This is as good as any, I suppose. It's from your grandmother."

Mellai frowned as she took the package and slowly unwrapped it. She had completely forgotten her birthday. Inside the parchment was a polished silver pendant of a ghraef with a tiny pearl at the tip of its tail. Mellai lifted it from the parchment by its matching silver chain.

"Your father gave this to your grandmother when he asked for Shalán's hand," Dhargon said. "I don't like bribery much, but that's a pretty little thing, isn't it?"

Mellai fingered the pendant, astounded by its careful detail and workmanship. "Thank you, Grandfather," she said, then placed the pendant around her neck and hung it over her dress. In the process, she inconspicuously felt for the other pendant hidden beneath the material.

"We'll miss it, but your grandmother figures that if anyone should have it, it should be a Beholder. Too bad ghraefs are extinct. It would give you a much faster ride across Appernysia than a donkey."

Mellai's chin dropped in contemplation. *Ghraefs aren't extinct!* she shouted in her mind. At first inclination, she wanted to tell her grandfather, but she changed her mind. Her instincts told her that few people would appreciate that she was capable of reading minds. It would be the ultimate violation of their privacy. As she fingered the pendant, a marvelous thought entered her mind. *Maybe I'll get my own ghraef someday.*

"Is that Kutad?" Dhargon asked as soon as they exited the tunnel through the outer stone wall. The man in question sat on a horse thirty feet to their right. He was dressed in Appernysian plate armor and talking to another soldier. "That can't be him, is it?"

Mellai cupped her hands around her mouth. "Kutad." The man turned his head in their direction.

"There's your answer," she said.

Dhargon clicked the reins and turned the donkeys in Kutad's direction. "What's he doing in armor?"

Kutad turned his horse toward them and the other soldier galloped away. "I never thought I'd see you two here."

"I bet you didn't," Dhargon said without hiding his suspicion. He flicked his chin at Kutad. "What's all this?"

"It's simple really; I was a soldier before I became a tradesman, and King Drogan convinced me to come back." He nodded at Mellai. "It's good to see you back on your feet. What brings you this far east?"

"Kaylen," Mellai answered. "I haven't heard from her in months. I'm worried about her."

Kutad's eyebrows rose. "You have perfect timing. She's in desperate need of a friend right now. Follow me." He turned his horse around and moved forward, but Dhargon didn't follow.

Kutad pulled back on his reins. "What is it?"

"Where's Kaylen?" Dhargon asked. "Somewhere nearby?"

"I'm afraid not. She's in the keep."

Dhargon shook his head. "That's fifty miles away, Kutad, and it sounds like you need to hurry." He turned to his granddaughter. "Go with him, Mellai. You'll ride much faster on his horse."

"Will you follow after us?" Kutad asked.

"No," Dhargon answered, still looking at Mellai. "She can take care of herself. She doesn't need me around anymore."

"That's not true," Mellai argued. "Follow us, Grandfather. You wanted to meet Kaylen, remember?"

"I did, but now doesn't sound like the best time." He took Mellai's hands, his eyes wide with insistence. "Go to the keep, but be careful."

Mellai returned his gaze. Tears filled her eyes and fell down her cheeks. It wasn't just the goodbye that tugged at her heart, but the overwhelming weight of the responsibility awaiting her at the keep. Time was moving too quickly. She still didn't feel ready.

Dhargon wiped the tears away with his thumb and pulled Mellai into his arms. "You have to be strong," he whispered, "for Appernysia."

"I don't know if I can," she sobbed.

Dhargon took hold of Mellai's shoulders and moved her away. "You must."

Mellai nodded and calmed her breathing. "I love you, Grandfather. I'll visit you and Grandmother as soon as I can."

"I know you will."

Dhargon helped Mellai down and gave her a travel pack from the wagon, then turned his donkey to exit the city. Mellai watched him leave, but he never looked back. After Dhargon disappeared through the gate, Mellai turned around and faced Kutad. His head was cocked slightly to the side, but he said nothing as he held out his hand.

She donned her travel pack, then took his hand and pulled herself up onto the horse's back behind him. "Let's get going."

Kutad smiled and nodded his head. "Aye. Hold on tight." He kicked his horse into a canter and rode down the middle of the street toward Itorea's keep, taking care to avoid any people who got in his way. About eighteen miles into their journey, they reached another high wall of white stone. Kutad had Mellai dismount, then swapped his horse for a rested replacement and climbed into the saddle.

"A lot has changed since I last saw you," Mellai said, pulling herself up behind him again. "Look at you, taking another soldier's horse like you're his superior."

Kutad only smiled as he continued through the gate.

"How much farther?" Mellai asked once they were through the gate. The white stone of the road looked orange under the rays of the setting sun, weaving between endless farming lands.

"Another thirty-five miles. Do you need to rest?"

"I want to keep going, but I'm afraid I'll fall asleep and slip off the saddle."

Kutad slowed his horse to a fast walk. "Tighten your hold around me and lay your head against my back." Once she complied, he let go of the reins and grabbed her forearms with his left hand. "Sleep, Mellai. I won't let you fall."

Mellai nuzzled into the thick fabric of his green cloak and closed her eyes. The repetitious click of the horse's iron-shod hooves on the stone path was soothing, lulling her quickly into slumber.

Chapter 30

Sergeant

When she opened her eyes, Mellai was still sitting on the horse behind Kutad. The dark of night surrounded them, broken only by the torch Kutad held in his hand.

Mellai pulled her arms free and stretched them above her head. "How long did I sleep?"

"A few hours," Kutad answered, retaking the reins with his left hand. "We're still a few miles away."

"I'm surprised I slept that long," Mellai said. "I must have been sleepier than I thought."

She glanced around, but could only see a few feet in front of them. She leaned her head back and looked at the sky, but it was completely black. No stars or moon appeared overhead. The darkness was disconcerting, and Mellai longed for her best friend's presence. "I would prefer to ride at a faster pace, Kutad, if it's safe."

"A slow canter," Kutad replied, then tapped his heels against the horse's side. Their speed doubled.

Mellai struggled to stay calm under the pressing darkness, but it became too much for her to bear. Making sure to stay hidden out of Kutad's vision, she summoned True Sight and observed her surroundings.

No wonder I couldn't see any stars, Mellai thought with relief. They were in another long, stone tunnel. "Where are we?"

"In the west gate into the keep," Kutad answered.

Moments later, a full moon and dazzling stars filled the heavens. Mellai took a deep breath and released it through her nose. "That was a bad place to wake up. It felt like we were trapped in a dungeon."

"Sorry about that," Kutad replied, then cleared his throat. "How do you feel?"

"Refreshed. Why?"

"I've had a question stuck in my mind ever since my caravan visited Pree last year, but no time has ever seemed right to ask you."

"What is it?"

Kutad shifted in his saddle and glanced over his shoulder. "Do you stay in contact with Lon?"

Mellai sighed. "No," she replied, but became immediately suspicious. "Why do you ask?"

"Just wondering," Kutad answered casually.

Mellai knew he was up to something. She could hear it in his voice. Besides, it was highly suspicious for any Appernysian to ask if she kept in touch with Lon. She looked up at Kutad, contemplating whether to search his thoughts, but she decided against it. Despite the suspicious circumstances, she trusted him as a friend of their family. He had kept many secrets for her, and he deserved reciprocation. Even so, she needed to make sure he knew where she stood regarding Lon. "You know I love my brother, right? I'll do anything I can to help him."

Kutad's body tensed, but quickly relaxed again. "Aye."

I knew he was up to something, Mellai thought, *but what?* She decided to let it go for the moment. She'd know soon enough, and it wasn't like he was a threat to her. Not anymore. Not with her power.

A few minutes passed in silence, then Kutad spoke again. "It surprises me that you traveled all the way to Itorea this late in the season just to see your friend. It's even harder to believe your grandparents sanctioned it and that Dhargon left you with me. You were right, Mellai. A lot has changed since I last saw you."

Mellai leaned her head against Kutad's cloak, dreading the life awaiting her in Itorea's donjon.

"You have no idea." She had hoped the probing questions would stay behind in Roseiri, but she realized that the thought was silly. The questions, whether innocent or sinister, would follow her for the rest of her life.

A half-hour later, they were outside a tar-filled moat surrounding the donjon. "Lower the bridge," Kutad shouted to the men on top of the outer wall.

"By whose order?" a man replied.

Kutad held the torch close to his face. "Sergeant Kutad Leshim."

Silence followed, then the creaking of thick steel chains as they lowered a heavy drawbridge over the moat.

"Leshim," Mellai repeated.

"What's that?" Kutad asked.

Mellai shrugged. "That's the first time I've ever heard your last name. You've always been just Kutad to me."

"Aye. I normally stick with Kutad."

"And you're a Sergeant?"

Kutad nodded.

The drawbridge groaned as it touched the ground in front of them. Kutad kicked the horse forward.

"Do they always keep it closed?" Mellai asked.

"Just at night." Kutad saluted the guards by placing his right fist over his heart and rode to the center of the bailey. He helped Mellai out of the saddle before dismounting, then a stable boy took the reins and led the horse away into the darkness.

Kutad glanced behind them, then offered his steel-covered arm to Mellai. "This way." He led her through the front gate into the castle and down a confusing maze of torch-lit corridors.

"Are we going to see Kaylen now?"

"I don't think that's a good idea."

Mellai let go of Kutad's arm and stopped walking. "Then why did we push so hard to get here?"

"I wanted to give you a safe place to sleep tonight," Kutad replied, still holding his arm out for her. "Sunrise isn't for a few more hours. There's an empty bedchamber up here where you can rest. I'll call on you first thing in the morning and take you to Kaylen."

Mellai narrowed her eyes. "You're lying to me."

Kutad didn't respond, but remained facing away from Mellai as he lowered his arm. She summoned True Sight and dug into his mind. One solitary word stood out above the rest.

Traitor.

Mellai brought her hands forward defensively. "What's going on?"

Kutad turned around with tightened lips, obviously startled by her masked eyes. "Why don't you tell me?" He reached for his sword, but Mellai captured him in a form-fitting pocket of air. She tried to push further into his mind, but someone threw a sack over her head from behind. Mellai connected with the sack's energy and flung it off her head, then stepped sideways with her back against the stone wall and created a shield around herself. Kutad and five other soldiers rushed at her with drawn swords, but bounced off the invisible barrier and fell to the ground. The torches suspended nearby on the walls dimmed as part of their energy resupplied Mellai's shield.

"Why are you attacking me?" Mellai growled. She wanted an answer, but was more concerned with escape. The question was merely a distraction to buy her time. She searched up and down the corridor, planning a retreat.

The six men slowly stood, obviously disoriented. Kutad tapped his sword against the invisible barrier, then sheathed it and turned to one of his men. "You said that would work, Jareth."

"That's what they told me," Jareth replied. "She's not supposed to be able to use it if she can't see."

"Jareth," Mellai repeated, realization striking her. He was the man who had summoned Kutad from Roseiri. She abandoned her escape plan and focused on him. "I know you. Was it your idea to mix Kaylen up in your plot to kill the chamberlain?"

The six men gaped at her.

"How could she possibly—?" Jareth started.

"Quiet," Kutad cut in.

"I was listening to your conversation in Roseiri," Mellai said. "I have nothing to hide. Do you?" She connected with Jareth's consciousness and pushed into his unguarded mind. Although his body didn't show it, he was filled with terror at facing a Beholder.

Indescribable power. Nearly impossible to defeat.

Ah, there it is, Mellai thought as she pushed into his mind.

Blind a Beholder to stop him.

Mellai's brow furrowed. *But who told him?*

Swallows.

Mellai shook her head. *That doesn't make any sense.*

Beyond that, Jareth's mind offered little immediate help. Long, boring days on top of Itorea's perimeter wall. Love for a girl in Sylbie.

Mellai reentered Kutad's mind. There was the same word again.

Traitor.

"Why do you think I'm a traitor?" Mellai said. "I came here to help you."

"That's not what it looks like to me," Kutad argued. His mind shifted to her twin brother and his crimes against Appernysia. Kutad believed Mellai was in league with her twin, suspecting her as an assassin sent to Itorea by Lon. Kutad was beginning to think her whole family was in on it—maybe even Kaylen.

"You're being ridiculous," Mellai shouted. "You know my family. And Kaylen? How could we be assassins?"

Worry filled Kutad's face, and his thoughts became erratic.

Reading my thoughts! pickled cucumbers . . . rainbows . . . Linney . . . tradesmen . . . Roseiri . . . No! Reading my thoughts! grassy plains . . .

rolling surf . . . Tayla . . . Linney . . . Kaylen . . . Lon . . . Beholder . . .
King Drogan . . . No!

Mellai's eyes narrowed. "How did you find out about Lon?" She kept her voice calm and deliberate, despite her need for answers.

"Kaylen," Kutad answered.

"Before or after she asked you to deliver the letter to me?"

Kutad returned her gaze spitefully. "Long before. She told me when I first brought her to Itorea."

Mellai clenched her jaw. "You betrayed her trust and took the information to King Drogan?"

Kutad winced. "I had no choice."

"Which is why King Drogan sent scouts to the Quint River," Mellai deduced, "and initiated such an aggressive draft into the army."

Kutad folded his arms across his chest. "You're awfully informed for a peasant living on the outskirts."

"Your efforts were all a waste of time," Mellai continued, ignoring his suspicion. He was misinformed, and that needed to be fixed immediately. "Even King Drogan can't stop a Beholder. Only I can."

Kutad opened his mouth, but stopped short, his brow furrowed in confusion. "What?"

Mellai clenched her jaw with frustration. "That's why I'm here, Kutad. Believe it or not, Lon joined the Rayders with good intentions. But he betrayed us when he led the Rayders into Taeja. I am not a traitor. I'm here to drive the Rayders *out.*"

Mellai pulled the flames from all visible torches and combined them between her hands. She had to convince Kutad of her power, even if it required another lie. "I could destroy this entire castle right now and crush everyone inside with its rubble." She hoisted the fireball above her head and flared it into a bright white flame, blinding the men, then shifted the energy protecting her to capture them. She hoisted the men into the air and moved them into a huddled mass in front of her. Their red faces were filled with terror as they fought against her control.

While it was tempting to gloat, Mellai was careful to keep her thoughts in perspective. It was all a show, after all. They weren't her enemies. She stepped directly in front of Kutad and glared into his wide eyes. With what little movement she allowed him, Kutad nodded, so she sent the flames of the fireball back to their torches and released the six men. "Take me to Kaylen. Now."

Kutad raised his palms toward her in defeat. "I'll take you to her, but we didn't put her in the dungeon. She chose to make herself a prisoner."

"Prisoner? Why would she do that?"

"She blames herself for Aely's death and won't be convinced otherwise," Kutad said as he turned down the corridor with his five soldiers. Mellai followed close behind, True Sight still filling her vision.

"She'll barely eat or drink anything," he continued. "It's been everything we could do to keep her alive the past few months. I was serious about how much Kaylen needs you right now. You might be the only one who can help her."

"Aely died? How?"

"I'll let Kaylen tell you. It'll be good for her to talk about it. It might help her work things out."

Mellai glanced over her shoulder for danger. "I'm warning you, Kutad. If this is some sort of trap, you'll be the first person I kill, and I'll do it slowly for all of your soldiers to watch."

The conversation ended with a nod from Kutad. While they walked, Mellai took the opportunity to search the minds of each man. They were all loyal to King Drogan and Sergeant Kutad. Their only desire was to fulfill their responsibilities with honor. Kutad also had strong ties to King Drogan. Although they had only been working together for weeks, their history went back decades—until Kutad's daughter died. *Linney,* Mellai repeated in her mind. *He gave me his daughter's name.*

Mellai stopped there. *Just because I'm a Beholder doesn't give me the right to invade people's privacy without consent.* She just wanted to know if she could trust the men. She had her answer. If only she could instill the same confidence in Kutad about her.

"Wait," she called. Kutad and the five men turned around and looked at her. "We need to clear things up between us. Yes, I can read your thoughts, Kutad. I don't make a habit of it, but it has its advantages. I know I can trust all of you. Unfortunately, none of you can read my mind. How can I prove my loyalty to King Drogan?"

Kutad stared at Mellai's clouded brown eyes. "You can start by releasing your magic."

Mellai dismissed True Sight. "Done."

"Now let us blindfold you."

Mellai shook her head. "Didn't you already learn your lesson? Blindfolds won't do any good."

"I don't know what else you can do, Mellai. I know your family. They're some of the best people I've ever met. Before now, I've always thought you were a marvelous person. Unfortunately, that's not enough to prove your innocence."

"Then talk it out with me. Why don't you trust me?"

Kutad sighed. "It started when Dhargon acted so strange at the west gate. He's never been the kind of man who would leave his only granddaughter in Itorea. I've moved past that concern, but what about your brother? You said you'd do anything to help him."

"And I meant it," Mellai replied. "I'll stop him, but I can't kill him. He's my twin. I have to believe he can be reasoned with. But I won't let him dictate control anymore. What I can do is take his ability to use True Sight."

Kutad's eyes narrowed and lips parted. His tongue fidgeted at the corner of his mouth, then slowly, his lips curved into a smile. "You have to understand. It's my responsibility to keep King Drogan safe. I'm already suspicious of everyone I meet, but you and Dhargon were being particularly vague. From my experience, most secrets hide something evil. I'm sorry for doubting you."

"I have a couple questions, too," Mellai said. "My first one is for Jareth. If I read your memories right, you learned about blinding Beholders from swallows. Can you really talk to birds?"

Jareth glanced at Kutad, who nodded in return. "No," Jareth answered. "Thousands of peasants defected during our battle with the Rayders. They and their families now live in Taeja. The Rayders gave them the nickname of Swallows."

Mellai turned her attention to Kutad. "You have spies in Taeja?"

"Aye, but that's a big secret. Only a few of us know about them."

"Who else? King Drogan? Kaylen?"

Kutad shook his head. "Neither of them, but it's not safe to discuss this here."

Mellai nodded. "Next question, still for Jareth. How long were you following us?"

Jareth looked at Kutad again.

"Stop staring at him," Mellai snapped.

"Go ahead," Kutad added. "Answer her questions."

"Kutad contacted us while you were asleep on his horse," Jareth said. "We were following you before you entered the keep."

"Then why were you and Kutad waiting for me at the west gate?"

"We weren't. He was just talking to me about . . . the Swallows."

Mellai turned to Kutad. "If you thought I was an assassin, Kutad, why did you bring me here to the castle?"

"Because I thought we could use you as collateral to persuade your brother. I knew he'd come for you and that the safest place to keep you from him was in the heart of Itorea."

"But didn't you think I was a Beholder?"

Kutad shook his head. "No. Jareth just acted on an impulse when he saw you using your magic."

Mellai glanced at him. "You just happened to have a sack with you to throw over my head?"

Jareth gave a guilty shrug. "Ever since the Rayders found their Beholder. I thought it might come in handy someday. It only makes sense."

"None of this makes sense," Kutad countered. "How are you a Beholder, Mellai? You're a woman."

A single laugh escaped Mellai's lips, part mockery and part elation. She felt like they were on the brink of a breakthrough, but she was still on guard. "That's what you get for reading too much, Kutad. I don't fit history's mold at all."

Kutad smirked. "Any more questions?"

"Just one more." Mellai licked her lips. "Do I have your complete trust?"

Kutad rubbed the stubble on his chin for a moment, then dropped to one knee with his fist over his heart. "I was wrong to doubt you," he said with a bowed head. "Please forgive us." Jareth and the four other men copied their Sergeant's actions.

"Don't do that," Mellai complained.

Kutad stood and smiled at her. "If you're really here to lead Appernysia against the Rayders, you better get used to this kind of thing. You'll have a hundred thousand men under your command."

Mellai grimaced. "That's worse than fighting my brother."

Chapter 31

Broken

Mellai looked down at her best friend, who lay curled up on a stone floor covered by a thin layer of moldy hay. Even in the failing torchlight, Mellai could see that the Kaylen she knew was lost. Her slim and graceful figure had transformed, now thin and frail. Her long blond hair—once so radiant and beautiful—was matted and filthy. Portions of it clung to her damp skin, while others wrapped around her tattered servant's dress down to her hips. Her breath came out in short bursts of frost in the chilled air.

"Get her a blanket," Mellai said to the warden, "and a cup of hot tea."

"We've tried," the man argued. "She won't take them."

"Yes, she will," Mellai answered, then knelt beside her friend and brushed the hair off her pale face. "Do it."

"This is my dungeon, girly. I don't take orders from you."

Kutad placed his hand on the warden's shoulder. "Do as she asks."

Jareth stepped forward. "She's a B—"

"—bout to get really mad," Mellai cut in, wanting to keep her identity a secret.

Kutad pushed the warden toward the door. "Go."

"Yes, Sergeant," the warden replied, then disappeared out of the dungeon.

"Make sure the tea is hot, but drinkable," Mellai called after him, then looked at Jareth. "As for you, let's keep this B-word stuff to ourselves for now." She winked at Kutad. "See? Not all secrets are evil."

"Aye."

Mellai watched Kaylen sleep and stroked her pale cheek with the back of her fingers. "She looks terrible."

"It's been a rough couple of months for her," Kutad replied with a frown, "ever since the chamberlain died. I've felt completely helpless, but that doesn't compare to her pain and misery."

Soon the warden returned with a steaming cup of hot tea and a thick woolen blanket. Mellai took the blanket and handed it to Kutad, then grabbed the steaming tea and, after making sure it wasn't too hot, threw part of it into her friend's face.

Kaylen sat up with a small scream and cowered to the back of her cell. "What do you want?"

"I want you to drink this," Mellai replied, "or do you want me to throw the rest of it on you?"

Kaylen wiped her face with her arm and squinted in the dim light. "Mellai?"

"One and the same. Kutad told me you threw yourself into another emotional ditch. I didn't want to believe him, but look at yourself. You're a bigger mess than when Lon left. Stand up."

"I . . . I can't."

Mellai pulled back her cup to fling more hot tea on Kaylen, but Kutad stopped her. "She really can't, Mellai. Her legs can't support her weight."

Mellai looked more closely and realized Kutad was right. The bottom half of her legs poked out from her dress, deformed and discolored.

"What did you do to yourself?" Mellai gasped.

"She didn't do it," Kutad answered, "but she wouldn't let anyone heal her."

Kaylen buried her face in her hands and burst into tears.

Mellai sat next to her friend and handed her the cup of tea. "Tell me what happened."

"Aely died," Kaylen answered through her sobs. She took the tea and set it on the ground. "It should have been me."

"How did she die?"

"We were just delivering food, but Lords Haedon and Anton . . . they were being tortured. I thought I had to help, but I wasn't thinking straight. I killed Aely."

Mellai's face twisted in disbelief. "*You* killed her? How?"

"I made her help. She didn't want to, but I made her."

"Do what? You're not making any sense." She took Kaylen's hand between her own, stroking it reassuringly. "Look at me, Kaylen, and tell me what happened."

Kaylen looked up at Mellai. "I made her help me kill the chamberlain. I stabbed him, then I just stood there gawking at my dagger in his heart. And then Aely saved my life." She pulled her hand free and broke into more sobs. "It should have been me."

Mellai sighed and looked up at Kutad. "A little help?"

"One of the lords threw a dagger at Kaylen," Kutad inserted. "Aely stepped in front of it."

With new understanding and empathy from her own suffering, Mellai leaned forward and embraced her best friend. "I'm sorry, Kaylen. What do you need? What can I do?"

Kaylen's bottom lip trembled, but she didn't answer. She only rocked back and forth in Mellai's arms, her tears flowing freely.

"She's never talked about it," Kutad said.

Mellai looked up at him. "Do you know what happened?"

"Aye. The steward, Lord Teph, told us."

Mellai turned back to Kaylen and kissed her on top of her head. "I want to hear it from you. Please?"

Kaylen's lips tightened, and she shook her head.

"It's alright," Mellai reassured her. "I understand." As she finished speaking, Mellai summoned True Sight and pierced her friend's

272

memories. Unlike the structure of the tree's consciousness, human memories existed in what Mellai could only explain to be an endless corridor. Doors lined both walls of the corridor, each guarding a thought, impression, or experience in Kaylen's life. Some doors were more difficult to open than others, such as her last moments with Aely. Kaylen had buried that memory in the dungeons of her consciousness, making it extremely difficult for Mellai to decipher. Eventually though, she succeeded.

Kaylen looked back to see Aely's eyes glaze over before she slumped to the floor. As blood began to pool underneath Aely, Kaylen was jerked backward by her throat and thrown onto the floor. Her mind wandered, dazed when her head knocked against the stone.

"Let her go!" The man's voice filled the hall with curses.

Kaylen turned her head and saw him nearby, pinned against the wall by several of the lords who once surrounded the table.

"Lord Teph," she whispered as her gaze wandered. Then she saw another man standing over her. His presence terrified her.

"Please, Lord Tyram," she cried, begging for mercy.

His tanned skin stretched as he opened his mouth and spit in her face, then he lifted his foot and stomped on her lower leg with his hard leather boot. She heard the bones crack and felt the pain surge up her leg.

"I'll make you pay," Lord Tyram shouted as he lifted his foot and stomped again, this time on her knee, then once more on her thigh. "You have no idea what you've done."

"Please stop!" Kaylen begged between her screams, but her cries fell on deaf ears. Lord Tyram continued his onslaught on her other leg, then moved over her head. As he lifted his foot to crush Kaylen's face, an arrow pierced his chest. He faltered and lost his balance, toppling sideways. Kaylen turned her head and saw a wave of armored soldiers. They slaughtered the only resisting sentry, Sergeant Ched, and poured into the great hall.

Mellai pulled out of Kaylen's mind, released True Sight, then closed her eyes and leaned her head back against the stone wall. Her body still shook from the pain she had experienced in Kaylen's mind. Mellai took slow, deep breaths to calm herself, then wiped the perspiration from her brow and reopened her eyes.

Kutad was squatting in front of her, his face full of concern. The other men stood behind him with the warden, who had his hands over his ears.

"Thank the stars, she stopped screaming," the warden proclaimed. "Are you trying to make us all deaf, girly?"

Mellai summoned True Sight and moved to stand up, but Kutad raised a warning hand to her. She sat back down and watched with pleasure as Kutad whipped around and knocked the warden unconscious with a powerful blow to his chin.

Kaylen's voice filled Mellai's ears. "Are you alright?" She turned and found Kaylen looking at her. Her eyebrows lifted, her head jerking up erratically from post-sob hiccups. "Your eyes. Don't tell me it's happening to you, too."

"It already happened," Mellai said with a shaky voice. "Don't worry. I'm past the dangerous part."

Kaylen blinked slowly, obviously trying to process the new information. "You were screaming. Why?"

Mellai leaned forward, touching her forehead to Kaylen's. "I read your memories," Mellai whispered. "Now I really do understand."

Kaylen gasped. "Could Lon do that?"

"Not when he left Pree," Mellai said, sitting back, "but he wasn't tutored by a Jaed. I was."

Kaylen's eyes widened. "A Jaed?"

Mellai nodded. "We have a lot to catch up on, but not yet. I'm going to heal your legs, and you're going to let me. I've seen what you've been through, Kaylen. Stop blaming yourself for Aely's death. It wasn't your fault, and your guilt only diminishes her sacrifice. She saved your life, and you saved countless others. Be grateful."

Kaylen's breathing trembled as tears reentered her eyes. It took a moment, but she finally nodded her agreement. "Are you sure you can do it? Lon . . . he hurt people with his power."

"I guarantee it," Mellai said, "but here isn't the place to do it. Can Kutad carry you, or does it hurt too much?"

"I'll let him try."

Kutad jumped forward, wrapping Kaylen in the wool blanket and lifting her into his arms with ease. She stifled her screams by burying her face in Kutad's chest. He kicked the unconscious warden, then stepped over him and led the way out of the dungeon.

Chapter 32

Healing

"Your bones healed wrong," Mellai said, "so I have to break them again."

Kaylen was dressed in a white nightgown, lying in the center of the bed in the royal bedchamber. Queen Cyra sat at her head, stroking Kaylen's forehead. Snoom stood over Kaylen, gripping her wrists, while Kutad held down her waist. King Drogan and General Astadem were at the foot of the bed, each gripping an ankle.

"She'll scream and kick," Mellai said to the king and general, "but you have to hold her legs straight or I won't be able to heal her."

The two men nodded.

"Are you sure you don't want Henry to give you an elixir to put you to sleep?" Queen Cyra asked. She indicated to the old healer, hunched next to Mellai at the side of the bed. The chambermaids Lia and Jude were behind them with bundles of towels and warm rags in their arms. The queen's three ladies-in-waiting stood at the far corner of the room.

"No, I need to do this," Kaylen answered.

"Why?" the queen said. "It's not necessary."

Mellai understood. Kaylen still blamed herself for Aely's death. She wanted to hurt, thinking it might ease her pain.

"The pain will stop as soon as I'm finished," Mellai interrupted, too impatient to argue with Kaylen.

"I'll believe that when I see it," Henry wheezed.

Mellai summoned True Sight and looked at each person in the room, giving them a chance to absorb the uncanny effect in her eyes before she started working on her friend. She looked at Kaylen last. "Ready?"

Kaylen clenched her jaw and nodded. Her eyes were filled with fear.

Mellai shifted her gaze to Kaylen's legs and searched the bone structure. The breaks on her lower and upper legs were clean and could be healed quickly, but the knees suffered more damage. Her kneecaps were dislocated and bits of bone still floated around in the swollen tissue. Many strands of tissue that usually held a person's knee together would also need to be repaired. She decided to leave the knees for last, knowing the pain might be too much for Kaylen to bear.

The Beholder wrapped her essence around the upper break on Kaylen's closest leg, then broke the incorrect bond. Kaylen screamed and bucked as Mellai knitted the bone back together correctly. The men tightened their grips on Kaylen to restrain her. Fifteen seconds later, Mellai finished and moved on to the other thigh.

"One," she said as Kaylen's body relaxed.

"Impossible," Henry commented, gawking. "This should take many surgeries."

Mellai broke the other thigh and repaired its damage even quicker, despite Kaylen's desperate attempts to escape the pain.

"Two."

"Enough with the counting," Kutad growled. "Just fix her."

Mellai moved to Kaylen's right calf and focused around both damaged bones. She broke and knitted them both back together simultaneously, then moved to her left calf and repeated the steps. Kaylen thrashed against the men's hold on her.

"Now the kneecaps," Mellai said. "These will take time."

"Be brave," Queen Cyra added, still stroking Kaylen's face. "Your friend is almost finished."

Mellai worked as fast as she could, but Kaylen's shrieks and wild thrashing made it difficult. She carefully pulled the broken shards of bone through her flesh and reattached them to the knee, then moved the kneecap in place and stitched the severed tissues back together. It took longer than the other four breaks, but she was still finished in less than five minutes.

Tears flooded Kaylen's face. "Please stop."

Mellai cringed at her friend's plea, and the accompanying memory of Lord Tyram's beating, but continued to the other knee. She couldn't let her emotions get in the way. It would only take her another few minutes, then Kaylen would be whole.

By the time Mellai finished, Kaylen's legs were returned to normal—thinner than usual, but normal. The deformities and discoloration were gone. But Kaylen's screams had been replaced by deep, quick breaths, and her body was shaking violently. She was also unresponsive to Queen Cyra's attempts to sooth her.

"Prop up her feet," Henry ordered, "and cover her with a blanket. Her body couldn't handle the pain. Unless her mind calms down, she'll die."

Mellai moved into Kaylen's mind and connected with her living consciousness. Henry was right. Her brain was overreacting to the pain, which was sending her body into shock. Mellai was about to intervene, but recalled Llen's council not to attempt mind manipulation. It was something only Kaylen could fix herself. Mellai released True Sight and watched the chambermaids bustle around. She reprimanded herself for pushing Kaylen too far, for not insisting Kaylen take a sedative. She should have slowed down and given her a chance to recover between each healing.

It took time, but eventually Kaylen did settle down. Her breathing slowed and her pale skin regained a little color while she slept. Once Henry announced that Kaylen was out of danger, he shuffled out of the room without a word to anyone.

"Don't mind him," Snoom told Mellai with a smirk. "He's just jealous."

Mellai returned the smile. "So what kind of name is Snoom, anyway?"

"It's a nickname."

"Are you going to tell me where it came from, or do I have to read your mind?"

Snoom raised his eyebrows. "Can you do that?"

"I won't—unless I have reason to."

"It's a boring story," Snoom said with a shrug. "I got it when I was a child because I liked the taste of charred rattlesnakes stuffed with mushrooms. Snooms."

Mellai giggled. "Sounds like a dangerous appetizer. If one won't kill you, the other will."

"Never heard that one before," Snoom said, rolling his eyes. "I haven't tasted it in years, though. Snooms aren't something you'll find in the king's court."

"And for good reason," Mellai mused. "They probably taste worse than a bloated toad. But you have me intrigued."

Snoom's eyes brightened.

"Don't encourage him," Kamron said as he walked over to Mellai. "Thank you for your assistance, Snoom. You may return to your post."

"He seems like a good person," Mellai commented after Snoom saluted and disappeared out of the bedchamber.

Kamron nodded. "I've known him since he was a young page. It's hard to think he's grown into a knight."

"A knight?" Mellai started. "How old is he?"

"Just turned sixteen last month," King Drogan answered as he crossed the room and stood by the general. "I'm glad Kaylen requested his help with her healing. I've missed him. He was a good page."

"He's an even better soldier," Kamron added. "Don't let his age fool you, Mellai. He's one of the best fighters I've trained. With a few years of good experience, he'll be nigh unstoppable."

"But enough about Snoom," King Drogan said and gestured to a nearby chair. "Please have a seat, Beholder. We haven't been properly introduced."

"You're maddening," Queen Cyra complained. After running her hand across Kaylen's forehead, the queen slid off the bed and crossed the room. "Now isn't the time for your silly formalities, Drogan. There's a Beholder in our room, and a woman, no less. Get over here, Kutad, and tell us where you found her."

Kutad reluctantly left Kaylen to the care of Lia and Jude. "She grew up in Roseiri with her grandparents," he said, "but moved to Pree after about a decade."

King Drogan's eyes narrowed. "That sounds very familiar."

"Aye," Kutad said. "She's his twin."

King Drogan's gaze bored into Mellai as his hand rested on the pommel of his longsword. "You're Mellai Marcs?"

Mellai nodded warily. The situation needed to be diffused, and Kutad was best suited for the task. She had no idea how much he had told King Drogan about her brother or the rest of her family.

"Bringing a girl like her into the royal chamber was a dangerous thing to do," Kamron chimed in, edging closer to the king, "especially when she's a Beholder."

"What do you mean, *a girl like her?*" Mellai asked as she glared at the general. She fought to control her temper.

Kamron returned her stare. "A headstrong sassmouth with a traitorous father and brother."

Mellai embraced True Sight and captured Kamron in an air pocket, then used her power to wrench his own sword from its scabbard and aim it at the general. She moved so fast that King Drogan didn't even have time to draw his longsword before Mellai had locked it in place. The king pulled on it with both hands, but it wouldn't budge.

"You don't know anything about my family," Mellai spat. She inched the blade forward until its tip touched Kamron's throat. "Or what we've been through."

Kamron's eyes widened, but he didn't speak. Mellai had sealed his mouth shut. She glared at him, ignoring the other astonished looks in the room.

"Stop," Kutad said and put his hand on Mellai's shoulder.

Mellai whipped the sword back and slammed it into Kamron's scabbard. "He's a hypocrite," she said, maintaining her hold on him.

"You have to understand where General Astadem is coming from," Kutad continued. "He fought against Lon at Taeja. He watched your brother kill hundreds of Appernysians."

"And save thousands more," Queen Cyra inserted.

"True," King Drogan responded, released from Mellai's power. He fingered his long sword, obviously distraught over Mellai's actions, but not enough to act. "But now those peasants and their families are a part of Taeja, bolstering the Rayder numbers."

"If our own men hadn't shot at them," Queen Cyra argued, "the peasants wouldn't have needed Lon's rescuing."

"You know Kamron had no choice. Lord Ramik gave that order."

"And why didn't you stop it?"

King Drogan sighed. "I didn't know about it. Now isn't the time to discuss this, Cyra." He turned to Mellai. "Release my general."

"Only after he apologizes," Mellai countered. She released her hold on the general's mouth, but squeezed tighter over the rest of his body.

Kamron opened and closed his freed jaw, furious over his imprisonment. "I have nothing to apologize for."

"She's right about you, Kamron," King Drogan said. "You *are* a hypocrite. You call her a traitor, yet you fled the battlefield and left my entire army to die. If it wasn't for your loyalty to me, and my desperate need for an ally, I would have left you to the executioner's blade."

Mellai's eyes widened, and her curiosity took control. She pushed into King Drogan's consciousness, quickly finding the memory at the forefront of his mind.

When King Drogan discovered that the council had ordered Kamron's execution, he took it upon himself to intervene. He left the safety of the royal chamber and rushed to the square. Despite the king's presence, the executioner tried to pursue his task anyway. General Astadem also caught sight of his king. He ducked under the executioner's blow and rolled out of the way. When the executioner attempted another strike, General Astadem disarmed him and broke his neck. An ugly encounter ensued, both king and general accusing each other of cowardice. Queen Cyra appeared and forced them back inside, out of the sight of the public. They eventually resolved their differences, but obviously not without residue. King Drogan had worried how he could unite his soldiers under Kamron's command again, but Mellai presented the perfect opportunity. With a Beholder at General Astadem's side, soldiers would flock to join the battle.

"You know her father ran away from the Rayders," King Drogan continued. "He's no traitor." He paused and glanced at Mellai. "And neither is she."

Kamron closed his eyes, then looked up at Mellai. "I spoke out of line." His expression was masked, making it impossible to tell whether the apology was sincere or forced. "But try to understand—"

"Understand this," Mellai cut in, releasing the general and dismissing her power. "No one feels the weight of my brother's actions more than my family. That's why I'm here. Someone has to hold him accountable. I just need to get close enough to stop him."

The king removed his crown and ran his fingers through his silver hair. "This is the last thing I expected to happen. It is great news, but changes everything." He paused for a moment and looked at Mellai. "It should be obvious by now that I haven't had control over my council for many years. Before Kaylen killed Lord Ramik, he had organized several attempts on my life."

"Why didn't you kill him first?" Mellai asked.

"I wish it were that simple. He had many supporters—both on and off of the council—who were men of high standing. I couldn't venture anywhere near the Crook without endangering my life."

Mellai looked at Kutad. "The Crook?"

"The southwestern region of Itorea," Kutad answered, "where the nobles live."

"Unfortunately," King Drogan continued, "even with Lord Ramik dead, I still have many enemies. But I refuse to govern my people by fear. That's not how my father ruled, and I won't do it either. That's where you come in, Beholder. Until now, I've thought the best way to regain the trust of the nobles was to defeat the Rayders. General Astadem and I have been working together on a plan to retake Taeja, but even with our superior numbers, one problem thwarts all of our planning."

"Lon."

"Exactly. Now with your help, the advantage lies on our side. We will drive the Rayders out of Taeja, but I believe we can unify my soldiers before we even go to battle." He paused and looked around at everyone, his lips slowly forming a grin.

"My theatric husband," Queen Cyra said impatiently. "Just tell us what's on your mind."

The king fixed his gaze on Mellai. "Do you know where the most heavily guarded place in Itorea is?"

Mellai's lips flattened. "I hate guessing, your Majesty."

"Fair enough," King Drogan said with a laugh. His behavior was becoming increasingly jovial. "You might think it's my castle, but you would be wrong. To the east of here is the royal garden. The gardeners keep it trimmed and beautiful all year long, but that's not what makes it so important. In all of Appernysia, it is the only place to find a very special flower. It has been guarded there since our ancestors brought it to this continent at the beginning of the First Age."

"For heaven's sake," Queen Cyra cut in. "He's talking about the Lynth flower. Have you heard of it?"

Mellai shook her head.

"Beholders had a unique marking on their face," Kutad added, "made from the blue petals of the Lynth. If I understand where His Majesty is going with this, he wants to make a spectacle of you."

"Precisely," King Drogan agreed. "My subjects are terrified of your brother, including my soldiers."

"But with a proclaimed Beholder of your own," Mellai inferred, "their fear would be quelled." She had been expecting and dreading this moment since the day she first met Llen. There would be no turning back.

"More than that," King Drogan replied. "Mellai, you're a blessing from the Jaeds. By announcing your presence and marking you with the Beholder's Eye, all of Appernysia will be unified. It will be like the First Age again. The Rayders will know we are coming, and with the power to drive them away. They may even flee before we get there."

"Don't count on it," Mellai said. "If you think I'm headstrong, you should meet my father. He's no longer a Rayder, but he's shown me a few things about their stubbornness. The Rayders won't give up Taeja without a fight."

"I agree with Mellai," Kamron inserted. "By announcing our Beholder's presence, it will give the Rayders time to prepare for our coming and change their tactics. We should move against them without identifying her. The Rayders' overconfidence will be their downfall."

"Your argument makes sense," the king replied, "but without a Beholder, convincing my army to go to battle will be impossible. You betrayed their trust."

"Then we only tell the soldiers," Kutad suggested. "Make them convince their families that it's the right thing to do, but without revealing the secret behind their newfound confidence."

King Drogan brought his hand to his face, massaged his forehead with obvious frustration. "Gaining the trust of my people will be the most difficult, especially since my council has already banished many peasant families. So many wrongdoings, all while I hid inside my chambers. I could have done more. I *should* have done more."

Queen Cyra rose and stood beside her husband. She took his hand from his face, kissed it, and held it against her cheek. "We did the very best we could, Drogan."

Silence overtook them. The sound of Kaylen's smooth breathing filled the bedchamber, rising and falling like the rolling surf of the Asaras Sea. Mellai sat on the bed and watched her friend, deep in her own thoughts. She felt stifled, like standing in the middle of a dense fog that only revealed a few steps ahead. Where her path led was anyone's guess. Well, except for Llen, but getting information out of the Jaed was a pointless venture.

King Drogan was the first one to stir. He stood and paced the floor. "You have given me much to consider, Mellai. Cyra and I will weigh the options and discuss them with Lords Haedon and Anton, if they're well enough. When we feel we have come up with an acceptable solution, I will call upon you to finalize our strategy. In the meantime, I'd like a squad of soldiers assigned to act as our Beholder's guard. She's the key to our success. Sergeant, do you have recommendations?"

Kutad stood next to Mellai. "Whom do you trust?"

Mellai glanced at him. "You."

"I'm honored and willing, but I can't be your only protector. Anybody else?"

"I like Snoom, and Jareth seems like a motivated soldier. Besides them, I will trust your judgment."

"In that case," King Drogan piped in, "take Ric and Duncan."

"They're your sentries, my king," Kamron argued.

The king nodded. "I realize that, but I'm expendable. If Mellai dies, no one else can rise up to take her place. I think one more person should do. Perhaps Thudly?"

"Not a bad suggestion," Kutad replied, "but he's a little heavy on his feet, if you get my meaning."

"True," King Drogan replied. "Who else?"

"Kaylen," Mellai said. "She's not a soldier, but there isn't a person alive whom I trust more."

"That's the best suggestion of all," Queen Cyra replied, "if she recovers."

"She's fine," Mellai answered and gave Kaylen's hand a tiny squeeze. "Right, faker?"

Kaylen smiled and opened her eyes. "I missed you."

"Me, too."

Kutad scowled. "How long have you been awake?"

"Since I finally found out where Snoom's name came from."

"I was surprised to hear that story," Queen Cyra commented. "He hasn't told any of us."

"Are you sure you still want him in your guard, Beholder?" Kamron teased. "I think he likes you."

"Not interested." The words shot out of Mellai's mouth like crossbow bolts.

Silence broadsided the room. Kutad and Kaylen knew about Theiss, but even they must have wondered over her outburst. Mellai refused to make eye contact with either of them. She didn't want to talk about Theiss. Not yet.

"Come with me," King Drogan said to his general and sergeant. "Let's gather the rest of Mellai's guard."

While the three men left the room, Queen Cyra sat on the bed opposite Mellai. "How are you doing, Kaylen? Can you move your legs?"

Kaylen lifted her knees and slid her heels slightly toward her hips. "Yes, but they're stiff."

"You haven't used them for months," Mellai said. "I healed the damage, but it will take time for you to strengthen your muscles again. I'll help where I can, but don't expect to dance anytime soon."

Kaylen rolled onto her side and wrapped an arm around her friend. "Thank you."

Mellai returned the hug. "I'm sorry about Aely. I know she was a close friend."

"She was," Kaylen sniffed. "I miss her."

"Don't burden her journey to paradise with your sorrow."

Kaylen leaned back and looked at her. "Where did you hear that?"

"A long story, but it's still good advice. We all choose how to react to life. You can choose to dwell on the agony of Aely's death, or on the happiness she brought you while she was alive. What do you think she would want?"

Kaylen smiled weakly. "That *is* good advice."

"Thank you for your help," the queen said to Lia and Jude. "I'll let you know if we need anything else." As the chambermaids left, Queen Cyra turned to her ladies-in-waiting, who were still standing at the far corner of the room. "You, too." The three women curtsied and followed after the chambermaids. Once all five women were gone, the queen leaned close to Mellai. "I have something I need to tell you before my husband comes back."

"What is it?"

Queen Cyra took a deep breath. "Everyone is so caught up in the evil of Lon's actions that they forget all the good he did."

Kaylen threw her hands up over her face. "I can't hear this again."

"Just hear me out," Queen Cyra continued. "I realize he led the Rayders into Taeja, but there's a lot more to the story. I've heard the reports General Astadem gave my husband about the battle. You heard me mention this earlier. Lon rescued thousands of fleeing Appernysian peasants from being murdered by our own soldiers. People talk about how terrible his power was, but he stopped the battle with threats and intimidation, not actual violence. Most of our soldiers returned from Taeja. There was even one point where Lon could have killed General Astadem, but he didn't."

Mellai raised an eyebrow at her queen. "Why are you telling me this?"

Kaylen elbowed her friend. "Your *Majesty*," she whispered.

"Forgive me, your Majesty," Mellai said, her eyebrows smoothing. "I'm still getting used to this place."

Queen Cyra smiled. "Thank you, Beholder. Now hear me out. I'm not convinced that Lon is as bad as everyone is making him out to be. As soon as our soldiers left, even the Rayders stopped fighting. They weren't out for blood. They just wanted Taeja."

"I'm sorry, my queen, but you're talking like Lon is something separate from the Rayders," Mellai said. "Did Kaylen tell you why he went to the Exile in the first place?"

"No, but Kutad did. He was seeking a way to control his powers."

Mellai's eyes narrowed, having again forgotten her manners. "Do you know what he promised to do when he learned how to control True Sight?"

The queen didn't answer.

"He promised to come home and marry Kaylen," Mellai continued. "She was the whole reason he left. I don't know what happened to him in the Exile, but somewhere along the way, he changed his mind. He learned how to control True Sight, but he still hasn't come home. That alone proves where his heart lies. He's a Rayder now."

No more was said until King Drogan returned with his general and sergeant, along with Snoom, Jareth, and five other men she didn't recognize. Wait. Three looked familiar from Kaylen's memories. One had been pinned against the wall. The faces of the other two were heavily bruised. They were the spokesmen for the king and queen.

King Drogan gestured to the group of men. "Lord Tephílst Thorverson, Lord Anton Vetinie, and Lord Haedon Reeth, may I introduce Mellai Marcs." The three men she had recognized stepped forward and bowed. Even though it was the middle of the night, they were still finely dressed with swords belted around their waists. "Lord Teph is our steward and acting chamberlain, Lord Haedon is my advisor, and Lord Anton is my queen's chancellor."

"Lord Teph," Mellai said, returning his bow with a curtsey. "Thank you for trying to rescue Kaylen."

He nodded. "I wish I could have done more."

"These other two men," King Drogan continued, "are Ric and Duncan. They are committed to your protection."

The two armored men placed their right fists over their hearts and bowed toward the bed. "Who is this woman we are protecting, my king?" Ric said.

"Why don't you show them, Mellai?" King Drogan suggested.

Mellai surveyed the room, scrambling for the best way to impress her audience without frightening them. A nearby pitcher of water offered the perfect solution. She summoned True Sight, pulled the water from the pitcher, and moved it above Ric and Duncan's heads. The two men tilted their heads back to watch with bulging eyes as the floating pool of water froze, shattered, then fluttered down on their faces as fluffy white snowflakes.

"Incredible," King Drogan said as he crossed the room and took Mellai's hand in his. "With your help, we cannot lose, Beholder."

Chapter 33
Swallows

"B ecause it's impractical," Lon said after warming his hands with his breath. "This is getting to be an everyday conversation, Wade."

"I am sorry, Beholder, but every section of this stone piping we unearth reminds me of how much work our ancestors put into the creation of Taeja. Perhaps if Omar were still alive—"

"It wouldn't matter," Lon cut in. "Even if he discovered an efficient way to repair the damaged pipes, there are way too many of them for me to fix alone. I've already told you. There's a complex web of piping under the entire city. Many of the stone pipes are too small for me to enter, which means I'd have to dig them up entirely. Even if I could walk through them all, doing so would be foolish. I need to be on the surface, where Commander Tarek can find me quickly."

"Of course," Wade said. "Our defenses would be crippled. This I understand, but I cannot bring myself to agree that destroying the pipes is the best course of action."

"We're not destroying them," Lon replied. "We're modifying them. This isn't the same Taeja that existed in the First Age. We're building it to fit our needs. We need stone to build our keep, and this granite piping is the perfect source. The Tamadoras Mountains are the next closest source of stone—sixty miles away. You know what's lurking in those forests, Lieutenant."

290 TERRON JAMES

Wade frowned. "Not for certain, and neither do you, Beholder. It has been three months since our squad's encounter. There has not been any further evidence to suggest the calahein are still around."

"Except for the feeling in the pit of my stomach," Lon answered, then turned away and summoned True Sight. He shattered another large section of piping within the riverbed, which had been exposed while the Rayders were collecting clay for the dome shelters, then lifted the chunks of stone, taking care to shake off the snow before placing it in the wagon. "Ready."

The driver glanced over his shoulder at the piled stone, then returned his attention to his team of horses. They were skittish, dancing in place as they waited for their master's signal. When the driver tightened his lips and gave a shrill whistle, the four horses lunged forward. Their muscles bulged and heads lowered, nearly touching their noses to the ground. Snow and dirt flew into the air from their shod hooves until the wagon was moving at a steady pace.

Dawes nickered beneath Lon and shook his black mane. Lon smiled and patted the horse's neck. "I know, Dawes. You could do better. Pull the whole wagon all by yourself, right?"

When he finished speaking, he shattered another section of stone pipe and moved it into another wagon. It was the last of a long line of wagons he had been filling for many hours. "This is much faster than quarrying stone in the mountains."

"But at what cost?" Wade inserted.

Lon and Wade tapped their heels on their horses' sides and trotted toward the heart of Taeja, followed by the rest of Lon's squad. Once they were moving, Lon released True Sight and turned to his lieutenant. "You're forgetting the necessities, Wade. We can't keep hauling in all of our drinking water from outside of Taeja. Removing the stone from this old riverbed will allow us to reconnect it with the active river. We'll have a constant source of water in the city again—without any flooding."

"I did not forget," Wade replied quietly, "but we are destroying so much of the city's history."

Lon nodded absently, having heard the same argument too many times to count. "I understand, truly. If Omar were here, he'd have a real problem with destroying the pipes. I'm glad you two share a love for the history of Taeja, even if it means I have to endure a little of your complaining. Unfortunately, this is our only option."

Lon's comment ended their conversation. His thoughts drifted as his squad followed the line of wagons. While creating the deep trench surrounding Taeja, Lon had exposed several sections of stone piping. He had removed the piping from the trench at the time, knowing that if the trench was filled with water, the piping would bleed into the city and create another flood. Now, once Lon had finished removing the piping from underneath the riverbeds running through the city, there would be no further threat of flooding. He would be able to route the rivers back into the city by filling the trench with water, which would strengthen their defenses. Taeja would have a moat instead of an empty ditch. But that presented other problems.

"We need drawbridges into Taeja," Lon said to his lieutenant.

Wade furrowed his brow. "Why?"

"If I'm killed or unavailable to raise a bridge at the north or south gates, everyone would be trapped in Taeja." What Lon didn't mention was the difficulty of raising land bridges if the trench was filled with water. He was tired of pointing out his weaknesses, so he kept the information to himself. When he saw Tarek, he'd pass the information along to him.

"I will not allow you to die, but the bridge is logical," Wade said. "I will order their construction as soon as we return to the keep."

"Good," Lon replied. "We'll also need iron grates along the inside of the ditch where the river flows into and out of the city. We don't want enemies swimming into Taeja."

Soon they reached the keep, where the stone-laden wagons cir-cled massive piles of granite rubble. Lon moved the stone from the wagons, then glanced at the sun reflecting low off the snow-covered terrain. Almost dusk.

"Return to your shelters," Lon told the horse teams, then dis-mounted and climbed to the top of one of the stone piles. Wade and the rest of his squad formed a spaced perimeter.

"Beholder?" Wade asked.

"I'm surveying," Lon said as he glanced over the surrounding area. High snow-covered domes made of Lon's brick solution littered the western plains of Taeja, each with a fifty-yard radius and housing about five hundred families. The domes worked as temporary solu-tions to help the civilians survive the winter, but they weren't a practical long-term solution. People couldn't live their lives clustered in lightless domes of brick. They needed their own land—a place to stretch their legs and cultivate. Come springtime, many of the Rayder civilians would move out of the city limits, which worked with Lon's plans. The Rayders would need many acres of farmland to feed their people. That farmland could never exist inside Taeja's walls while the underground pipes still existed. Irrigation canals would bleed into the pipes and flood the city. No, the crops would have to be raised outside Taeja, perhaps for years to come.

Closest to Lon was a smaller but sturdier dome—the temporary keep of Taeja—where Tarek, Lon, his squad, and Flora's family dwelt. Braedr Pulchria was also imprisoned inside on a raised pillar of earth encircled by a deep trench. When Tarek became commander, one of the first things he did was revitalize the Rayder army. The soldiers worked in shifts to protect the keep, guard the silos, and enforce the peace in Taeja.

Lon peered north and saw a small armored unit approaching on horseback. It was Tarek's guard, consisting of fifty of his finest soldiers. They were escorting him from the Swallows, where the commander had spent most of his time over the previous month.

"If those Swallows want any hope of surviving," Tarek had argued, "they'll need to learn how to live as Rayders. It wouldn't hurt if they learned to fight, too."

Lon wanted to talk with Tarek, but they were still miles away. Lon picked up a granite fragment and showed it to Wade. "Granite is strong, but if we try to build the keep by piecing this stone together with mortar, a catapult's rock would plow through it with little resistance."

"What do you suggest, Beholder?"

"I'm not sure," Lon replied, "but I noticed something today. Have you been paying attention to the rubble we're bringing back? There aren't mortar lines in any of the stone piping, like it was cut from one solid piece of stone."

Wade glanced around, then returned Lon's gaze with raised eyebrows.

"Somehow," Lon continued, "this stone was molded together. Beholders did this."

"Can you?" Wade asked.

"Again, I'm not sure," Lon answered with a sigh. Pain filled his heart as he once again missed his mentor. Omar had always seemed to know the impossible. Even when Lon discovered how to do something on his own, Omar wasn't surprised. He had just smiled knowingly, like a father whose son figures out how to tie a new knot. If Omar were still alive, he would have a solution. Lon was sure of it.

"Rock has to form somehow," Lon said aloud. "Think, Lon." He rubbed the top of his head with frustration. "Seems like the easiest solution would be to melt it, but have you ever seen rock melt?"

Wade shook his head. "Only rocks with ore deposits. Is it even possible to melt granite?"

Lon summoned True Sight and suspended the rock between his hands with an open bowl of air. "I'm going to find out. You might want to get behind me, Lieutenant."

While Wade stepped behind him, Lon created a ball of fire and wrapped it around the stone. He started adding more heat to it, but paused to create another protective wall of air between himself and the stone *before* adding more pressure and heat. As the temperature increased, the fireball changed from red to orange, then to blue and white. Finally, the rock hidden within the fireball also turned white and softened into a spongy mass.

Lon reeled at what he held between his hands. He removed the flame to see it better. The melted granite quickly changed from white to red, but cooled very slowly. Lon thought to pour water over the mass to cool it quicker, but remembered back when he threw a river rock into an open fire as a young boy. The rock heated quickly and exploded. Luckily, neither he nor his father was hit by the flying projectiles. *If a wet rock reacted like that to heat,* Lon thought, wincing with his head tucked to one side, *I don't want to see what water would do to this.*

Rather than using water, Lon concentrated on the stone's speeding energy and soothed it. Moments later, the spongy mass had transformed into a black stone. He lowered the cooled rock into his hand, then dismissed his power. The low sunlight reflected off its shiny surface.

"It doesn't look anything like granite now," Lon complained, then hurled the rock against the stone pile. It shattered into many jagged shards. "And look at that. It's as brittle as glass. Useless."

"Obsidian?" Wade asked as he picked up one of the shards.

Lon shrugged. "What's obsidian?"

Wade's eyes bulged. "Obsidian is very rare in Appernysia. It is worth more than gold. You could buy an entire village with the fragments you just created." He gave Lon a sidelong glance as he gathered the remaining black shards. "A tradesman would know this, Beholder. I wish you would trust me with your childhood."

"I don't bother you about your past," Lon said pointedly as he climbed down the rock pile. "You don't need to know mine."

When he reached the bottom, Lon's squad circled around him. They obviously recognized the obsidian in Wade's hand and glanced between him and Lon.

Lon took the obsidian, placed it in one of Dawes's saddlebags, and swung onto the horse's back. "If history has taught us anything, it's that greed brings the downfall of nations. It happened to Bors Rayder and the rest of the Taejans in the First Age, and the same thing will happen now if anyone discovers the obsidian. This secret stays with the seven of us. I don't even want Tarek to know about it. He doesn't need the pressure of corruption weighing on his shoulders."

"Yes, Beholder," the six men agreed, then kissed their fingers and moved them to the King's Cross on their right temples.

The squad followed after Lon as he rode to meet the commander's guard. Tarek was in the middle of the group, his face drawn with exhaustion.

"Rough day?" Lon teased.

"Funny," Tarek growled. "Those Swallows' skulls are as thick as my neck. They try hard, but teaching them our way of life is about as difficult as galloping on the back of a cat. They're too used to Appernysian lifestyles. Don't even get me started on the weapons training."

"Like the training grounds back in the Exile?" Lon asked, remembering the pathetic display he had witnessed when he first met Tarek.

"A perfect comparison."

"Sorry to hear that."

Tarek smiled. "Speaking of stone walls, how's the keep coming? I see big piles of stone over there, but have you started piecing the puzzle together yet?"

"No," Lon complained. "I'm worried about using too much mortar. It'll really weaken the structure."

"We have to do the best we can with what we've got," Tarek replied. "Any solutions?"

Lon eyed Wade, then shook his head. "Not yet."

Tarek shrugged. "Don't worry about it. I have some good news for you, though." He led Lon a short distance away from his guard and spoke quietly. "One of the Swallows has relatives in Itorea, one of which has a position in the king's court."

"How's that going to help us?" Lon asked. "Our Appernysians were cut off from their families when I rescued them."

"Not all of them. I'm sending the family to Three Peaks to coordinate with Lieutenant Thennek on how to get into Itorea unnoticed."

"You're using them as spies?" Lon said.

"Absolutely," Tarek proclaimed, "and they're more than willing to help. They hate King Drogan more than Commander Rayben did."

"Did you ever consider that King Drogan is using the same technique against us? We've been letting in a lot more Appernysians refugees. There's a good chance some of them are spies, too."

"Probably," Tarek said with a smirk, "but they can't report back to Appernysia, can they? They're trapped here unless you let them out."

"Maybe they're this family you're talking about. They might be using you."

Tarek scrunched his eyebrows and twisted his thick beard between his finger and thumb. "But if they are honestly on our side and willing to help us, think of all the advantages. Even so, I'll have to ask them a few more questions before I let them go."

Lon laughed. His breath came out in tiny cloud bursts before disappearing into the chilled air. "Just don't turn them against us with your interrogation."

"Hey, I'm a new man," Tarek said with a shrug. "I haven't hurt anybody since I've been commander, unless it was part of their weapons training."

"A whole month? That has to be some kind of a record for you."

"Don't push me, or I'll end it right now."

Lon threw his hands up with feigned innocence. "No argument here."

Tarek signaled for his guard, then rode toward the keep, Lon and his squad riding alongside. Two hundred armored soldiers surrounded the dome, all standing at attention as their commander and first lieutenant approached from the north.

"I've decided not to assign a new general," Tarek said as they rode. "Call it convenience, or believe it a courtesy to your *Unite Appernysia* goals, but if generals weren't needed in the First Age, I see no need for them now. We'll run things how the Taejans did. One commander with a Beholder lieutenant, and all of our other lieutenants, of course."

"Excellent idea," Lon replied. "I was struggling to choose your replacement."

As they neared the keep, Tarek nudged Lon with his elbow. "Think Flora will be in?"

Lon only rolled his eyes.

"It's perfectly fine to like her," Tarek continued. "You haven't seen Kaylen in eleven months, and you hardly even think about her anymore."

"You don't know that," Lon replied. "Besides, I can't be interested in Flora. I'm only eighteen, and she has three children."

"Eighteen?" Tarek asked. "When was your birthday?"

"Last month. A week after the tournament."

Tarek shook his head. "It seems like only last week when you first arrived at the Exile with Wade ready to kill you. That duel between you two is still the best one I've ever seen, even if you did cheat a little."

"Not on purpose," Lon said. "I had no control. True Sight was killing me."

Tarek became more serious. "I'm glad you changed, Lon. You've developed quite the talent for saving people's lives. Especially mine."

"My pleasure, Tarek. You're my best friend." He glanced over his shoulder. "Except for Wade, maybe. My own shadow spends less time chasing me around."

"Be grateful for such a loyal guard. Someday, he might be able to repay everything you've done for us."

Lon slumped as he thought of Omar's sacrifice. "Enough people have died at my expense."

"Listen," Tarek said, leaning closer to Lon. "I know I've complained a lot about the Swallows, but I think it's time."

"To brand them?"

Tarek nodded. "They've been with us for over three months. Commander Rayben was a good man, and I played a key role in many of his plans, but I never felt right about the training grounds. It was nothing more than a prison camp with a fancy label. Only a few of those men ever had a chance of actually defeating a Rayder in combat, no matter how hard I tried to help them. I can try to justify it, but I'm really just doing the same thing here. The Swallows are nothing more than prisoners."

"The north blade is a safe haven for them," Lon countered. "That's not a justification. It's a reality. They'll never fit in."

"Perhaps not," Tarek agreed, "but they still have a right to belong somewhere. They've earned it, just as you did, and you don't fit in any better than they would."

"Exactly my point. If you brand the Appernysians, you'll have just as many enemies as I do."

"Being a good leader isn't about doing what's popular. It's about doing what's necessary."

As Lon stared at Tarek, he knew the commander had already made his decision. His mind wouldn't be changed, but another idea popped into Lon's head. "You don't have to do it, Tarek. You're the commander. Your word is the law."

"I'm not going to change twelve hundred years of tradition and stop branding people," Tarek argued. "Besides, they want the Cross."

Lon shook his head. "That's not what I meant. *You* don't have to do it. A lot of Rayders hate me already, so let me brand the Appernysians. I'll be a lot quicker about it than you anyway, since

I can keep the branding iron constantly heated. I'll even do it right now, while the rest of Taeja is turning in for the night."

Tarek shook his head. "This labeling system is getting really confusing. Go ahead, Lon. Brand them. No more Appernysians. No more Swallows. Just Rayders."

"Hopefully that's not your only reason for branding them," Lon said with a smirk. "It must be hard to be an empty-headed simpleton."

Tarek swung a fist at the Beholder's head, but Lon pulled Dawes away and kicked him into a gallop toward the Swallows.

"Don't you want to give Flora a goodnight kiss before you leave?" Tarek taunted, but Lon ignored him. He had learned not to give in to Tarek's berating unless he wanted to end up bruised and bloodied.

As always, Wade and the rest of Lon's squad followed after the Beholder at a close distance.

Chapter 34

Reunited

"That's the last time I saw him," Mellai said. "Grandfather and I left that same day."

"How heartbreaking," Kaylen replied. Tears streaked down her cheeks. "No wonder you haven't talked about Theiss until now."

"I told you I just needed a few days. We're pathetic, you know? You're easily the most beautiful girl in Appernysia, but you're already seventeen and I'm a year older. We both should have been married years ago."

Kaylen smiled through her tears. "You've changed. The Mellai I knew back in Pree never would've said something like that. She despised men."

"I know. It serves me right that now, when I've finally found a man worth marrying, he doesn't want me anymore."

"Don't give up on Theiss yet," Kaylen said, lying sideways on her bed. "There's a good chance he'll still be around when this war blows over. Who else is he going to marry?"

"There are plenty of other girls in Roseiri," Mellai responded, "and you're wrong about my place here in Itorea. Even if Lon stops helping the Rayders, I'm too valuable to King Drogan. I'll have to stay here the rest of my life." That thought twisted in her stomach even as she said it. She doubted she would ever get used to the idea.

"If you decide to leave," Kaylen whispered, "he couldn't stop you."

Mellai sat back on her bed and stared at her friend with exaggerated surprise. "Listen to you, servant of the court, conspiring against the king."

Kaylen lifted her nose and stuck out her chin. "Not anymore. I've been promoted to lady-in-waiting, thank you very much, and to a Beholder, no less."

Mellai laughed. "I'm glad to have you." She looked around, absently sliding her fingers over the silk of her upholstered chair. The room used to be the quarters of Lord Ramik Gunderott, chamberlain of the king's council. "This room was too big for me to stay in by myself." Aside from her oversized bed, which was large enough to sleep five tradeswomen, Mellai's new quarters also had a smaller bed for Kaylen. A carved desk and ornate wardrobe—both made of polished oak—stood near the window, and a birch dining table large enough to seat eight people filled the middle of the room.

"I miss my old quarters," Kaylen said with a frown, breaking the silence. "I miss having Aely in the room next door."

"I know," Mellai replied, reaching over to give her friend a reassuring squeeze on her hand. "I'll make you a promise. As soon as we drive out the Rayders, I'll take you down to Wegnas, and we'll visit her."

Kaylen smiled weakly. "Thank you."

"Then after we leave the burial grounds," Mellai continued, "we'll take a ship out to sea and let the wind blow through our hair." She longed to touch the Asaras Sea. She hadn't even seen it yet, but she could often smell the salty air carried to her by the wind. It was hypnotic and refreshing.

A soft knock at the door cut off their conversation.

"Come in," Mellai called.

Kutad poked his head inside. "They're ready for you, Mellai."

Mellai thanked Kutad and stood to leave, but Kaylen remained lying on the bed. Mellai turned to her friend. "Aren't you coming?"

Kaylen shook her head. "Sorry, but I can't. I never want to see the great hall again."

Without argument, Mellai exited the room after Kutad. Kaylen's response didn't bother her. If she were in Kaylen's shoes, Mellai would have felt exactly the same way.

The other four men in her guard were waiting with Kutad. The five of them formed a tight circle around Mellai before stepping away from her door and crossing the seating area of the royal chamber. A young page opened the door for them, bowing his head respectfully.

"Thank you, Ernon," Mellai said to the young man.

Ernon placed his fist over his heart and nodded at Mellai, then closed the door after she and her guard had exited the royal chamber and started down the stairs.

Kutad led them down the spiraling staircase, past the sentries posted at the bottom, and into the confusing maze of corridors. As they passed one of the many cross-corridors on their way to the great hall, Mellai glanced down it and saw two people. They were at the far end of the long hallway, too far away to recognize or hear, but judging by the way they threw their arms around, they were in the middle of a heated discussion.

"Wait," Mellai told her guard, then stepped back to peer down the hall again. She summoned True Sight and pulled the conversation to her ears, her instincts shouting it was a conversation worth eavesdropping. The two people were still arguing and their voices were rising.

". . . forget about the necklace already. The council has been dead for over three months. We don't need the trinket anymore."

"Says who?"

"Says Lady Netsey. She's on her way to Taeja right now."

"But that's suicide, Verle. They'll kill her."

King Drogan's page, Mellai thought with anger.

"Don't you understand?" Verle said. "She doesn't care. Her father's dead, along with all their plans. She doesn't care about anything anymore, except ruining King Drogan."

"How will joining the Rayders hurt the king?"

There was a pause in the conversation as Verle stepped sideways, blocking Mellai's view of the other man. "She knows about the king's Beholder." His voice slithered out in a whisper.

Mellai had heard enough. She captured Verle in a pocket of air and threw him aside to grab the other hidden man, but she was too late. The other man's body fell on the ground, void of its glowing essence and blood pouring from his chest.

The vision shocked Mellai, enough that she loosed her hold on Verle. As soon as the page was free, he thrust a bloody dagger into his own chest and buckled to the floor.

"No!" Mellai screamed as she ran. Her guard followed after her, shouting for her to wait, but Mellai ignored the warnings. She had to get to Verle and heal him before he died. She had to read his memories. Just when Mellai drew near enough that she thought she could start repairing Verle's wound, his essence lifted out of his body, hovered for a brief moment, then disappeared.

Mellai released her power and slowed her pace until she was standing still. Her guard surrounded her and Kutad rushed forward to check on the two men. They were lying in their own pools of blood. The only visible weapon was the dagger sticking out of Verle's chest.

"Do you know him?" Kutad asked Snoom, pointing to the man next to Verle.

Snoom stared at him for a moment. "No, Sergeant. He's probably a servant of the court."

Kutad returned to Mellai. "What happened here? What did you see?"

"Verle killed the other man," Mellai answered, "then stabbed himself when I tried to capture him."

"Why would he do that?" Snoom asked.

Mellai turned and sprinted down the corridor. "Leave them. We need to talk to the king." She led the way back to the intersecting hallways, then let Kutad pass and followed him as they hurried to the great hall. When the sentries posted at the great hall's entrance saw Mellai and her guard running toward them, they pushed the doors open and rushed to Mellai's aid, thinking she was under attack.

"Lock the doors behind us," Mellai ordered as they entered the great hall. She ran straight to the king, who was sitting at the far end of the room with Queen Cyra, General Astadem, and Lords Teph, Haedon, and Anton.

King Drogan jumped to his feet. "What's going on?"

"Send your fastest riders for Taeja," Mellai shouted between gasps for air. "Lady Netsey's on her way to tell the Rayders about me. She has to be stopped."

The concern on the king's face transformed to confusion, then contemplation, and finally satisfaction. "Let her go."

"What?" Mellai gasped. She bent over and placed her hands on her knees, blindsided by the king's calm reaction. "Why?"

"Because they'll kill her, which will do us a favor."

"But what about the information she'll give them?"

King Drogan tilted his head at Mellai. "Where did you hear this?"

"I just caught Verle arguing with a servant about it," Mellai answered. "He killed the servant and himself before I could learn anything more."

"Did anyone else hear this?" King Drogan asked.

Kutad shook his head. "They were out of earshot."

King Drogan moved in front of Mellai, his eyes intense and probing. "Are you certain this is what you heard, Beholder?"

"Without doubt, your Majesty."

"Then that is unfortunate news indeed," General Astadem inserted.

"Verle," Cyra repeated with shock. Her hand drifted to the glowing stone hanging around her neck. "Our circle of trust continues to shrink."

"I agree," King Drogan said, "which is why I've made my choice. I'm not worried about Lady Netsey because the Rayders are going to find out anyway. Mellai, I will announce your presence to Itorea before we go to battle."

Mellai looked at Kamron. "You feel the same way?"

"I didn't at first, but now I do."

"As do I," Kutad added. "It was foolish of me to think we could tell our soldiers about you and expect them to keep it a secret."

"We need an army," King Drogan said, "and the only way to reassure them that we can win is to tell them they have a Beholder on their side."

Mellai sighed. "As you wish, your Majesty."

King Drogan arose and stood before Mellai. "We'd also like to mark you with the Beholder's Eye. You'll be a beacon of hope to our kingdom."

"With all due respect, your Majesty, that's going too far." Mellai straightened and folded her arms. "I don't want a big *I'm a Beholder, Kill me* sign painted on my face."

"Tattooed," Snoom inserted.

"A *permanent* target?" Mellai said, her eyebrows raised. "My answer is definitely no."

Kutad put his hand on her shoulder. "Just listen—"

"No, *you* just listen," Mellai cut in, pulling away. "I don't care if Beholders had the marking in the First Age. They lived in a completely different time where they were respected and safe. This is a different age. My ability to use True Sight isn't affected at all by what's tattooed on my face. And you don't need me as a beacon to rally your army. That's what flags are for. If you want to inspire the people and give them confidence against the Rayders, then I can demonstrate my power for them. I don't need a tattoo."

"But Mellai—" Snoom tried to intercede.

"I don't even know what the Beholder's Eye looks like," Mellai continued, "and I doubt you know anyone experienced in giving tattoos. It's a lost art. I'd come away from it looking uglier than Braedr."

Everyone stared at Mellai.

"Who's Braedr?" Snoom finally asked.

"It doesn't matter," Mellai said. "My answer is still no."

The king was silent for a long time, a little too calm and collected considering Mellai's tirade.

"I disagree with your choice, Beholder. Henry is a talented surgeon, with years of experience with needles. I'm sure he could manage. However, I realize we cannot force you if you refuse. We will have to be satisfied with a public display of power. Lord Teph, begin preparing heralds to carry the news throughout the kingdom."

"And the villages, your Majesty?" Mellai asked.

"Well spoken," King Drogan agreed. "Send runners along the trade routes as well, Lord Teph. Tell them that a Beholder has joined my army, but keep her identity a secret. If Lon Marcs discovers Mellai is our Beholder, he might try to use their family to sway her."

Lord Teph bowed. "Yes, my king."

"I apologize again for my rash behavior," Mellai said as she curtsied, "and it probably won't be the last time. But if I may, I would like to make one more request. Send a portion of your army to protect Réxura. It's a key trade port for Appernysia, and it's the closest city to Taeja. They are completely defenseless."

"You are forgiven," King Drogan replied, "and I have already taken your suggestion under consideration. I don't mean to doubt your abilities, but I will not underestimate the Rayders again. Every available soldier must fight in this battle. Don't worry about Réxura. We will move swiftly and drive the Rayders out of Appernysia before they have a chance to attack."

The king took a slow breath. "I think we are finished here. Thank you for coming, Beholder. You may return to your quarters."

Lord Teph followed after Mellai as she exited the great hall. "Where is Verle's body?"

"This way," she answered.

Lord Teph signaled for the two sentries to follow, then trailed behind Mellai and her guard. She gestured down the corridor to Verle's body, then continued back toward the royal chamber while Lord Teph turned down the hallway with the sentries.

"He's a busy man now that he's filling Lord Ramik's shoes," Kutad commented as they walked. "Lord Teph has to be overwhelmed."

"You can stop the pointless conversation, Sergeant," Mellai replied. "I made my decision about the tattoo."

"As you wish," Kutad said. No one else spoke until Kutad opened the door for Mellai to enter her room in the royal chamber. "I will let you know once Lord Teph has completed his proclamation for the heralds. You might want to start thinking about what you could do with your power to reassure our people."

"Kutad?" Kaylen called from inside the room.

Kutad leaned inside after Mellai. Kaylen was sitting upright on one of the upholstered chairs, her legs hanging straight down.

"Your range of motion is returning," Kutad observed. "That's great news."

"Only because of Mellai's help," Kaylen said. She smiled at her friend, but Mellai ignored her and plopped face first onto the bed.

"Is she alright?" Kaylen asked, her voice filled with concern.

"She's fine," Kutad answered. "We just ran into Verle outside. He turned out to be a traitor."

Kaylen gasped. "What did he do?"

"Besides kill himself? I'm not sure. He died before Mellai could read his memories."

Mellai turned her head toward Kaylen, unburying her face from the comforter. "Hurry up. I want to be alone."

"I don't have to do this now," Kaylen replied. "I can talk to him later."

"About what?" Kutad asked.

"Ugh," Mellai complained, rolling onto her back. "Would you at least come in and close the door?"

Kutad complied and sat in the chair next to Kaylen. "What is it?"

"I want to know why you changed your mind," she replied. "You used to hate King Drogan."

"Aye, I did." He glanced warily at Mellai.

"Relax," Mellai said. "I'm not reading your memories. It would be pointless. Kaylen already told me everything."

"And Mellai told me everything, too," Kaylen added. "Why did you do it, Kutad? Why did you betray my trust? Why did you tell King Drogan about Lon?"

Kutad licked his bottom lip and frowned. "To protect Appernysia. I abandoned my role as a soldier after Linney died, but it was only because of differences between the king and me. I have always cared for our nation, though. You can't serve in an army without developing an unshakable love for the people you're protecting."

"It had nothing to do with earning King Drogan's trust?" Kaylen asked. "To become a soldier again?"

"Not at all, but my attitude toward him has changed. I learned King Drogan has been ruled by his council for decades. It was his council that denied me audience when Linney died, not him. I've forgiven him."

Kaylen frowned and lowered her eyes. "Lon must love the people he's protecting, too. He's never coming back, is he?"

"I thought you didn't want him to come back," Mellai replied, but she didn't wait to hear Kaylen's answer. She didn't want to hear it.

Mellai stared up at the ceiling while she thought back on the conversation between Verle and the other man. They were talking about a necklace. From the way Queen Cyra reacted when she heard Verle's name, it was obviously her necklace they were talking about. Why did they want it so badly? Mellai focused on her memories of the necklace and how it put off a constant glow of soft white light. It had to have been made by a Beholder, which means it must be an heirloom passed down from queen to queen since the First Age. No wonder Lady Netsey wanted it.

The riddle of the stone's creation stuck in Mellai's mind. She knew how to bend light to make herself appear invisible, but if she did so and closed her eyes, the bent light would return to normal. As she pondered possibilities, a possible answer formed in her mind. The glowing light had been contained within something solid—something that didn't require a Beholder's constant attention to maintain its shape. The crystal had been formed around the light, sealing the light permanently within. The solution seemed simple enough, but the process sounded impossible.

Mellai had to try it. Her eyes clouded over as she summoned True Sight, but before she had a chance to experiment, Llen appeared. He was hovering over the foot of her bed, his white eyes radiating with furious light.

"You have shamed me, Mellai," the Jaed boomed, "along with every other Beholder of the First Age."

What did I do? Mellai asked in her mind.

Llen's voice calmed, but his intensity remained. "What is your only purpose as a Beholder?"

To serve Appernysia.

"You refused the highest honor Appernysia's king can offer you."

The tattoo? Mellai asked.

"Leadership requires selflessness, Mellai."

I wasn't just thinking of myself, Mellai argued. *A permanent marking would make me a public target for traitors. What good would I be to King Drogan if I were dead?*

Llen's eyes narrowed. "Personal safety is the last of a Beholder's priorities. Do not justify your pride. Your refusal had nothing to do with Appernysia. Think of your king's argument. You will inspire his people to unite, which is the greatest need pressing upon you. And regarding your personal safety, your argument will be short lived. Tattoo or not, your description will wash through Appernysia quicker than a rushing waterfall. Everyone will know you at sight, with or without the Beholder's Eye."

Mellai sighed. It wasn't easy to admit to herself, but the Jaed was right—mostly. However, one part of her hesitation hadn't been self-ish. *Who gave Beholders and the Phoenijan their tattoos in the First Age?*

"Other Beholders," Llen replied, "which was partly why the Rayders began branding themselves instead. Aside from their loss of the Lynth flower, there were no more Beholders left to mark them."

Then who is going to tattoo me? If the Beholder's Eye is as honorable a symbol as you say it is, then should it be given by anyone other than a Beholder? Before Mellai even finished asking, the answer had entered her mind. She raised her eyebrows with emphasis. *Llen, would you do it?*

The Jaed hummed. "I would be honored, Mellai, but my involve-ment must be kept a secret. I will assist only because it is a matter of necessity and honor, not safety or protection. Appernysians must not be led to believe that Jaeds will intervene on their behalf."

Thank you, Llen. This will work perfectly. I'll get the Beholder's Eye, and everyone watching will have their display of power. To them, the needle and ink will be flicking around by magic.

"All I will need," Llen countered, "is the dried petals of one Lynth flower."

You'll have them, Mellai replied with a smile, anticipating the shock on everyone's faces when she received the mark.

Kaylen's voice interrupted their conversation. "What are you smiling about, Mellai?"

Llen nodded and disappeared, then Mellai released her power. "I was just thinking how happy King Drogan's going to be."

"Why's that?" Kutad asked. Mellai could hear the anticipation in his voice.

Mellai sat up and swung her legs off the edge of the bed. "Send Ernon to the great hall with a message for our king. Tell him I will tattoo myself with the Beholder's Eye in front of anyone he wants to invite."

Chapter 35
Light of Appernysia

"Last time I stood in front of a crowd this big," Kamron whispered to Mellai, "I almost lost my head."

Mellai smiled inwardly, trying to keep a composed disposition in front of so many people. She knew the general was referring to his near execution. She admired him, along with Kutad. Both had loathed King Drogan at some point for a decision that wasn't really his. Yet, they had let go of their anger when they learned the truth. It must have taken a lot of faith and courage.

"I hope I don't lose mine," Mellai replied.

"That's what we're here for," Kutad said. In addition to Kamron, Mellai's guard, and the king's sentries, another fifty soldiers protected the snow-covered platform outside the castle. They wouldn't let their Beholder come to harm. Of course King Drogan and Queen Cyra were there, along with a fully recovered Kaylen.

King Drogan stepped forward and raised his hands. "Welcome Appe—" He faltered as Mellai projected his voice through the air to the ears of everyone gathered inside the keep. After glancing back at the Beholder's clouded eyes, King Drogan smiled and spoke again with renewed vigor. "Welcome Appernysians!"

A deafening roar erupted from hundreds of thousands of nobles, peasants, soldiers, and the countless heralds who had been scattered across the fifty square miles to pass along their king's words.

"Today," the king continued with Mellai's assistance, "I bring you the greatest news to reach our kingdom since the First Age. Today, I bring you a Beholder."

Cheers did not follow, but a wave of frightened and angry whispers. Mellai tried to separate some of the comments as she pulled the sound to her ears.

"The Rayder Beholder?"

"Did they capture him?"

"Which one is he?"

"We can't control him."

"He'll kill us all."

Amid the scattered talk, Mellai also realized that many people attributed the enhancement of King Drogan's voice as a trick of the Beholder, perhaps to enter their heads and kill them from the inside. She passed everything she heard to King Drogan.

"This isn't going at all like I hoped," the king commented. He threw his hands up in the air and indicated for Mellai to project his voice again. "Rest assured, the Rayder Beholder is not the Beholder here with us today. In fact, our Beholder is not a man at all, but a young peasant woman."

Mellai listened to the people's responses as they changed from fear to curiosity. Most of the people were soldiers, families of the soldiers, or had heard firsthand accounts about Lon from the soldiers. They knew the Rayder Beholder was a man. Those who couldn't see Mellai's clouded eyes watched Mellai and Kaylen with raised eyebrows, wondering if either was the woman King Drogan meant.

"She holds more power than the Rayders or their Beholder could possibly imagine," King Drogan continued. "She will lead our army into Taeja and drive them out. Never again will the Rayders plague this land."

Cheers finally came. Mellai continued listening to and relaying their comments, though many were unsettling to her. They would have their revenge for their fallen loved ones. The Rayders would pay a terrible price.

King Drogan raised his hands once more. "But first, I would like to recognize three men. Step forward Ric Jois, Duncan Shord, and Banty Prates."

"Who's Banty?" Mellai asked Kamron, but she discovered her answer when Snoom joined the two sentries on the front of the platform. *No wonder he uses his nickname,* she thought to herself.

"Despite an aggressive attempt on my life and my queen's," the king continued, "these three knights stood against overwhelming odds to protect us. I award them with the Lynth pendant, so that all may know their courage, bravery, and loyalty to Appernysia."

Mellai was stunned at the crowd's silence, thinking it disrespectful and wanting to intervene. However, as King Drogan slowly moved between the three men and hung a silver pendant around each of their necks, Mellai quickly realized the silence was not disrespectful, but revered.

"The Lynth pendant is the highest honor a soldier can receive," Kamron whispered in her ear.

Mellai nodded. "And well deserved, in this case." Her hand drifted to the ghraef pendant around her own neck, and her mother's hidden pendant underneath her dress. She marveled at their origins, crafted by her enemy.

King Drogan stood to the side and dipped his head toward the three men, who brought their fists over their hearts and bowed before stepping back to their positions behind Mellai.

"Now," the king continued, addressing the crowd, "we will honor our Beholder as she has honored us. Today, she will receive the Beholder's Eye."

King Drogan gestured to Kaylen, who held a gold platter covered with white lace. She placed it on an ivory pedestal at the front of the platform, then the king invited Mellai forward. She moved next to him, directly behind the platter. She squirmed under the probing stares of innumerable glowing figures below and tugged at the tight bodice of her gown, suddenly feeling very self-conscious.

King Drogan stepped to the side and gestured to Mellai. "Unlike the sorceries of the Rayder's amateur Beholder, you will now witness the power of *True* Sight."

A hush of anticipation fell over the crowd. Mellai knew that none of them were aware of the Jaed hovering in front of her, nor could they hear his voice as he appeared and began a private ceremony of his own.

"Mellai Marcs," Llen spoke. "Today you bring honor to your parents, Aron and Shalán Marcs, who raised you as one worthy to receive this gift. Today I mark you as a Beholder, wielder of True Sight, and protector of Appernysia."

Using True Sight, Llen removed the lace from the silver platter, carefully folded it, and placed it on the ground. Five blue petals rested on the tray, each the diameter of a baby's fist. Llen raised the petals from the platter and organized them into an evenly spaced halo. The ring moved up and slowly rotated in front of Mellai's face.

One of the petals broke out of the circular formation. It dissolved into a liquid, then transformed into the tiny form of a flying blue ghraef. At the tip of its tail was a sparkling white light. The ghraef circled around Mellai's head before descending in front of her left eye. Mellai squinted into the light shining from its tail as the ghraef opened its tiny jaws and let out a deafening roar, then buried itself headfirst into the skin below her left eye.

Mellai glanced at her reflection in the breastplate of a guardsman kneeling at the front of the platform. Two downward-facing claws of blue had formed on her left cheekbone, just below her eye. She breathed deeply. Her skin tingled, but without any pain.

"The mark of the ghraef," Llen said, his eyes gleaming with pride. "Let it bring you strength from a loyal friend and remind those who oppose you of his matchless power."

Mellai's mind reeled as she once again thought of riding a ghraef.

"Remember this, Beholder," the Jaed continued. "Ghraefs are not pets, but powerful creatures with knowledge that in many ways surpasses our own. Should one honor you with his presence, you would be wise to join yourself with him as an equal companion, bound together by friendship and respect."

Mellai nodded, grateful for the crucial information.

Another petal moved out of the circle and shifted into the shape of a blue King's Cross. It hovered in front of Mellai for a moment, then twisted sideways and spun into the skin of her forehead.

In her reflection, Mellai saw the top blade of the King's Cross appear on her brow, traced in blue. It was centered above her left eye.

"The mark of the King's Cross," Llen said. "Let it fortify your loyalty to Appernysia's king and sustain your kinship with your fellow Taejans."

Mellai frowned. In her excitement of reading the oak tree's memories in the clearing, she hadn't processed all of the information she gleaned. She was a pure-blood descendent of Taejans, and thereby Rayders. Not only Lon, but every other Rayder in Taeja was her kin—and she was going to battle against them.

The three remaining Lynth petals rose high above the keep, pulling Mellai from her thoughts. She leaned her head back and watched as they began spinning around each other, steadily increasing in speed. As they did, a small white light appeared in their core. Its intensity swelled so greatly that Mellai wanted to shade her eyes, then they burst into a ring of light that raced over Itorea.

In place of the dispersed light was a large sphere of blue dust, swirling within itself. The sphere lowered in front of Mellai, then shrunk in size as it curved around the left side of her face and splashed into the skin of her temple.

Mellai marveled at her reflection, which showed a blue arc connecting the mark of the ghraef to the mark of the King's Cross. Five solid triangles pushed outward from the arc, evenly spaced from each other.

"The mark of True Sight," Llen said. "Let it endow you with the power of your unparalleled gift and give you the courage to do what is necessary."

Llen hovered closer to Mellai. "You have seen much and struggled often, Mellai, but it has not been without cause. Above all else, remember that Beholders are not chosen idly. Follow your pure heart, Beholder. It will not lead you astray."

Mellai's emotions swelled as Llen finished speaking and disappeared. Tears filled her eyes, but she maintained control of her power and nodded to King Drogan, indicating that she was finished.

King Drogan faced the crowd. "I'm at a loss for words," he said solemnly, "but what more could I say? You have seen for yourself what this Beholder is capable of doing. General Astadem, assemble my army. We march for Taeja!"

Chapter 36

Mobilized

A whistling spear shrieked through the air. Lieutenant Thennek Racketh looked up to see the spear flying at him from the southeast summit of Three Peaks. It landed only a few hundred feet from his guardhouse. A moment later, another spear shot from the hidden ballista atop the mountain crest. It left a long trail of flame as it arched through the air toward the south.

"Another one?" Thennek said as he mounted his horse and galloped toward the first spear. When he reached it, Thennek pulled the shaft from the snow, unscrewed its steel tip, and retrieved a rolled piece of parchment from its partially hollowed core. He unrolled the parchment and read its message.

Carriage with light escorts. Heading toward Taeja. Fast pace. Thirty-five miles south.

Thennek tossed the note aside, climbed onto his horse, then pulled a spyglass from his saddlebag and placed it against his eye. He aimed it south, in the same direction indicated by the flaming spear. A tiny cloud of dust rose into the sky, just at the limit of his vision.

He placed the spyglass back in his saddlebag and kicked his horse into a gallop. As he rode past the guardhouse, Thennek shouted for ten men to follow.

"More 'Nysian refugees?" one of the Rayders asked when they finally caught up to him. "It has been months since we saw the last group of them."

Thennek shook his head. "This is a carriage with escorts, and they are in a hurry."

"An embassy?"

"Perhaps," Thennek answered, "but we need to stop them before they reach Taeja. They cannot see our defenses and take that knowledge back to Itorea." He angled farther west and urged his horse faster, anxious to intercept the carriage.

A few hours later, at the waning light of dusk, Thennek and his men reached the approaching carriage. It was trapped in the middle of the reopened south river with a broken wheel, still twenty-five miles from the east bridge into Taeja. Under the brutal whips of its master, the team of horses tried to pull the wagon from the icy river, but it was stuck fast. The river was too deep, too cold, and the horses kept slipping on its stony bed.

The six carriage escorts were on the river's north bank and preoccupied with their predicament. They didn't seem to notice the Rayders until they were nearly upon them. The closest escort unsheathed his sword and rode at them. Thennek calmly slipped his composite bow from his shoulder and loosed an arrow at the man, piercing his heart. As the man tumbled to the ground, the other ten Rayders pulled their glaives from their saddles, formed a wedge in front of their lieutenant, then charged the remaining five.

"Wait," a woman's voice screeched over the splashing river.

Thennek ordered his men to halt. He searched for the source of the voice, unable to find it.

"I'm up here, you wreaking pile of dung," the voice continued, then a pudgy face poked out of the baggage stored on top of the carriage. "I thought Rayders were supposed to be intelligent."

Thennek smiled at the woman's rash behavior. "Bold words for a woman so far away from home."

"Lady," the woman snapped. "Lady Netsey D'Lío."

Thennek bowed low in his saddle with exaggerated mockery. "Pleased to meet you, Lady Netsey. What can we, your humble servants, do for you?"

"You can get me out of this blasted river," Netsey screamed. She tried to stand up and nearly toppled over the side of the carriage. Her face went ghostly white and she plopped back down on her rear.

"I would, my lady," Thennek continued, "but I don't want to get my polished boots wet. And I just gave my horse a buttermilk bath." He patted his horse's neck, sending clouds of dust puffing into the air from its mane.

"You wouldn't treat me like that if you knew why I was here."

"Why *are* you here?" Thennek said with a yawn. "This conversation bores me."

"I have crucial news for your commander," Netsey said. "I must see him immediately."

"That will not happen," Thennek replied, his sarcasm gone. "Best to hop down from that carriage and follow the river back to Itorea."

Netsey's face turned red. "How dare you. Never in my life have I been treated so—"

Thennek nocked another arrow in his bow. "You are not welcome here."

Netsey's escorts, who had been watching from their horses, moved to attack Thennek. The other ten Rayders raised their glaives. The escorts tossed their weapons to the ground and threw their hands in the air.

"Should I give the kill order," Thennek asked Netsey, "you spoiled 'Nysian cow?"

"We have a Beholder," Netsey screamed. "She's in Itorea right now, preparing King Drogan's army to attack Taeja."

Thennek pulled back on his bowstring and aimed the nocked arrow at Netsey's forehead. "Do not lie to me."

"I'm not. She came to Itorea three weeks ago."

"Women cannot be Beholders," Thennek shouted back, his frustration growing.

"She's staying in the king's royal chamber."

Thennek was about to loose the arrow, when a change in the horizon caught his attention. The eastern sky, which should have been darkening under the setting sun, looked as though it was growing brighter. Yes, like another sun was rising. The light pushed into the sky and became so intense that the lieutenant had to avert his eyes.

Quicker than it came, the light suddenly disappeared, leaving them in the reddish hue of dusk.

Thennek lowered his bow and gaped. Whether that light came from within the walls of Itorea or not, one thing was certain. Another Beholder was in Appernysia. There was no doubt, and from the powerful display of light, it appeared he—or perhaps she—was extremely powerful.

Thennek refocused his attention on Netsey. "Who is this Beholder?"

"I never met her," Netsey answered, "but I've heard she's really good friends with a handmaiden from Pree."

"Who—"

"No need to ask me for the handmaiden's name," Netsey interrupted, obviously enjoying her control over their conversation. "I had the displeasure of meeting her many times in the king's court. Kaylen Shaw." She spat out the name like a rotten potato.

Thennek pondered the name, wondering if this Kaylen might be related to their Beholder, Lon Shaw. "Why are you telling us this?"

"My name is Lady Netsey," she snapped, "and I'm telling you because I hate King Drogan. I'd rather see him destroyed by Rayders than reign over Appernysia another day."

Thennek returned the arrow to his quiver and slid the bow over his shoulder. After signaling his men to follow, he galloped west with as much speed as he could force out of his exhausted horse.

"What about me?" Netsey called. "I'm still stuck here."

Thennek ignored her as he glanced at Three Peaks. All three crests were glowing red.

*　*　*　*　*

Lon peered through the darkness. "Eleven men on horses."

"Rayders?" Tarek asked.

"I can't tell from this far away," Lon answered. He watched as the men continued around the south end of Taeja and up the corridor leading to the south gate.

"Open the gate," a voice called when they reached the trench, "by order of Lieutenant Thennek Racketh."

Rather than waiting for the soldiers to lower the drawbridge, Lon filled the wide trench with a land bridge and created an opening through the high barrier of dirt. When Thennek and his men burst through the opening, Tarek and Lon were waiting for them on the other side.

"Why is Three Peaks lit?" Tarek asked. "What was that burst of light?"

Thennek saluted. "I am not sure, my Commander, but—"

"If I find out my entire army is assembled because of an accident," Tarek growled, "I'll hold you responsible, Lieutenant."

"Yes, my Commander. We had a visitor right before the light appeared. A Lady Netsey D'Lío, who claimed Itorea has a Beholder."

A thick silence swept over those who heard Thennek's news.

"Who's the Beholder?" Lon asked. His voice was calm and his eyes were still clouded with his own power.

"Netsey did not know who she was, but—"

"*She?*" Tarek cut in again. "Don't tell me you believed her?"

"Not until I saw the light, my Commander." Thennek saluted again. "Although we do not know her identity, Netsey said she has a friend from Pree. My Commander, you were from that village. Do you know Kaylen Shaw?"

Lon eyed his friend and saw the fire in Tarek's eyes disappear. "Yes, but it's been over a decade." As he finished speaking, he returned Lon's gaze.

Thennek turned to Lon. "She has your last name, Beholder. Do you know her?"

Lon flexed his jaw, then forced himself to relax. "How does Lady Netsey know her? Nobles don't travel to the outskirts."

"According to Netsey, Kaylen is a handmaiden in the king's court."

Lon's eyes widened. He turned away, lost in his thoughts. *I never heard of Kaylen or Scut having living relatives, in or outside of Pree. Is this Kaylen someone different from my Kaylen?* As the last thought ran through Lon's mind, a chill ran down his spine. He had no claim to her anymore. He didn't have the right. A year had passed since he had left and news of the Rayder Beholder no doubt reached Pree. Kaylen would know it was him. She would see him as a traitor. She must have moved on and forgotten him, just as he had constantly forgotten her since reaching Taeja. From the sound of it, Kaylen *had* moved on, all the way to Itorea.

"Lon?" Tarek said, placing a hand on his shoulder.

"I don't know," Lon whispered, quiet enough that the surrounding men couldn't hear him. "I don't know if it's her, but something tells me it is. It would've taken something really important to make her leave Pree. She's all Scut has left."

"Agreed," Tarek replied, "and from the way you've talked about her and Mellai—"

"Mellai wouldn't let Kaylen leave without her," Lon cut in, then a terrible thought entered his mind, so terrible that it churned in his stomach and crawled up the back of his throat. Spasms shook his abdomen. He brought his hand to his mouth, barely keeping himself from retching all over the ground.

Wade came running from the shadows with his hand gripped around his sheathed sword. "I recognized Kaylen's name, Beholder. She shares your last name. Is this the same woman? Is she your wife?"

"Not quite," Tarek answered as Lon struggled to regain his composure. He wrapped his thick arm around Wade's shoulders and pulled him close. "You're a good man, Wade, and the two of us are getting along better than last year. What I'm about to tell you doesn't leave your lips, understand?"

Wade kissed his fingers and placed them against his brand. "By my honor, my Commander."

Tarek nodded. "Kaylen and Lon share the same last name because Shaw isn't his real last name. It's Marcs."

Wade's eyebrows lifted with understanding. "Aron Marcs?"

"His father," Tarek replied with a nod. "Now you know why he kept his name a secret."

"My father's a great man," Lon interceded, having finally gained control, "the best man I know. I never want to hear his name and traitor in the same sentence."

"You do not have to worry," Wade replied with a bow. "He would have to be a father of renown to raise a Beholder son."

Lon wiped his mouth with the back of his hand and stepped close to the other two men. "*And* daughter. I think my twin sister is the other Beholder." His throat twitched and he turned away, distracting himself from another pressing wave of vomit.

"Was she a Beholder before you left?" Wade asked.

"Not that he knew of," Tarek answered.

"How can we be sure it is her?"

"Good question." Tarek looked over his shoulder. "Lieutenant Thennek. Where's Netsey?"

"I left her at the river," Thennek answered. "Why, my Commander?"

"Did she tell you what the Beholder looks like?"

"She never met the Beholder."

The commander cursed and stomped away in Thennek's direction. "She was probably lying. You should have brought . . ."

Tarek's voice faded in Lon's mind. He lowered himself to the ground and sat with his legs crossed, breathing deeply through his nose and pushing it slowly out of his mouth.

"Beholder?" Wade asked.

"Give me a moment," Lon said.

He closed his eyes and thought of his sister. It had been months since he had felt for her, so it took a few minutes to reestablish the connection. Before he could sense any of Mellai's emotions, Lon was bombarded by an overwhelming sense of . . . *something*. He could only describe it as authority . . . or power. He worked around the wall, searching for a way through. It took a few minutes, but he eventually found it. When Lon entered his twin's emotions, they were smothered with anxiety. Lon had felt a similar emotion in his sister before. Mellai had felt that way before her fifteenth birthday celebration in Pree, when she had come of age. It should have been exciting, but Mellai had complained to Lon many times about the opportunity it would give Braedr to court her.

Mellai is anxious of something to come, Lon thought. He couldn't read her thoughts, but he guessed her anxiety stemmed from a pressing battle with the Rayders. Even worse, it would be a battle against another Beholder. A battle against her brother.

Lon reopened his eyes and called for Tarek. The commander returned, red-faced and gruff. "What?"

"It's Mellai," Lon told Tarek and Wade. "She's the Beholder, and a powerful one for sure. You saw that light. It lit up the sky as bright as the sun; I don't have the power to do anything like that. Even with me fighting against her, she'll push through Taeja's defenses without breaking a sweat."

"We won't run away," Tarek asked. "We fought and died for this city."

"I know," Lon answered, "but staying here will be a deathtrap. I can't defend Taeja against her."

"Forget about winning," Tarek said. "Can you even bring your-self to fight against her?" His words were calm and collected, but loaded with venom.

Lon tried to process the idea, but found it impossible at that moment. "I can't answer that yet, Tarek, but it doesn't change the fact that we have to leave."

"Ride out and meet them head on in an open-plain battle? Ten thousand versus a hundred thousand, no defenses, and against a Beholder who's even stronger than you. Not the best odds in the world, Lon."

"Fourteen thousand," Lon countered. "You have an extra four thousand Rayder soldiers now."

"Maybe so, but they aren't anywhere near as skilled as the rest of my men, and we don't have armor made for them yet. They would better serve here, protecting Taeja while we're gone."

An idea suddenly occurred to Lon. "Mellai's never been in battle before; she won't be used to all of the death and suffering that comes with it. She won't want to kill people. Even if she does, she won't kill her own soldiers. We'll do exactly what you said, Tarek. Ride out and meet them, but we won't meet them head on. We'll have to close with the Appernysians as quickly as possible so Mellai can't distinguish between the two sides. It'll catch Appernysia off-guard as well. It's the only chance we have."

"An all-out brawl with Appernysians," Tarek said. A grin slowly formed on his face. "I've never heard of a better idea."

Lon tried to smile. "I thought you'd like that."

*　　*　　*　　*　　*

Since the Rayders had already mobilized their army, they marched out of Taeja an hour after Thennek arrived. A runner had been sent to Bryst Grayson to have him load supply wagons and catch up to the army, while a separate runner had been sent to the Swallows. They would remain behind.

"Think they'll survive?" Tarek had asked as they led their army of ten thousand Rayders out of Taeja.

"The Appernysians?" Lon replied. "You've been training them hard. I'm sure they'll be fine. We're the ones marching into battle, not them, and we had to leave somebody to protect the civilians. Not to mention Braedr. He can't be trusted, even in prison."

"I know, but they're still Swallows. If the calahein decide to attack while we're gone, they won't last very long."

"None of us would."

Early the next day, Tarek and Lon met one of Lieutenant Thennek's men at the crossing where they had left Lady Netsey. Her crippled carriage was still in the river, with her bloated corpse dangling over one side. Her bags had been torn open and scattered on both banks of the river. None of her escorts were in sight.

Lieutenant Thennek immediately chimed in. "What happened?"

"They grew tired of Lady Dictatorship," the Rayder replied with a shake of his head. "They looted her possessions and fled south toward Itorea."

"How many approach?" Tarek asked.

"None that we could see from Three Peaks before nightfall, my Commander," the Rayder replied with a salute. "But after that light from the east, we had feared the worst and lit the beacons."

"As you should have," Tarek replied, then directed his attention to Thennek. "Return to Three Peaks, Lieutenant, and tell your men to defend it with their lives."

Thennek saluted, then he and his soldiers galloped north.

Chapter 37

Underground

Bryst Grayson stole along the perimeter of the Rayder fighting arena, hiding behind the low wall of packed dirt. It was there that Tarek Ascennor had become Rayder Commander after besting all comers, including Bryst's own lieutenant, Braedr.

The defeat had come as a surprise to all of Lieutenant Braedr's supporters, which made the defeat even more humiliating—not just for the lieutenant, but for everyone who followed him, too.

Many had defected from Lieutenant Braedr's cause after his defeat. Even as one of the lieutenant's leading agents, Bryst had wrestled with his own doubts. Ultimately, though, he stuck with Braedr's plan to take over leadership of the Rayders and had rallied enough men to fight in his behalf.

Bryst peeked over the low wall at the lieutenant's prison. Bryst knew that it was hidden in the nearby brick dome, stabbing into the air higher than six full-grown men. The entrance into the dome was guarded by a circle of at least fifty Swallows. The Appernysian refugees stood in crisp rows with glaives in their hands and swords at their waists. The display was impressive, perhaps even intimidating to someone who didn't know better. But Bryst had seen much of their so-called training. He knew their weaknesses and exactly how to exploit them. By the end of the day, Braedr would be free. By the end of the week, he would be the Rayders' new commander.

Bryst spit on the muddy soil in disgust. Tarek had given those Swallows weapons. And not just any weapons, but Rayder glaives. He glowered at the guards, visualizing the fresh brands on their right temples. Such a thought infuriated him. They had fought for the enemy during the Battle for Taeja—forced or not, it didn't matter. Besides the two thousand Lon had pointlessly saved during the fight, the rest had defected *after* the Rayders had proven themselves supreme in battle. Now they were depleting Rayder resources without giving anything noteworthy in return. They did not deserve the mark of the King's Cross. They deserved to die, along with the other slaves Captain Vance had disposed of at the Zaga Ravine.

This fight will be a good leg-stretcher, Bryst thought, knowing the guards would offer little resistance to his own band. The real fight would be later, out on the plains. Assassinating Lon and Tarek would be hard enough, but doing it in the middle of a battle with a hundred thousand Appernysians would seem impossible to most. Bryst smiled wryly. *All the more reason to do it. I will be remembered eternally for what I accomplish today.*

After glancing back at his own men—thirty-five strong and armed with swords, bows, and diamond-shaped shields—Bryst altered his choice of attack. They could easily defeat the unshielded men with a few volleys of arrows, but where was the honor in that? Direct combat was a much better option. It would prove his loyalty to Lieutenant Braedr and secure himself a place at the new commander's right hand.

Bryst signaled for his men to stow their bows and draw their swords. Word passed between them until all were donning their shields in one hand and their swords in the other. The time for stealth had passed; the time for action was at hand. Revenge would be their reward.

Bryst stood with his men. They vaulted over the wall and moved slowly toward the defending lines. The enemy began to panic; many of the guards dropped their weapons and fled, while the remaining

looked about dubiously, exactly as Bryst had expected. In his haste
to battle the Appernysians, Tarek had forgotten to assign the
Swallows a leader.

"This will be even easier than I thought," Bryst shouted proudly.
He licked his lips and broke into a run.

✳   ✳   ✳   ✳   ✳

Another day passed as Tarek led his army along the south river out
of Taeja. The supply wagons caught up to them partway through
that day, and the Rayders greeted the supply wagons with enthusiasm. The wagoners responded with their typical threats of dis-
memberment and murdered children should anyone touch their
wagons. The Rayders calmed quickly. All eyes looked south, but
there were still no signs of movement on the horizon. No warning
of an approaching Appernysian force.

"How far have we traveled?" Tarek complained to Lon. "I'm no
good at keeping track of long distances."

"About fifty miles," Lon answered as he looked toward Three
Peaks. They were just east of the faraway mountain.

"Looks like a great place to lay a trap for the 'Nysians," Tarek said.

"I disagree," Lon argued. He knew it made sense to stay close
to a source of water, but he was still learning how to wield it with
True Sight. He feared his sister's ability and how she might be able
to use the river against him. "No, we have to keep going, Tarek.
We can't stay by water."

Tarek stretched his back. "Whatever you say, Beholder, but you
realize that there's snow everywhere, right?"

Lon nodded. Tarek had guessed his anxiety. "Yes, but it's frozen.
I only struggle with the liquid."

"You don't struggle with anything." Tarek blew out his breath.
"Stop fearing her, Lon. If you keep this up, she'll win the battle

before it even starts. I need your confidence. I need your skill. I need your power."

Lon nodded. "That's exactly what worries me."

"But the same goes for her," Tarek countered. "She has *no idea* what you're capable of. Let me be in charge of catching their army off-guard. You do the same thing to her." Tarek turned to cross a shallow section of the river. "It'd be nice if you could freeze the water, then I wouldn't have to get my boots wet."

"I can't," Lon replied as he moved Dawes into the knee-deep river. "Once again, you prove my point."

After another day of travel toward Sylbie, Lon finally agreed to a halt.

"We should be right in the middle of their path," Lon said. "Now we're ready to lay our trap."

Tarek signaled his lieutenants, then dismounted and pulled a shovel from his saddle. "About time."

Chapter 38
Conflict

"Rayders sighted!"

The proclamation roared through the Appernysian army until it reached King Drogan, who rode near the rear.

"Follow me," he ordered as he kicked his horse into a gallop toward the front line of their army. Kamron and Mellai both followed on their own horses, along with the king's personal guard and the Beholder's escort. Kaylen was among them, too, sharing a horse with Snoom.

"What do you hear?" King Drogan asked Mellai as they rode.

She summoned True Sight and pulled the voices near the front line to her ears. "A small camp. Maybe ten Rayders."

"Be on the lookout," Kamron cautioned. "This could be a trap, my king."

"I'm sure it is," King Drogan replied and pushed his horse faster through a break in the formations.

Mellai followed the king for a mile through the ranks. At the front line, she scanned the surrounding terrain, searching for glowing essences or footprints in the snow. With the exception of the Rayder camp, everything was clear. Reassuring as well as unnerving. As her father had taught her, if there was one thing Rayders liked to do, it was ambush.

"Beholder?" King Drogan asked.

"Nothing," she answered, shaking her head. "Only the small camp."

The king stared at the canvas tents, still miles away. "Would Rayders send an envoy?"

"I don't know," Mellai answered, "but Lon might. He was raised an Appernysian. He knows how to play fair." She glanced at Kaylen as she finished speaking. Were they really about to meet him? On the field of battle? After a year of separation?

"But he's been a Rayder for a year," Kamron countered. "I don't like this. It doesn't feel right."

King Drogan agreed. "Fair or not, I won't play the fool. We will stay with our army until we reach the envoy. If the Rayders really have something important to say, they won't flee. To the camp," he ordered, pointing his hand at the Rayders.

Mellai pulled back on her reins and waited with her king and general until a few rows of pikemen were in front of them, then kicked her horse forward in the midst of their ranks.

Mellai sighed, grateful the horse had responded correctly. When she had first mounted the horse in Itorea, she had earned a few chuckles from her guard, though not nearly as many as Kaylen received. It was the first time either woman had ridden a horse, but Kaylen definitely fared worse. Despite Kaylen's love for horses, she had fallen twice before they had exited the stable, and eventually had to ride with Snoom. King Drogan had suggested Mellai ride with Kamron or Kutad. She had refused stubbornly. She eventually found her rhythm, but it still had been a very long ride from the keep.

She scanned the plains one more time, then closed her eyes and felt for her brother. Lon was calm and relaxed, the usual feeling he projected when he was asleep. Mellai reopened her eyes and continued her search. King Drogan and Kamron were right. Something was off.

By the time the Appernysians reached the outpost camp, the Rayders had broken down and packed their canvas tents. Eleven men sat on horseback, watching the approaching army. The men were dressed in traveling gear—cloaks, composite bows, arrows, swords, and glaives, but no armor. Their swords were sheathed and their glaives were stowed on the sides of their saddles.

"Would you like me to ride ahead and meet them?" Kamron asked.

"They can listen to us just fine from here," King Drogan answered. He raised a hand to stop the advancing army a hundred yards from the camp, then nodded at Mellai. She carried his voice to the eleven men. "You expect much to think you are privileged to the rules of war, Rayders. Envoy or not, I should kill you all where you stand."

"To whom are we speaking?" the center man replied. "Even from this distance, I recognize the coward general riding next to you, but your face is unknown to me."

"Don't answer," Kamron whispered to the king. "They're trying to single you out."

"I have nothing to hide," King Drogan replied. He glanced at Mellai.

"I'll keep you safe," she assured.

He puffed out his chest and returned his attention to the Rayders. "I am Drogan Jagonest, King of Appernysia."

"The *king?*" the man replied, his voice full of sarcasm. "Allow me to introduce myself, as well. I am Thennek Racketh, a lieutenant in my Commander's army. He sent me to warn you. Halt your advance and return to Itorea, or he will be forced to destroy your army. He will not show the same mercy he extended during our last battle. How do you respond?"

"You can tell your commander that his empty words don't frighten me," King Drogan replied. "Much has changed since we last met. It's you who should fear us. We won't stop until Taeja is purged of your filth and every last one of you dies or flees to the Exile. You have my warning."

"And here is my response," Thennek replied. In the blink of an eye, he pulled his bow from his back and loosed an arrow at the king. Kamron moved to protect King Drogan, but the king held up his hand.

The arrow arched through the air toward the king. Just as it was about to reach King Drogan, the shaft of the arrow shattered as it struck an invisible barrier.

King Drogan smiled at the Rayders. "Take *that* message back with you, too, if you make it back alive. Charge!"

Mellai released the air pocket protecting her king and watched with satisfaction as the front row of pikemen sprinted forward. It was more of a show than anything. The Rayders galloped away long before the pikemen got anywhere near striking distance.

"Thank you," the king said to Mellai after a deep breath. "I don't know if I'll ever get used to that."

"Good," Mellai replied. "That's only for emergencies, your Majesty. I can't protect you that way constantly."

King Drogan nodded and watched the retreating Rayders. "I don't understand. Why would they send an envoy all the way here to warn us?"

"Lady Netsey, my king," Kaylen answered from the back of Snoom's horse. "She must have reached them, which means they also know about Mellai."

"That's why they shot an arrow at you, my king," Kutad added. "It was a test to see if there was a Beholder among us."

"They're afraid," Kamron concluded, "and now they know they are no match for us."

A massive explosion erupted behind them. Mellai jerked forward from the concussive force of the blast, then turned around to see a large cloud of fire billowing into the air. Screams followed, echoing across the rear of their army.

"What was that?" King Drogan shouted.

"On the ground, Kutad," Mellai screamed to the sergeant.

He slid off his horse. "Ready."

Mellai lifted him high into the air on a pillar of dirt.

"We're under attack," Kutad shouted as he pointed at the rear of their army. "Rayders are pouring out of holes in the ground. They've destroyed our catapults and mixed into our ranks."

Mellai brought him down. "I can't stop them?"

"No," Kutad replied. "It's chaos back there. It's already dissolved into melee—there's no line separating them from us. It looks like a tavern fight gone terribly wrong. People are swinging at whoever's closest."

The situation was far worse than Mellai had expected. She had hoped to fight the Rayders from a distance. Now there would be unavoidable bloodshed—too much of it—and she would be standing in the midst of it, hunting for her brother. She had lost a tremendous advantage.

"Then let us retaliate," King Drogan shouted as he drew his sword.

✳   ✳   ✳   ✳   ✳

As the first ranks of Rayders charged out of the caverns Lon had dug, he summoned True Sight and hoisted a cask of oil from a supply wagon near the Appernysian catapults. With a mental squeeze, he shattered it and dispersed the oil in a fine mist over the nearby siege weapons, then he reached out with his essence and yanked a torch out of an Appernysian's hand and set the oil alight. A concussive blast shook the ground, destroying most of the catapults lining the rear, along with many of the Appernysian soldiers positioned there. The remaining catapults were then quickly crippled by small clusters of Rayders that were still pouring out of the caverns.

"Watch out," Lon shouted with alarm as the snow lifted in front of him. A hatch made from wooden planks flipped open, along with a foot of dirt and snow that had been packed on top of it. More Rayder men emptied out of the angled hole in a sprint toward the Appernysian rear.

"Still think this'll work?" Tarek asked as he donned his shield and drew his sword.

"It's a little late to ask," Lon replied, retrieving his own sword and shield. "As long as we stay mixed with the Appernysians, she can't stop us." He ran forward with Tarek, followed closely by Wade and the six remaining members of his squad.

"For Taeja!" Tarek shouted.

"For Taeja!" the Rayders echoed.

As they neared the destruction, a horrible sight caught Lon's attention. A small cluster of Appernysian soldiers stood together on their right flank, obviously holding down an unopened hatch. Two other Appernysians were hauling a full oil cask to it, followed by a third with a torch.

"They're going to burn them alive," Lon shouted and veered to the right.

Just as the Appernysians carrying the cask reached the hatch, Lon shattered the cask with True Sight. Oil spilled all over the snow. The torch bearer panicked and dropped his torch, igniting the spilled oil and engulfing the offending Appernysians in flames.

The men screamed and swatted pointlessly at the fire heating their chain mail. Without thinking twice, Lon knocked the men to the ground and smothered the flames in snow. The hatch they had been guarding burst open. The first Rayder out searched the ground and stabbed the nearest soldier, who was still lying on the ground in steaming armor.

Lon ground his teeth and moved to intervene, but his commander grabbed his shoulder.

"Whose side are you on?" Tarek shouted in anger.

"They're defenseless," Lon argued.

"They're dead anyway," Tarek countered. "Focus, Lon. You're a Rayder now, remember?"

✳   ✳   ✳   ✳   ✳

"I told you to stay in Itorea," Mellai screamed at Kaylen, who had fallen off Snoom's horse and sat shaking on the ground with fear. "I can't stay here with you."

"Go," King Drogan ordered the Beholder. "General Astadem and I will stay behind to protect Kaylen. Take your guard. Save our army."

"We'll protect your flank," Kutad affirmed as he rode alongside Mellai toward the fight. "You concentrate on squashing the roaches."

At first, there was little resistance as Mellai and her guard galloped toward the rear of the column. Appernysian soldiers stepped out of their way and the Rayders seemed oblivious to the approaching danger. That soon changed, however. The Appernysians became less aware of Mellai the farther she moved, and the Rayders finally noticed her coming. It started with one or two arrows from the Rayders, but with every foot Mellai and her guard pushed forward, more Rayders caught sight of them.

"We can't stay up here," Mellai shouted as she stopped a volley of arrows and thrust them back at the attacking Rayder archers.

"Aye," Kutad agreed and slid off his horse. He chuckled after Mellai dismounted and stood next to him. "Down here, you're at least a foot shorter than the rest of us."

Mellai smirked and continued forward.

✳ ✳ ✳ ✳ ✳

"Did you see that?" Lon shouted.

"Yes," Tarek answered as he crushed his forehead against the Appernysian in his grip.

Hopefully everyone else did, too."

"That had to be at least fifty arrows. She didn't just stop them. She flung them back at us. I can't do that." Lon ducked under a swinging halberd, stabbed the man with his sword, and looked back toward the Beholder. She and the men riding with her had disappeared. "Where'd she go?"

Tarek lunged at the next closest Appernysian. "Probably got wise and hopped of her horse. Beholder or not, she was asking for it up there. Did you get a good enough look at her yet?"

"No." Lon cursed and swung his diamond-shaped shield at another soldier. "I still can't tell if it's her."

"Stay hidden," Wade counseled as he guarded Lon's flank. "If you use your power, she'll know right where to find you."

Lon lost his footing on the slippery snow and fell onto his back. An Appernysian seized the opportunity and swung his halberd at the Beholder. Lon barely managed to roll out of the way before swinging his sword into his enemy's ankle. "That's easier said than done," Lon argued as he regained his feet and finished off the offender.

"Bide your time," Tarek shouted. "She'll make a mistake sooner or later, then you'll have your chance."

"But what if she's Mellai?" Lon argued. "I can't kill my own sister."

"You'll have to," Tarek replied, "or she'll kill us all. Now watch for her to use True Sight. She doesn't know any better."

*   *   *   *   *

Mellai ducked behind Kutad, glad that Kaylen had stayed out of the fray. "I'm not a soldier. This is suicide!"

"That's why I told you to stay behind me," Kutad answered. He knocked a Rayder's shield to the side and thrust his scimitar into the man's chest. "Surround her."

The rest of Mellai's guard encircled her while she provided support. Two Rayders charged at them from her right. Mellai peeked under Snoom's arm and with careful concentration, created a large energy blast under the attackers' feet. The two Rayders shot into the air a hundred feet while those surrounding the blast crashed to the ground from the force.

"Yes," Snoom shouted triumphantly. "I like this a lot better."

Mellai continued to spin around from within the protective ring of her guard. She watched the glowing energies surrounding them, hunting for danger and searching for her brother. Another three Rayders attacked on Ric and Duncan's side. She caught hold of the Rayders' armor and crushed it around their bodies. The men screamed in pain before they were finally silenced.

Mellai recoiled at the horrible deaths she caused. She watched the essence of the three dead Rayders float above the other glowing forms of the two fighting armies. A gasp escaped her lips. Hundreds of men were dying around her. Their essences hovered over the battlefield and disappeared, only to be replaced by hundreds more.

Without warning, the vision was blocked. A thick dome of earth formed over the top of Mellai and her guard, blocking out all light.

"What is this?" Snoom shouted in the darkness.

Mellai tried to force the barrier back into the ground, but she was met with strong resistance. The barricade wouldn't budge. She clenched her jaw and pulled more energy from the ground beneath her, adding it to her strength. The glowing dome vibrated in her vision, then suddenly gave way in front of her. She thrust the dirt back into the earth on one side with such force that the ground rippled out like a rock thrown into a pond. Men toppled over the rolling dirt for fifty feet in front of her.

Mellai turned around and forced the remaining section of the dome back into the ground, but all signs of Lon's connection to the dome had disappeared. He was nowhere to be seen.

"Your brother?" Kutad asked in the temporary silence around them.

"Yes," Mellai answered, rattled by her brother's tactics. She had been taken completely by surprise. "I'll have to be more careful. I forgot how clever he can be."

*   *   *   *   *

"What happened?" Tarek shouted as they pushed further into the Appernysian ranks.

"She's too strong," Lon replied. "I couldn't hold it."

Tarek knocked a soldier to the ground with his shoulder and stomped on his exposed neck. "You did your best, Lon. Time to end it."

"Didn't you hear me?" Lon asked. "I said she's too powerful."

"If you can throw a dirt mound over her, you can kill her. You caught her totally by surprise."

Lon didn't answer. He concentrated on the fight immediately surrounding him. Now that he had seen the Beholder and knew it was his sister, he couldn't bring himself to finish her off. There was no way he could do it.

✱　✱　✱　✱　✱

"That way, Lieutenant," an Appernysian pikemen shouted, jerking his head to the right. "Be careful. He's surrounded by the best fighters I've ever seen. Only a few Rayders, yet they slaughtered my entire unit."

Kutad tightened his lips. "Come on, Mellai."

They wove between the fighting, avoiding confrontations wherever possible. While Jareth and Snoom helped Kutad push forward, Ric and Duncan guarded their rear. Mellai continued to search the soldiers from the midst of her guard, but quickly realized that the glowing essence of everyone looked basically the same.

"I have to stop using my power," Mellai shouted, but only loud enough that her guard could hear. "I can't recognize him like this. I can't even tell between our forces and theirs. Everyone is moving too fast."

Her guard tightened their circle around Mellai and continued forward, pressing through the crowded trail of dead bodies. Mellai released True Sight, and nearly vomited at the sight of so much blood surrounding her. The scene was more gruesome than she could have imagined.

"What are we doing?" she shouted to Kutad. "All this killing. It's pointless."

"Don't lose your head," Kutad replied. "These are Rayders we're fighting, Mellai. If we don't drive them out, they'll create this same carnage in every village across Appernysia. The death around us is horrible, but not pointless. It has to be done."

Mellai turned her head to the side, trying to avoid the inescapable slaughter. Twenty yards to her left was Lon, protected by full-plate armor and wielding his sword and shield with lethal accuracy. Appernysian men fell everywhere that he and his guard moved. They were all deathly skilled. It was no wonder that the Rayders created such havoc in their previous battle. Their fighting was far superior to the Appernysians.

One particular man in Lon's group caught Mellai's attention. He was a red-bearded brute, broad and powerful, but it was the symbol on his breastplate that she cared about most. A blue King's Cross. He was the only Rayder with such a marking. Mellai had found the commander.

Mellai's first instinct was to kill the commander, but she changed her mind as she watched. He and Lon never strayed far from each other, moving in unspoken synchronization as they repeatedly saved each other's lives. They were obviously good friends, and a strong fighting team. If Mellai killed the commander, Lon would become irrational. He wouldn't listen to a single word she said.

She summoned True Sight, grabbed the commander with her essence, and dragged him through the fighting until he was prostrate at her own feet. The man cursed and tried to spit at Mellai. She stopped the saliva, formed it into a frozen dart, and aimed it directly at the commander's eye.

"I dare you," the man ranted as he struggled against his invisible bonds. "Go ahead and do it, Mellai. I dare you."

The commander's shouting must have caught Lon's attention. He turned and summoned True Sight.

"Don't do anything foolish," Mellai shouted over the fighting as she watched the energy flare in Lon. While using True Sight, his essence glowed brighter, like a Jaed. "You already tried to overpower me once, Lon." She moved the projectile closer to Tarek's eye. "Is another failure really worth his life?"

One of Lon's guard charged at Mellai. Kutad stepped in front of her, but it was unnecessary. She used her power to grab the Rayder by the blond ponytail hanging out of his helm and throw him to the ground. The man's face dragged for many feet across the snow, then he stood up, obviously dazed, and backed away with his shield up.

While Mellai was distracted, Lon struck. He compressed the air around her, but she flicked it away with one hand. He tried to shift the earth beneath her, but Mellai severed his connection to it before he could do anything. The more he tried and failed, the more obvious Lon's frustration became. Finally a head-sized sphere of energy formed in his hands and shot out at Mellai.

"Grab the commander," Mellai shouted as she focused her entire essence on controlling the sphere. The power of the blast nearly overtook her; she barely managed to stop it. She watched Lon, waiting to see what he would try next, but he only stared at her with a slacked jaw. He obviously had no control over the sphere.

Mellai carefully molded the energy into a shield, which she encircled around her brother. "You're imprisoned, Lon. Give up. I just want to talk."

Lon ignored her warning. Although she knew he couldn't control the energy he manipulated, he could still affect it. He fought against the barrier, desperately trying to free himself. With every attack, Mellai was forced to pull massive amounts of energy from her surroundings to supply the energy shield. She couldn't see it, but she knew that things were disappearing. It was as Llen had warned her, but something even more concerning caught her attention. Lon was glowing brighter, and continued to flare with every attack. He was absorbing the energy shield into himself. If he didn't stop . . .

"Stop fighting, Lon," Mellai screamed. "You'll kill us all."

Lon ignored her.

"I swear I'll cut out your eyes if I have to. I just want to talk."

Lon lifted his hand again to strike, glaring at his sister. She returned his gaze, pleading. Death and suffering surrounded her. Too much to bear. This battle had to end.

Lon's expression softened. Mellai connected with him, sensing overwhelming frustration and desperation. But in the midst also dwelt defeat. He released his excess energy through his palms, then let go of his power.

By then, most of the nearby fighting had stopped in an unspoken truce as both armies watched the faceoff between their Beholders. The Rayder Commander was sitting on the ground while Ric, who was just as large, kneeled behind him with the commander's neck locked in his arm. Duncan crouched in front of the commander, his sword at the commander's face. Mellai's gaze shifted from the captured commander back to Lon. She slipped into his mind, finding the same emotions she had already sensed through their connection. He wouldn't fight her again unless he felt threatened.

Mellai released the energy shield encasing her brother. Raw energy whipped about in all directions, uniting itself with the closest entity. "I removed the barrier, Lon, but don't try anything foolish." She maintained her connection with True Sight.

Lon crossed his arms over the top of his bent knees. "Send back my Commander, Little Sis, then we'll talk."

Mellai nodded. "Let him go, Ric."

"But Mellai—" Kutad argued.

"This isn't a debate," Mellai snapped. "Release him."

Ric released his grip and stepped back, but Duncan kept his sword at the ready while the commander sat up.

"Nice spit dart," the commander said to Mellai with a wink and a laugh, then walked back to the circle of his own men, searching the ground. "Where's my sword?"

"It disappeared, my Commander," the blond Rayder answered, "along with your shield."

Mellai searched the surrounding soldiers, finding many similar circumstances accompanied with terrified expressions. Missing swords, halberds, and shields. One nearby Appernysian soldier stood bare-chested, his chain mail and tunic nowhere in sight.

The commander looked suspiciously at Mellai, a hint of alarm showing through, then turned to Lon. "Options?"

Lon shook his head. "We have none, Tarek. She's stronger than me."

"Tarek?" Mellai interjected. The name struck her as a ghost from her past, from when she and Lon used to live in Pree. "Tarek Ascennor?"

"One and the same," Tarek replied with a wide grin and a low bow.

"I thought you were dead," Mellai continued, grateful she had decided not to kill him. "When did you become Commander? What happened to Rayben Goldhawk?"

"Long story," Tarek replied. "Why don't you come sit on my lap, and I'll tell you all about it?"

Mellai scowled and used her essence to quickly curl Tarek's frizzy beard into perfect ringlets. "Tempting, but I'm already promised to someone else, Lady Prettybeard."

"I can't believe I never thought of that," Lon said with a hint of amusement, while Tarek frantically clawed at the curls. Lon looked up at his sister and pointed at her face. "Nice tattoo. When did this happen?"

"It's a long story," she replied with another quick glare at Tarek. "Sounds like we both have a lot of catching up to do, Lon. Did that brand sink too far into your head?"

"Talking isn't going to change anything," he responded. "As long as you keep attacking Rayders, we're still enemies."

Mellai's expression softened. Her eyes plead with her twin brother and fellow Beholder. "We don't have to be—"

A small commotion erupted behind Lon, then a soldier leaped into the midst of his group and flung a glaive at her brother. Lon tried to roll out of the way, but wouldn't have survived without his sister's intervention. Mellai caught hold of the glaive and thrust it into the ground, then imprisoned the culprit in a mound of hardened dirt up to his neck.

Now it was Mellai's turn to be surprised. "Braedr?"

"*Lieutenant* Braedr," he spat back, his face dark red as he fought against the earthen prison.

She shook her head. "You're a Rayder, too? How'd you survive?"

"You wouldn't believe it, *witch*," Braedr replied, but turned his attention away from Mellai as Tarek stepped forward and slugged him hard in the face with his steel gauntlet.

Mellai lowered her brow, confused as her brother's voice filled her ears.

"Stay out of this, Mel. It has nothing to do with you." Lon's face was deathly serious, warning her not to get involved.

Mellai assented, watching as Tarek folded his arms and paced around Braedr. "How did you escape? Who brought you here?"

Despite his broken nose and watery eyes, Braedr laughed. A full, roaring, belly laugh. "You'll find out when you get home. Might have to do a little cleaning up, though. There's an unfortunate mess of Swallows in the keep."

Tarek reached forward and wrenched Braedr's head sideways with a loud pop. Mellai swept Tarek's feet, knocking him to the ground, but she was too late. She watched, brimming with anger and disgust at Tarek's actions as Braedr's essence lifted into the sky and disappeared.

Mellai peered at her brother, and was shocked to see him looking on without any apparent reservation. She wondered how he could condone such brutality, but didn't care what his excuses were. He had changed. No, he had degenerated. He was a true Rayder.

Chapter 39

Hindsight

Just a little farther, Rypla thought. He glanced up at the inter-
mixed Rayder and Appernysian armies, then stumbled forward. *Why did they stop fighting?*

He forced his feet to keep moving—one foot, then the next. His
strength waned. He kept one arm over two gaping wounds in his
stomach to keep his insides where they belonged. His other arm
hung uselessly at his side, barely held to his shoulder by a thin layer
of dissolved and cauterized flesh. Such strange poison. Similar injuries had already killed his horse, which had bravely brought him as
close to the battle as possible before collapsing into the snow.

I'll die, too, Rypla thought, *but not yet. Someone has to warn them.
It has to be me.*

Three hundred yards. Two hundred. One hundred. Stumbled into
the snow. *Crawl. Keep moving. Don't stop. Almost there.* Collapsed.

Someone rolled Rypla onto his back and lifted the top half of his
body. "A tradesman," the man called over his shoulder, then turned
back to Rypla. "Where did you come from?"

Appernysian soldier, Rypla thought as he looked up at the man. *Good.*

With his last ounce of strength, Rypla lifted his free hand and
gripped the soldier's chain mail. "Réxura is destroyed. Everyone's dead."

Worry and confusion flashed across the soldier's face. "What
happened?"

Rypla's eyes glazed over. He felt so calm. So peaceful. Was it finally over? Had death finally come?

"No, you don't." The soldier smacked Rypla hard to bring him back to his senses. "You can't die yet. Tell me what happened. Was it Rayders?"

Rypla refocused his eyes on the Appernysian soldier, mouthing empty words until one finally escaped his lips.

"Calahein."

A final gasp escaped his lips, then Rypla joined his horse in the world beyond death.

Glossary

<u>Pronunciation Guide:</u>

\ā\ *as* **a** *in ape*   \ər\ *as* **er** *in person*   \th\ *as* **th** *in thin*

\a\ *as* **a** *in apple*   \ī\ *as* **i** *in ice*   \ū\ *as* **u** *in union*

\ä\ *as* **o** *in hop*   \i\ *as* **i** *in hit*   \uh\ *as* **u** *in bug*

\ch\ *as* **ch** *in chip*   \ō\ *as* **o** *in go*   \ü\ *as* **oo** *in loot*

\ē\ *as* **ea** *in easy*   \qu\ *as* **qu** *in quiet*   \ů\ *as* **oo** *in foot*

\e\ *as* **e** *in bet*   \sh\ *as* **sh** *in shop*   \zh\ *as* **si** *in vision*

Aely Leeran – (ā´-lē | lē´ran) friend of Kaylen Shaw, servant in Itorea's donjon.

Allegna Ovann – (uh-leg´-nuh | ō´-van) wife to Dhargon Ovann; mother of Shalán Marcs.

Appernysia – (a-pər-nē´-zhuh) the kingdom in which this story is set, established at the beginning of the First Age.

Anton Vetinie – (an´-tuhn | Ve-tē´-nē) chancellor to Queen Cyra.

Aron Marcs – (ä´-ruhn | märks´) husband to Shalán Marcs and father of Lon and Mellai Marcs.

Banty Prates – (ban-tē | prāts) birth name of the king's page, Snoom.

Battle for Taeja – a battle between Rayders and Appernysia for the city, Taeja; during the Second Age; won by the Rayders.

Beholder – a person with True Sight who can manipulate the world's energy.

Beholder's Eye – the tattoo surrounding the left eye of Beholders.

Bors Rayder – (bōrz´ | rā´-dər) a Taejan who led the Phoenijan rebellion against the king and Beholders at the end of the First Age; all Taejans who followed him took the title of Rayder.

Braedr Pulchria – (brā´-dər | půl´-krē-uh) son to Hans and Ine Pulchria; raised in Pree.

Bryst Grayson – (brist´ | grā´-suhn) Rayder supply wagon overseer.

calahein – (ca´-luh-hīn) ancient enemy of Appernysia; exterminated from their home in Meridina near the end of the First Age; composed of kelsh, seith, and one queen.

Cavalier Crook – the southwestern quadrant of Itorea that houses the city's nobles.

Channer – (chan´-ər) member of Lon's twelve-Rayder tactical squad; cousin to Keene.

Ched Trelnap – (ched´ | trel´-nap) sergeant of Appernysia; bailiff of the king's council.

Clawed – (clād´) leader of a Rayder uprising; also known as Claude.

Coel – (kōl´) village leatherworker in Pree.

coming of age – an important transition from adolescence to adulthood in Pree, enabling a person to participate in village councils, start their own trade, build their own home, and marry and start a family; age fifteen for girls and age seventeen for boys.

Cortney Baum – (kōrt´-nē | bäm´) young Rayder daughter of Gil and Flora Baum.

Cyra Jagonest – (si´-ruh | ja´-gō-nest) queen of Appernysia; wife of Drogan Jagonest.

Dawes – (däz´) Lon Marcs's Rayder horse, previously owned by Gil Baum.

Dax – (Daks´) Omar Brickeden's horse.

Delancy Reed – (de-lan´-sē | rēd´) village brewer in Pree; father to Sonela Reed.

Dhargon Ovann – (där´-guhn | ō´-van) husband to Allegna Ovann; father of Shalán Marcs.

donjon – (duhn´-juhn) the central keep of Itorea where the king and queen dwell.

Dovan – (dō´-ven) member of Lon's twelve-Rayder tactical squad.

Drake – (drāk´) a member of Gil Baum's Rayder squad.

Drogan Jagonest – (drō´-gen | ja´-gō-nest) king of Appernysia; husband of Cyra Jagonest.

Duncan Shord – (duhn´-cuhn | shōrd) sentry to the royal chambers of Itorea's donjon.

Edis Ascennor – (ē´-dis | uh-se´-nōr) deceased wife of Myron Ascennor.

Elie Swasey – (el´-ē | swā´-zē) member of Clawed's Rayder rebellion.

Elja – (el´-zhuh) member of Lon's twelve-Rayder tactical squad.

Elora – (ē-lōr´-uh) village alfalfa farmer in Pree; widow with four sons.

Ernon – (ər´-nuhn) a page to King Drogan.

First Age – the time period which began when Appernysia was first settled; ended after the Rayder revolution and banishment to the Exile; reference Second Age.

Flagheim – (flag´-hīm) fortress city of the Rayders; located in the Exile about thirty miles north of the Dialorine Range.

Flora Baum – (flōr´-uh | bäm´) Rayder widow of Gil Baum; mother of Cortney Baum and two older sons.

Furwen Tree – (fər´-wen) a massive tree with wood as hard as stone, grows over six hundred feet tall; located in the Perbeisea Forest.

Gavin Baum – (ga´-vin | bäm´) oldest son of Flora Baum.

Geila – (gā´-luh) young pureblood Rayder woman executed for fornication with Sévart; gave birth to a child in the wilderness.

Gera – (ge´-ruh) head cook in Itorea's donjon.

ghraef – (grāf´) a large beast with thick, hardened skin that is covered in fur and an armored tail with a unique crystal on its tip; served as companions to Beholders, but disappeared after the end of the First Age.

Gil Baum – (gil´ | bäm´) the deceased Rayder husband to Flora Baum, killed by Lon Marcs.

Gorlon Arbogast – (gōr´luhn | ar´-bō-gast) father to Theiss Arbogast; lives in Roseiri.

Hadon – (hā´-duhn) village farmer of wheat and oats in Pree, along with Landon.

Haedon Reeth – (hā´-duhn | rēth) advisor to King Drogan.

Hans Pulchria – (hänz´ | půl´-krē-uh) village blacksmith in Pree; husband of Ine Pulchria and father of Braedr Pulchria.

Henry – (hen´-rē) personal healer to King Drogan and Queen Cyra.

Ine Pulchria – (īn´ | půl´-krē-uh) mother of Braedr Pulchria and wife of Hans Pulchria.

Itorea – (ī-tōr´-ē-uh) the capital of the Kingdom of Appernysia; also known as the Fortress Island or City of the King.

Jaed – (jād´) an ethereal being; regulates the balance of the world's energy; only visible by Beholders.

Jareth – (jer´-eth) soldier in the Appernysian army; friend of Kutad.

Jude – (jüd´) chambermaid in the royal chambers of Itorea's donjon.

– a portable Rayder bridge used to span the Zaga Ravine.

Kamron Astadem – (kam´-ruhn | as´tuh-dem) general of Appernysia's army; fled during the Battle for Taeja.

Kat Jashfelt – (kat´ | jash´-felt) female spymaster of Appernysia.

Kaylen Shaw – (kā´-len | shä´) betrothed of Lon Marcs and daughter of Scut Shaw.

Keene – (kēn´) member of Lon's twelve-Rayder tactical squad; cousin to Channer.

kelsh – (kelsh´) the ground troops of the calahein.

King's Court – an entity consisting of the seat of government and the royal household.

King Drogan – (drō´-gen) current king of Appernysia.

King's Cross – branded into the right temple of all Rayders; in the First Age, it was tattooed into the right temple of the Phoenijan from the blue petals of the Lynth Flower.

Kutad Leshim – (kü-täd´ | le´shim) leader of the Appernysian trading caravan; close friend to Mellai.

Landon – (lan´-duhn) village farmer of wheat and oats in Pree, along with Hadon.

Lars – (lärz´) deceased member of Lon's twelve-Rayder tactical squad; oldest member of the squad.

Lia – (lē´-uh) chambermaid in the royal chambers of Itorea's donjon.

Linney Leshim – (lin´-ē) deceased daughter of Kutad; the name Mellai Marcs uses to disguise herself while in Roseiri.

Llen – (len´) a Jaed; appeared to Mellai Marcs.

Lon Marcs – (län´ | märks´) twin brother of Mellai Marcs and son of Aron and Shalán Marcs.

Lon Shaw – (län´ | shä´) nickname used by Lon Marcs to hide his connection to his father, who was a defecting Rayder.

Lynth Flower – (linth´) a rare blue flower that grows only in the center of Itorea's donjon; its petals were used to tattoo Beholders and Phoenijan in the First Age; replicated as a silver pendant that is given to honored soldiers in Appernysia.

Mellai Marcs – (mel-ī´ | märks´) twin sister to Lon Marcs and daughter of Aron and Shalán Marcs; also known as Mel.

Meridina – (mer-i-dē´-nuh) underground city of the calahein; destroyed near the end of the First Age.

Myron Ascennor – (mī´-ruhn | uh-se´-nōr) deceased father of Tarek Ascennor and prior village delegate of Pree; died protecting the Marcs family from a Rayder assault in Pree.

Nellád – (nel-ad´) younger of Flora Baum's two sons.

Netsey D'Lío – (net´-sē | d-lē´-ō) lady of Itorea; daughter of Lord Tyram D'Lío.

Night Stalker – a tactical game created by the Rayders to test their stealth and skill; one team of five men tries to capture a diamond from a separate team of fifteen men without detection.

Nik – (nik´) member of Lon's twelve-Rayder tactical squad.

Nybol – (nī´-bōl) village sheep and goat herder in Pree.

Old Trade Route – abandoned trade road in Appernysia that runs from Humsco to Pree before returning to Roseiri; reference Trade Route.

Omar Brickeden – (ō´-mar | bri´-ke-den) respected Rayder scholar; acting Rayder commander after the death of Rayben Goldhawk; personal tutor and confidant of Lon Marcs; raised Aron Marcs.

Perbeisea Forest – (per-bā´-zhuh) sacred woods located west of Itorea; made up of Furwen Trees.

Phoenijan – (fēn´-i-zhan) elite guard of Appernysia in the First Age; composed completely of Taejans and led by Beholder lieutenants; after the Rayder revolt at the end of the First Age, the role of the Phoenijan was dissolved.

Pree – (prē´) a small village located in the southwestern corner of the Western Valley in Appernysia, 5 miles east of the Tamadoras Mountains.

Preton – (pre´-tuhn) member of Lon's twelve-Rayder tactical squad.

Ramsey – (ram´-zē) village farmer of vegetables and fruits in Pree, along with Wellesly; father of Tirk.

Ramik Gunderott – (ra´-mik | guhn´-dər-ät) chamberlain of the king's council; dwells in Itorea's donjon.

Rayben Goldhawk – (rā´-ben) deceased Rayder commander; accepted Lon into the Rayder brotherhood and made him First Lieutenant.

Rayder – (rā´-dər) title acquired when the Phoenijan followed Bors Rayder in a revolution against their king and the Beholders at the end of the First Age.

Rayder Commander – leader of the Rayders; functions similarly to the king of Appernysia.

Rayder Exile – the land north of the Zaga Ravine and the Dialorine Range; where the Rayders were banished at the end of the First Age.

Reese Arbogast – (rēs´ | ar´-bō-gast) younger brother of Theiss Arbogast.

Réxura – (rex´-ər-uh) a major trade city located at the eastern tip of the Vidarien Mountains.

Ric Jois – (rik´ | jois´) head sentry to the royal chambers of Itorea's donjon.

Riyen – (rī´-yen) member of Lon's twelve-Rayder tactical squad.

Roseiri – (rōs-ēr´-ē) a village located twenty miles south of the Vidarien Mountains, along the West River; home to Dhargon and Allegna Ovann, as well as Mellai Marcs.

Ryndee – (rin´-dē) lady-in-waiting to Queen Cyra.

Rypla – (rip´-luh) right-hand man to Kutad in his trading caravan.

Sátta – (sä´-tuh) soldier in the Appernysian army; friend to Aely.

Scut Shaw – (scüt´ | shä´) village dairy farmer in Pree; father of Kaylen Shaw.

Second Age – the current time period in the story which has been in existence for one thousand two hundred years.

seith – (sēth´) flying calahein; great bane of the ghraefs.

Sévart – (sā´-värt) young pureblood Rayder man executed for fornication with Geila.

Shalán Marcs – (shuh-län´) wife to Aron Marcs and mother of Lon and Mellai Marcs; village healer in Pree.

Snoom – (snüm´) a page serving under King Drogan; see Banty Prates.

Sonela Reed – (suh-ne´-luh | rēd´) daughter of Delancy Reed.

Sylbie – (sil´-bē) large city that handles shipments from Réxura to Itorea; located at the connecting fork of the Sylbien River and Prime River.

Taeja – (tā´-zhuh) ruined city in the Taejan Plains; home to the Taejans and Beholders in the First Age; retaken by the Rayders after the Battle for Taeja.

Taejan – (tā´-zhuhn) title of the Rayders before their revolution at the end of the First Age; from the Taejans came the Phoenijan and Beholders.

Taejan Plains – (tā´-zhuhn) the northwestern region of Appernysia between the Tamadoras Mountains and the Nellis River.

Tarek Ascennor – (ter´-ek | uh-se´-nōr) son of Myron Ascennor; Rayder general; best friend to Lon Marcs.

Tarl – (tärl´) deceased member of Lon's twelve-Rayder tactical squad.

Tayla Leshim – (tā´-luh | le´shim) deceased wife of Kutad.

Thad – (thad´) member of Lon's twelve-Rayder tactical squad.

Theiss Arbogast – (tīs´ | ar´-bō-gast) young man who lives in the village of Roseiri; courting Mellai.

Thennek Racketh – (then´-ek | rack´-eth) Rayder lieutenant responsible for maintaining control of Three Peaks.

Thorn – a conical watchtower situated north of the Zaga Ravine.

Three Peaks – solitary watchtower mountain located in the Taejan Plains; Rayders took control of this watchtower just prior to the Battle for Taeja.

Thudly – (thuhd´-lē) sentry in Itorea's donjon.

Tirk – (tərk´) son of Ramsey, one of the village farmers of vegetables and fruits in Pree.

Trade Route – trade road that extends from Itorea to Pree, then circles around the Western Valley of Appernysia; reference Old Trade Route.

Trev Rowley – (trev´ | rō´-lē) current village delegate in Pree.

True Sight – the ability of a man to see the world's energy.

Tyram D'Lío – (tir´-uhm | d-lē´-ō) member of the king's council; father to Netsey D'Lío.

Vance Talbot – (vans´ | tal´-buht) deceased captain of the Rayder cavalry.

Verle – (vərl´) a page to King Drogan.

Wade Arneson – (wād´ | ar´-ne-suhn) loyal member of Lon's twelve-Rayder tactical squad; Rayder Lieutenant; Lon's personal protector.

Warley Chatterton – (war´-lē | cha´-ter-tuhn) Rayder lieutenant over siege weapons.

Weeping Forest – a boggy forest of weeping willow trees situated at the northern base of the Dialorine Range.

Wellesly – (wel´-es-lē) village farmer of vegetables and fruits in Pree, along with Ramsey.

Wegnas – (weg´-nas) burial grounds south of Itorea.

Western Valley – the southwestern region of Appernysia between the Tamadoras Mountains and the Pearl River.

Zaga Ravine – (zä´-guh) a deep gorge that extends from the Tamadoras Mountains to the western tip of the Dialorine Range; marks the northern edge of the Kingdom of Appernysia.

Zaxton – (zax´-tuhn) Appernysian scout at the Quint River; killed by Lon's Rayder squad.

About The Author

Born in the wrong age, Terron James continually fantasizes of shining steel, majestic stone architecture, thundering cavalry rushes, and opportunities to prove his honor. Under the direction of his queen, Terron labors diligently in his kingdom, striving to prepare an inheritance worthy of his five heirs.

When he finally graduated from the University of Utah with his English BA, Terron had become besties with most of the English department staff, as well as the employees of Brio, who make a wicked cup of hot chocolate.

Terron currently resides in Tooele, UT. His dream is to capture every sunset with his wife, fingers interlocked, the reflection of his soul in her brown eyes, and the ocean surf rolling over their bare feet.

Terron is a junior high English teacher at Excelsior Academy and a former Tooele Chapter president of the League of Utah Writers.

Visit www.TerronJames.com

Made in the USA
Lexington, KY
09 December 2019